ADELAIDE;

OR,

THE TRIALS OF A GOVERNESS.

BY

GABRIEL ALEXANDER,

AUTHOR OF " WALLACE, THE HERO OF SCOTLAND," " BRUCE, THE HERO KING OF SCOTLAND,"
" LILIAS, THE MILLINER'S APPRENTICE," ETC. ETC.

WITH BEAUTIFUL WOOD-ENGRAVINGS.

DRAWN BY W. H. THWAITES.

LONDON:
JOHN DICKS, 313, STRAND; AND ALL BOOKSELLERS.

ADELAIDE;

OR, THE TRIALS OF A GOVERNESS.

CHAPTER I.

THE BULKY BARONET.

"SERVE you right! This comes of your sense-less, Jehu-like driving, to pamper pride, to puff up the vanity of the blundering Sir Vaux.

But there are women-folks in the case, and in danger, so that I must do my best to assist, although they may be akin to Sir Arrogance himself."

Thus did a man of many years mutter his sentiments, as he hobbled to the edge of his property, which was skirted near the spot where he had been standing, by a fine level, private

road, that led to the still more carefully constructed and stately avenue, within a massive gate, not half a mile off, by which Wartham Hall was approached, the seat of Sir Vaux Waldgrave.

The circumstances which had so much moved the aged soliloquist were certainly startling. He had been paying attention for some minutes to the progress of a carriage and four, and saying to himself it was a shame to drive or ride horses in harness at such a merciless speed as that which arrested his notice. At length one or both of the leaders stumbled and fell, necessarily, at the rate they were running, causing the other pair to roll over upon them, breaking the pole, and capsizing the vehicle.

It was a sad and frightful sight, and would have taken more than even the misanthropy of the old man to look upon it and talk only of the folly and pride of any one. The riders and the ridden were thrown into a heap; they were in horrid disorder. The horses lashed out, utterly regardless how or where they might strike; the feet of some of them reaching the body of the carriage with thundering blows, fracturing it dreadfully, and the travellers within screaming for assistance, and shrieking from mortal fear.

The startled and snarling old man was fortunately up to the scene of disaster in time to lend his aid in extricating one of the ladies from the perilous position into which they had so unexpectedly been thrown, by lifting her clean out of the capsized coach; the other, who was the elder of the pair, having already got to the ground and away from the disorder, in safety. As for the postilions, they had enough to attend to in liberating themselves and putting the cattle to rights, without paying heed to the fair, one of whom felt herself greatly indebted to the aged stranger who came to their succour, even while their alarm was upon them. And yet something else than either gratitude or alarm was instantly to move these ladies, in consequence of certain exclamations which burst from the old man's lips, as he gazed upon the young creature he rescued.

"The very picture, I declare, of——but it matters not now who she was," ejaculated the old man, giving a sort of growling sigh as the accompaniment of his consternation. " I little thought," added he, after a short pause, during which the two ladies regarded him with a growing amazement, "I little thought when I parted from her fifty years ago, that I should ever look upon her like again;" and having thus spoken, without adding another word, he hobbled away, leaving the travelling party to their own resources, without once casting a look behind.

"What can that strange-looking old man, who has yet acted so humanely towards me, mean by his words?" inquired the younger lady of the other, as the aged individual withdrew from them; she who put the question having caught at some not unpleasurable romantic idea as being connected with his mysterious ejaculation,—her interest in the expressions being increased on perceiving that they seemed to have suddenly troubled her companion. "Know you anything, mother, of that person, or of what he can have been thinking of, when he spoke as he did?"

"Not I; how should or could I, girl?" answered the elder lady, with an air of offended feeling. "It would be more to the purpose, Adelaide, if we considered of the manner in which we are to approach the Hall, and accost your stately uncle, seeing that the carriage is disabled, and the men have their hands full of work with the horses. Indeed we have no alternative but to proceed on foot, and to leave our luggage to the care of our people to bring up at their leisure. A sorry plight it will be held by Sir Vaux, I dread, to find us trudging to his princely mansion on foot. Would that the ugly old brute who so unceremoniously just now left us, had gone before to announce at the Hall our mishap, or that he had undertaken to furnish us with some country lout to perform the office."

"Oh, mother, I dare say that singular-looking, yet to me not uninteresting person," observed the young lady, "may be somebody that is quite above acting a servant's part; at any rate, I should never think of characterizing him as an ugly old brute. In fact, I shall be curious to learn something concerning him, which is natural for me to do, after the efforts he made to assist me out of peril. He is not an every-day or very ordinary individual, I conjecture."

"Have done, girl, with such stuff and about such unworthy objects," said the mother, in her reproving tone; "and think how you are in less than half-an-hour to carry yourself in presence of your exacting uncle, who will be vastly disturbed, I fear, by our approaching his mansion as if we were poor pedestrians, and perhaps construing our mischance and alarming accident as an evil omen. However, there is nothing left for us but that we hasten towards our destination."

While the ladies are tripping along the smooth gravel towards Sir Vaux Waldgrave's noble residence, now shaded by the stately trees of his avenue from the heat of a summer day's meridian sun, and next pacing it, in their travelling robes through the openings which relieved the sombreness of the other parts, to the enhancement of their beauty,—let a word of introduction be said relative to him whom the mother stigmatized as an ugly brute.

And truly Mr. Peter Plumtree had few exterior attractions to recommend him to the finical and the artificially delicate. He was above the middle size, with high stooping shoulders, sharp elbows,—usually projecting behind his back when he stood or walked,—a somewhat stormy blue face, and small gray eyes, surmounted by shaggy brows. He ordinarily wore a red woollen night-cap, which had not a little to do with the grotesque figure he cut when out of doors, he hobbled from one point to another of his small estate of Red Cot, as he called it, because of the colour in which he had plastered or painted the dwelling. In addition to the mentioned peculiarities, he had a course, growling voice. He was also left-handed, which lent a further uncouthness to his ungainly form and awkward deportment.

Very different was the wealthy baronet, whom the pair of ladies were about to visit for while Sir Vaux Waldgrave had no strong natural sensibilities, he was most keenly alive to what he called propriety. Accordingly, he regarded as of most undue importance the trifles of life, magnifying mole hills into mountains; so that he was one of those whom small sorrows place below the world, instead of great encounters raising him above it. The love of power and the desire of human applause were powerful principles within him; principles, which with his weak contracted mind, moving in the narrow sphere of domestic life, rendered him often intolerable. Such authority as his, which can only find exercise through a thousand little ways, may be made very sensibly to increase or to impair the happiness of those around. To direct and control every man, woman, and child, who came within his range, was his hobby; and this he contrived to accomplish in the most tedious and tormenting manner.

Sir Vaux was by no means a petty tyrant; for his aims were benevolent, according to his code of laws—laws, which as observed and administered by him,—he deeming himself an impressive speaker, and given besides to the explaining of everything,—made him one of the most tiresome bores that ever breathed. As for the two ladies who were on their way to the baronet's domicile, it was fortunate that some account of their mishap had gone before them by another route than that which they circuitously pursued, and also that the great man at the Hall happened to be languishing for subjects upon whom he might exercise and execute his code of form and delicacies; in short, the system of proprieties, which, in his self-assumed idea of his consummate wisdom, was fit and necessary for all that were of his order.

"Welcome to my ancestral residence, Mrs. Wilford Waldgrave; for it is my uniform way to be particular, even to the minuteness of names and designation," said Sir Vaux, on receiving his sister-in-law with her daughter, as they neared the porch of Wartham Hall, Yorkshire, to take up, according to his own special arrangement, their residence with him. "Let bygones be bygones," continued the pompous baronet, "except in so far as it is necessary for the well ordering of my affairs that I bear in mind passages of the past. And as for my pretty niece here, whom I have the pleasure of beholding for the first time in all my life,— as you well know, Mrs. Wilford Waldgrave,—I say doubly welcome;" the formalist clenching his latter words by stiffly saluting the cheek of the beautiful damsel. "And now," added he, "let me conduct you to my private parlour, that you may refresh yourselves with the choicest delicacies my ample means can command; after which you will be shown to your suite of apartments appointed by me for your sole and undisturbed accommodation, no matter how mighty or how numerous may be my visitors and guests."

Sir Vaux Waldgrave was an old bachelor, and the representative of an ancient Yorkshire family. He was besides a bulky and portentous-looking personage, with nothing characteristic about his countenance, except a pair of very elevated eyebrows, which lent an unvarying expression of astonishment to his physiognomy. He was on all occasions, when

he could command listeners, an egregious egotist; his voice being husky, and elocution feeble. He was imperious and obstinate to the uttermost extent of his power when opposed, or when the parties who dealt with him had not the tact to make him feel and believe that the thing they were anxious to bring about emanated entirely from himself. Do this, and he would yield almost anything and go anywhere; so that amongst his numerous tenantry there were few who did not in a short time contrive to render him a good and accommodating landlord. There was one other feature in the stupid career of Sir Vaux that may be here noticed; he looked upon himself to be not only a profound politician but a patriot of the first water. He never talked to any extent without bringing in by the shoulders his parliamentary influence and his avowal of the consciousness that his special talent was for statesmanship; although all the while his utmost reach either as regarded the amount of his sagacity or sway was to oppose change and progress with the pig-headed stubbornness of the most ultra-Toryism of the country party. Now, as this blundering Yorkshire baronet, at the period when our story begins, happened to be struggling against common sense and civilization, and while hostility to alteration was most rampant, it may very readily be credited that his equanimity was more than usually disturbed, and that the inefficacy of his opposition in one quarter, and this, too, in his view, the grandest, served but to render his mode and species of intolerance and despotism the more marked in every other direction where he could make these be felt.

"Our policy, daughter, is to humour your opinionative uncle to the uttermost in every notion or whim, and on all occasions," said Mrs. Waldgrave to the lovely Adelaide, as soon as they were fairly within their appointed apartments; "and to this end nothing will be more conducive than to give him a constantly patient and acquiescent hearing,—that is, so far as appearance goes, no matter how prosy or how absurd his talk may be. Let him but have to all-seeming everything his own way, and you, with my vigilant help, may wind him, large and ugly as he is, around your little finger."

"Oh! dear mother, I wish that you would not continue to talk to me so often and so urgently in this manner, as of late you have done," returned the generous and ingenuous Adelaide, who, whatever might be her deficiencies or wrong constructions, had still a heart which was not yet perverted from the love of truth, open dealing, and respect for age, by her selfish and artful parent. "I would fain cherish and cultivate tender affection as well real esteem for my lamented father's brother, who, with all his peculiarities,—and who has not censurable peculiarities?—I am sure, is a highly worthy man. Besides, how can I stand well with myself, or avoid contracting a dangerous and vicious habit, if I set about practising duplicity towards my kind, though, perhaps, headstrong uncle? I think you ought not to persist in commanding me to observe such sinister and unfair courses."

"You *think*, far too often you do, Adelaide

Waldgrave, as a fool," replied the mother. "Surely my trials, my experience, in life,—I being not only your parent but twice your age, —should give me wisdom as well as a title to instruct, to sway,—nay, to impose my commands upon you; especially when I am assured that the course I adopt will be eventually for your great worldly advantage. In fact, I am cognizant of a great deal more than you yet can, or shall, with my consent, be made acquainted with for a long time to come; and this bearing too upon your most important interests, and perhaps not distant prospects. Remember you are not only the heiress by law as well as by special testamentary settlement, or entail,—as I believe they call it,—of your uncle's ancestral splendid estate, but ought to be so wholly the object of his personal affections as that he will never think of willing away from you the bulk of his own vast accumulations. I enjoin you, at the peril of forfeiting more of my love and confidence than will be conducive to my own peace for you to do, to bear what I have have just stated constantly in mind; keeping in view, besides, that the sacrifices which through the flower of my life I made for the sake of your ungovernable father, not to speak of the perversity you seem to inherit from him,—with which I also have had to contend,—entitle me to issue such mandates to you, as will result in some obvious advantages to myself ere it be too late altogether, to learn that I ever became allied to the Waldgraves. But it is high time for us to repair to your uncle's presence, Adelaide; so you will follow me, like a good girl, without farther remark at this turn concerning that of which we have just been discoursing."

"My heart revolts at the tendency of my mother's mode of thinking and behaviour," the young lady mentally ejaculated, as she mutely accompanied her parent to the baronet's favourite apartment. "And hardly less am I repelled from her by the unkindliness of her manner to me,—I who have so long panted for such reciprocal endearments as should and do pass between most mothers and daughters. But, alas! it seems to me that I never knew what it was to have had a fond mother's heart to pillow my head even when I was an infant; no soothing mother's hand ever wiped away my childish tears,—all this having been left for my kind nurse to do,—tenderer and kinder than was she who gave me birth. Yes, I am repelled, my heart revolts, and surely the time is near, if not now, for me to stand out and firm upon my claims of conscience,—to assert my birthrights and some measure of freedom of will; otherwise it may be to relinquish myself to a dictation which I feel to be cruel, and to the observance of a course that must lead to misery here and hereafter."

Although the Waldgrave family was of ancient and elevated rank, neither national history nor provincial records supply any accounts of a single member of the line, for generations, having become distinguished through public services, or by the display of talent, in any one department. On the other hand, something not far removed from notoriety as well as unenviable publicity had attended the conduct and career of certain of the race, subjecting them to ridicule, and even to contempt and scandal, by persons of their own heraldic station.

Sir Vaux's elder brother, Reginald, who wore the family title for some time,—being several years the other's senior,—made a run-away marriage, or, as was generally said, formed a more questionable connexion with a beautiful girl in the neighbourhood of Wartham Hall, but who was of most obscure origin and without a shilling of fortune; and this folly was perpetrated during the life of his proud father, who, had it been in his power, would have for ever disowned him as a son, and disinherited him as a successor to title and estate. The reckless and passion-guided young gentleman sped him with the syren charmer to New England, where there was territory owned by his family, —the war between the American colonists and the mother country having by this time broken out; Reginald's gallantry, not only as regarded the beautiful young woman whom he took with him, prompting him to the withdrawal from his offended kinspeople, but also to struggle and fight for the rights of his race where they were actually menaced. In this service and enterprise he bore himself bravely; the death of his father taking place in the meanwhile. At length, however, he fell in battle in the New World; the tidings of his decease being wholly unaccompanied with any reference to Maria Bremner, the lovely creature who had been sc ill-fated as to run away with him.

Of course the next brother stepped into the vacated heirship, and from that date Sir Vaux showed himself resolved on maintaining the dignity of his line; bearing himself not only with the aristocratic pretensions of the proudest of his ancestors, but making it a matter of arrogant boasting that never would he ally himself by marriage with any but such as the world should acknowledge to be his equal by birth, wealth, and personal consideration; making it his practice at the same time to traduce the sex, as well as to hold out his own merits as being unapproachable.

The nuptials of the pompous baronet's younger brother, Wilford, with Jemima Chaloner, another provincial beauty, of questionable gentility,—being but a country surgeon's offspring,—seemed to feed the pride of Sir Vaux, and to embitter his railing against the tender sex,—so that he not merely determined to disown his now nearest kinsman for all time as brother, but to die a bachelor; the ungainliness of his person and manner, and his ridiculous pretensions, having a much greater deal to do with his *blessed singleness* than the stupid possessor of Wartham Hall was willing to understand or ready to acknowledge.

The dazzling but heartless and artful Jemima having contrived to win, if not to inveigle, Wilford Waldgrave into a matrimonial alliance with her,—weak-minded and at first a love-sick youth,—being Sir Vaux's junior by several years, —they withdrew to France. Here, upon some two hundred and fifty pounds a year—this being the amount of his patrimony—they lived in comparative affluence; the lady assuming and maintaining from the commencement of their union the supremacy over the feebler and more frivolous party, and acting the not unskilful manager.

It fell within the scope of Mrs. Waldgrave's discernment and ambition to work through the stupid and preposterous Yorkshire baronet, in causing her husband to practise upon the other's credulity and perversity by a continued and consistent system of professed subserviency and humiliation to him, and by a very constant urgency to have his advice concerning all things. Thus she flattered, in the most effectual way, the egregious pride and vanity of him who perhaps was the greater of the two simpletons, namely, Sir Guy, who mightily plumed himself upon the idea that he was the potent as well as invoked arbiter in respect even of every momentous national question.

The result at length of this cunning policy of Wilford's beautiful spouse was, at any rate, that Sir Vaux took his brother into considerable favour. Nay, after the lapse of several years of apparent estrangement and repudiation, he invited the faulty one to pay him a visit at Wartham Hall. This friendly and forgiving procedure was adopted again and again,—Mr. Waldgrave's sojourn at his birthplace being sometimes prolonged for a number of months together; and it was during one of those absences that Adelaide first saw the light.

"It is a girl, and therefore next best to a boy, that I am to place in your arms, beloved Wilford, when you return to Paris," wrote Mrs. Waldgrave. "It is a most charmingly stout and healthy babe, so that do not hurriedly quit your excellent brother's hospitable roof; that is to say, until the most sagacious of men, and influential of the people of title in Yorkshire, has condescended to suggest the name by which he would have our darling child baptized I am extremely anxious to have such an important circumstance settled, as being indebted to the accomplished baronet for a mellifluous appellation to our babe, in order that she may be reared in the daily inculcated knowledge of the fact. I trust you will not return to me until you bring with you the longed-for announcement and prized gift!"

"I have not lived till now, Wilford," said Sir Vaux, on a perusal of Mrs. Waldgrave's epistle, communicating the news of her child's birth, with the earnest requests concerning the name by which she should be christened, "without having evidence from your lips, as well as her letters, of your spouse being, after all, a superior woman, as women now-a-days run. The fact is, brother, there are, as I find in the course of my wide experience, among the commonalty and such as are hardly any distance removed from the ignorant, sordid, and brutish multitude,—there are, I say,—at rare times, to be sure,—some individuals who prove superior to the vast majority of their vulgar class, just as there are, amongst our own exalted and privileged order, melancholy instances of degeneracy and degraded taste. I must consider of your sensible partner's expressed anxiety, and indeed will write to her myself; so that ye shall not, brother, know what the charming appellation is by which your babe is to be called through life; or at least until perhaps I myself provide a suitable husband for her,—ye shall not be made acquainted with it except from the lips of the mother."

The baronet wrote to Mrs. Waldgrave, styling her sister-in-law, for the first time, either orally, or in legible terms; directing that the euphonious name *Adelaide* should forthwith, with all due solemnity, be given to the infant. "A name of hallowed significance and memorable occurrence," he asseverated, "in the archives of my celebrated ancestors." A hint had been suggested to, as well as a mandate sought for, in regard to the choice of nurse to the babe; nor was the black eyebrowed authority above giving instructions in this particular; the immediate reply from Mrs. Waldgrave to her brother-in-law being that she had found a young woman who was recently bereaved of her first-born, that in every respect answered admirably to the characteristics insisted on by her "far-sighted counsellor."

Adelaide proved a thriving child, and was the delight of the father, so far as a very weak-minded and unstable man in his habits, and also as respected his place of residence, could feel. In fact, he came to be fully more in Yorkshire with his egotistic brother, than in Paris with his usurping spouse; but the baronet could not bring himself so far to succumb to the impeachment that he could ever retreat a jot from his patrician creed as to acknowledge Mrs. Waldgrave publicly to be his sister-in-law. Accordingly, he refused to countenance her return to England. The child grew in beauty as she advanced in years, greatly indebted to her constant nurse and attendant, Maria,—such was the woman's name,—until the girl was bereaved of the vigilant care by the death of her guide. The mother had bestowed all along but a slight share of parental fondness upon the young creature, except as regarded an ample provision of tuition for her; such indeed as the artful calculator deemed would prove serviceable to herself should the great and proud uncle die without issue.

Adelaide had seen nine summers when she lost her daily, it might be said her hourly, attendant,—the thoughtless father being at the time with his brother; this proving, as usual during his absence, a relief to the self-willed spouse. At this period the charming child was held to be uncommonly beautiful. With a skin of dazzling whiteness, a profusion of golden ringlets, large blue eyes, and a sylph-like figure, she had an air of distinction, such as—the gently and fashionably trained will tell you,—although not always the accompaniment of high birth, is rarely to be seen except among the true patrician orders. As she advanced in age, and got to girlhood, her beauty did not, as is often the case, forsake her, but expanded and increased with her stature. Happily, also, her mind was of a character not to retard the progress of her loveliness, or to diminish its effect; a frown of displeasure, or an expression of evil passions, seldom passing over her face.

Up to this era in her life she was a creature of an open heart and buoyant spirits. But a change now began to come over her. She mourned her loss, and felt as one who had no bosom to repose upon,—no genial voice to respond to the artless outpourings of her curious inquiries or juvenile anxieties. Her features seemed to grow more soft and delicate; her countenance became milder and more expressive of thoughtfulness; and her manners more grave than is common at her age.

Her mother, though neither a dissipated nor gay woman, was so selfishly absorbed in carrying out her own plans in her Parisian *coterie*, and in regard to becoming thoroughly possessed of the Yorkshire baronet's confidence and approval, that she proved no parental companion to the girl, nor did she anything to adequately supply the place of the deceased Maria. The father, as already told, was at least half of his time with his brother; and when at his proper home, in consequence of being supplied incautiously by Sir Vaux with funds, he took so to debauched habits, that his arms were seldom open to the maiden. The domestic peace, even such as it had been in his less infatuated days,—which, after all, had nothing to boast of in the way of harmony,—was sadly broken by his headlong career. Disregarded or checked in the natural development and expression of her feelings, and not seldom shocked or insulted, Adelaide gradually learnt to repress her thoughts and confine her emotions to her own breast. And thus it came, that while to careless observers the feelings themselves seemed wanting, the roots were really striking deeper into the heart, though the shoots were rudely trodden down.

While the husband was acting the fool, and running a ruinous course, in respect at least of health and reputation, and the daughter was growing into womanhood and intelligent thoughtfulness, the wife had been advancing from the blooming hoyden which she was on quitting her birthplace, at the period of her nuptials,—with her awkward habits and provincial dialect,—into the beautiful woman, graceful in her movements, and polished, though elaborate, in her manners. At length a great and sudden change was to occur in the circumstances of Wilford Waldgrave's spouse, for he was cut off by apoplexy in the midst of his orgies; a fate which, instead of deeply afflicting the heart of his widow, rather facilitated her purpose, and strengthened her hopes in regard to her acceptance with Sir Vaux.

"I shall now have it all my own way with the bulky baronet," thought she; "and cannot fail, if I play my cards skilfully, of being invited,—nay, commanded, to take up my residence in England; perhaps in my native county, not remote from his princely seat; nay, peradventure, along with my daughter, to be domiciled in the Hall itself, until she succeeds to Sir Guy's immense wealth; after which event I'll take care to reign paramount over the spiritless thing, for such it pleases me to find her. Even a husband's sway and authority shall not readily upset a dominion which I have studied to obtain and to establish over the simpleton; especially as my confidence is complete,—if once the pompous, but, after all, weak and easily managed baronet comes within my cultivated influence, whatever his earlier exclusive sentiments may have

been towards me,—that I shall wield him to my liking, and to the fulfilment of my most far-sighted designs."

In perfect accordance with the cold-hearted and artful widow's ends, the breath was hardly out of the nostrils of her husband, when she set about concocting an epistle to Sir Vaux, conceived and expressed with all the glow which could be lent to feigned sorrow and sense of bereavement. It was a falsity of which the dull feelings of the stupid man could take no heed; she throwing in, at the same time, such inuendoes concerning her sufferings through the misconduct of the deceased, as she thought would stir up additional sympathy for her condition.

"I shall adopt no step," said she, in her tear-stained letter, "with regard to the manner, the time, and the place of interment of the mortal remains of the dear, though ofttimes imprudent, departed one, without your paramount special directions, Sir Vaux Waldgrave; save taking the necessary measures of immediate moment for the solemn preservation of the sacred dust in its leaden dwelling, within the chamber where Wilford breathed his last. Perhaps, sir, you will condescend, along with your instructions concerning the burial of my beloved one's ashes, to afford me some directions respecting my future conduct and location,—directions and commands which I humbly pray for from you mainly on account of my charming and highly accomplished Adelaide. Is it your will and pleasure, sir, that I quit Paris, and even this un-English country, with her; or do you require that we be entirely separated, and for ever,—she repairing to my admired native Yorkshire, and I remaining amongst foreigners? The slightest expression of your mind on these and other points momentous to me, as well as my child, will be regarded as a resistless injunction, without a single reluctant word; knowing that, however much my feelings at the first might rebel against your decisions, those decisions would be dictated by consummate wisdom, and in a manner that must eventually work for the greatest good of all concerned."

CHAPTER II.

THE SUPERLATIVE SUITOR.

SUCH were the terms in which a portion of the elaborate letter was couched, and which, to be brief, took the bulky baronet exactly in the manner wished for by the writer of it. Sensibly enough, he ordered that his brother's corpse should, without ostentation, be consigned to its last resting place. At the same time he transmitted a liberal allowance of money, to enable the widow to carry out his directions; also to clear off all debts which the deceased or she might at any time have honestly incurred in the city of their more than twenty years' residence; and, lastly, to bring her and Adelaide to Wartham Hall in suitable style,—"a style," the baronet added, "that is to have respect rather to the position and character of the living head of the Waldgrave family, than to the condition of any of the inferior or remote connexions, whether they be dead or alive."

Of course, it was not long after this when the managing mother and the serene, pensive daughter quitted the capital of France for the English coast. Arrived in London, they made haste to leave for Yorkshire, as nearly in the manner indicated by the baronet as the widow could imagine.

We have seen how it fared with them towards the termination of their land journey——Sir Vaux exonerating them from all blame in connexion with the disaster which occurred to their travelling equipage—and, also, how they were welcomed at the Hall by its ponderous owner. In short, he was entirely pleased with the taste and discretion they manifested; giving credit, at the same time, to the docility of his sister-in-law, because of her having acted in perfect conformity with his deliberate directions.

"She is not only a most sensible and discreet woman, I find," said the head of the Waldgraves to himself, the moment that mother and daughter left him, after enjoying refreshments, to take possession of their allotted chambers—"but she is really one of the most lady-like and mannerly of her sex that this country has produced. As to Adelaide, I at once discern that a sense of her beauty has not spoiled her; that she is meek, and trained to obedience,—the very qualities I desire to work with and mould to my considerate purposes. I shall treat her, if she prove and continue tractable, as were she my own offspring; and, seeing it cannot be too soon to commence my system of instruction and fatherly discipline, I shall begin this same afternoon, when dinner is over; knowing that the influx of visitors tomorrow and for days thereafter, no doubt, in consequence of becoming acquainted with the fact of the arrival of my presumptive successor, may interfere for a period with my directing influence over the damsel."

On the mother and daughter descending to the baronet's private parlour to dine with him there, — the three forming the entire party on that occasion, for a wonder,—and from everything which came under the observation of the two ladies that evening, and, indeed, afterwards, they were struck with the air of stiff propriety and splendid discomfort that reigned throughout everything in which the directing voice of the baronet was supreme. Now, this was so different from the ease and polish, together with the light-heartedness, with which the widow had been familiar for more than half of her years, and Adelaide all the days of her life, that it seemed to them as if they had been suddenly transported to the antipode of the gayest city of the world, and under an entirely opposite system of civilization to what prevailed there.

"These are beautiful and most inviting walks of yours, Sir Vaux, stretching far among the shrubberies, I perceive, after taking many a fantastic turn, though, no doubt, in strict keeping with the lines and laws of beauty and ornamental gardening," observed Adelaide, not unaccompanied by a sigh, as she turned from gazing at the massive furniture, and the almost antique features of the baronet's favourite parlour, and, indeed, *sanctum sanctorum*, to feast her eyes with the charms of nature, as seen through the window. "I shall have much delight in traversing your pleasure-grounds, and penetrating yonder thickets."

"Sit by me, Adelaide, while I read you a wholsome lecture, taking my text from words which you have now let drop," said the ponderous baronet,—the harsh tones of his voice, his coarse, yet feeble, elocution, and the startling elevation of his black bushy brows, combining to make the maiden tremble, as she turned to meet his address. "Sit by me, and listen. I am to inform you that it has long been a practice of mine to render *trifling occurrences*, and even the most *commonplace observations*, as the ignorant and unthinking name what people of understanding and penetration regard as *memorable events*, and *reprehensible sayings*,—to render, I say, such things the pegs, as it were, upon which to hang, or from which to start, the teachings which reading, meditation, and great experience have stored me with: it is my practice thus to act with persons younger than myself, ay, and sometimes with my elders, when they have the sense to be silent and patient. Having stated this much, I have to proceed to comment about your fancy for traversing my pleasure-grounds, and penetrating my picturesque thickets, all which reprehensible notions, I doubt not, you contemplated fulfilling by yourself, and alone, without such an escort as I must appoint for you. Well, then, to proceed: it is my positive, my imperative command, that you never upon any occasion, any pretence whatsoever, go beyond the threshold of Wartham Hall,—in one of the most admired chambers of which you happen to be now seated,—unattended, unaccompanied, and unescorted by such individuals or personages as I in due course of time will appoint and mention for you."

"Does England, then, so abound with ruffians,—do the magistracy and gentlemen of Yorkshire so feebly wear the sword of justice,"—cried Adelaide, alarmed and amazed at the portentous speech of her uncle, although her mother was affecting, by her smiles and gestures, approval and hearty acquiesence all the while,—"that a female cannot safely during day traverse your pleasure-grounds alone? I could hardly have credited this, sir, if the testimony had come from any other quarter."

"You are young, niece, you are inexperienced, and the laxities of our French neighbours may have infected you," replied the baronet, drawing himself up, with the greatest pomposity he could assume, and throwing into his voice all the rotund solemnity he had at his command. "But, first of all, let me set you right with regard, at least, to the territory which belongs to me. Whatever the rest of England may be where radical reformers abound—a most ruffian multitude, I allow—I say, with regard to my ancestral possessions, there is not a transgressor who can with impunity set foot upon them, the entire country knowing that Sir Vaux Waldgrave is 'a terror to evil-doers, and a praise to them that do well.'"

"Then whence the danger, dear sir," inquired the damsel, "of a person like me traversing of a morning or of an evening your charming park and other ornamented grounds, —I who have had in crowded Paris few opportunities of viewing cultured nature and expansive landscapes, upon the scale which the near vicinity of your noble mansion presents?"

"The danger! do you ask, my novice?" exclaimed the baronet, with a sardonic smile. "I spoke not of danger, peril, or jeopardy of any sort; but you ought to know that there are proprieties and delicacies which it is most necessary for a young lady with your prospects, and in your present position, to attend to, such as to be careful not, while alone, to expose yourself to the vulgar gaze even of any one of my out-door labourers. My code of conduct for such as you denounces the levity; it is, in a word, sufficient for me to issue my mandate to you, knowing full well the soundness of my reasons for issuing the same; so that I must, and shall be obeyed."

"I entirely agree with you, Sir Vaux Waldgrave," the mother chimed in. "In fact, we encountered a singularly rude and grotesque-looking being at the time that the mishap occurred to our horses and carriage on nearing the Hall. I certainly would not wish that Adelaide should fall in his way again;" the widow intending effectually to repress any curiosity which the mysterious manner and utterances of the almost grotesque Peter Plumtree had excited.

"Who was he, sister by affinity?" the startled baronet impatiently inquired; "his manner, his looks, his whereabouts? I must know more of this, and will know,"—the peremptory speaker affecting mightier interest in the matter by every sound he uttered, as well as by the lusty strokes he inflicted on the table before him.

The lady promptly supplied the required information so far as suited her purpose; representing the old man's proceedings as merely the result of impertinent curiosity, and as having been of no service. This was a view very different from that which the daughter took, although she felt she must not interpose a defence of the individual, seeing the temper in which the baronet chose to figure at the moment.

"Why," cried he, "it must have been that old wretch, Peter Plumtree, of the hideous Red Cot, as he names and has made his dwelling, in order to spoil the noblest view and most romantic scene of all my spacious and picturesque estate. He is a vile pest,—a thorn in my side, in fact, and this most literally; for possessing, as he does, a tongue of land—a mere slender wedge, as it were—that cleaves into my most charming grounds—viz., opposite to the Cauldron Cliff,—he, like as did his obstinate father before him, refuses to dispose of the same to me,—no matter what the sum I offer for its purchase. Nay, more, he has erected, plastered, and painted the eye-sore spoken of merely to vex and spite me,—monstrous radical that he is, and leveller that would be of the grandees of my country. In short, a vile democrat and outrageous revolutionist, whom it would be but justice to cut off. Indeed——"

"A letter, sir, delivered by a servant on horseback, who desired that it might be instantly handed to you, sir," said a lacquey.

"All right," cried Sir Vaux, the moment the note was put before him; "and this *event*, not *commonplace occurrence*, as fools of the unthinking sort might deem it, will concern you, Adelaide, more nearly and interestingly than you dream of in your philosophy, or even my discourse relative to your walking alone in my pleasure-grounds could directly have done. And yet with that subject you will find that I connect this document in a manner that is striking. This welcome and pleasing letter," continued the tedious and tormenting baronet, after a pause,—"this elegant epistle, I say, which I hold in my hand, is from no less considerable a person than he who has long held a high place in my favour and affections, and who, for the future, will have to be regarded by you, Adelaide, with still higher and tenderer partialities, if you ever have the hope and desire to enjoy my countenance and regards. I allude to my nephew, by my only sister, Gertrude,—whose name, by the bye, I, at the first, had thought of ordering for you, my dear,—the Hon. Ludlow Chesters, of the noble house of Chesters, a most gallant and meritorious officer in the most *crack* corps of his gracious Majesty's household troops,—the First Regiment of Life-Guards. You ought to be informed that the Chesters' family is one of the most ancient, renowned, and potent in the British peerage, and whose weight and political influence, when combined with, and supported by, mine, as well as by my experience and foresight, has not seldom made the first minister of the crown to yield to us, or to those of our friends whom we have chosen to recommend and patronise, valuable grants, privileges and promotions. Let me inform you that a great deal goes by favour in the high places of the state, and this is just as it ought to be. People of my standing and stamp are generally better judges of merit, and what ought to be done in particular quarters, than the members of the executive. However, it is of my high-souled nephew that I am more immediately to speak. Hem! Where was I?" and the baronet cogitated for a few moments in order to collect his ideas and to come at his discourse. "Yes, as I was telling you," continued Sir Vaux, "Ludlow is a pattern for our young patrician order. He is now in his twenty-eighth year, is a gentleman in the properest acceptation of the term, handsome, highly accomplished, witty, and truly brave. In short, he is a man, in the flower of his age, and of first-rate fashion—a star, I may say, of greatest magnitude in the galaxy of the wonderful London world, during the *season*. Indeed, there cannot be a doubt, had our present George been in his prime, at this era in England's history, my nephew would have shone as an associate of the first gentleman in Europe, and been already high in office in the court of the monarch to whom I have affectionately referred."

The ponderous talker had reached the climax of his figures of speech, when he got among the heavenly orbs, and also of his praise and exultation on planting himself by the side of the Fourth George. No further could the Yorkshire baronet go, and, therefore, he had to betake himself to a series of *hems*, and then descend into more homely announcements.

"In short," said Sir Vaux, on obtaining his

customary volume of breath, after the flight of eloquence, "the Hon. Captain Ludlow Chesters, of the First Regiment of Life-Guards, is to be with us here, at Wartham Hall, at no more distant a day than to-morrow; he being on a visit to a neighbouring gentleman for the present,—hovering about, so to speak, in order to alight at my mansion at the period of my niece's expected arrival, to take up, along with her prudent mother, her residence with me. We shall soon have many other arrivals. Even already, and since I gave you my welcome in the porch and at the threshold of my house, have I issued invitations to sundry of my best and most notable neighbours, to join me here without delay; so that you will perceive, Adelaide, how important and imperative it is that you be governed and directed by me in everything,—your good mother coinciding,—aware,

No. 2.—THE GOVERNESS.

as you must be, that I am the best judge of all that relates to my own character and dignity, as also the character and delicacy of those through whom I shall be beheld and be judged of."

But, not further to fatigue the reader with the dead weight of the bulky baronet's discourse on this occasion, let it be understood that he had fixed upon and pronounced with all the assurance and irreversible decision of one who acts the autocrat, that Adelaide was to wed Captain Chesters; intimating, at the same time, that if she perversely refused to be guided implicitly in this matter by her uncle, or even if she evinced the semblance of reluctance to the arrangement, he, the talker, knew of a method whereby to render the nephew his substantial successor, vastly to her own loss and injury. From this height, Sir Vaux clumsily passed on to the subject of walking in his ornamented grounds, and penetrating to the romantic spots of his large and unquestionably picturesque estate; pointedly and plainly announcing that it would be at the peril of incurring his "highest displeasure," if ever she so ventured abroad, or forth from the Hall, while the Hon. Ludlow was a visitor and guest of his uncle, except when leaning on the gallant officer's arm.

"And does not this decision of yours, Sir Vaux Waldgrave, amount to making a prisoner of me whenever Captain Chesters may be absent from Wartham Hall," half playfully, half seriously, inquired Adelaide, looking coaxingly in the face of the high-browed baronet as she spoke.

"You do not mean to insinuate that the privilege of enjoying the expanse at will of this mansion and noble Hall, or even of having only the scope of your proper suite of apartments, can ever be likened to incarceration!" croaked the bulky, lumbering man. "Yet, to relax my rule, I have to add that when Ludlow may chance to be with his regiment, which will scarcely occur before the solemnization of your nuptials, I myself will attend you in your peregrinations; or, when this is impossible, your good and approving mother there will be your companion. Upon no account, let me once for all announce to you, are you to stray from my threshold at unseemly hours with any one—not even with your parent or the captain either, so long as you remain unwedded; and further, at no hour of the day are you to transgress my edict as regards your escort—that is, to have one or other of the three responsible persons named by your side. It must not be that such a lovely, priceless jewel expose herself to the possibility of any impertinent, rude, or vulgar gaze, until she be clothed with a husband."

"More anxiously considerate, affectionate, and complimentary vigilance has never been devised by parent or guardian than that of which Sir Vaux Waldgrave has given you a foresight, Adelaide, thus early," breathed the mother, pointedly addressing her daughter, and throwing into her manner the tokens of admiration and surprise. Then, turning more directly to the baronet, she added, "I think I may promise from my child implicit obedience to your slightest wish, Sir Vaux; she has not known what it is, hitherto, to go counter to legitimate authority."

"We shall see, we shall see. I have not yet had time or opportunity to test her," returned the husky, heavy copyist of the law of the Medes and Persians, Adelaide, meantime, biting her lip. "But I must pay immediate heed to concerns which Ludlow's letter has rendered of paramount importance; so that you may have the range of the Hall till next meal, always excepting my sleeping and dressing-rooms. Few are allowed access to the apartment in which we have now been enjoying ourselves, but which will be ever open to you until contrary orders are given."

We shall not for a time burden our story with much more of the baronet's heaviness—passing also over a great deal which occurred between the widowed mother and her daughter, in consequence of what they had so soon learnt from Sir Vaux's matter and manner of discourse. Mrs. Waldgrave declared herself greatly strengthened in her previous views of the mode in which she and Adelaide ought to carry themselves towards the young lady's uncle, of whom the utmost that a maiden's ambition could contemplate might be made, the widow declared, by exceedingly trifling sacrifices—merely amounting to a disregard of truth and honesty, the adoption of deceit and duplicity of bearing and speech, and the abandonment of all natural, juvenile feeling.

As for the individual whose virtue and happiness were thus prospectively trifled with, everything that she had witnessed, during but the few hours she had been under her uncle's roof, served to invigorate her design of taking such an early stand in defence of some measure of independence and free will, as appeared to her to be far more desirable possessions than any that could descend to her from her father's brother or her living parent's principles, counsels, and example. In regard to Captain Chesters, the ingenuous Adelaide strove to withhold herself from forming any preconception, although it was impossible for a young creature of her thoughtful habits not to be rather scared than enticed by the baronet's representations concerning him. However, the maiden was not long to be left to mere hearsay relative to the man whom Sir Vaux had fixed upon for husband to her—there being beheld by her next day from the window, through which she was feasting her eyes on the beauties external to the mansion, and before the meridian hour had arrived, a grand display in the shape of arrivals.

"Look yonder, Adelaide!" cried the mother, with unusual fervour; "it is a barouche and four, driving up with splendid pace and parade, nobly emblazoned, with riders and liveries most dazzling, and, in short, all the *eclat* of an equipage which at once denotes great wealth, admirable taste, and lofty rank. There is one lady and one gentleman. What a flattering compliment to us, dear, were the testimony borne by no other circumstance than that they must have been abroad at an unusually early hour for people of their quality. What say you, daughter? What makes you so demure?" added the parent, with something of a displeased and upbraiding tone. "I fear that Adelaide Waldgrave was not made for a life of brilliant bustle, or to sustain the honours of Wartham Hall."

"I am sure I was not; I feel that I am unfited to uphold a part, not to say to shine, among such people as these, judging from their display," was the maiden's return to the designing and unfeeling mother.

"Poor soulless thing!" exclaimed the widow. "Yet, spite of yourself, wreathe that face in smiles, and carry yourself, girl, as if you really merited to be the splendid heiress which it requires only a little spirit and common sense to render you. But what do I next behold? Why, a most sprightly cabriolet, with its calash thrown quite back, and a fine high-spirited bay dashing hitherward, his veins starting through the silky skin, and proclaiming the excellence of his blood. A magnificent fellow, with his dove-coloured kid gloves, dexterously and gently manages the noble courser. It must be—it cannot but be—the Hon. Ludlow Chesters!" And the widow was right,—the equipage was that of the Captain, and the charioteer was no other than he himself.

"But who is this that comes trudging on foot across the lawn," exclaimed the widow with some surprise, on perceiving a gentlemanly young person sedately approaching in that unpretending fashion. "No doubt it is some bore or another, for the gratification of the baronet's peculiar tastes; most probably some sombre parson whom Sir Vaux, the formalist, has invited to say grace at dinner. But I hear the footsteps of the ponderous, may I not add, portentous baronet," the widow sneeringly whispered, next moment, with affected humility and sweet cordiality, curtseying her apparently joyful reception of him.

The mother and daughter were speedily conducted to the grand saloon, where the visitors were anxiously waiting to meet and congratulate them on their safe arrival. Here was Lord Adolphus Rivers, and his sister, Lady Augusta, members of a ducal house. It was their magnificent equipage that had at first so transported Mrs. Waldgrave, when viewed from her window. For the present, it is sufficient to say of his lordship that he looked a man of forty years; that he had a not undignified and a placid aspect; and that his few first words were not only handsomely conceived, but they carried a remarkable fulness of meaning with them. The lady, his sister, might be five years younger, with a strong resemblance to Lord Adolphus every way.

But it was the Hon. Captain that must have chiefly arrested the attention of a stranger on entering the chamber, not merely because of the graceful, high-bred ease of the man of fashion that he at once showed himself to be, but of a certain *hauteur* in his bearing, which was yet so qualified by the light gaiety and sportive good-nature of his manners, that it seemed nothing more than that elegant sense of his own exterior superiority, to which, without arrogance, he could not be insensible.

Assuredly, the Life-Guardsman was not merely formed according to the first model of manly beauty, but he had a high hereditary air of gentility and freedom, and which bore the impress of nobility and distinction. His address to Adelaide was fitted at the first to remove any special embarrassment she might be expected to experience, for it had at once the polished facility and the pleasant composure of one who was not only conversant with accomplished society, but who understood his title to talk to her, as both a near kinsman, and as one that was specially endeared to him. He kissed her hand, took her arm within the bend of his; and, while leading her from one to another of the party, spoke much and well,—no doubt, knowing his powers in this way, as also how uncommonly agreeable his voice and accents were. There was most significance, however, in what the captain uttered to Montague Mildmay, the young gentleman who came on foot—he whom Mrs. Waldgrave had characterized as "some sombre parson," and one whom "Sir Vaux, the formalist," had invited to say grace at dinner.

"I have the privilege, I trust, as well as the pleasure," said Chesters, "notwithstanding our kind uncle's previous courtesy, of introducing you to Montague Mildmay, of Mildmay Park,—of recommending him to your good graces, Miss Waldgrave. And this I do, not only because, as you have learnt, of his relationship to ourselves, but of his many superior qualities both of head and heart. He is saintly as well as scholarly; and, although he looks as modest and retiring as a young lady on her *debût* at our London *season*, he has yet all the self-possession and coolness of a man of the world;" all this being said with such a smiling facility, and yet carelessness whether it gave offence, or not, as indicated a self-assuring confidence on the part of the speaker, and a patronizing sense.

"I am proud to be recommended to the friendship of Miss Waldgrave, valuing it on its own account," answered Mildmay. "Yet I must not seem ungrateful to him who has had his part in affording me the happiness, especially as he has furnished at the same time what he conceives to be a comprehensive and graphic sketch of my properties;" this being spoken in a tone that was bland and measured, and with an unaffected bearing, although unequal, in point of apparently conscious superiority and polished training, to Chesters' carriage.

Some deficiency in dress and gentility of figure, as compared with the other, no doubt had its effect on Adelaide's first judgment. Still, the young lady fancied she perceived in Ludlow's look and manner, when Montague spoke, indications of his being unwilling to prolong discourse with him who could claim "relationship to ourselves;" for though it was with a supercilious smile that he listened to the quiet reply, he immediately led her away to another quarter, where he might maintain his part in a more general conversation. In this the Life Guardsman took the lead,—in fact, starting the topic, in a tone and spirit, besides, characteristic of him; his intention and motive no doubt being to bestow indirect flattery upon his lovely cousin, to whom he paid not only the most marked attention, but upon whom his eyes were ever turned with what appeared the expression of delicate homage and admiring love.

CHAPTER III.

THE CAULDRON CLIFF.

"WE had rather too much of warmth where I was yesterday at dinner, my Lord Adolphus," observed Captain Chesters, "about hereditary rank and titles, family honours, pride and ancestry, and kindred subjects. You may be sure I lent my voice to that side to which I naturally by birth and relationship belong; that is to say, speaking in general terms, and of mankind as we find them in classes. But we had two or three millmen,—cotton-spinners,—at table, each one of whom I believe, had belonged in his boyhood to the working orders,—all radical reformers,—who as earnestly, at least, combated my patrician notions. In the course of the contention we diverged in some measure from our first theme, making *beauty*, female beauty, our topic, where I proved myself consistent; although I am aware, had my friend

Mildmay, there, been one of our number, I should have had him for an antagonist as well as the cotton-spinners and calico-printers."

"And what, may I inquire of you, Captain Chesters, might be your *consistent* notions respecting female beauty?" inquired Mildmay, who had been so pointedly referred to, "what the terms and tone in which you expressed yourself? for much depends upon the latter. Was it triumph, or truth, which formed your aim and end, I should like also to be informed, before I enter into anything like collision with you on so interesting a subject?"

Adelaide felt, from the twitch of Chesters's arm, that he winced as the other spoke, although his countenance betrayed no emotion, so complete a master was he of show and manner. The discovery in some degree astonished her, as the other gentleman's questions were mildly and naturally put. Her knowledge of them, however, was necessarily far too limited at the moment for understanding their characters and histories; otherwise she must have known that in disposition, accomplishment, and pursuit they were widely different; and that although they were both connected by blood with Sir Vaux,—the one more remotely than the other, —that although also they had been playmates in boyhood, fellow-pupils and scholars, and on familiar terms up to that hour,—yet they had never been bosom friends, in the true meaning of the language; the attachment, such as it was, having gradually slackened as they advanced in years. We have already outlined Ludlow's character, attainments, and aspect. Montague merits a similar sketch, and this is it:—

In him there was nothing so remarkable as to arrest a stranger and the careless eye, or to call forth instant admiration. Yet his figure was good, being tall and well proportioned; his head and features were well formed, having altogether that intellectual aspect,—that sort of classical cast, which, although not conspicuous, is uncommon,—that air of calm repose, which indicates a mind of an elevated order. Nevertheless, if seen only on a first occasion, and for but a short time, beside the Hon. Ludlow Chesters, Montague Mildmay would have been overlooked by most people; for he had little of that patrician bearing, and still less of that brilliancy of address, which distinguished the other. And yet he had what is still more rare,—that unaffectedness of manner which borrows nothing from imitation; few peculiarities being more striking or admirable than such a want of effort. His character was noble, his sentiments sincerity itself, and great was his simplicity of motives and aims.

We return to the subject of female beauty, and the questions it elicited; to the first of which Captain Chesters answered directly, without, however, finding it convenient to take any notice of the inquiries in regard to the tone, manner, and motive of his expressed views.

"My consistency of notion was this, friend Mildmay," returned the Life-Guardsman, "and will continue to be—that female beauty, as a general fact, belongs alone to the true aristocracy; a fact, indeed, which is in perfect accordance with what we know of birth, breed-

ing, training, and civilization all over the world."

"I cannot go along with you, Captain," said Mildmay, "to the extent you carry your views However rare beauty may be, to confine it to the higher orders appears to me arbitrary and unjust."

"I hold," returned the gallant officer, "that not only does female beauty specially belong to people of our condition and ancestry, but that it is nearly alone that such people can properly appreciate the quality, leaving out, of course, the professional class. How indeed can one of the unwashed, of the *canaille*, possibly com prehend the fine antique cast of such feminine features as you and I have seen, and do see,— the classical contour of the head,—the swan-like neck,—the inimitable moulding of the cheek, of patrician beauty; this comprehension, I maintain, having a very considerable influence towards the production, in the course of time, of the features so judiciously and tastefully admired?"

"The mass of the people,—the *canaille*, as you name them, Chesters," observed his antagonist,—"may not discourse so fluently, so elegantly, so artificially, on the present subject as you do. And yet they may be as fond and proud of their wives and daughters as the greatest lord in the land; for many of these wives and daughters are as admirable in mind as in person."

"The notion is absurd; the assertion contrary to fact; the thing is impossible," cried the Hon. Ludlow, affecting to be moved as if by the feeling of offence, desiring to be thought by the ladies present the champion of the sex, and also, by his manner to Miss Waldgrave, endeavouring to evince an unusual quantity of superlative love.

"Undoubtedly," said Mildmay, in continuation of his views, "it is difficult to conceive finding the artificial refinement of what you, Captain Chesters, regard as high life in a person of humble birth and lowly breeding. Yet why may not a female's manners be as true to the more natural and sincere standard of the working classes, and her mind as noble, though met with in the plain cot of a peasant, as what may be found in the palace of a prince?"

"Do you really profess to say, Montague Mildmay," demanded the Life-Guardsman, rising in his warmth, "that the offspring of a country lout or a town mechanic,—beings who tread the ground in hob-nailed shoes, or that have sat all their lives cross-legged with their noses at a grinding-wheel,—can possibly possess or have acquired the same lofty as well as refined spirit as the descendants of heroes and statesmen? The very thought of being so descended must elevate the mind and imbue it with a superiority over the low-born drudges of the earth."

"Where are your facts, my friend?" quietly inquired Mildmay. "You made reference to facts and possibilities a little while ago. Alas! these are beyond all question against you. According to your argument, you would have us to conclude that Shakspere, Milton, Burns, and a multitude more, both ancient and modern, of nature's nobility, were of high descent, but which was not the case. In one view, I regard it as rather a brand upon the aristocracy of this country,—families of wealth, honours, and power for centuries,—that the order can present so few really great names. How numerous are the *old families*, as they are sometimes called, who have not furnished the world with an historical—nay, even a provincial celebrity! On the other hand, it seems to be ordained, and if so, it must be wisely, that genius is not hereditary. Were it so, in the course of ages under what an oligarchy and despotism should mankind labour! A word or two more, for I feel earnest and sincere on such subjects as Captain Chesters has thought fit to start this forenoon. Let it never be forgotten that there is a taste in moral as well as in physical beauty; the privileged, exclusive, and artificial, being apt to suppose that both kinds are principally to be met with in the saloons of the rich, and under court-dresses, where stars and coronets principally glitter. However, depend upon it, that the purest beauty can as little be found in what is unsatisfactory to the eye of reason and the voice of truth, as real happiness is to be discovered in what the world calls pleasure,—*happiness!* that rare thing, upon whose name I have stumbled, which is such a generous, diffusive, sentiment, that it gladly seeks to impart a portion of its own blessedness to all around."

More than once, something like a sigh had escaped Adelaide's breast, in response to the pulse of admiration felt for him over whom her cousin would fain have had that day's triumph; her feeling heart being encouraged by the glistenings of delight with which Lady Augusta Rivers regarded the amiable and bland speaker.

"What say you, my Lord Adolphus, concerning the difference of views between me and Mildmay?" impatiently inquired Chesters; expecting that the member of an ancient ducal house would at least help him out to some extent.

"Why, I would and must say," answered his lordship, "be grateful if your descent is from worthy ancestors; especially if they have not only done the state some public service, but been patterns of good conduct in their private lives. It is your duty to be thankful and to congratulate yourselves, if you find that you are the descendants of such forerunners. Yet, be most jealously on your guard, lest this lawful satisfaction degenerate into arrogance, or a fancied superiority over those nobles of God's creation, who, endowed in other respects with exalted qualities, cannot point to a long line of titled ancestry. Pride is, of all sins, the most foolish as well as hatefully mean; and even of the proud, who is so despicable as he who values himself on the merits of others? Remember, besides, that never yet was there a stainless family.

'Where, then, is boasting?
Only the actions of the just
Smell sweet, and blossom in the dust.'

One word more. Times are changed, and, in many respects, we are blessed with knowledge beyond our fathers; yet we must not, on that account, deem ourselves better than they were. On the other hand, we should not assent to the opinion so often hazarded, that the virtues of chivalry are necessarily extinct with the system they adorned. Chivalry, in her purity, was a holy and a lovely maiden, and many a heart was refined and ennobled by her influence: nay, she proclaims to us no one virtue that is not derived from, and summed up in, Christianity. The 'age of chivalry' may be past—the knight may no more be seen issuing from the embattled portal-arch on his barbed charger,—his lance glittering in the sun, and his banner streaming in the breeze,—but the spirit of chivalry can never die; still that spirit burns, like love, even in what some would characterize as the mechanical and material nineteenth century—lights up its holiest shrine—the heart of that champion of the widow, that father of the fatherless, that liegeman of his God and his country—the noble-hearted, but practically-minded Christian man of England."

At the suggestion of some one, the day being charming—a delicious breeze tempering the sun's heat—it was proposed that the party should take a stroll in the baronet's beautiful and extensive pleasure-grounds. Sir Vaux himself seeking to be excused, for that he had pressing domestic matters to see to. There were thus three couples: Adelaide and Chesters, Lady Augusta and Mildmay, Mrs. Waldgrave and Lord Adolphus. They traversed the meandering walks through the shrubberies, they paraded avenues, visited grottos, struck into paths formed amongst the plantations, and even extended their excursion to the bolder features of the baronet's wide possessions, some of which had rugged and massive scenery to recommend them to attention, together with tragical traditions.

The most remarkable of these spots presented a precipice of stern and noble aspect, consisting of a huge and towering sandstone pile of nature's masonry; the greater portion of the boldest of its facings being abrupt and precipitous, with a far-sunk foundation, much below the general level, through which a rapid stream drove with boiling and foaming fury; giving the name of the Cauldron Cliff to the frowning scene. The vehement waters washing the suddenly dipping stone-work deep into the soil, had, in the course of ages, gradually increased the descent, or the perpendicular surface of the rock. As the bold masonry,—to repeat the term,—neared the summit, it broke into huge fragments, piled beside and above one another; forming a superstructure of beetling and, in some instances, such nicely poised portions,—each of them many tons in weight,—as added not slightly to the grandeur of the features. What served still further to enhance the picturesque aspect of the romantic scene, were the gnarled oaks, which for centuries had been growing out from the fissures of the frowning superstructure, together with many a smaller branch and numberless brambles. And then the locality was hallowed to the imagination by certain stories, not only of vengeful bloodthirstiness, but narratives of warrior-deeds, together with sundry tales of adventurous love.

"I never beheld a scene like this in nature," cried Adelaide, as soon as she was led to the rugged summit of the precipice, "and have only conceived of it from my reading, or, perhaps, still more vividly from having at rare times witnessed theatrical displays, in which such wild pencils as Salvator Rosa have characterized the painted representations. And how much it adds, at this instant, to the perfection of the bold and rugged—the almost savage—features of the landscape, to find yonder grotesque being in what may be treated as the foreground, down below, with his red night-cowl upon his head, and his figure as well as posture the uncouthest. Ha! it is the same singular and mysterious personage who came to my deliverance when our carriage was upset, on our way from York to the Hall,—a service for which I will ever hold myself his deep debtor. But how comes he to encroach upon our uncle's grounds, and especially so near to his cherished scenes?—a question I ask you, Captain Chesters, with the greater curiosity, having not only learnt something of Sir Vaux's watchfulness over his ornamented territory, but of his dislike to Peter Plumtree, as I think he named the individual?"

"You are perfectly in the right, Miss Waldgrave," answered the Life-Guardsman, "with regard to our uncle's jealousy about uninvited feet venturing to tread upon his pleasure-grounds, and also both as to the name of yonder queer wretch and the hatred of him that is entertained by the baronet. But know that the owner of the neck of land upon which a frightful square box of a bright scarlet colour stands, as you will perceive through the branches a little way off, is as seldom upon the lands of Wartham Hall as our uncle is upon his; he stands upon his own property; but more of it and him at another time. I long to hear the story of the upsetting of your carriage, of which I am entirely ignorant."

"At another time, also, Captain Chesters,— at another time," said the young lady. And gathering courage of spirit as well as fluency of speech, she added: "I must endeavour to obtain Sir Vaux's leave to sketch this noble feature in his possessions,—in fact, to paint it elaborately, with the exception of the redness of Plumtree's cottage; Paris, with all its wealth of subjects, never having supplied me with one of this kind in reality. I'll show you, cousin, one of the points from which, if I can judge when standing here, I should wish to take a picture; commanding, as I imagine it does, a most striking view of the boldest aspect of the precipice and its adjuncts. I doubt not of the position giving me, besides, a sufficient command of the stream whose hoarse brawling reaches our ears, but whose crystal waters we cannot here behold."

As Adelaide thus talked, she had withdrawn her right arm from leaning on the captain's, in order to point accurately to the position far below, on the opposite side of the water, where she thought the spot most favourable for her sketching would be afforded. The motion of her arm and pointing finger, directed through an opening between the upshooting branches of stately trees, whose roots were embedded in crevices and fissures fathoms lower down among the piled masses, naturally was accompanied with a corresponding leaning forward of the entire person, more especially, as it

seems she hoped to get a glimpse of the stream, of whose turbulence her hearing gave her partial knowledge. So far, all was well; but something more was to be instantly witnessed. Partly, perhaps, from a giddiness which might have seized her,—a turning, as it were, of the brain,—a sudden impulse to throw herself off, and away into the void before her,—but still more from the instantaneous yielding and crumbling of the material upon which was her gentle footing, and also from a sense of having been propelled by her companion,—from one or all of these causes, it so happened that her weight precipitated the maiden, with headlong force, down towards the base of the awful steep; Mildmay and his partner having come so near at the instant as to be witnesses of the appalling event.

During the long stroll and varied courses which the three pairs that day had taken in the delightful grounds of the baronet, Captain Chesters had not lost one moment in forwarding his views and suit, as he flattered himself, in reference to his fair cousin. He brought the force of all his artillery, in the shape of polished flattery, of affected ardour, of diversified and splendid displays of conversational powers,—sometimes in romantic descriptions, again in exuberant bursts of generous or gallant sentiment, and again, in withering sarcasm applied to the absent,—Mildmay coming in for his full share,—to bear upon the serene, yet, as the Life-Guardsman flattered himself, the admiring listener,—sweet simpleton, as he set her down to be. Nor was the experienced man of the world of courtesy and gaiety, in which he had achieved many triumphs amongst the fair, wholly in error when he fancied he was making an impression upon the gentle one whose arm pressed his; although that impression was not exactly such as he had calculated upon. He even talked, at last, of their uncle's fixed arrangement as to their early union; and thence easily passed on to the subject of such alterations in regard to objects they were viewing as, he said, had often occupied his mind during his sojourn at Wartham Hall.

"But this was before I had enjoyed the ineffable pleasure of beholding her," he ejaculated, as they paused at one quarter where he knew they should be unseen and unheard, "compared with whom all is trivial and of no account which the world otherwise or elsewhere holds. Much had I heard of your merits and attractions, much more had I figured to myself of your priceless worth; but now that I have beheld you, and listened to you, all that was said and all that was fondly fancied shrink into nothingness in presence of the reality. That psalm-singing yet stoical Mildmay, who is somewhere behind us, when I have, on occasions, broken out in my raptures concerning my destined bride, would rally me about my heroics, and as being premature in my adoration—ay, and extravagant at any time. But he is a dolt, whom we shall be obliged to tolerate, with this forewarning to you, dear cousin,—soon to be addressed by a tenderer title,—that while priding himself in saying that he loves truth on all occasions, and honest dealing, he is one of the most deceitful and designing fellows in existence."

The captain thought that he held it all his own way, fancying that he had nothing but a creature little more discerning and sensible than a prettily-painted doll to deal with—a mistake into which he had the more readily fallen by observing that, though she said but little in the course of his heartless and common-place rhapsodies, her eyes at times sparkled, and her countenance gave out tokens of surprise and admiration, as he believed; especially when he repeated, as he several times did, "that the reality infinitely transcended all that had been reported and imagined" concerning her; "her matchless beauty," it was added, "being even inferior to the charms of the rarest intelligence," as the mental attribute was found in his cousin.

"This is a wonderful discovery of yours, Captain Chesters, that of my surpassing intelligence," quietly observed Adelaide, on his repeating the asseveration for the fifth or sixth time, and just as they were nearing the precipice already described, which, according to tradition, had proved fatal to the innocent or the misguided on sundry occasions. "I will not say wonderful at present, in respect of your discovery of that which does not exist, for it is unnecessary to go so far. But the marvellous matter is, how you can have so soon and rapidly made that discovery; for I have never yet, in your hearing, uttered half-a-dozen consecutive sentences. In short, I look upon Mr. Mildmay's views as being the best and most trustworthy, where he recommends the observance of truth and fair dealing above all other courses, including courtship as essentially as commercial transactions."

How far the staggering of the gallant captain, or rather feather-bed soldier, which overtook his notions on listening to the still, small voice, that had not only reached his outward ear, on hearing the maiden's few words, but had also spoken to his conscience,—how far this may have affected his physical energies and rapidity of action when Adelaide slipped, first, from his arm, next, heedlessly pointed and bent forward, and lastly, was launched towards the abyss below,—a shriek announcing her sense of the treacherous nature of her footing, as the soil gave way,—these are inquiries to which we do not at this part of the story address ourselves. It is sufficient for the present to be told, that she, who a little while before had been described as priceless, was allowed not merely to shoot out and away from him without an outstretched arm of his being offered to arrest her descent, but that, even when out of sight, he only wrung his hands, like one incapacitated for exertion by utter despair,—roaring out the while for assistance.

Nor was the proffered help far distant, however ineffectual it might prove. Quick as the speed of a winged creature, was the rush of Mildmay to the brink of the precipice. The grasp of the first branch he could reach, and a look of agonising eagerness downwards, were the doings of the next moment.

"Have heart, and hold fast, Adelaide!" were the words that he shot down to the dreadfully perilled maiden, on perceiving that she had been arrested by a number of out-stretched branches, upon which she lay,—the elastic materials swinging in response to their burden's weight, and keeping her spread over the tremendous void below, which terminated in the rugged channel of the noisy stream. "Have heart,—lose not your self-command,—hold fast, as you are doing, and succour and safety are yours," were the utterances that the adventurous young gentleman kept repeating, whilst, at great personal risk, he contrived by means of the inequalities in the face of the precipice, the up-shooting branches, and the fantastic bendings of many a tough root, to gain nearly to the quarter where the damsel swung.

"I have heard your words, Mildmay," said Adelaide, her eye turned towards him during his dangerous descent, "and my confidence has not quite gone; but you must not come nearer, for it is I who must endeavour to get to you, finding that the branches which support me have not strength to sustain additional weight. Oh! I shall have faith and assurance while you are in sight."

It was in broken utterances and snatches that the wondrously self-possessed young lady thus spoke; her simultaneous efforts to near the spot where Mildmay held himself being greatly guided as well as encouraged by his directing voice. And, delightful to be told, she succeeded in crawling and scrambling towards him along the stems of two or three of the stoutest of the outshot branches, until she got to where he could lend her the aid of his hand and next of his arm. A moment or two later, and she stood on a narrow footing in his embrace, within a fissure, where, whilst they both were able to maintain their self-command, no immediate danger threatened.

"Miraculous!" cried some one below. "Be strong and trustful! She's the very picture of ——no matter who:" the speaker the while being upon his bended knees, and his arms earnestly uplifted, as if to receive her should she drop. It was Peter Plumtree.

"Yes, be strong and trustful a little longer," breathed encouragingly the young gentleman, neither of them thinking of other than the most familiar, and, in the circumstances of their position, the most affectionate form of mutual address. "Very shortly we must essay our ascent. Meanwhile it may serve to occupy your energies when I tell you, that there are more perilous precipices for a young lady to stand upon than that from which you so lately dropped."

"I understand your meaning, Mildmay, and I believe in their import," answered Adelaide. "I could not have credited any one, had he told me a few hours ago how much I was to discover since we left the Hall. Why did not Captain Chesters put himself foremost to succour me, if it be all true which he has this day said? Why did he not stretch out his arm to prevent me dropping headlong as I did, for I screamed in time, I now remember, to advertise him of my danger, and to secure his adequate assistance, I believe, had he been prompt to offer it. How can you account for his negligence—his inability?"

"Cannot you yourself, Adelaide Waldgrave, account for his conduct?" was the reply

"Perhaps he was suddenly paralyzed by the appalling accident," returned the maiden, with a strange gaze, as if a wondrous light had on the instant broken in upon her.

"If he was not paralyzed at that dreadful and, by me, never-to-be-forgotten moment,—for I heard your shriek, and got a glimpse of you as you disappeared,—be assured he is now," was Mildmay's significant remark; "paralyzed not alone at the thought that you live, but at that of finding I have done something towards your deliverance."

"I have wanted firmness and decision of character on many occasions, ere quitting France," ejaculated the young lady; "and even during the brief period I have been at Wartham Hall, my silence and manner must have induced a belief that I am to be wholly at the will and dictation of others. But no longer shall it be so. Come, Mildmay, let us ascend; I am strong and resolute for the effort. At this instant, it seems to me, I could dare anything. Who knows, besides, but that my present trial and peril may prove useful in training me for other and, perhaps, more severe difficulties—exacting far greater moral courage than to hang over a tremendous void, into which to fall would be but to have an instantaneous death instead of a protracted persecution and eventual wretchedness? Yes, let us ascend. I would now have no other helping hand than yours, adventurous friend, who, though but an entire stranger to me this morning, can be no longer such. Hark! they call from above that ropes shall be forthcoming to assist us. But no, I would have no other arm to lean upon this day than that of him whom I heard sneered at not an hour ago, because he professed a love for truth and honest dealing. Come, I am strong and resolute!"

Mildmay, from the first moment that his eyes alighted upon the maiden, had, with his usual sagacity and genial spirit, felt an interest in her, such as it was not in the nature, much less consistent with the habits, of Captain Chesters to entertain. There was much of kinship in the character, modes of thinking, and manners of the two, although the young gentleman, whose education and mental discipline had been far more systematic than Adelaide's, as well as rich and profound, was fitted to be her guide and instructor for a long time to come. And well would it be for her, if she should have to pass through no other school than that of which he might be the master.

The ascent of the pair towards the summit of the precipice was accomplished with much greater ease than they had anticipated. When within a yard's length or two of the landing-place, the Captain, with a great show of commiseration and ardour, stretched down with one arm, whilst those behind him kept hold of the other, in order to afford the heroine, as we must now term her, some measure of assistance.

"No!" cried she, with firmness and an animation that surprised the witnesses of her self-possession and decision—and none more than her mother. "No! There is not need for that now; it is too late—for ever too late. Withdraw your proffered aid, sir, for ye but keep me in peril while you extend your arm,

seeing that it scares me from clinging to a safety-spot."

There was no resisting these declarations and commands. Adelaide gained the platform at the summit. She rushed into her parent's arms, who wept over her; and then holding out her right arm to Mildmay to assist her homeward, the three, abreast, took the lead to the Hall.

———

CHAPTER IV.

THE QUELLED QUARREL.

ADELAIDE, along with her mother, sought retirement and repose in their own chambers the moment they reached the Hall, after the occurrences of the strange and frightful events described towards the close of the last chapter. And they deemed it fortunate that they gained their rooms without encountering the peremptory master of the house, had it been for no other reason than that from them the first account of these events was not to be derived. Once within her privileged apartments, indisposition, during several days, formed not only a sufficient excuse for Adelaide not appearing in the company of the baronet's visitors, but for a man of such punctilious etiquette and unbending propriety, as he fancied himself to be, not insisting on intruding into her privacy. Still, in the circumstances of the appalling accident, and from the position of the parties most intimately connected with it, it was not possible that Sir Vaux should, for any considerable space of time, remain in ignorance of what had so remarkably happened; with immediate results, too, which to him, perhaps, might appear no less astounding. In fact, the persons most directly concerned in the extraordinary affair, leaving out Miss Waldgrave, were those who put the elderly gentleman in possession of the surprising particulars; and this they did, too, without either of them suspecting, at the time, that he had a hand in the service.

"Why, what does this mean?" said Sir Vaux, to himself, on hearing loud and angry words, the sounds issuing from an apartment near to the passage of his spacious mansion, which he was traversing at the instant. "An altercation — a quarrel — deadly threatening bandied between my gallant nephew, the Hon. Ludlow Chesters, and my more distant kinsman, the peaceful Mildmay! It cannot be, and yet it is; and it behoves me to judge equitably between them, although it is impossible that my sister's son can be in the wrong. I'll act the eaves-dropper."

While these thoughts were rapidly coursing through the brain of Sir Vaux, he, as softly as it was possible for a man of his weight to do, moved close to the entrance of the room in which the altercating gentlemen were holding themselves—the door being but partially shut; at the same time that any noise made externally to the pair was wholly drowned by what was passing within.

"What a spirit has that nephew of mine," thought the baronet, as he leant his ear to the necessary point for overhearing what was said

within,—his first impression having been incorrect, in so far as he concluded that both gentlemen had a share in making the frightful noise. "He is a lion for courage, for he speaks daggers; then what must he be when armed for the fray? Hark!"

"Thou art a crawling parasite, an insidious viper, a dastardly wretch, I repeat," bellowed the captain; "and, also, that unless thou dost accord to me the satisfaction, by an ample and witnessed apology, for having studiously this day insulted me, or, as the laws of honour dictate, I shall horsewhip thee most wholesomely, and have thee posted publicly, as a coward and poltroon into the bargain."

The *gallant* threatener was by this time, apparently, so transported with passion, that his speech was weakness itself, from its inflation, as well as its poverty; his rage having increased as he beheld the other remain comparatively

No 3.—THE GOVERNESS.

unmoved, and to look upon him with unaffected contempt. Mildmay, in fact, had not yet gone beyond manifesting a silent scorn, excepting by the utterance of a simple *yes* or *no*.

"The cowardly thing has not even a refuge of lies to fly to," exclaimed the nearly breathless feather-bed soldier; "he cannot—he dare not—open his lips," the maddened officer of the Life-Guards stamping and striding through the room at the time, followed by the unquailing eye of him who was the object of so much frothy and impotent fury.

"I'll take care that the brave captain does not kill Mildmay on the spot," inwardly ejaculated the baronet, as he listened to the noisy strides and menaces of his nephew. "What terrible thing can the frightened, speechless creature have done? Yet, no matter what the enormity, for I promise him that he will find Sir Vaux Waldgrave's wrath still more awe-striking than that of my unquestionably wronged and magnanimous Ludlow. But, hark again! the guilty creature ventures, after all, to open his lips. It were wiser to keep mute, and throw himself upon his knees, I trow."

"You seem, Captain Chesters, to think," quietly but firmly said the abused one, " that because I do not imitate your bluster, but choose rather to allow you to exhaust yourself nearly to bursting by your real or affected bravado,—and I care not which, for neither the one condition nor the other can lower you farther than what you already are in my reckoning, or the reckoning of all who shall become acquainted with your cowardly, your criminal conduct this day, towards your unsuspecting cousin, Adelaide Waldgrave,—you seem to suppose that I stand in awe of you."

"Ha! Mildmay begins to turn the tables with a vengeance," exclaimed the baronet within himself. "What can this mean? But the youth proceeds."

"You have, sir, with an impotence of phraseology which I did not expect even from you," continued Mildmay, "reiterated till you have become breathless that I am a parasite, a viper, a coward—with equally elegant expletives and adjectives. Now, I dare you to the proof that I am either one or other of these three characters; at the same time, that I undertake to convince your friends—if you have any, after knowing a tithe of that which I am cognizant of in regard to your history, that you are all three at one and the same time."

"Liar! libeller!" shouted Chesters," as if about to crush the other in an instant.

"Silence, captain, and allow me as much space, without rude interruption, as I have accorded to you at this turn," was the other's command, he still preserving calmness of demeanour and speech. "Well are you aware that gentleness of voice is much more for your advantage than for mine, at present. What if you should bring your uncle to be a hearer of what passes between us? Oh! you do well for yourself to shut the door, and thereby to prolong, probably, the impunity you unjustly enjoy."

"Does he?" thought Sir Vaux; "but the keyhole may serve me as completely for my end as a wider opening, and offer withal a safer medium of discovery for the eavesdropper."

"You, Chesters, are the unprincipled parasite," said the wrongfully accused one, "for you have systematically paid court to and indulged in fulsome flattery to your uncle, in order to make advancement in his estimation, and for the most sordid ends; while, behind his back, you have as constantly ridiculed him,—at the same time, recklessly squandering away the money with which he has supplied you; and in what manner? In gross dissipation; in facilitating your infamous career of seducing the young, the susceptible, the unsuspicious. Silence, sir, for nothing will prevent me from now speedily adopting steps, which perhaps have been too long postponed, in order to lay bare your character to your over-indulgent and generous kinsman, whom you so habitually mock, traduce, and wrong, whenever you imagine that you can thus conduct yourself with-

out injury to your prospects. Answer me, yea or nay,—dare me to the proof. Is it not your persevered in practice amongst your associates, and before every person upon whom you mean to impose, to represent Sir Vaux Waldgrave as being too stupid, and too obstinately set in his confidence and love towards you, ever to listen to the slightest charge that might tend to your disadvantage? And yet, immediately afterwards, you are the sycophant who stops not at any baseness or falsehood that you may worm from him gold, for the gratification of your tastes in the vilest walks of infamy. What is your constant story to the money-lending Jews,—for Sir Vaux's liberality, great as it is, does not keep pace with the career of your unprincipled folly,—but that Wartham Hall, and all his large accumulations, are as assuredly yours, and this at no distant date, whether your cousin Adelaide lives or dies,—cool calculator as you are about death, --as that there is a sun in the firmament?"

We shall not impede the account of the quarrel between the two gentlemen, by recording all the exclamations and interjections which rioted in the baronet's breast, as Mildmay proceeded. Had it been from nothing than the calmer and more intelligent manner in which the young gentleman delivered himself, even the dull owner of Wartham Hall must have soon felt on which side the superiority lay, and that it was possible for mildness of tone to subdue ruffian-like bluster, and simple truths to overwhelm the most audacious falsehoods. At an earlier part of the scene, he had reluctantly been compelled to own that there was a turning of the tables taking place; but by the time the contention had reached the pitch at which we have arrived, the astounded man's ejaculatory utterances — had these been audible— would have been pronounced certain evidences, by those most familiar with him, that his mind was distracted beyond all precedent; that it was as if, by some tremendous convulsion of nature, a new world had been opened to his vision, by means of which all his former impressions were driven into wild disarray,—all his arrangements and fondly-cherished plans contradicted and destroyed. As for Chesters, he was stunned in a manner that was not to be looked for, one would have thought, from his haughtiness and past history, unless by supposing he felt that it was nothing but the truth to which he was unexpectedly forced to listen.

" Had I no other test whereby to ascertain that you, a soldier and gentleman by birth, are morally a consummate coward," said Mildmay, " than this, that you bluster about the laws of honour—as these are understood by many—to one whom you believe and know holds those laws and their frequent results, as well as continual tendency, in utter abhorrence, and that I am, and ever will be, an anti-duellist,—I could not fail to be thoroughly convinced of your being swayed not only by a sordid but the most despicable of spirits. I claim no merit for rushing, in the excitement of the moment, to the rescue of Miss Waldgrave, when she was in the most imminent and appalling danger. There was more of the unthinking and physical man than the moral, perhaps, in the action. No; slight is the credit for doing that which I believe the great majority of my sex—even amongst the orders you so habitually contemn, and so grossly misrepresent—would have done or attempted, had they been exactly circumstanced as I was providentially at the instant. But what should be thought of the young lady's proposed lover,—her affianced one, it may be said,—who, having first led her to the summit of the precipice, and planted her on a spot where he must have known the footing was remarkably treacherous, owing to the nature of the soil,—who, having villanously done this, let her slip from his arm and hold, and next, without stretching out a succouring, rescuing hand, when her piteous shriek rent the air, permitted her—ah! hideous thought!—to be precipitated headlong towards the yawning gulf below, at the bottom of which, had she alighted there, her frame, though it had been made of brass, must have been crushed into shapelessness! Hear me out, Chesters; ye shall not escape my remaining words, which will be few. I call you not only a coward, but a villain of the deepest dye. Adelaide Waldgrave stood in the way of your heirship of Wartham Hall, and you were not quite sure, when your career was brought to light,—as in a brief space must have been the issue,—that she would have you for a husband at all. What, then? It is this—that you meditated being virtually her assassin, as in reality ye were this day. She regards you, in short, as nothing other than her deliberate murderer, as assuredly you are in the eye of God. Now go, and bluster about your honour and your valour, but be sparing of accusing others of cowardice, for the feeblest and tamest of your sex are your masters in all that is manly."

"He shall not go, Montague Mildmay, till I have done with him," cried Sir Vaux, throwing open the door, outside of which he had been standing, and bounding into the room with all the haste with which one so lumpish could rush forward, being dreadfully infuriated. "It might have been possible to forgive him for his gross ingratitude; his squandering away of money kindly given, that he might maintain himself in a manner worthy the son of my lamented sister, and of his generous living uncle; he might have borrowed from usurers upon a large expectancy, and been, in spite of his folly and recklessness, even on the discovery of his naughty ways, tolerated and forgiven by me, perhaps, as other men of the world and of fashion have been pardoned by their elders and their affectionate kinsmen. Who knows but that, even after I had my ears offended and grievously hurt by being forced to believe that he mocked and traduced me behind my back, —though the fawner and flatterer in my presence,—who knows but that in my old age I might have grown silly enough to take him into favour?"

The import of all this was uttered, though in broken sentences and with numerous repetitions, before either of the hostile gentlemen had an opportunity, or were expected, to throw in a word. The vehement baronet kept himself between them and the door, so that neither could have effected an escape from the torrent, had he wished to do so, without upsetting the bulky speaker; who, owing, no doubt, to the

extraordinary excitement which surged him, was no longer, it seemed, the dull, formal, and dilatory individual, as on most other occasions. Promptitude and propriety for once characterized his views and decisions.

"Ludlow Chesters, take you up or not the challenge which my remoter kinsman has thrown in your teeth, daring you to the test and trial?" demanded Sir Vaux. "Let it be a yes or a no that you return to me: I will for the present have nothing of comment,—not a morsel of explanation."

"I do take up the challenge, and call my accuser a vile calumniator," replied the captain, resuming something of his wonted carelessness and prideful mien.

"This, at least, has the appearance of greater manliness than your bearing a moment ago entitled me to expect," cried Sir Vaux, "or than was your demeanour during the latter part of your altercation with Mildmay,—I judging by hearing only,—I, who am determined to decide equitably between you, in order that I may visit him who is in the wrong, not only towards me but to the other of you, with my highest displeasure. Ye resent, repudiate, and flatly deny Mildmay's story; but this is a secondary matter. What distracts me most is the alarming affair of this day, and which, when my ears were torn with the first notice of it, on overhearing your accuser, was all a mystery—but not all mystery now. Then be it as I fear, judging from Mildmay's tone and your style of replying to him. Ludlow, mark me! never another shilling of mine more shall go into your pocket, for you shall henceforward be disowned by me to my dying hour. And now to the testing of the matter."

Sir Vaux, who had calmed greatly,—the direct and sensible way in which his views ran, of course, tending to regulate his excitement and pacify his passion,—proceeded to ring the bell of the room in which he found himself, ordering that Lord Rivers and Lady Augusta, and also that his sister-in-law, Mrs. Waldgrave, together with her daughter, should, as quickly as possible, be requested to attend him.

A pause of some little endurance now took place, not a syllable being dropped by any of the three individuals who were in the predicament described. Nevertheless, the baronet did not fail to take note of the carriage and air of both the gentlemen; drawing certain conclusions, in his own mind, from the different ways in which they bore themselves,—conclusions at which no stolidity could have prevented any one from arriving.

Mrs. Waldgrave was the first to make her appearance; and the reader need not be told that she came unaccompanied by her daughter, but not without her views having changed regarding the person fittest for being her son-in-law, her feelings having set in strongly against the captain. In fact, from the moment she had at first scanned him and paid heed to his carriage and conversation, the conclusion of the mercenary woman was, that he would prove a tyrannical husband and an imperious master in his own house, to the utter overthrow of any third person's influence who might attempt to rule through her partner's facility, so as to control him. On the other hand, in the meekness and modesty of Mildmay, she fancied that she discovered the very elements upon and with which she could best work out her ends, should he become wedded to her daughter. Not that, in reality, she cared anything about Adelaide's personal interests and happiness; the selfish and cold-hearted widow having by far the keenest and most direct eye to the establishment of her own eventual supremacy at Wartham Hall, and the advancement of the consideration in which she was ambitious to be held in her native county.

The scowl which the intriguing widow directed towards the Life-Guardsman on entering the chamber of trial, as it might be regarded, and the burst of apparent gratitude and favour with which she,—yielding to a flood of tears,—threw herself upon Mildmay's bosom, were alone conclusive against the captain; whereupon Sir Vaux, with greater vehemence than he had shown since bounding into the room, pronounced that the accused was wholly guilty of everything advanced by the other party. Still, he resolved on having his judgment buttressed by further testimony.

"Adelaide has not accompanied her mother to my presence, at my citation," observed the baronet, as soon as the widow in some measure recovered from her simulated condition of overpowering emotion; the speaker gradually relapsing into his wonted pomposity, as the lady's apparent agitation became moderated,—his sympathy, to the utmost depth of which his heavy nature was susceptible, having also been experiencing a return to its habitual insensibility.

"No, Sir Vaux Waldgrave; my poor daughter has not accompanied me to your presence," breathed the mother, who seemed, to the apprehension of the baronet, to perform her part as only a parent could do, although it was much of a theatrical effort all the while; "and I know not that she will ever descend your stairs, until carried to the tomb. It is from one swoon to another that she is kept, each fit looking as if it would be the last; nor should I be from her bedside for a moment, were it not that your summons was sent me, and this, too, at one of her recovered intervals, when she implored of me that I would immediately repair to you, in obedience to your wish."

"Then I have heard nothing but the truth," cried the uncle. "Montague Mildmay has not exaggerated the affair; I having been witness of a contention between these two gentlemen, without, however, either of them being cognizant that I was near, and a listener to what passed. The truth was then made manifest enough to me, although the particulars were not all detailed."

"Exaggerated, Sir Vaux!" exclaimed Mrs. Waldgrave, recovering her energies and acting more in the magnanimous strain than before. "Mr. Mildmay I am sure is quite incapable of dealing in exaggeration to the perversion of truth and the misrepresentation of facts; but further, it is impossible to exaggerate the character of the hideous accident and danger which my dear Adelaide encountered through the studied negligence, to say the least of it, of him who should have been the last to expose her to peril,—the first to boldly adventure his life to save hers But no; having conducted the girl, who was wholly a stranger, to the pinnacle of the giddy steep, he lets her tumble over, no doubt, in the hope of one who stood so much and so directly in his way being dashed to pieces, he remaining stationary thereafter, and wringing his hands, forsooth, while another manfully, at the imminent risk of his existence, descends to her assistance, hapless girl, who, half-way down the precipice, hangs dangling upon the bed of branches that arrested her progress. Wondrous presence of mind and of self-command on the part of my child, whose eye at one moment is looking down to the rugged floor far below, and next, upwards to heaven, and to him who, with encouraging voice, is rapidly descending to her succour, still preserves her senses, and strains the last effort of her all but exhausted energies to reach his outstretched hand! It is caught; she is planted for a few minutes in a fissure of the rock, upheld by her deliverer, in order that she may recover her strength,—a doubtful matter, and still more doubtful if she can ever climb aloft; when the conviction, along with certain recollections, flashes upon her mind, that she has just been the victim of a murderous design. Now it is that she feels nerved for the exploit, with Mr. Mildmay's helping arm and inspiriting voice, of climbing the steep. The thing is all but achieved, when that gallant gentleman there, a Life-Guardsman, vouchsafes to proffer his assistance. But it is scorned: Adelaide again stands upon the summit of the dizzying height, but with not the same by her side as held up his head there when she was precipitated. With further strained effort, protected and supported by her succourer and myself, she gains the Hall; when, as she reaches her couch, her timid and tender nature resumes its sway, and she is the prostrated victim of cowardly and assassin-like outrage. My Lord Adolphus Rivers, upon whose arm I leant prior to the awful occurrence, had been entertaining me with accounts of certain romantic traditions which are intimately associated with the Cauldron Cliff, and the adjacent singularly picturesque portions of your splendid estate, Sir Vaux, but little thought I that the day should not close before my own darling daughter was to figure in a more marvellous scene in the same vicinity than any described by the noble lord."

"So much, and directly, in his way! Truly spoken," exclaimed Sir Vaux; "I see it all; it is as clear as noonday; Adelaide did, and does, stand between me and the wretch in regard to the inheritance of Wartham Hall, and therefore he deemed it politic to rid himself of her. And having murderously disposed of my excellent niece,—the offspring of my beloved and lamented brother Wilford,—what next could remain to be done but to get myself, Sir Vaux Waldgrave, removed?—which, though not accomplished by tossing me over a break-neck steep, might be more quietly contrived and perpetrated by drugging me,—by mixing my cup, or powdering my food. Monstrous to think of such perfidy! But I'll bring to naught his villany. I henceforth disown him; and as an unmistakable measure of promptitude and completeness, I now open this chamber's door for him to make his exit, never to darken my mansion with his presence while I am master here."

The captain sought no other dismissal. Having resumed his cold stateliness and haughty mien, he threw looks of defiance and revenge towards each of those who remained behind; muttering something about a time of reckoning yet to come, and reminding his uncle that his lease of life was not eternal; then, hurrying from the place, he sought to hide his head and chagrin in the world of London.

"I'll have Montague Mildmay for my niece's mate, and forthwith shall the nuptials be celebrated," was the imperative utterance of the baronet, as soon as he was freed of his nephew's company; the speaker being a personage who regarded the assertion of his authority with much greater favour than any claim of blood-relationship. He had no feelings of endearment for any one that were half so profound and operative as his notions of self-importance, his hereditary rank, and the maintenance of his political influence. Having very summarily disposed of Chesters, he dreamt not of any difficulty that could occur in the matter of nominating his more remote kinsman to take the discharged one's place; being of the mind that thus, by a mere expression of his will, the strange and unexpected severance that had happened might, in the most simple and immediate manner, be healed. "Mildmay, you shall wed her as soon as Adelaide has recovered from her untoward mishap, and thus will all the mischief that has been so suddenly wrought,—threatening a complete derangement to my long-cherished views,—be remedied in a twinkling, to the admiration of the world as respects my resources of wisdom, and the dismay of him I have just now repudiated and disowned for ever."

Such was the reiterated sentiment which fell from Sir Vaux's lips, as Lord Rivers and his sister entered the chamber in which the baronet was, with amazing confidence and rapidity, setting everything to rights; not for a moment calculating that any obstacle could mar his cut-and-dry scheme, and priding himself greatly on the fertility of his judgment. But the young gentleman to whom he addressed himself specially had a way of thinking of his own, which was not only widely different from that in which the discharged Captain indulged, but from that of the owner of Wartham Hall himself.

"Do not allow yourself to run away with the notion, Sir Vaux Waldgrave," said the young gentleman, "that I can be dictated to in regard to marriage. Nay, I feel assured that your charming niece would as little respect me, were I to renounce my independence of mind in a paramount matter of this kind, as I should be grievously disappointed to find that she was capable of relinquishing her rights of self-government. However admirable the young lady may already appear in my estimation, or however gratefully she, together with her mother and uncle, may look on my efforts in her behalf this day, neither of us can or will, I am convinced, dispense with that probation of temperament and character in the other, which time and social intercourse can alone afford."

"Are you as mad as Chesters was wicked, Montague Mildmay?" cried the baronet, with mingled astonishment and displeasure. "I had rather expected that you would, young man, have fallen upon your knees, in token of your gratitude to me for my condescension, Have a care; speak but once again as ye have now done, and never more shall you have the same tempting offer which I now make you—you shall lose for ever the prospect of wedding the heiress to Wartham Hall and my accumulated wealth; and while I find a worthy husband for her elsewhere, you will be but the poor owner of your deeply mortgaged lands of Mildmay Park—a dependent thing to the end of your days."

"Not so, I trust, Sir Vaux Waldgrave," mildly, but yet with a decisive tone, replied the young gentleman. "The truth is, we are not of one mind in relation to what constitutes wealth and independence. It is true that Mildmay Park—a small estate compared with Wartham Hall—was so deeply drowned by mortgages when I succeeded to the property, as rightful heir, that it became a question with me for some time whether I should not allow the lands to be brought to the hammer, in order to relieve myself from many anxieties and much trouble. But I have two sisters, who are much attached to the family seat; and finding, besides, from my literary tastes and pursuits, I could earn for myself a fair income for a person of my habits, I at length resolved on keeping the property, were it but that those sisters should have their birthplace for their home whilst they remained unmarried. I have not spent one shilling of the rental since the estate came into my hands. The incumbrances are gradually disappearing. My sisters and I eat the bread of independence —that is to say, of my earnings by my pen; and I assure you that no morsels can ever be so sweet to the lips as those that are thus yielded and procured. Besides, again, my powers, whatever these may be, I intend to devote to the service of my species—a service which, while it brings me remuneration sufficient for my wants, delights me exceedingly from its nature;—my ambition being to raise my fellow-creatures in the scale of intelligence—to lend assistance to the cause of progress—and to emancipate what are called the lower orders from every species of thraldom to which they are exposed. I claim for myself and all others perfect independence from all arbitrary and irresponsible authority; and however flattered my vanity may be by your preference—and this preference, too, in relation to one whom I feel assured is every way inestimable,—yet I cannot agree to any premature understanding or arrangement on the subject, especially as this would be as derogatory to the feelings and prudence of her who has the tenderest claims upon your consideration, as to my own sense of justice and right."

"Then you, Montague Mildmay, scorn my offer and commands," cried the baronet. "But I'll give you a week to consider of the subject; during which period, I trust you will not only have ample opportunities of judging of my niece's merits, but she of your whimsicalities, young man. If, at the end of that period, she has not cured you of your error in the matter of marriage to her, and of your vile radicalism to boot, then I'll clear my hands of you—I'll find for her a worthier spouse; or, should any disastrous accident befall the maiden, I'll take a wife to myself, and have offspring of my own, rather than any degenerate kinsman should ever inherit a farthing's-worth of my property. Yes, I vow by ——; but no, no! I never now swear—it is unseemly in high life, and for a personage of my years; but I vow I'll get wedded and have a family. This hand, which was never offered to womankind, shall be at the refusal of some lady of exalted rank. What say you, Lady Augusta Rivers? Shall it be a match between us, should this wrong-headed and ungrateful youth persist in his obstinacy?"

Sir Vaux had wrought himself into an unusually high pitch of fervour once more, for an individual of his dull and ponderous character; nor did he perceive how ridiculous he was making himself. As for Lady Augusta, she perfectly well understood the man, and had far too much good sense and tact to do otherwise than treat with light humour the absurdity of the bulky and ungainly baronet.

"You would not, Sir Vaux, have me to accept of any such conditional wooing as you have proposed?" said she. "You must come forward with a distinct avowal and an ample declaration, without any implied or possible hindrance, and then we shall be in the fitter position to come to definite terms."

Taking this answer in a light as favourable and propitious for him as could be looked for at the first starting, Sir Vaux declared it was high time to think of dinner; and, accordingly, each one retired to prepare for a meal, which the gourmandizing baronet had never been in better trim for enjoying.

———

CHAPTER V.

THE HOMELESS HEROINE.

MRS. WALDGRAVE, on returning to her daughter, could not have been the bearer of more acceptable tidings to the young lady, or anything which was likely to prove more medicinal, than was afforded by the account she had to give of the peremptory dismissal of Captain Chesters. There appeared, however, to be another source of real gratification to Adelaide; and this was in the statement of what had transpired in presence of the mother, while absent from the maiden, between Sir Vaux and Mildmay, relative to the latter's substitution in the place of the Life-Guardsman, as the husband of the young lady,—every word which had fallen from the lips of the young gentleman delighting the ear of the thoughtful and eager listener. True, she refrained from giving audible expression to the happiness she experienced on being informed of the modest, but decisive bearing of him who had so recently risked his life in her behalf; being, however, not the less sensible of the extreme difference of his views and conduct, from what had characterized her truthless cousin's behaviour during the short time it had been her misfortune to be

near him. So pleased and renovated did the indisposed one find herself in consequence of what was detailed to her, that she insisted her mother would join the baronet's small dining-party, were it but that this might serve as a token of her sure recovery. And Sir Vaux, as well as the others, regarded the circumstance in this light, which, indeed, tended not slightly to enliven them all—the baronet actually going beyond his ordinary freedom with the wine-cup, and growing wondrously generous and happy the while. He did not even seem to recollect Mildmay's discourse about independence, leisure—taking in the matter of deciding on marriage; neither his new-fangled ideas about society's progress, and a determination to devote himself to the cause of the people. All went smoothly and amazingly well; and at length, at the supper hour, when the great and opulent man produced a splendid pearl necklace, which had belonged to his mother—the gift to her, he said, of royalty when she was in the bloom of beauty,—the precious article was forthcoming for the purpose of being sent and presented to the convalescent niece, who, "it was hoped, would wear it on the day she became wedded to him who had been her deliverer from sundry precipices." Adelaide could not now but be making rapid progress to perfect health and tension of nerve. In the course of two days, at most, she should be able to appear in company; and then, thought the baronet, everything would go merrily as the marriage bell.

It was the day on which the young lady had intended to join her uncle and his guests at the dinner-table, that a note was put into her mother's hands, at the moment, too, that the latter was talking in the most sanguine terms of their brilliant prospects. But no sooner had Mrs. Waldgrave's eyes alighted upon the signature of the epistle, than she betrayed stronger signs of agitation and alarm than her daughter had ever known her evince. It was, in fact, some considerable time before the widow would return an answer to the passionate inquiries put to her; nor was this done without still more exciting the anxieties of Adelaide.

"What terrible thing is it, dear mother?" the young lady had repeated several times in effect, when Mrs. Waldgrave, in an angry impatient tone returned, "You disturb me, girl; leave me—begone!"

"Leave you!—and why? Can I do nothing for my mother?" were the maiden's next words.

"Much, very much; and unless you promptly perform it, my destruction—nay, and your's—is certain," cried Mrs. Waldgrave, with vehemence.

"What would ye?" inquired the trembling Adelaide, feeling at the moment how powerless she was in her parent's present state of excitement.

"I would have every farthing of money you possess, girl, and every trinket besides, handed to me, and no questions put as to what I intend to do with the trash," was the stern reply.

"If parting with such baubles will preserve you from evil, or afford you any satisfaction," observed the daughter, bursting into tears, "you will have all, excepting, of course, the pearl necklace given me so recently by my uncle."

"So be it, then," muttered the mother; "but I have something further to require of you, if you wish me to live,—if you do not long to see me dead."

"Have you ever found that I deserve to be spoken to in such terms, or in such a tone?" gently inquired the maiden. "Only name how I can serve or assist you, and you shall be obeyed—unless, indeed——"

"Unless what?" fiercely demanded the widow.

"Unless by the sacrifice of what is just and right," answered Adelaide. "But my mother must be incapable of soliciting from me any such sacrifice or wrong-doing."

"Wrong-doing! no, assuredly," replied Mrs. Waldgrave, "but only obedience, no curious questions put, and also that, this very night, at a late hour, you do accompany me to a certain spot in Sir Vaux's neighbouring grounds,—not to the Cauldron Cliff, I do assure you," interjected the lady, on observing the glow that rushed into the maiden's cheek, and the start of deep surprise which shook her frame. "Ha! you retract. Be it so; you repent your promise of obedience, in order that my ruin may be sudden and complete. Say—for once, and for all time—whether you are ready to hold yourself at my dictation at a most trying crisis; believing that your parent can ask of you nothing that is unworthy, however carefully her reasons for the present may be kept secret as regards the faith required of you. Pronounce against my requirement; and a few hours will find us separated for ever, and that you are motherless."

Adelaide, upon this, felt more poignantly than ever that she had become a mere tool in the grasp of one who had never regarded her with a genial love, and that it was vain on the present occasion to contend with such despotism; only remarking that it might have been better, after all, that she had been dashed to pieces at the precipice than live to be at the control of any such tyranny. She could have added, with perfect truth, that could she have taken counsel of Montague Mildmay at the moment, she would have felt strengthened towards the performance of whatever he might name for her guidance. But no such opportunity was afforded the damsel; so that, with bitter misgivings, she felt forced to whisper an acquiescence in her mother's proposal and demand of unqualified obedience; the peremptory announcement being, that not only should she be obeyed at her daughter's direst peril, but the argument used, that it was purely for that daughter's sake alone that the entire adventure was to be made. On hearing this, Adelaide became convulsed with deep emotion; she figured to herself her dying parent; all fear vanished from her mind; and reiterating her promise that she would implicitly obey in everything required, she strove to nerve her mind for readiness to undertake, along with her mother, the midnight enterprise.

A considerable amount of manœuvring was employed by the widow, in order that she and Adelaide might go forth from their suite of apartments, unobserved and unsuspected by any one, at the midnight hour; it being very distinctly understood and painfully felt by Mrs. Waldgrave that the knowledge of such an adventure as she contemplated, should it ever come to the ears of Sir Vaux, might thereafter peril her interests with him to the end of his days. By means, however, of a turret-stair in their wing of the spacious mansion, and a judicious use of muffled cloaks and other stratagems, the pair at length found themselves threading the shrubberies; the mother proceeding with such a degree of certitude to convince the daughter that she had made herself acquainted during the reign of sunshine with the route they were taking, and the exact locality to which they were proceeding. The weather still continued beautiful; the sky was cloudless and serene, and so finely did day and night seem blended, that the charms of both might have been felt to be enhanced, had the minds of the adventurers been attuned to respond to the associated influences. But no such susceptibility was theirs at this juncture. Adelaide scarcely dared to breathe as they passed along, and might have yielded to weakness, had not the expression of her parent's countenance, whenever she caught a glimpse of it, pourtrayed powerful, ay, and fearful emotion, growing at length so terribly agitated that the maiden was about to say, "This, dear mother, will prove your death, in spite of all that I can do in obedience to your wish and commands," when a voice arrested her purpose and speech.

"More punctual than I had expected of such fine ladies as you be," said some one, in a rough voice, and before the person was at all visible. "I must speak to you both, and this, too, at first, separately, I reckon," added the party, as he emerged from a clump of bushes. "It will be advisable to begin with the older one, and on matters of substantial business, I shall then know how to talk to the girl."

As he thus spoke he put out his arm, seizing hold of the muffling gear of her who was the nearer of the two to him, this being the mother, whom, on identifying her, he tapped on the shoulder with vulgar familiarity, telling her, after removing a few paces farther away from Adelaide, to name and show the things she had got for him. What the lady's answer was did not reach the hearing of the trembling daughter; but after some apparently dissatisfied observations used by the fellow, he drew from the proffered bag sundry articles not only in the shape, it seemed, of coin, but of jewellery, among which, as Adelaide could distinctly perceive, the lately gifted necklace figured conspicuously; taken, it must have been, she immediately felt to her consternation, from a secret keeping-place of her own, and therefore, to all intents and purposes, theftuously abstracted by her parent. The discovery was a new blow to the maiden's heart, nearly extorting from her a cry of astonishment and displeasure. But the man's observation at the instant checked the utterance.

"What may this be?" demanded he in an offended tone; "for unless it makes amends for the other trash, I'll not only keep the whole, but stand to my first notice to you; thus serving you right for the nasty trick you have played me, after all the toil and anxiety I have had in finding out where my real and most precious jewel was hidden."

What the whisper conveyed by Mrs. Waldgrave was, in reply to this ruffian speech, did not reach Adelaide's ear, but it must have been something to the effect that the necklace was of great value; for the fellow instantly conveyed it to one of his pockets with an air of gratified importance, saying aloud that it might stop a gap for the present, although it was the substantial and permanent to which he would, after all, and at no very distant date, look, unless his first demands were acceded to.

"And now," added he, "I must have a talk with my darling," turning from the mother to approach the daughter, but yet not so as to prevent the former from rushing past him and whispering in the latter's ear with passionate earnestness that she would maintain her self-command a few seconds longer, for that then the trial and the danger would be over. The maiden would have remonstrated; but before, in her grievous excitement, she had power to speak, the man was not only by her side, having pushed the widow away, but had taken Adelaide's gentle hand with such a hurtful pressure in his as to force a cry from her.

"Beg your pardon, darling," returned the ruffian, relaxing in some degree his hold. "I did not mean to give you pain. You must set down my roughness to my seaman's practice and my affection."

"Horrible!" exclaimed the young lady. "What further insults am I to endure from this stranger—this ruffian? I must be the victim of some monstrous conspiracy, in which an unnatural mother is a principal."

"Not so fast, darling," cried the man, still keeping hold of the maiden's hand, and clinging closer to her,—the other lady meanwhile seeming to writhe from still more merciless treatment, to judge from her anxiety and agitation, for she stood hard by. "You wrong your female companion in charging her with a mother's cruelty. There's never a bit of that character about her, so far as ye are concerned. But say, did'st thou, darling, never behold me before? Take a good look; and if now thou canst not remember me, I'll make daylight serve for the renewing of our acquaintanceship. No remembrance, eh! of thy nurse Maria? No keeping in mind of him who stood by her death-bed when she acknowledged me for her husband? Maria was thy true mother, girl; and now what canst thou make of this but that I am thy real father, the long lost father, who has been robbed of thy sweet society, merely to serve the ends of a designing woman who never had the heart to love thee, and who now would keep thee and make an heiress of thee for her own sake, without any proper remuneration, for the loan, to him who can and will claim thee, spite of the world, unless handsomely bribed to the contrary."

"It is all false; you are an impostor," screamed Adelaide, who was now struggling to escape from the loathed embrace of the man, as he persisted in kissing her. "Unhand me, or the cries of murder will bring, even at this dead and dreadful hour, succour to my side."

"Succour is near," cried Montague Mildmay, springing forward at the instant, and felling the ruffian to the ground; "to the Hall with you, mother and daughter, while I keep the villain at bay. Alarm the servants, in order that we may secure the scoundrel, and make him answer for this outrage."

"Refrain from sounding an alarm,—for Adelaide's sake, if not for mine, refrain," implored Mrs. Waldgrave, as she clung, with embarrassing embrace to the young gentleman's person; the maiden meanwhile taking advantage of the opportunity to run towards the Hall, convinced that the woman whom she had been accustomed to address as mother had not given her birth, but had long been acting some deep and dangerous part. Indeed, so numerous and alarming were the surmises that flashed through the damsel's mind, as she hurried to the neighbouring mansion, that it was with the vehemence of a distracted person she sought for admittance, at the same time declaring that murder, in all probability, would be perpetrated near at hand, unless assistance reached Mr. Mildmay without delay; for him it seemed to be that she alone thought of succouring. And away, in the direction indicated, did the alarmed people hasten, even Sir Vaux himself at length joining in the race, though far behind the others; the young lady also persisting now in repairing to the spot, where the earliest comers found the widow reduced to insensibility from the discovery of the truth, while Mildmay and the stranger were grappling with one another in deadliest conflict. To separate them, and next to convey the ruffian fellow as a sort of prisoner to the Hall, were measures which, along with taking charge of Mrs. Waldgrave, occupied some time.

And now unparalleled was the baronet's amazement, when he came to listen to Jared Jobson's story, as the fellow named himself, who had so lately and unexpectedly laid a parental claim to Adelaide; the account which he gave of his past history, and of the young lady, being in no particular denied or contradicted by the widow.

"It is all true," said she, "and long have I been as one in a measure prepared for the discovery being made; hardly now sorry at the disclosure, when I consider the agony of uncertainty to which I have been accustomed, and the guilty shifts to which I have felt obliged to betake myself. Nor is it the slightest horror that tears me, to think of the unkindly manner in which I have acted to the poor maiden," continued the hypocrite, "the child of obscurity and misfortune,—whom I bribed her mother to nurse as my offspring, with the prospect and promise of her inheriting my brother-in-law's vast property and wealth; the infant having been taken by me, and reared from the first as my own, when my husband was far away, and long absent from me. Jobson,—Jared Jobson,—is the father of the lowly-born and disowned girl, as was acknowledged by the dying mother, when very near her last extremity, in my dwelling at Paris; and when he, too, deeply swore never to trouble me with the story of his relationship to the child, until she was lady of Wartham Hall; when, for the purpose of securing a moderate annuity, he might, perhaps,

make himself known to me again. I flattered myself that he had been lost at sea, mariner as he is, and that I should never be dismayed and tortured by his re-appearance. But I reckoned rashly, and am utterly undone. What more would ye of me? I sever myself from Adelaide, and the whole of you, now and for ever; only allow me some undisturbed repose before I depart. Fare ye well; I seek that which has lately been my bed-chamber, for some brief rest, from which I pray none will before day-break awaken me."

It must have been from the agitation that prevailed throughout the Hall on this remarkable and distracting occasion, that no particular or immediate heed was paid to the wretched woman's language, and that its ominous import passed without attention. The condition of Adelaide, and, still more, the hurricane of rage which surged Sir Vaux, in a

No. 4.—THE GOVERNESS.

sense absorbing the observation of the spectators and witnesses of the extraordinary scene.

Jobson also required to be looked after, had it only been to deprive him of the ill-got money and trinkets with which he had been so unrighteously supplied; Mildmay taking care that the coins, as well as the jewellery, which had belonged to, and been wrested from, the young lady, should be returned to her forthwith; and, also, that the pearl necklace should promptly find its way back to the baronet, its proper owner. Thereupon, to dismiss the alleged parent of the now motherless maiden to seek redress and the recovery of the young lady as he best might, became a proceeding that was speedily set about and effected. And at length it was, too, that some regard came to be paid to the parting speech of the wretched Mrs. Waldgrave.

Alas! it was too late. True, she slept, but

it was the dreamless sleep of death. She had been long armed with a fatal soporific, to be at the service of the unprincipled woman at an emergency. The drug had been swallowed at last, and she ceased from troubling, as well as to be delivered from the weariness of this wicked world.

It was now waxing near to the morning twilight hour; and, while measures were adopted by some of the more thoughtful of the amazed inmates of the Hall, in relation to having Mrs. Waldgrave's body secured against all interference, until the coroner should hold his inquest upon it, poor Adelaide, more alarmed and disconsolate than all the rest taken together, stole to her room, and to which she had for several days been confined by indisposition,—caused by her fearful accident at the precipice,—in order to decide upon the course she should adopt in her perplexing position. Nor was the gentle, yet resolute, girl, slow to come to a determination. With no small amount of heroism, she speedily proceeded to collect her more serviceable raiment, after dressing herself in the fittest manner her opportunity permitted, for the purpose of travel; her design being to carry under her arm the compact bundle, while she clandestinely withdrew from a mansion which she felt could no longer,—not, even, for another day,—be a home for her. And yet it seemed to the maiden impossible to take her departure, without leaving behind an expression of deep gratitude to Sir Vaux, for his kindness to her, as well as of her extreme distress at having been,—though innocently on her part,—made the cause of such vexation and disturbance to him as he had endured.

"But let my going forth into the world, unknowing and unknown, with all expedition," added she, "so that I may no more be a trouble to you, and an offence in your eyes,—prove to you how grieved I am on account of what has passed, and also how ready I feel to encounter danger, trial, and privation, rather than cause you a moment's misery which it is in my power to avoid inflicting."

"To you, Mr. Mildmay, I must tender my devoutest thanks," she next hurriedly wrote, "for your generous aid and opportune deliverances on dreadful occasions. I go forth alone, and I know not, for the present, whither. Yet I feel that it will please and comfort you to find me saying that I am resolved to strive against despair; also, to believe that it is my interest, as well as my duty, to put trust in Providence, and that every vicissitude to which I may be exposed,—while uninvoked by my own evil acts,—will yet be made to work together for my good; and, moreover, that the probation to which I am to submit may, in the course of time, render me worthier of the esteem of the discerning than had I been fated to bask in the sunshine of prosperity for the remainder of my days. If I can be sustained in these views and resolves, it is probable, I think, that my friendless and, in a sense, outcast condition,—that my going forth this morning—alas! how memorable,—all unknown and unknowing,—making a renunciation of all claims upon the kindness of any, just as all must renounce poor me,—I say, it is possible, at least, that the immediate loss and agony

may in a measure find a recompense through the goodness and mercy of Him whose pitifulness is ever over the homeless, and who never deserts those who earnestly seek the paths of virtue. Thus,

'All our ill
May, if directed well find happy end.' "

To these brave sentiments,—hoping against hope,—the fair writer intended to add some touching expressions in the manner of farewell taking, and had used means to brace herself for the effort. She had, after writing so far as to cite the little snatch of poetry, which seemed to invigorate her heart, gazed into the mirror, and, while gazing, fancied she experienced an inward power,—a sense of influence supporting her. She smoothed her hair, which was somewhat dishevelled, and bathed her face, which looked feverish. "The more solitary and the more friendless,—the more unsustained I am by others," thought she, "the more I will respect myself; and thus, though frail, I shall be indomitable."

But the damsel was still ignorant of herself, and of the nature of the human heart; believing that to will and do were the same thing. She was soon to be taught in part that she reckoned rashly; for no sooner did she set herself to the writing of the postscript, in which she had thought of putting the pith of her note to Mildmay, than fast-coming tears blotted the paper, and a suffocating sensation obliged her to relinquish the effort. To divert her emotions, she flew to the wardrobe in which her dresses were, to select the fittest,—the neatest and plainest,—for her new exigencies. Had it been in her power to lay her hands upon some sordid garb,—one made of the coarsest stuffs,—it would have been preferred to all other dress. She tied up her few selected things in a bundle,—she gathered into her hand what money she possessed once more, and her trinkets; resolved that now she should be able to indite the postscript,—not another moment being her own for the delicate office, seeing that day was dawning and streaming the orient beams through the casement.

But her ear is startled by sounds as if of people astir, and perhaps approaching her chamber, in order to have her mind, or some matter of information respecting the suicidal widow. Not one second is to be wasted or thrown away about her bundle,—hardly about the coins and trinkets which, on the instant, she had thrust into the folds which enveloped her bosom. Dashing everything else from her, she hurries as if from a pest-house; winds her way down the same turret stair, which had so recently before been trod when going forth to meet Jobson. Having got into a court-yard, the latched wicket of the locked gate affords her a stealthy egress, and in a few minutes she is beyond the view of the Hall. No reflection was to be allowed at this stage of her flight; not a glance to be cast back, scarcely one to be thrown forward. She dives through shrubberies and into plantations; skirts fields, hedges, and lanes; she strikes into screening thickets once more, as the sun gains power, and the idea of encountering one of her own species gains upon her.

But the exertion cannot long last, especially considering her recent sufferings and encounters. She is weeping wildly as her pace becomes slow and distressing; a weakness beginning inwardly, then extending to her limbs, is upon her, seizes her, and she can no longer resist sinking to the ground. The visionary in her teens has already some foretaste of the truth, that to will and to do are not exactly the same things, however identical they may appear at moments of excitement, and under the impulse of youthful enthusiasm.

The homeless girl, no longer sustained by heroic purpose and self-reliance, clove to the earth, weeping bitterly; oppressed with the idea of being all forlorn, and more sensitively alive than she had yet been of the extreme reverse of fortune to which she was doomed. It was a wrong thought, an unhallowed wish, and only to be accounted for on any excusing grounds, by the desolate condition to which she so suddenly had been reduced, when she now gave utterance to the lament that she died not at the Cauldron Cliff. She even felt a temptation to invoke dissolution, speedy and final; or, at least, to be delivered from the remembrance of the past, especially of her who, while affecting to be her mother, had never been a genial and tender parent to her. Fatigue, and a multitude of memories and dark forebodings, overwhelmed her. She felt unable longer to weep aloud, or to act desperately. She sobbed, and at length sank into a slumber.

"Montague Mildmay! save me from the ruffian-monster—from the false man of violence!" were the screamed words, the very sounds of which rang through her own ears, serving to awaken her from the short and troubled sleep, in which her dream was of the fellow whose sudden appearance, at a midnight hour, had wrought such a revolution in her position and prospects, and brought disaster to others. The shriek had been wrung from her, but not alone by a dream; for, as she raised her head, and opened her eyes, and became conscious of the reality, she discovered that Jobson was beside her, and also that he had actually been rifling her person of such precious property as she carried; the villanous act having mainly served to awaken the young lady.

"Thou art not of age, and hast no property, darling, over which thy father shall not take care," said the scoundrel. "Scream away, and take thy fill of crying; for the longer and louder thou dost thus exercise thy lungs, I shall just have so much the less remorse in carrying thee to my proper country and home, and for making thee my toiling help; that is, after bringing to their account the folks that, a few hours back, took the law into their own hands, driving me away from my own flesh and blood, as anybody with but half an eye in his head may see that thou art. There's no denying the kinship, girl; so prepare thee for trudging it along with me, after I have taken an accurate inventory of the gear I now hold."

The ruffian, while he thus ran on, threw himself upon the grassy ground close to the spot where he had found the homeless maiden; who, however, no longer invoking death, but most eagerly set on escape from danger and destruction, had sprung to her feet, alarmed at being in contiguity with such a person as her eyes scanned, no matter whether parent or impostor. He sat him down, and began deliberately, under the plantation's shade, to count the coins and to examine the jewellery; not appearing the while to pay the least heed either to the feelings or the movements of the maiden. These feelings and movements were how most effectually to fly from him. Accordingly, gliding away from the seemingly absorbed fellow, she soon gained such a distance from him, as encouraged her to take to her heels in good earnest; the sense of fatigue, the feelings of despair, the desire to die, yielding to a love of life and frantic efforts to be delivered from peril.

CHAPTER VI.

THE ECCENTRIC SAMARITAN.

THE early stir at the Hall, which had so greatly alarmed the young lady, and caused her confusedly, and even recklessly, to fly from the mansion, was not wholly made without a reference to her condition. The fact is, that Mildmay had never closed an eye in sleep,—no remarkable circumstance after what he had witnessed since sunset,—had not undressed, or thrown himself upon a couch; on the contrary, from the moment he dismissed Jobson, he had traversed his room,—his thoughts mainly occupied concerning Adelaide. Indeed, his anxieties in that direction were deep, growing more intense as the time sped; a terrible feeling gradually gaining upon him, that probably she too, in her anguish and woful position, might rush into some awful act. This idea at length grew so strong, that he could no longer resist hastening to the housekeeper, in order to have her to visit the young lady's room and see how it fared with her. The visit was paid, and this very shortly after the damsel's flight; and now the confusion of the apartment, the left tied-up bundle, the written notes stained with tears, unmistakably established that she had not only stealthily left the Hall, but that it had been only very shortly before the housekeeper repaired to the deserted chamber, that the young lady fled,—and startled, too, it was evident, at the instant when she took her departure. These discoveries greatly moved the young gentleman, stirring him to prompt measures to ascertain whither she had directed her course; nay, more, to recover her,—distracted, as he felt she must be,—to rescue her from evil, whether of her own invoking, or of such as prowl for the innocent and helpless; and to plant her at a genial hearth, there to enjoy and adorn life.

"Unknowing and unknown! friendless, and houseless, truly!" exclaimed Mildmay, on perusing what the young lady had written for his reading. "I would travel the kingdom to succour her. With my sisters she should find a kindly asylum,"—and away he hurried, while yet it was but the dawn of day, with some faint hopes—being accompanied by a servant—of arresting her in her hazardous flight.

It was hither and thither that they ran, penetrating the baronet's extensive plantations and woods in many a direction, and spending hours in the pursuit, which, however, proved unavailing in respect of Adelaide's recovery; although not as regarded the assurance that her misfortunes had become greatly enhanced since her adventurous flight from the Hall.

"Hark! was it not a scream, friend, as if of one in distress or danger, that echoed through the wood this instant?" eagerly cried Mildmay, suddenly standing stone still, on a sound of the kind mentioned smiting his ear; "and I think it resembled that of a female voice,—ay, and this too, of the unhappy, misused, Adelaide."

The surmise was more than sufficient to put fresh mettle into the young gentleman's heels, who was with alacrity seconded by his attendant. Away they sped in the direction whence the stirring sound came; nor was it long before they came to the spot, where, no doubt, it had been uttered; the discovery of the ruffian Jobson counting coins and examining trinkets, convincing the pursuers on the instant that the articles had shortly before been wrested from their unfortunate and helpless owner.

"Once more relinquish that ill-got gear," were the words with which Mildmay accosted the robber ere the wretch could conceal the articles, or spring to his feet from the ground where he had been examining the plunder; a scene of violence immediately taking place between the villain and his challengers,—despair and utter recklessness now rendering the fellow almost a match for the pair of assailants. Yet the struggle was at length brought to a close by his discomfiture, which included a fractured arm; when, to the conviction of the young gentleman, the valuable pieces of jewellery, which he again took the liberty to handle, proved to be identical with those that had a few hours earlier been returned to Adelaide at the Hall; the gold pieces seized this second time being of the exact same number as were handed to her.

"What have you done with the young lady whom you have so cruelly robbed, you lurking villain?" demanded Mildmay.

"I am not her keeper, as you may see," was the sulky and unsatisfactory answer.

"Neither are you her father; no true parent would act the monster as you have done to her,—she who can never have harmed you,—believed you she was your child," was the vexed observation; the enraged speaker adding, in the bitterness of the moment, "your looks, as well as your conduct, repels the thought."

"You think yourself a judge about such matter," returned the ruffian. "I am not answerable for your errors."

"I waste time," impatiently cried the young gentleman; "show us the route the unhappy one took, and this gold shall be yours the moment we overtake her."

"A very likely thing, after ye have maimed as well as plundered me," was the insolent and scornful remark. "Yes," continued the villain, "and you would have the wench to witness against her father to the bargain." Then, after appearing to cogitate for a moment or two, the fellow subjoined, "Let me have back all the things, and I'll not only show you the direction the runaway lass took, but inform you of more than I have yet disclosed about her,—more a great deal than her pretended mother ever knew."

"This is absolutely trifling away the time with us, villain," cried Mildmay; "and were it not that we have a more important object in view than immediately bringing you before a magistrate, I should have you tied hand and heel, in order to be duly punished for your felony;" these last words being spoken as the young gentleman and his attendant darted forward, still in the hope of overtaking or of falling in with the fair fugitive.

Their pursuit and searchings were in vain; neither could tidings be obtained of poor Adelaide from any one whom they met in the course of their eager inquiries, whether travellers or mere passers by. Mildmay's vexation was extreme; for he had not only taken up the idea that she was, after all, not the offspring of the ruffian he had more than once assisted to master; but that if she could be brought to confront the fellow, and to accuse him of the robbery, he would purchase an escape by revealing truths which he deemed it not his interest frankly to divulge without some tempting consideration.

What rendered the anxious young gentleman the more disappointed and vexed was, that while failing in his efforts to discover, and also to recover, poor Adelaide, he necessarily lost sight of Jobson, who had contrived to disappear from the quarter in which he was so unexpectedly found. Thus it was, that as surely as the fair fugitive would be exposed to untold hardships, in consequence of her heroic resolves, the chance of confronting her with the escaped villain might be for ever lost. As one overpowered by despair, Mildmay returned to Wartham Hall, where he knew there would be nothing to gladden his spirit; while the thoughts of Adelaide, penniless and friendless, being abroad in the hardened and reeling world, to face its dangers, and to be dismayed by its courses, wrung his heart to its utmost depths.

But what of poor Adelaide all this while? She was the victim of a villain, and now of privation also, as well as fatigue and exhaustion. She had no other resource than once more driving through lanes, along hedge-rows, down into ditches, and again wherever a thicket offered to screen her from the ruffian prowler's eye, to the great damage of her dress, of which, in her distraction, she had become utterly regardless. Alas! there was nothing else left for her after all this than to sink to the ground, to cling to it as before, until insensibility relieved her from conscious despair. How long she continued in this deplorable state and position she herself could never have been able to report; nor indeed is it certain that ever the unhappy maiden would have been again seen alive, had not a spectator of as singular a description as could possibly have been found in all the Ridings of Yorkshire, happened to obtain a glimpse of her as she dropped down amongst some brushwood.

No wonder that the young lady opened her eyes, to be transported with new terrors and strange imaginings, on perceiving that she was in the arms of a being whose complexion was not more outlandish than her garb, and whose ways were as extraordinary as either. It was a deaf and dumb creature that had Adelaide in her keeping, and one of African blackness, of the coarsest negro features conceivable for an elderly female; her dress consisting of a flaming red kirtle, her sort of jacket of a deep yellow, and her head-gear of whiteness as pure as the driven snow. Not a scrap of darkness was to be seen about this remarkable object, save what her large face, her wrinkled throat, and her huge hands presented; so that it was no wonder, on gazing at such an extraordinary object, as she grasped the damsel and held her up in her arms,—just awakened from stupor, too, at the instant,—that Adelaide shrieked aloud, in her momentary delirium, thinking that she had fallen into unearthly hands.

Indeed, it took some little time for the recovering young lady to look around her, and also into the sable face, as well as to the numerous humane assiduities of the mute housekeeper of the eccentric Samaritan,—for it was Black Martha, the only domestic, of the human race, whom Mr. Peter Plumtree had allowed for years to sleep under the roof of the Red Cot, besides himself.

Fortunately, heaven was about to temper the storm of disaster to the shorn lamb,—the mute negress having been the witness who noticed the unhappy maiden's distracted course when she rushed into the thicket where she dropped; her race and flight having been so wholly without guide or compass that she had actually not only thrown herself upon Peter Plumtree's neck of land, which shot into the heart of the bulky baronet's territory, and into one of the eccentric old man's cherished clumps of shrubs, but under the very shadow of the Cauldron Cliff itself. A safer quarter to free her from the pursuit of any one belonging to Wartham Hall could not have been found in all England; the cynical owner of the Red Cot and its surrounding grounds, being as hostile to Sir Vaux and his associates as it was possible for the proud and peremptory baronet to be to the oddity, whom he regarded as being the vilest pest in the world, and as an absolute thorn in his flesh.

It took not long for mute Martha, not merely to assure Adelaide that she was a being of flesh and blood, and of a benign nature, but to conduct the forlorn one to the threshold of the Red Cot; the sagacity of the good creature, though bereft of the sense of hearing and the power of speech, quite independently of some previously acquired knowledge of the interest which the lovely girl had already created in her master's house, informing her that the fugitive would find a kind asylum in the cynic's dwelling, even although she had come from the neighbouring Hall, and been for a period an inmate there. The negress, it is true, had not been an eye-witness either of the breaking down of the carriage, or of her dreadful peril and wonderful rescue at the Cauldron Cliff, and yet she had somehow obtained an accurate inkling and conception of the incidents, and also that it was

the very same beautiful being upon whom her eyes now alighted for the first time, who was the delivered damsel on each of these occasions, to the amazement and delight of her master. In these circumstances it was not other than might have been expected by any one who had the slightest acquaintanceship with the eccentric gentleman's sable yet gaudy housekeeper, when she was seen by him approaching his fantastic habitation, gibbering and capering from the excess of her gladness; half carrying, too, and most affectionately caressing, the object of her sympathies at the same time.

"The very picture, I declare, of——," exclaimed the red-cowled and uncouth-looking old man, as he hobbled out from under the roof of his porch, to assist the negress in her efforts of kindness and hospitality,—his words being the same that fell upon Adelaide's ear when he so opportunely assisted towards her deliverance from the broken-down carriage, and also when he witnessed her appalling predicament at the Cauldron Cliff; there being the same halting in his speech, and the same sort of mystery; for he again added, while he lent his assistance with all the tenderness and alacrity he could muster, "I little thought, when I last parted from her fifty years back, that I should ever look upon her like again."

Peter Plumtree's history, his character and peculiarities, merit some notice. He was the only child of a man little less eccentric than himself, although in his old age the father was far from being equally opulent. In fact, the stripe or tongue of land which proved such a sore in the side of Sir Vaux Waldgrave, extending only to some twenty acres of ground, was the amount of the sire's possessions, and the only source of his income; his culture and the use which he made of this piece of soil having been injudicious and unprofitable. The very house which he inhabited upon it was only a miserable thatched hut, until the more fortunate and enterprising son built the fantastic Red Cot, which, after all, was a poor affair, excepting what might belong to its vile colour and certain other fantasies in respect of shape and accommodation. Yet, though pinched with poverty, the father, with characteristic obstinacy, would not accept of an offer for the purchase of his small property, even when thrice its value was named by Sir Vaux; the stubborn feeling arising in part from the fact of the piece of land having belonged to his predecessors for generations, none of whom, however much hampered, would ever part with it, but chiefly because of the keenness with which he could spite the pompous baronet by keeping it as a thorn in his side.

Now Peter, the son, had been bred up with all the same prejudices, dislikes, jealousies, and stubborn sentiments. He was not, however, without energies of other descriptions; for on reaching the period of manhood, after wooing and winning a beautiful girl in the neighbourhood, who was of still lowlier origin than himself,—and after cherishing for her a passion of romantic, warm, and unwavering constancy, so generous and heroic were his purposes, that he most solemnly bargained with her they should remain unmarried whilst he went and remained abroad, in order to better his fortunes, and that she might have a husband who should be able to take her to a more hospitable roof than that under which he had been born. They plighted their vows of everlasting fidelity, and interchanged the recorded terms of their troths, on paper, written with what was taken from their own veins. Peter then steered his course for the New World, and had his destination in Jamaica, where his energies and excellent character ere long were the means by which his prospects were much improved. To have his betrothed one with him in his new home, and there to make her his wife, was now his prideful and happy thought. But ah! the reply to the honourable offer and earnest invitation was, that the object of his ardent constancy had proved fickle and false, and could never be his.

Terrible was the blow to the young man, who now directed all his powers, with a sort of desperate and savage energy, to other engrossing subjects,—that, chiefly, of amassing wealth; there being, however, all along, ever after, more of the Mammon than the Moloch in him. For years and years he strained himself, body and soul, to heap up riches; but for far the greatest portion of the lengthened period with little progress towards independence. At last, the soured man, when not less than threescore years of age, by a lucky speculation in a vast quantity of tobacco, which was shipped for England, resolved likewise on returning to his birthplace, there to spend the remainder of his days. Fortunately, as regarded the increase of his wealth, during the passage homewards of himself with his property, a very considerable advance of duty was made by the minister in power on the article in question; thus, at a word, as it were, creating for Peter Plumtree a large independency, amounting to many thousands. Yet the sudden accumulation brought not happiness: it chased not even away from him his long-cherished species of misanthropy and unsociability; one of his main objects now being, how most effectually he could vent his spite on such as were rich by inheritance and boastful of family titles; above all, how most keenly he might show his dislike towards the owner of Wartham Hall, not merely because of his preposterous pretensions, or because the speculator in the weed had been bred to dislike Sir Vaux above all others, but because the baronet, who was pretty nearly of Peter's years, had treated him with an extremely provoking indignity when they were young.

Peter Plumtree, as may be inferred from the foregoing statement, was a man of fair character, strong understanding, but peculiar temper, and unpleasing manners. Endowed with a good deal of penetration,—which experience had of course improved,—this had come to do him little better service than to disgust him with his species. He had returned home laden with wealth, which he had no longer the wish even to enjoy. He felt that he had lived in vain; for to a childless, cynical old man great wealth is, perhaps, more galling than poverty. He had no one to love,—no one to share in his possessions; the only constant associate, if she could be called one, whom he allowed to be near him, being the old mute negress whom he brought from the

West Indies, and whom he had selected for his future housekeeper and domestic, as much on account of her being wholly bereft of the sense of hearing and the power of speech, as her known honesty, gentleness, and docility.

Yet there were good points in Peter's character, and in his ways; and perhaps, had he been a husband and father, and had his heart been kept alive to the charities of life, he might have proved an amiable man and an agreeable, useful member of society. He possessed strong natural affections, which, though they had long lain dormant, were not yet extinct. He had, however, been disappointed in love. The mistress of his heart had married and was dead, he believed; and the sanguine, adventurous youth had grown into the cynical, soured old man. He lived alone, with the exception of the mute negress being always near, and those errand people from the nearest town as were required to come to the Red Cot with such things as he required,—amongst which a copy of the "Times" newspaper was the most regular, and the most prized; this being the journal, at the date of which we are speaking, that he took in, on account of the ability with which it advocated the liberal views of the Whigs,—although Mr. Plumtree would have gone much further towards the sweeping away of political and governmental abuses than eventually did the Russell Sponge.

Peter's were the habits of a recluse, and he had also most of the forbidding peculiarities which are supposed to belong to single and soured gentlemen of a certain age. In particular, he had an extreme dislike to receiving those delicate attentions which are sometimes so assiduously rendered to the rich who are childless. The self-same parlour, the self-same arm-chair, the self-same small, staring, red house,—with a plot of long, bottle-green grass in front, and a narrow border of the coarsest flowers, interspersed with weeds, growing thin and straggling, out of a slimy-looking soil,—these were his continual associates; while as for indulgences in pleasure or luxuries, besides the everlasting "Times," were his pipe and his bowl. Of too long standing were his tropical habits for the keen air of the north, and for him to dispense with the fragrant weed, so that he dozed away life pretty much as he had done during his last years in the West Indies; except that he generally smoked at the fireside, instead of being in the verandah, and now preferred whisky-toddy to rum-punch,—his stomach resisting the stronger and more perfumed mixture.

In short, Peter Plumtree's feelings were hardened, and he was rendered too suspicious, by the circumstances of a varied and trying life, for him to think there was any good in human nature. His benevolence, accordingly, was mostly frozen over; but when it thawed, the verdure of a generous character came quickly forth.

"What! turned out from the great man's hall already?" growled he, as he assisted the old negress to conduct Adelaide towards his poorly-furnished parlour. "But there is room in the Red Cot for one that has thy looks, notwithstanding all that I have gone through for the sake of falseness that was exactly in the guise of such another face. No, not the parlour, Martha," continued he, leaving off his mysterious allusions on finding that the young lady was again about to sink in a fainting-fit to the ground, and just as if the deaf and dumb creature heard every syllable he uttered, or had the capacity to answer him and to put questions; Martha every moment casting her looks from the maiden to his lips, in order to construe what he said,—shedding tears, too, while she *neighered* and laughed. "Not the parlour, Blackie; but my sleeping-room, and into my bed at once. I'll make the parlour floor do for me, till I provide for her more fitly. She's famishing, I'll be sworn; bring me my cordial bottles, Martha, ye nigger! and then I'll set thee over the poor thing for nurse, as soon as I see her restored to sense, and in the way to take sound rest. There now," as they delicately and gently laid the damsel upon the bed, and threw a thin covering over her, the weather being warm. "Fetch the bottles; not a word of idle talk, Blackie, for fear of disturbing the innocent creature. Let them but dare to set a foot upon my ground in search of her, if she have a wish to fly from such a pack as would be her death. Peter Plumtree's bull-dog, Cerberus, and his two pair of spitfires, will answer for her, for me, and for themselves, in a twinkling."

In this way the recluse ran on, happier than he often of late years had been, in thinking that he was doing good and bringing comfort to one in whom he had already taken a deep interest; not being, at the same time, insensible to the less pure and amiable gratification, that of spiting his titled neighbour. With judgment he administered the cordials, and with equal discretion indicated to the mute and serviceable negress what to do in regard to loosening the maiden's dress, the bathing of her hands and forehead, and the preparation of some light food. A mother could not have been more fertile with succouring expedients for her daughter, or more tender in their application, than was this rough son of Adam, and cynical old man; nor could a more willing and expert handmaiden have been found in the chambers of the great, for the fulfilment of his orders, than the mute Martha. So judicious and prompt, indeed, were the measures adopted in behalf of Adelaide in the Red Cot, that before its uncouth-looking owner thought of relinquishing the damsel to the sole services of his sable housekeeper, she had begun to express her sense of deep obligation for such unexpected and, as she felt, undeserved kindness.

"Now, be obedient, young creature, and let me have the command," cried he, when he found she was going to talk, and also what was to be the course and nature of her speech. "Learn that I am as wilful and obstinate in my own cot as ever the frothy Sir Vaux can be in his great house. I must have my own way in everything; and one of those things for the present is, that thou, poor creature, do not open thy mouth about a single circumstance before the arrival of a new day, excepting to signify what thou would'st have to comfort thy frail and exhausted body. I

must be both the peremptory father and the prescribing physician for thee, until, at least, the morrow comes."

Adelaide felt the kindness and the wisdom of the old man, whose ungainliness, like that of the mute Martha, was quickly passing away. She accepted of whatever was recommended to her in the way of gentle stimulants and light nutriment; she resigned herself as best she could to slumber; and while the old negress watched with unceasing vigilance and assiduity at her bedside, the aged recluse kept wandering about his cot, as if to be its guardian against the approach of hostile or stranger-feet; lamenting, amid his sense of happiness in acting the part of the good Samaritan, that he had not some dear one, like the invalid who occupied his couch, whom it should be his right to call daughter, were it but as an adopted one.

"It will be her own fault," he at length ejaculated, time after time, as he paced backward and forward, and sometimes close to the half-open window of his bed-chamber, in which the young lady now lay,—it being one of old Peter's peculiarities not only to think aloud, but to talk to himself in a singularly high and noisy key, the deafness of his domestic having encouraged him in the ludicrous practice. "It will be her own fault if she does not become mine adopted bairn, that is to say, also, if nothing worse turns out for me to learn than what my hopes and wishes are. She shall be my child, and everything which is mine shall be her's that survives me, Blackie and all; only never shall she have it in her power to part with the Red Cot, were it to please the king himself, and all the lords and knights of the kingdom."

The eccentric Samaritan had so frequently come over these sentiments, and growled them out in such a high key, that the sounds and their import at length reached the hearing of Adelaide,—startling her from her slumber,—which, owing to her recent distractions and exhaustion, had been far from profound or properly refreshing. The nature of the soliloquist's language could not but interest her, and keep her awake, at least, while his talk came to her knowledge. And yet she was soon destined to overhear discourse that still more excited her.

"Who are you, that has got unbidden so close to my cot?" were the words which the maiden caught at, uttered with no complacent or welcoming growl,—she listening with redoubled eagerness, in the hopes of gathering the terms of the answer, and half anticipating by whom it would be returned. Nor had she been in error, for she at once recognised the bland speech of Montague Mildmay, when he said,—

"I am in search of a poor, distracted, and fair fugitive, who I imagined might have strayed in this direction. Have you, sir, had any knowledge of such a person in the course of to-day?"

"From whence has she fled? what the cause? and to what quarter was it her wish to escape?" were old Peter's harshly put interrogatories, instead of deigning to afford the inquirer any satisfaction.

"To your first query I have to reply," said the young gentleman, "that it was from your neighbour's mansion, Wartham Hall, the unhappy young lady went. As to your other interrogatories, I hardly think you can either desire or expect me to make answer."

"Ay, this is just like the impertinence of the blundering Sir Vaux's sort of folks," returned the cynic, growing more uncouth and uncourteous as he spoke. "But you ought to know, young man, that I do as little allow of such gentry intruding themselves upon my ground as the pompous baronet is willing for me to go into his fine shrubberies; so the sooner ye decamp, the better. Were it not that I suppose you ignorant of the kind of love that is between him and me, I should probably give it in charge to my surly four-footed housekeeper, Cerberus, to show you the way to where ye came from. A late inmate of the Hall to be a fugitive to old Peter Plumtree's neck of land that is such a thorn in the vain Sir Vaux's side! why, this would be a marvel, indeed; and be sport for me through a month to come. Nothing more unlikely; therefore be off, or I'll not parley another moment with you so gently as I have done."

"Shall I rush to announce myself to my late deliverer?" was the question which the again distracted Adelaide put aloud to herself, on hearing Mildmay exclaim, "Savage and inhospitable man!" But at the instant the sound of his withdrawing steps reached her ear, and she withheld herself, to be again poignantly agitated with renewed anxieties.

CHAPTER VII.

THE WOOING OLD BACHELOR.

How fair and promising had certain of the airy fabrics seemed which the castle-builders at Wartham Hall erected for themselves! and how suddenly were they dashed to the ground by the appearance and pretensions of the ruffian who took the name of Jared Jobson! But of these several adventurous architects who had soared into cloud-land, in connexion with the arrival from France of the now unhappy Adelaide, there was not one who could merit less sympathy than Sir Vaux Waldgrave himself,—the blundering tactician in the entire business. As for Captain Chesters, his case had already been to a great extent disposed of, yet was it, by the strange discoveries made relative to the parentage of the young lady, rendered much better than prior to his first sight of her. Had the baronet indeed manifested a sense of his stupid manœuvring in the management of the marrying affair, and been forward to confess that he was a clumsy contriver for himself as well as for others, the painful events—some of them deeply tragic—which threw gloom upon his house and disgrace upon his policy, might have evoked compassion towards him. But so little was the ponderous, petty despot conscious of his own miserable incapacity, as regarded foresight and delicacy of control, and so prompt and wide-mouthed at the same time was he in throwing all the blame upon others, as concerned the failure of his tortuous and bungling schemes, that the most tender-hearted must have felt it to be a waste of sensitiveness to bestow pity upon him. It could not but afford a very bad aspect as respected his discernment, as well as generosity, that his wrath found expression chiefly against the poor fugitive maiden, who had been made,—although innocently on her part,—the victim of a vile plot; and that, instead of making his intriguing and unprincipled sister-in-law the main object of his loud fury, he directed his rage towards the unhappy damsel, who scorned to be his debtor in aught from the moment of her origin's exposure; just as if the girl ought to have been made responsible for that origin. Besides, it spoke little for his principles and sympathies, and certainly as slenderly for his wisdom, that hardly had he got the self-slaying Mrs. Waldgrave committed to the tomb,—which was as hurriedly done as could be allowed, — when he trumpeted forth his pretensions and purposes as a wooing bachelor; giving it out, that he was resolved on having offspring of his own, in order to inherit his fine estate and large accumulation of wealth.

"Now that I have no niece, and that I never had, except in the shape of a pretending beggar," said he, "I'll raise a race of my own, in order to spite and to spoil that libertine and sensualist, Ludlow Chesters, who would not scruple to be my finisher, and who, no doubt, is already crowing mightily on learning how a smooth-faced minx has been caught in her pranks to impose upon me, and to mingle her worthless blood with that of our ancient line. No time is to be lost. Would that something short of nine months served for my intents and ends; seeing that there is many a slip between the cup and the lip, quite independently of what the Life-Guardsman may essay and conspire to perpetrate. Yes, I shall contribute to the renown of the Waldgraves by uniting myself to a noble stock. The ducal house of Rivers shall, in all probability, supply me with a helpmate. Lady Augusta has already been sounded,—nay, she has as good as smiled an acquiescence in my prospective suit. I'll forthwith put the question, plump and plain, to her; and should she reject me,—a thing for Sir Vaux not to contemplate,—why, it is but to cast my line and lay myself abroad in some other and still loftier direction, and to chagrin the old maid by my success there."

Full of these oft-conned aspirations, between the death and the burial of the unprincipled Mrs. Waldgrave, no sooner had her remains been interred, than the bulky baronet started on his wooing adventure to the country residence of Lord Adolphus and Lady Augusta Rivers,—a brother and sister whose attachment to one another was so twin-like and enlightened, that it would have taken an individual of far higher intellectual and moral attainments than ever Sir Vaux displayed, to sever or slacken it, even by the mere circumstance of interposing any sort of distance between their respective habitations. So arrogant was the vain-glorious man in his hopes and pretensions, that, without allowing days to

MR. PETER PLUMTREE.

elapse between the burying solemnities and the courting enterprise, the hurried hearse had not well quitted the porch of the stately Hall, with its burden of misused mortality, when he, in the gay garments of a suitor for a wife, was helped into his carriage, leaving his mansion to the care of domestics, who knew how to profit by his absence.

"You cannot either be ignorant of, or surprised at, the purport of this visit to your noble residence, my dear Lord Adolphus Rivers," said Sir Vaux, on finding himself ushered into the presence of that nobleman, who happened to be alone on the arrival at the moment of the confident baronet's matrimonial visit. "You are too well and painfully acquainted with the sad events which so lately occurred at Wartham Hall, to require of my undertaking the task of recapitulating them to your lordship. Suffice it for the present that I inform you of the fact of these horrid matters having actually

No. 5.—THE GOVERNESS.

changed my position, my prospects, and my determinations. In short, I am upon a wooing and marrying expedition; and, as a piece of courteous neighbourhood, were no stronger motives swaying me,—as, indeed, they do,—I should hold myself in honour bound to proffer my hand, in the first place, to your fair and admirable sister, the Lady Augusta Rivers Allow me to add, although you must already be cognizant of the recommendatory circumstance, that this hand of mine never before was offered for the acceptance of any one of the daughters of Eve; and that, therefore, in reality,—although there be gray hairs in my locks, and a wrinkle may have planted itself on my brow,—my proffered hand, in a sense, is as juvenile and unengaged as that of any youth in his teens, or who may have just come of age, can ever pretend to have been. May I, my lord, since such be the facts, have your recommendation as a passport to your high-born sister, Lady Augusta Rivers', kind consideration; assured, as I am, that your ducal house can in no way be lowered in the estimation of the aristocratic world by an alliance with the head of the Waldgrave family?"

During the deliverance of this prosy speech, Lord Adolphus manifested — although the stolid baronet perceived not the alternations —very opposite states of mind; a sense of the ludicrous contending with disgust. In what way or terms he might have responded to the palaver is not very clear. Probably he knew not himself how most fitly to begin, or to end. But, fortunately for him, as he felt it, he was relieved from performing the task; the lady to whom the gray-headed wooer so pointedly referred, coming into the apartment where the two gentlemen were seated, but being quite ignorant of the baronet's presence there.

"You hesitate, my lord, as respects returning an answer to my explicit and unquestionably courteous statement,—master of all the proprieties, as I hold myself to be," observed Sir Vaux, with some degree of warmth. "It will, Lord Adolphus, be regarded by me as nothing more than politeness, if you will accord me a response of some kind."

"Oh! here comes my sister herself," cried his lordship, obviously thankful for her appearance at the moment. "Women," continued he, "have far quicker wits on an occasion of the present character than I, at least, ever possessed. Let me turn you over to Augusta, for whose information I trust you will be so kind as to rehearse the long harangue you have just finished."

The baronet, after exercising himself in bowing, ejaculating sundry ponderous "hems," and reiterating that he had always been a stickler for the nicest proprieties, commenced his prosy speech again, without perceiving how Lord Adolphus marvelled at his repetition in nearly the exact same words of his stupid story; the only material addition being, that he wished to have offspring of his own, in order that direct descendants might inherit his many broad acres, be benefited by his accumulated wealth, and transmit, "through many future ages, the issue of the houses of Rivers and Waldgrave, in consequence of the felicitous matrimonial alliance of the Lady Augusta and myself."

During this rehearsal, the fair one who was so pointedly addressed, had her mind gradually changing from surprise to indigation, and next to revulsion. The simple appearance of the baronet, without a symbol of mourning upon his person, — being on the contrary, rather showily attired,—on the very day when she understood the body of the suicidal Mrs. Waldgrave was to be consigned to its last resting-place, would have startled her. When, however, she was forced to perceive that the ponderous talker's egotism and selfishness were more intolerable and offensive than she had ever found them; and that he, a stickler about courtesies and a vain boaster of his regard for the nicest proprieties, not only was most palpably violating the commonest decencies, but discoursing with formal coldness of matters which outraged her feelings of delicacy, she deemed it her duty to deliver to him such a

lesson, which, if properly received, might save him from less ceremonious treatment on future occasions. And yet it was not until the wooer somewhat warmly pressed her ladyship for an explicit and prompt answer, just as he had done in the case of the hesitation of a response from Lord Adolphus, that words readily came to her lips.

"My brother was pleased," said she, "to give credit to my sex for the possession of far quicker wits, to the answering of such discourse as you have now addressed to me, Sir Vaux Waldgrave, than he is gifted with. And yet you have so wholly staggered me by your mere outward appearance here this day, and still more by your carriage and tone of manners, but most of all by your talk, that nothing short of your peremptory call for a reply from me could have prevented me from retiring from your presence and taking care that I never encountered it again. However, I am not a girl in my teens, and my middle age may excuse me, especially when in the company of my brother, — who, I perceive, approves of the course,—if I administer a few words of counsel and also reproof, which it vexes me to discover even the hoary-headed Sir Vaux Waldgrave stands in need of."

"You are personal! you are all at once growing abusive! Lady Augusta," exclaimed the baronet, bounding as nimbly and pompously as he was able from his seat: "you ought to have some respect for yourself, if not for me."

"Some respect!" her ladyship exclaimed. "What say you, Sir Vaux, to the proprieties in coming hither as a gay suitor within a few hours of the time at which the remains of your unhappy sister-in-law have been carried to the grave, and though not to your grief as regards her end, at least to the grief as well as consternation of my brother and myself, who could have wished to have been spared any idle visit to-day, and certainly, above all, by him who should have been the deepest mourner on the occasion,—we who were so terribly shocked on looking on the suicide—on the discovery of the horrid act."

"Oh! I wished to show to the world," impatiently responded the baronet, yet with a lowered tone, as he resumed his seat,—"I wished to prove to all that I despised the wretch who had brought such vile trouble into my mansion, and that it might be known there was no kinship between the low-born widow of my infatuated brother Wilford and Sir Vaux Waldgrave, the lord of Wartham Hall. Nay, more than this, I was desirous, and am resolved, to manifest to mankind that the discovery of the base trick which the self-murderess's reputed daughter,—beggarly baggage,—played me, sat not sorely upon my spirit, and that I had resources within myself which are capable of contending with far greater difficulties than any I have ever yet encountered through woman's wickedness or man's either."

"Worse and worse, sir!" indignantly cried the lady. "You not only proudly profess yourself to be destitute of religion, but to be without the ordinary sense of moral duty and the commonest sort of humanity. I trust there are few in Great Britain who cherish the barbarous sentiments professed by Sir Vaux Waldgrave, whatever station in life you go to. Of this, at least, I am assured, from what I have seen and learned of the misused Adelaide,—that even in the most forlorn of conditions she would repel the wooing address of the noblest of the land, were he, though a youth, to profess the principles and the utter want of natural sympathies which I have heard a man of three-score and ten this day vauntingly proclaim as his. Happy, after all, I must hold it to be for the amiable young lady whom I have just named, that she is not to dwell in a school where such a teacher and exemplar have a peremptory control as Sir Vaux Waldgrave would exercise at Wartham Hall."

Lady Augusta paused, for she perceived that if the blundering baronet felt not ashamed of himself and convinced of the miserable figure which he had made, he was at least struck dumb for the time. On perceiving, however, that he was about to rally, and to attempt a further defence, she interposed.

"I had intended, in my reply to you, Sir Vaux Waldgrave," said she, "to have touched on the terms and style of your matrimonial expedition, when you talked of your motives and the ends of your suit. But it better accords with my sense of delicacy that I conclude my lecture and reproof, by advising you, when next time you go a-wooing, old bachelor that you are, to remember the *proprieties* somewhat better than you have this day done in your address to Augusta Rivers."

Her ladyship upon this withdrew; nor was the stupid baronet slow to take his departure for his home, more especially as he could not remain blind to the acquiescence which Lord Adolphus manifested in the sister's sentiments.

"We have for ever alienated the heart of Sir Vaux, such as it is, from us," observed his lordship, on joining Lady Augusta.

"Not at all, brother," was her reply; "for whenever he wishes to pamper his pride by a show of intimacy with members of the ducal house, as he dubs us, when on his high-horse, or has some political crotchet to gratify, he will be as he was wont, a mere bore, with little good or evil about him, because of his want of power in either way. As for me, I shall study to avoid him, were it for no other reason than that his buckskins and top-boots, his white waistcoat and light-blue upper garment, as beheld this day, will be ever present to my imagination."

Sir Vaux was not a man to be driven from his absurdities and vulgar errors by any lecturer. He was too strongly hedged round by his codes and prejudices to yield an assent to any doctrine which squared not with his sense of the *proprieties*. Nor could there be a surer way of confirming him in his ludicrous, and often mischievous proceedings and creed, than to offer him direct and unmistakable opposition. If Lady Augusta expected to cure him of his selfish pride and pig-headed obstinacy, or to render him a more tolerable wooer in any other quarter than he had proved to herself, she was widely mistaken. In fact, as he rode homeward, he resolved more strenuously than he had yet done to take to himself a wife, in order to have a progeny of his own, and in order, as he flattered himself, to spite the ducal house.

"Neither shall I stand so nicely punctilious about my choice," said he to himself, "but have more respect to youth, beauty, and health, than any middle-aged old maid can furnish for me. I shall not even be greatly squeamish about widowhood, provided the dame be of a breeding sort, and afford me the promise not only of proving a good nurse in my latter years, but of implicit subserviency to my fixed rules and established methods."

In following up these views, Sir Vaux resolved on making a sojourn in the great world of London, where he had not been for many years, and where he knew there would be abundance of opportunities not only for a man of his substance meeting with marrying ladies who were on the wrong side of thirty, but prolific widows, to judge from their preceding fecundity. Nor was he without the prospect of vexing and turning into contempt his dissipated and profligate nephew, the Hon. Captain Chesters,—that Life-Guardsman of high fashion,—by a residence of several weeks in the metropolis.

After having been in London only a few days, during which short period Sir Vaux seemed to have been too proud or indolent to take any active measures for the accomplishment of his matrimonial project,—leaving it entirely to chance, time, or circumstances to carry it into effect,—his more marked notice was directed to the Lady Clementina Villiers, who, however, had in the first place paid him particular attention in certain large parties where he happened to find himself much in the background. Indeed, but for the fair one's notice, the ponderous Yorkshire baronet would probably have remained to the termination of his metropolitan visit a star of the smallest magnitude. To be rendered greater than, to his deep disappointment, he discovered himself to be in the saloons of the titled, was an occurrence not to be neglected. Still, to have this greatness conferred upon him by means of a wife,—of a woman, and one, too, who could not count a descent that went half so far back as that of himself,—she the widow, too, of a fashionable spendthrift, whose father had been a saddler who enriched himself by army contracts during the late most expensive war with France,—these were startling circumstances to the mind of Wartham Hall's owner. Still, the baronet's stay in town was protracted. Somehow or another hardly a day or evening escaped without his finding himself in juxtaposition to Lady Clementina, who never failed to render herself not only most affable and agreeable to him, but to assist in attracting notice from others to his merits and pretensions. She professed a wonderful admiration of a country life; declared that Yorkshire, of all the quarters of England, had endearingly recommended itself to her imagination in regard to rural beauty and felicity; that, in fact, the Riding in which Wartham Hall formed such a conspicuous feature was to her fancy the garden of the kingdom, —her delightful associations therewith being closely connected with the name and fame of Sir Vaux, long before she had the extreme happiness of meeting him in society. The baronet was captivated as much as it was in his nature to be. He also came to the conclusion that he would not be the worse for connecting himself with the splendid families amongst which Lady Clementina formed such a brilliant ornament. Although she was on the wrong side of thirty, she was still only about half his age, and a showy-looking woman, who might be the mother of a series of children, as had been the case during her first wedded period. In short, from being an admirer, Sir Vaux became a suitor, and ere long he seemed to think that he was a lucky man when he found himself an accepted lover?

Nor were the baronet's proposals made at a period inconvenient to the gay and manœuvring widow; for her infatuated husband, Sir Arthur Villiers, had closed a brief career of folly and extravagance by leaving his widow with a son and daughter,— the survivors out of half-a-dozen of children,—almost wholly to the charity of relatives. The new union was therefore warmly approved of by her family and connexions; so that as soon as the men of law and the milliners had done their parts, the marriage was celebrated with the greatest splendour. There was present a prince of the blood; the benediction of an archbishop was pronounced upon the alliance; peers and peeresses, lace and pearls, a magnificent saloon, an elegant *dejeuner*, and a line of splendid equipages, adding to the grandeur of the occasion.

Much was said by the glittering marriage party of the virtues and charms of the lady of whom Yorkshire was about to become the envied possessor, and also of the wonderful luck of Sir Vaux, of whose noble mansion she would become the fitting glory, and of whose wealth she would be found the liberal yet considerate distributor. She had been accustomed, it was added,—without at first alarming the aged wooer,—to a fashionable London life, and she had also lived abroad. She had seen a great deal of the world, and the world had seen a great deal of her. She had been lauded for her talents, her manners, her music, and her taste in dress. True, the admiration had been gradually on the wane for years; but then the craving still continued. In fact, and to dispense with all flattery, this lady, when taken without her adventitious aids, was a mere showy, superficial, weak woman; with a fretful temper, irritable nerves, and a wondrous sense of self-importance; the last-mentioned feature being that alone in which there was any community of principle, feeling, or habit, between her and her ponderous lord. In all things else they seemed not only to be directly opposed, but destined to remain in complete opposition; a fact which Sir Vaux began too soon for his peace of mind to discover, or rather, too late; seeing that, by the time he prepared for going northward with his spouse, he found cause to take objections to the magnitude of the lady's bridal train and early requirements.

"I really must give it as my decided opinion, which, you are to understand, never changes after I use the term *fixed, decided,* or *established,* my dear Lady Clementina," said the baronet, on observing the extent of preparations which she had ordered for her proceeding to Yorkshire, "that however much I approve of pomp and retinue in the display of persons of our station, yet that something more moderate should have sufficed, in pretension, and less alarmingly expensive, than what your arrangements, apart from mine, prognosticate for our travel to my ancestral home. Why should there be a separate equipage for your offspring by your deceased husband, with maids and footmen, I know not how many,—besides a French governess for my step-daughter, and a tutor for my step-son,—mere children,—the former not nine years old, the other some eighteen months younger? At this rate, Wartham Hall will prove too limited a dwelling for our own particular family, if we are to allow of suites of apartments for our distinguished visitors. Then, alas! for my pleasure-grounds, gardens and plantations, with so many senseless idlers ever racing about,—one only helping another in the work of mischief."

"You astonish me, Sir Vaux Waldgrave!" was Lady Clementina's response to a speech which appeared to her to be overbearing and coarse; beginning already to expatiate largely upon her tasteful consideration in regard to the manner in which she intended to confer upon their union honour and celebrity to Sir Vaux's domestic display. "Indeed," continued she, "I imagined that by such an importation as I am making to Wartham Hall, I was taking the most effectual means to secure your approval and gratitude, were it merely by allowing the separate equipage and retinue for my offspring to have a temporary show there, in order to dignify, with due rejoicings and magnificence, our nuptials at your ancestral residence."

"The show must be temporary, I warn you, my dear Lady Clementina," growled the baronet, "otherwise I'd feel shame at the huge and exorbitant addition,—*importation,* you call it,—there being no deficiency of fitting state and pageantry at the Hall in bygone times."

"We shall see! we shall see, whether the adition will be temporary and transient, or not," were the words which the new-made wife,—lately the gay widow,—muttered to herself, without, however, permitting the stupid baronet to be cognizant of her implied threat. "I am determined to begin as I shall end."

Nor, indeed, did a day elapse from that of their arrival in the Riding without Sir Vaux making the painful discovery that he had not drawn the capital prize in the marriage lottery; his first faint misgivings beginning to assume a less questionable shape, as the features of the lady's post-nuptial character became developed,—these, in less than two weeks after their arrival at the Hall, resolving themselves into tastes and forms, pursuits and habits, diametrically different from those of her peremptory husband. Above all the two spoilt children by the former marriage, with the French governess of the one, and the London-bred tutor of the other, together with their special servants, as well as those of the mother,—all these being subservient to her ladyship's immediate authority,—above all, did this formidable body of imported strangers prove troublesome to the baronet.

"Your mischievous son, Lady Clementina, although he were my legitimate offspring also," one morning cried Sir Vaux, on lumbering up to his spouse in a terrible fume,—"I say, your boy shall not on any account be permitted to

crop the flowers of my most valued and beautiful exotics with impunity, neither to uproot my
choicest shrubs, nor mar the regularity of my
arrangements in the garden or lawn, by driving
through and over them at will. You hear my
fixed and unalterable decision; so that unless
your ladyship adopt measures to prevent the
injuries he inflicts upon my feelings and cherished
property, it will be necessary for me to step in,
and take a severe initiative with him in the
way of imprisonment and stripes."

"Touch but a hair of my dear and beautiful
boy's head in anger or reproof, Sir Vaux Waldgrave," replied the lady, "and I will resent the
cruelty more than if you lifted your big arm
against myself. Learn that such is my fixed
and unalterable decision,—my unequivocal
forewarning."

CHAPTER VIII.

THE CONTENDING TEMPTATIONS.

AT the period when Sir Vaux Waldgrave was
commencing his matrimonial pursuits, poor
Adelaide was prostrated on a bed of sickness
within the walls of Mr. Plumtree's Red Cot.
And no wonder, considering her recent trials
and perils. The appalling affair at the Cauldron
Cliff, the distractions at Wartham Hall consequent on the discovery of the story of the ruffian Jobson, and the toils as well as the terrors
attendant on the maiden's flight,—whither, she
knew not,—were more than sufficient to overwhelm her,—and prostrate her with an illness of
a serious character, as soon as she had a bed
to recline upon. Even the incident of Montague Mildmay's coming to the exact quarter
in which she was housed with such eager sympathies in her behalf, as her ear drank in, together with the reception he met with from the
cynical recluse,—even this particular occurrence
was calculated not slightly to add to the perturbations of her mind. That fever, with its accustomed ravings, should follow her various and
distressing encounters, was nothing but what
was to be looked for in the case of such a tender and inexperienced person. She became ill,
alarmingly ill, immediately after the rude dismissal of the young gentleman for whom she
already entertained fervent affections, and who
manifested a no less ardent interest in her welfare. Day after day during the course of
nearly a fortnight the unhappy damsel was the
subject of such delirium or of such weakness as
to render it dangerous for the patient to converse
or put herself to any effort; Peter Plumtree's
caution being nearly as exclusive in this respect
as if he had been equally dumb with his sable
domestic. At the same time his skill in regard
to the treatment of the young lady rivalled
what a regular medical practitioner would have
recommended. At length her sickness reached its
climax. It subsided, and the recovery became
rapid. At the close of another fortnight, the
maiden was able not only to discourse at length
with the owner of the asylum in which she had
received so much kindness, but to relinquish
the bed except at the usual hours of rest. And
now came the questions how she was to dispose

of herself, and in what manner to choose between such contending views as had each strong
temptations in their aspects, and promises to
deeply perplex her in regard to selection.

Old Peter's pressure was the most immediate
and tangible, offering the young lady the prospect of most substantial benefit without further
risks and difficulties. He was wishful to adopt
her as his daughter, and, in the case of her survival of him, to make her the heiress of all he
possessed, — a liberality and extent of kindness, the amount and nature of which she
strove in vain to acknowledge with anything
which appeared to her of adequate gratitude
and warmth of admiration. To be at such an
easy rate invested with wealth as were the terms
upon which the recluse was willing to adopt her,
—namely, the taking up her abode in the Red
Cot while he lived, and thereafter preserving
the little property from being alienated from
her and her lawful successors, and also that she
should devote her love to him as if he really
were her father,—bestowing much of her time
also and the exercise of her accomplishments
for his entertainment and profit,—these were
the only things which the eccentric yet affectionate old man alone named as the returns to
be exacted for the proffered benefits. What
rendered his generosity the more touching were
not only the tears with which, as he held the
hand of the thoughtful and lovely girl in his
great grasp, he urged his fervent requests, but
the yearnings with which he ever accompanied
his appeals towards some long lost one of whom
he was constantly declaring that Adelaide
was a perfect picture; without, however, once
allowing himself to make farther disclosures
concerning the wondrously loved *original*, so
to speak; Peter Plumtree being a personage
who liked to deal in obscurities, and to heap
mystery upon mystery.

Now, it was not in the nature of the ingenuous
and generous girl to be insensible to the promised advantages, and yet there were strong
drawbacks to her yielding herself up to the
presented temptations. She could not, for
instance, but feel that before she could bring
herself to fall in with the habits and modes of
thinking of her benefactor, her mind and manners must undergo such a change as would
amount to a severe sacrifice,—to the entire
forgetfulness almost of what her upbringing
had been, her associations, her prospects and
sympathies. With all his sterling benevolence,
Peter Plumtree was a rough and uncouth subject. He had strange ways even for a vulgar
and coarse man, which were far more repulsive
to our young and fastidious lady than his ungainly figure, features, and attitudes. His pair
of voluminous eyebrows might be overlooked,
when tears of tenderness were found to issue
from beneath them; his huge round shoulders
arrested not the attention, when he stooped to
the performance of a beneficent ministry. What
though his gait was hobbling, or his unshapely
large fingers did their office awkwardly, when
it was seen that he ever felt ready to lend his best
energies in alleviating pain or removing distress? Still he was in many respects far from
attractive,—going beyond the ugliness of his
everlasting red and greasy cowl, and the oddity
of his other portions of dress,—a series of the

most frightful waistcoats that were ever seen being of the number. He chewed as well as smoked tobacco; he slobbered when he took his victuals; he walked up and down with creaking shoes, evidently enjoying this species of sound; he drummed upon the table with a snuffy hand. Worse still: with that same obnoxious, besmeared paw he would pat the shoulders, head, and chin of Adelaide as often as she came within his reach. And lastly, under this head of disagreeables, the Yorkshire brogue and the Yorkshire dialect, which the young lady detested, never can have flourished anywhere more rankly than these did in our eccentric Samaritan's mouth.

"Thou'lt get a husband as proud and high-born as the stupid Sir Vaux himself, girl, if thou'lt be mine adopted; for my dross will purchase the like for then," the cynic would say with a snarl and growl, although never a bitter or angry expression passed his lips towards the maiden, for not one grudging or displeased thought arose in his heart in relation to her. "If I mistake not, thou hast a fancy for that meddling fellow that came from the Hall in search of thee; then say that thou wilt be my daughter, and he'll shortly woo thee for his bride."

"Oh! call him not a meddling fellow, the amiable and excellent Montague Mildmay, of Mildmay Park," cried Adelaide; "for he it was, and no other, who adventured his life to rescue me from a dreadful death at the Cauldron Cliff, as you yourself were witness;"—this being communicated regarding the young gentleman as if reluctantly and extorted, after numerous allusions had been made to the event without drawing from the maiden the confession.

"Who? what? how?" exclaimed the recluse. "Why not call to me from thy bed when I angrily ordered him about his business? Why not cry the youth had been thy deliverer? The news comes too late now, darling," added old Peter, as he hobbled away in a suddenly agitated manner to another quarter of his fantastically built and oddly garnished dwelling.

"What can he mean?" ejaculated Adelaide, on observing the man. "All his movements, emotions, and sayings are strange, though full of intents. But now, as to my future, my best and wisest course for the time to come," continued the soliloquist, addressing herself to her own most immediate concerns, and the temptations which old Plumtree held out to her; "in what way would Mildmay look upon my principles and conduct, were I, from a sordid motive, to bury myself in this Red Cot, most hospitable although its eccentric owner has been to me, and were I to burden him with my further support? This assuredly could not be the sort of probation which Montague would expect or exact from me; not such as he himself would encounter, in order to purify and elevate his views. There must be noble sacrifices to win his approbation, and to earn my own self-reliance and respect. No; I will go forth and strive for myself, employing what talents and acquirements I possess honestly and strenuously. I will daily invoke the blessing of heaven upon my virtuous efforts; nor

shall I forget suing for the countenance and the encouragement of the good Samaritan, under whose roof I now find myself, in order to strengthen me in my enterprise and exertions. There have been young women worse provided for than education has done for me towards passing through life reputably, yea, honourably, and to their true renown. This will be the way to reap the applause of Mildmay, should he ever become acquainted with my trials and my triumphs,—ay, should he ever bless me with a sight of him."

It was in such a channel that Adelaide's meditations ran during the brief absence of the master of the Red Cot, after his manifesting the excitement mentioned, when he learnt that Montague Mildmay, of Mildmay Park, had not only been the individual whom he rudely turned away from his door, when the young gentleman was in search of the fugitive damsel, but that it had been he who at fearful peril to himself rescued her from appalling destruction at the Cauldron Cliff. Yes, the cynic returned to where he had left the young lady, looking even more troubled and melancholy than when he went out from her, carrying in his hand a file of the *Times* newspaper, with a large fold of one of the numbers, nearly a fortnight old, where was found the following notice:—

"Sailed, on Monday last, for Calcutta, attached to the suite of the newly-appointed Governor of India, Lord Paget Rivers, of the ducal house of that name, Montague Mildmay, Esq., of Mildmay Park, Yorkshire, in the capacity, it is understood, of private secretary to his lordship; the young gentleman's attainments in general literature, and the oriental languages besides, being understood to have greatly recommended him to the important and, no doubt, lucrative post of honour."

"And now he is lost to thee, girl," added Peter Plumtree, with one of his growled-out sighs, on reading the paragraph; "lost, in a measure, or perhaps wholly, through my rashness. Surely thou hast deservings for kindness from the owner of the Red Cot for this. Thou must not,—thou can'st not, refuse my offered terms of adoption now; for thy gallant deliverer will either die of a bad liver in the East, or return so withered a nabob, to lay his bones in Yorkshire, that he shall not be worth thy having, even though he made thee the offer, and thou hadst length of days sufficient to witness his coming back." And as the old, uncouth man uttered these latter words, sobs began to suffocate him,—the big tears also racing down his coarse wrinkled cheeks; the fate of the young gentleman, no doubt, in some way assimilating itself with the recollected history of his own fortunes in foreign and far distant parts.

Was it from a sympathy simply with the eccentric Plumtree that Adelaide wept also? or was there some other subject of sorrow, disappointment, and bereavement, on account of which, throughout a great portion of the remainder of that day, she felt as if there was no more comfort for her,—no further hope? The filed newspapers meanwhile, at her own request, were allowed to be near her; her intention being to peruse the important paragraph.

cited, as indeed she felt it to be to her, and yet, hour after hour, being without the fortitude to consult it for herself. At length she mustered courage for the effort; but instead of her eye alighting upon a notice which was so arresting to the young lady, it fell first upon an adjoining announcement, which was of the nature of an advertisement, and which was couched in these terms,—

"Wanted, a young lady, who is not only competent, from her upbringing and habits, to form a suitable companion for two girls of rank, who are on the eve of sailing for Bengal, but who is such a proficient in the French and Italian languages,—especially the former,— that she can speak and write it with Parisian purity. At the same time, the applicant for this very desirable situation must be of English extraction, with the usual admirable characteristics of that nation. It is expected that the pair of pupils,—the one fifteen years of age, the other considerably younger,—will make progress in the two foreign languages named during their outward voyage. Their mother goes with them;" the place for the applicants to present themselves, and the limit of the time for so doing, being added.

"It is the very chance for me!" ejaculated Adelaide, after perusing the tempting advertisement with dilating vision. "I'll forthwith start for London, and yet not without the consent of the eccentric Samaritan; and now, too, I can peruse with some composure the announcement of Montague Mildmay's departure for Calcutta:" and having done so, without, however, the purpose of confiding her precise intentions to the recluse, or saying a single word concerning her Indian anticipations, she repaired to his presence, with the file of newspapers under her arm.

"Is it as my adopted that Adelaide comes to me now, or as one of a more adventurous and independent spirit?" eagerly inquired the benevolent cynic, on seeing the lovely damsel approach him with an air of unexpected composure; the old man manifesting a dignity and elegance of deportment, as well as employing a phraseology superior to what she had ever before listened to on his part; the severity with which he blamed himself on account of his conduct to Mildmay, and also the pensive gravity which characterized the manner of the young lady, serving to elevate his feelings and speech. "Ah! I think I see how it is, my good girl," continued he, extending his hand to her in a style of almost refined courtesy. "I have been looking anxiously forward to the time; and even the hour, which I knew to be near at hand, when I should learn your determination for the future. That hour, I perceive, has arrived. I shall meet it with firmness, not as the bear which I have, too often of late years, seemed; but as an old man, who, in spite of his age, is yet resolved to cultivate some measure of gentleness to his kind."

"Why speak you, sir, in such a self-accusing tone, with regard to your gentleness and courteous character?" cried Adelaide, seating herself beside the man whom many scowled at and regarded as the misanthrope of the Red Cot; "you, who, whatever your outward carriage at the first may seem to those who look no further than to smooth phrases and fashionable dress, are all true-heartedness and benevolence to the destitute and helpless."

"Ah! we shall both leave off the flattering strain, and proceed to more rational matters," Mr. Plumtree interjected. "Your mind is made up to leave me, Adelaide,—is it not?" he added.

"Yes, for the present, sir; but it may not be for all future time," responded the young lady.

"Ah! many years, at the most, cannot be meted out to me, darling," said Peter. "I am threescore and ten, and ye know who tells us about that limit, and, also, what he declares."

"Long beyond it may you live, Mr. Plumtree," subjoined the maiden, "were it but that you may minister good to the needy and the deserving, even with a more unsparing hand than you have ever perhaps yet done. I feel assured that it requires but the exercise of your clear intelligence, with that of your abounding humanity, to render you such a benefactor to your species as cannot readily be expected of any successor who may inherit of your wealth."

"What! would'st thou, girl, have me to squander away what property I may have," demanded the old gentleman, relapsing into something of his wonted bluntness of manner, "and have nothing left for thy benefit, should'st thou ever return to me? But why go at all? Speak plainly and explicitly; and if thy reasons seem to me sound, I will approve of thy conclusions, however much I may have to grieve at being forced to acquiesce in what will prove a great loss to me."

"No one on earth has such a just claim upon my candour," answered Adelaide, "as the good Samaritan who took me in when I was like to perish; feeding, clothing, and nurturing me, as the fondest parent only could have done. No one on earth shall ever receive from me a more willing and plain reply. You have heard, sir, something of him who gallantly came to my rescue at the Cauldron Cliff, when I was the victim of an unprincipled man's villany. Upon this, Sir Vaux Waldgrave, with his wonted peremptory and overbearing authority, commanded that my deliverer from the hideous danger should woo me for his bride,—should wed me, in fact, without wooing, or even of our knowing more of one another than an hour's intimacy or so had supplied; for that in such a case we should inherit all his vast wealth. 'No,' said Mildmay, 'I must have what I deem a sufficient probation of the character and temper of her who is to be my wife; just as I cannot suppose it possible that Adelaide would dispense with a similarly trustworthy basis to found her matrimonial hopes upon.' Such being the reported sentiments of the young gentleman, the admiration which I naturally felt on account of his gallantry in risking his life to save mine, grew into a more absorbing character, with a rapidity which seemed strange to myself; my inmost resolve being that, whatever should befall me, my chief effort in the cultivation of human friendship and love, should be, really by my own acts and conduct to merit such blessings. Alas! certain distracting disclosures, of which you have already obtained sufficient information, drove me to shifts, bordering on despair, that happily brought me within the scope of your sympathy and unsurpassed kindness,—a kindness and sympathy which you would crown by adopting me as your daughter, with other extraordinary advantages."

Adelaide here paused, in a measure exhausted by the physical effort of saying so much, but still more by her swelling feelings. Having gained breath, and a degree of composure, she again proceeded thus,—

"I have not much more to add," said she, "yet I must reverently beg,—implore of you, sir, that you judge of these concluding sentences with your wonted liberality.   Listen! Although, I feel that my heart responds to your marvellous kindness and proffered gifts in a way that is ineffable, yet I know there ought to be a higher mission and end for my study than how I may most surely obtain gold or great wealth.   This is but, comparatively, a sordid purpose and object,—one, I believe, which could never secure the countenance of Montague Mildmay,—nay, more, which could never earn for me a high degree of self-respect or of self-reliance.   No : I purpose, with your benign wishes, to go forth as a worker,—a serviceable woman,—a teacher of, to the extent of my abilities, and an example to, those younger than myself of my own sex, over whom I may obtain a superintendence.   In short, I have resolved on offering myself as a governess ; and as soon as I have gained the approbation of my conscience in respect of my endeavours in that exacting line, I will not despair of obtaining your's also, sir."

Adelaide was incapable of adding, on the instant, another word.   She threw herself upon the bosom of the uncouth old man, feeling that, with the exception of her nursing mother and Mildmay, there never had been a human being whose affection so warmly responded to hers as did that of the cynical Peter Plumtree.

"How frail a thing, and yet how heroic!" ejaculated the recluse.   "Oh, had she, whom she resembles, been but——Yet, hush! no more of that!——I have not strength at present to touch further on the story.   To-morrow morning we shall consider of the arrangements for your departure, which, compelled as I am, to yield to your reasons, Adelaide, I will not for an hour hinder.   Good night! Heaven bless you!" added the old man, as he retired to his sleeping apartment, speaking these words in the tone of a breaking heart,—distress and despair living in his face.

Adelaide retired to rest that evening,—having got over, more easily than she had anticipated, the explanatory scene with the eccentric Samaritan, —and, consequently, with invigorated spirits; her hopes for the future receiving an accession of warmth, and careering bravely.   She could not, to be sure, remain insensible to the sterling qualities of the singular old man whom she was about to leave.   She perceived how deep his feeling of desertion seemed to be, and also that she was the occa-

sion of memories which were profoundly embedded in his bosom being most touchingly awakened.   Still, it was with the enthusiasm natural to her age, and with the roseate colours with which the young picture coming events, that she looked forward to her new sphere of life ; at the same time with great confidence transporting herself at a bound to the far-off East, and lavishing upon her expected position there enjoyments in perspective, such as oriental descriptions had associated with her ideas.   Above all, the probability, as she reasoned, of being planted in a situation which might not be remote from that occupied by Mildmay,—or, at least, the great likelihood, as she presumed, of being so conditioned that her efforts and merits should not long remain a secret to him,—threw around the enterprise to which she had bent her mind, and the approaching remarkable change in her history, an enticing halo, and many gilded promises.

"None but myself can ever know," breathed the young lady, "how unfit my past course and acquired manners have rendered me for mingling with those to whom polish is unknown, and whose coarseness and monotony are most opposite to that life in which I have of late been luxuriating, as the expectant heiress of Sir Vaux Waldgrave.   However genuine and excellent may be Mr. Plumtree's attributes, my habits and associations require that I throw myself into circumstances similar to those familiar to me ;" and not doubting but that these circumstances would, to a great degree, be attractive,—affording her also an enviable opportunity for the exercise of her noble resolves and fervent aspirations,—sleep, at last, on that, to her, not uneventful night, sealed the maiden's eyelids in sweet slumber, during which she basked in realms of bliss and sunshine.

Not such were the same hours to the owner of the fantastic habitation under whose roof both dwelt,—the rich, but childless, old man, whose nature in many ways had become hardened and ungenial.   Bitterly did his thoughts, throughout the livelong night, revert to his trials, many of them long passed, and to his desolated condition; but chiefly did his unwitnessed wretchedness find scope in the direction of anxieties on account of Adelaide,—his knowledge of the world, and the reverses in the history of his affections, to which he had been exposed, giving a very different turn to his forecastings concerning her, than she, as yet, yielded to.

"The poor creature's destiny, after all," said he to himself, "is to eat the bread of dependence, in the most precarious and hazardous of all its shapes,—that of a governess:" the cynic's wide observation while in the West Indies, and a naturally sagacious mind, enabling him to take a far juster view of the subject than those who knew little of him, or only beheld him in his ordinary and forbidding aspects, could have imagined him capable of doing.   "With the education, feelings, and tastes of a gentlewoman," continued he, "she will find herself treated as if she had no such merits and advantages.   How can a mother know the difference between a good and bad

teacher of her daughters, if she has not been well taught herself? In many instances, this is not the case; all that is looked for or desired being mere showy accomplishments. Indeed, till mothers know that the very best part of what an accomplished, wise, and virtuous young gentlewoman can give her daughters, are the thoughts of her head, and the movements of her heart, neither will governesses be treated as they ought to be, nor be generally qualified for their situations. Truly, I pity the wilful yet sound-minded creature. She will now go forth forlorn, yet gifted with such beauty as has often proved most fatal."

Morning came, when the recluse and the resolute girl again met; she, greatly refreshed, as if she had been bathed in bliss, but he, weary and perplexed,—prepared fully, too, for their parting.

"There is no variation, I perceive, darling,"

No. 6.—THE GOVERNESS.

said he; "and therefore, the sooner we put a finish to our few necessary transactions, the better for both it will be. Here is gold, and take thy will of it, girl. When it runs short, come back to me, and thou shalt have more, if the grave has not my old bones in keeping by that time."

The negotiations of the morning, between Peter Plumtree and Adelaide, ended in her acceptance of fifty sovereigns, though much more was pressed for her taking, and again on her departure for the nearest stage where a direct conveyance towards the metropolis was to be found; the old man intimating to her, that he would much rather have a glimpse of her pretty face than of any letter she could write, for that, indeed, he was very little of a correspondent on paper.

"It will probably only be when I have cheerful tidings to convey to you, sir," replied the maiden, "that I shall have the courage to address to you a single line. I would not trouble you with much more, nor for a less purpose."

"How frail, yet how wilful! how gentle, yet how heroic!" was once more old Peter's ejaculation, as he turned away to avoid a longer lingering look after the lamb for whom the tempered winds of Heaven were so much needed.

CHAPTER IX.

THE WANTED GOVERNESS.

ADELAIDE'S journey from Yorkshire to London was performed with due expedition, as also the process of providing herself with a fitting dress to appear at the quarter mentioned in the advertisement, concerning which her views were so sanguine. It was to a fashionable district of the West End to which her steps were directed; her anxieties seeming to increase every pace she advanced, and a presentiment at length taking possession of her, that, after all, she might be rejected, from some impression being conveyed that she was not equal to, or well-suited for, the situation named. She had, however, attired herself, though in the plainest manner, yet with every regard to gentility; and as she viewed her person in the mirror, she might without arrogance have whispered to herself, that her beauty was of too decided a character to be dependent on adventitious aid; while, as to her air, it was too distinguished, even in humility, to escape attention. There was one preliminary, that has not yet been mentioned, which she had studied. She had resolved on changing her name; for to that of Waldgrave she held that she had no claim.

"Neville shall be the appellation I hereafter take, this being my loving nurse's name," she said to herself. "The change, besides, will serve to conceal me from the knowledge of all who have been in any way acquainted with me when I was envied as one supposed to be born to a splendid fortune; my only other addition to my account of myself being that, by a sad and most sudden reverse, I have been reduced from a state of great expectations to one of dependence upon my own exertions."

Thus armed, the maiden proceeded to the appointed mansion, in reply to the advertisement respecting the teaching of French and Italian to the two young ladies who were on the eve of sailing, with their mother, to India; when, to her grievous disappointment and dismay, she learned that the enviable situation had already been obtained by a somewhat earlier applicant. What added not slightly to the maiden's vexation, was not only the circumstance that the outward-bound ladies were members of one of the most respected families of England, but that their destination was Calcutta; the head of the house, in fact, forming one of the officers in the establishment of the new Governor-General of India, Lord Paget Rivers, and therefore, in a sense, a colleague with Montague Mildmay at the capital of the British Eastern Empire.

These discoveries being made all at once by the young creature, and almost immediately on her arrival in London, where she was wholly a stranger, were felt as hardly less intensely distressing than the extraordinary revelations which were consequent on the appearance at Wartham Hall of the ruffian Jobson. How she found her way back to the inn in the City to which she had been brought by the coach from Yorkshire, she could not distinctly tell. She took to her bed-room, almost invoking despair, for hours together, or at least yielding herself up to severest self-upbraidings, for having quitted old Peter Plumtree and the Red Cot. Yet, a day or two of rest and reflection brought the thoughtful and sound-hearted girl to a better state of mind; a conscious power of triumph gaining the ascendancy over the temporary prostration of her hopes.

"The recluse of the Red Cot shall not hear from me of my discomfiture and discomposure," the maiden said to herself; for the old man was the only soul whom at the period she could think of as a confidant. "He is not a letter-writer nor letter-reader, unless it be in the shape of any legible print, and in the columns of the 'Times' newspaper. No, I must lay myself abroad, and look out for some other situation than the one near the court where Mildmay will be so fully appreciated. What right had I, at a first bound, to expect rising beyond penury and drudgery? It was the rashness and inexperience of childhood for me to calculate, with anything like the assurance I did, concerning my acceptance by the titled lady who, with her daughters, is bound for India. The reproof conveyed by the disappointment must be remembered, and ought to do me good. I'll be wiser hereafter."

Having come to reason thus with herself, Adelaide felt her mental vigour renovated, and began to make the discovery, practically, that, in the school of adversity, there might be more useful and fruitful teaching than when all was seeming bright and flourishing as a summer pageant, or when the young fancy themselves bathed in bliss. She went to work; had recourse to every accessible advertising medium; and on the very first occasion of her consulting the columns of the "Morning Post," read a paragraph, at the commencement of which her eyes glistened with delight, and her fair countenance became radiant with pleasure. Yet, as she read sentence after sentence, hope more than half died within her.

"Wanted, a governess,"—thus commenced the article. "The advertising party here is of the very highest respectability, having a town residence in a courtly suburb, being within a few minutes' walk of Kensington Gardens."

"A charming locality," thought our eager reader, whose information, from books, was extensive concerning the British metropolis, even before she had ever set foot upon English ground.

"Any young lady possessing a thorough English education——"

"A thorough English education!" ejaculated Miss Neville, observing, in the next place, that it was the attainment of comparatively few to possess a thorough knowledge and use of any one language.

"Any young lady possessing a thorough English education, a competent acquaintance with the theory of instrumental music, and, above all, in this department, who is mistress of the art and science of singing, may entertain hopes of finding her services acceptable in the most desirable of situations; supposing, at the same time, that she both writes and speaks the French, Italian, and German tongues, with accuracy and elegant fluency."

"Then I have not the slightest chance in the courtly suburb of Kensington," thought poor Adelaide, "if all this be exacted; neither any young person throughout England, unless there be some Admirable Crichton among the living daughters of Eve, in Britain's isle. But what more?"

"As there is a fine, spirited, and inquisitive boy in the family, the governess must have considerable familiarity with both Latin and Greek grammar."

"Oh! the young governess," thought Adelaide, "must have graduated at Oxford or Cambridge, a thing which I have not done. Really, I am amazed, but not unlikely to be more so, from the length of what is still unread."

"The principles, as well as practice, of drawing must be clearly understood and illustrated by the applicant. She must be a most accomplished teacher of dancing; while an indispensable addition to the whole is a capability of fitting the young folks put under her charge to keep up with every new thing that occurs in the circle of the sciences. Last of all, as to her requisites, the applicant's character must bear the strictest investigation."

"Heigho!" ejaculated the reader of the verbose advertisement, nearly out of breath, and no longer having either eye glistening with delight, or a radiant countenance. She, however, again directed her attention to the paper, and found the following noticeable statement in a postscript:—

"As the lady will be treated as one of the family, a high salary is not to be looked for."

"As one of the family!" muttered Adelaide. "Perhaps the writer regards the scullion's assistant as one of her family, which indeed, in a Christian sense, the humble handmaiden assuredly is. At any rate, I doubt not that the governess in such a house, though in a courtly suburb, will be treated as some nondescript person, holding an ill-defined or intermediate position; as a creature too high for the kitchen, but too low for the drawing room, and perhaps, even for the breakfast-parlour. Out upon them! And yet I have a mind to present myself at the mansion named, instead of writing, were it merely to have an opportunity to look upon the advertising party, especially as 'post paid' must be the written applications."

Miss Neville not unnaturally considered her circumstances at the period when she perused the advertisement about the *wanted governess* to be such as to warrant her not only to exercise for herself a course of selection, and of allowing of some time in order to make her choice in regard to the dependent situation, but of studying the various characters to whom she might have the opportunity of presenting herself. The light thence derived, she thought, might be found serviceable to her, before she wholly committed herself in any engagement of considerable permanency; the care with which she applied the money so generously gifted or lent to her by the recluse of the Red Cot, affording the prospect of a measured independence for a good many weeks from the day of her arrival from Yorkshire in the capital of the kingdom.

It was, to say the truth, with something of a keenly critical, if not satirical, intent that she resolved on wending her way to the courtly suburb of which mention had been so pointedly made; arraying herself with considerably greater attention to display than when she proceeded to the other residence, and where her disappointment about the situation in India, and during the outward-bound voyage thither, had been deep and intense. Somehow, the young lady concluded that the advertising party of "very highest respectability" was extremely ignorant and decidedly vulgar; being at the same time, she considered, proud, though probably wallowing in plenty. Even the very name that was announced to the maiden by the porter at the porch of the large and dashing mansion repaired to, as that of owner and controller of the establishment, sounded prophetically in Miss Neville's ear and to her imagination, Mrs. Puffendorff, as she thought, having an ominous sense.

This advertising lady was a widow, the relict of a Dutchman who had amassed a vast fortune in the City of London, in the course of a life of success in trade. He may be said to have grown from small beginnings to be one of the merchant-princes of the British metropolis; one whose probity was unquestioned, and whose passion was business, with an inordinate desire to amass wealth. That his intellectual acquirements were high will not be concluded from what has been stated concerning the man; neither that his tastes were refined, as the act of making in his advanced age a young, coarse woman, who was in his service, his spouse, illustrates; whom about five years afterwards he left in widowhood with three children—two girls and a boy.

The opulent man of trade having died, it was found that he had bequeathed to his relict the means to cut a great figure in the world, or, in other words, to be eminently vulgar; a vulgarity not only of person,—though in that she was, at the period our story finds her, remarkable,—but vulgarity of mind. She thought most extravagantly high of herself, of her children, and of her thousands a year. Her mansion in the courtly suburb had been the object of gaudy adornment to the amount of a fortune, together with her gardens, her hot-houses, pineries, conservatories, &c.; in short, in whatever way the very many good things which money can procure, was it lavished. And yet she thought still more highly of titles and ancient pedigrees, of knighthood and nobility, than of aught she was mistress of; so that the servile court which she paid to the great by descent was the most nauseating of her propensities and practices, always excepting the scorn and the grinding tyranny with which she loved to bear herself to all who were under her and subject to her control. To all who refused to besmear her with loathsome flattery, or to lose their dignity and self-respect, by humbling themselves meanly to the caprices of this unwieldy lump of bone, muscle, and fat, she was a sort of she-dragon.

"Here is another young lady, ma'am," said a lackey, bedizened with gold-lace, addressing the *vrouw*, Mrs. Puffendorff, whose page the lad was, as that big personage was endeavouring to maintain her part in a conversation concerning the requisites and characters of governesses, with a pair of visitors of her own sex. "She's after your situation, ma'am, as I have learnt from her own lips."

"If she be lady-like, Jem, show her into the breakfast-parlour; but if of a so-and-so appearance, let her remain in the hall," returned Mrs. Puffendorff. "I'll ring for you when it suits me to speak to the young woman."

"Oh! very lady-like, indeed," observed Jem; the reply to this being in effect that he knew in that case what was to be done.

Now, no sooner had the footman withdrawn, than the discussion by the trio of ladies,—all of them mothers, and the pair of visitors titled ones to boot,—became more animated and characteristic than previously; the announced circumstances of being *young* and *very lady-like*, stirring the talkers to say their very best for the time.

"*Very lady-like!* I like not that," said Lady Gorewell, playing upon the recommendatory term. "Fine feathers make fine birds; or if all the pretensions be not in the attire, ten to one but it depends upon the mere fact of the girl being some clergyman's or officer's daughter, —some of your decayed gentlewomen,—than whom nothing is so intolerable, if in the shape of a governess. Why, such a one is only a school-room princess, who will do nothing she is desired to do. If indeed such creatures do obey you and prove serviceable, they are so high-toned in their manners, and so careful never to give you a contradictory word, as to render them doubly disagreeable; for, from their very silence and affected courtesy, they prevent you from being quite at ease with them in your own house. No, I will never again have either a lady-like governess for my charming daughters, nor one that is both young and pretty. Sir William Gorewell is a gentleman of character, and a good partner besides. But husbands are but husbands, after all; and you know the world is very depraved; so much so, in fact, that I would repudiate and dismiss any female teacher of my children, who plays, sings, or dances, in finer style than one's self. You cannot think what a painful difference arose between me and Sir William through the last accomplished *slut* I had for the management of my school-room. Since that distressing occurrence my spouse has never been as he was prior to it to me; so that I now employ a tidy-kind of woman, who not only has her home exterior to my house, but gives me her services during most of the day for a small monthly allowance, and does other work besides than benefit her interesting pupils. In a word, she is a most obliging person; for she arranges my hair for me every day, nor ever grumbles at any drudgery. Mrs. Puffendorff,

my dear lady, you should have looked out for just such a woman as I have got. I might have assisted you in your choice."

"Mrs. Puffendorff, ought not, according to my judgment, to have looked out for any such woman as you employ, Lady Gorewell," lisped the other visitor, Lady Lymington. "I never would have any governess I may engage for instructing and proving an example to my girls to officiate as my maid, much less as a drudge in my household-work. I would rather have a lady in my school-room, from whom my children may learn to be lady-like, and, I hope, some day, well educated and polished. Besides, I like nice-looking people, and will make no exception even as regards the teacher of my daughters. It never enters my head to be jealous of Sir Matthew Lymington, I assure you, ladies."

"Jealous! I named not the word," exclaimed Lady Gorewell, fired at the stroke which the other had lent her. "And yet, had I made use of the expression, it would have become me better, than had it been let fall from the lips of any female whose husband may happen to be twice her own age, seeing that my dear spouse, Sir William, is nearly as juvenile as myself."

Mrs. Puffendorff, who was always most forward to do the amiable in behalf of people of station, and was also aware how opposite the tastes and tempers of her two visitors were, on finding that the pair were rushing into a conflict of personalities, bounded from her chair, to intercede with both the titled ones, that they would not disagree upon such a trifling subject to people of their position as that of the age, the looks, or the qualifications of creatures who were only governesses. She deprecated the idea of their lowering themselves by talking longer for the present on the matter; alleging besides, that her own circumstances were so unlike those of persons who were clothed with husbands, as to excuse her from taking into consideration the arguments of either of her dear and highly admired friends.

"I will have an eye both to looks and to labour," cried the mistress of the gaudy establishment, as, with portly presence, rustling silks, and consequential vulgarity, she moved from the one to the other of her visitors; "and should the female that receives my money for teaching my children be really as proud, or affect to be, as if she were a real lady, call me fool if I do not find a way to bring her down a peg. In the meantime, I am extremely obliged to both of you, dear ladies, for the views you have now and at other times laid before me about the creatures that are to furnish my young ones with sufficient knowledge and accomplishments, and also to be proper examples. What say you, then, to my ordering my page to bring up the *very lady-like person* below, that we may judge of her for ourselves, and likewise that I may have the benefit of your further advice."

It was not an ill-timed suggestion on the part of the Dutch merchant's widow; for it not merely allayed the gathering storm which she dreaded, but introduced some more pleasant object for the treatment of our pen than any that could have been supplied by the trio of mothers who were to sit in judgment on the merits of poor Miss Neville. And yet, ere bringing the maiden to the gorgeous drawing-room, it seems needful to afford the reader a little more insight than has yet been lent as respects the characters of the said trio.

With regard to the mistress of the house,—the portly Widow Puffendorff,—we have already given certain intimations which cannot have served to exalt her in the reader's mind. She was, as stated, wallowing in wealth and material delight. She had everything which money could procure, and yet she was far from happy. No sooner was one whim gratified, than another was entertained, and had to be sated; and to be told that any one had things more splendid or more highly-priced than she, threw the woman into a fit of discontent and a rage for rivalry. She purchased articles, not because she needed them, but because others were in possession of the like; and numerous were the things she bought, of the use of which she was either altogether ignorant, or of the qualities of which she could be no judge. Her passion for rivalry, and her ambition to outshine all to whom she had access, were constantly sources of painful anxiety and effort to her. Then she had never-ceasing minor annoyances to bear up against.

Not seldom, to give an example, was there turbulence in her spacious, garnished, and crowded mansion,—crowded even by needless domestics,—for Mrs. Puffendorff was utterly incapable of superintending such an establishment as she vaunted of, and in her folly had brought together. Familiarly sitting and gossiping with the obsequious and cringing members of her household one hour, and the next coarsely lecturing and scolding others of them with most insufferable disdain, were usual alternations with her. She was perpetually dismissing domestics for not manifesting towards her proper respect; an omission which it never enters the head of a lady to conceive possible. It was a matter of course, that as soon as the nature of the household became known, respectable servants seldom were betrayed into it; and consequently also all sorts of frauds and peculations came to be committed by such as were hired, which, when discovered, raised the wrath of the *vrouw* to the highest pitch. The result also followed that she was kept in a state of continual suspicion, which alone would have been a vile torment. Inconsistent as it may at first seem, yet not a very unnatural effect of her jealousies and suspicions with regard to the extent and manner she got plundered by some of her people, was her meanness in the way of wages and allowances, even although all the savings in these directions for a twelvemonth might not amount to a tithe of what she expended upon some ridiculous frivolity, month after month.

Had Adelaide been aware that the person who last filled the situation of governess in the family of Mrs. Puffendorff,—last prior to her procedure to the courtly suburb, as already stated,—had she known that the said young lady,—a pretty, interesting-looking girl,—was made to sit at the table with the puffed-up mistress of the establishment, and be the only individual of the party to whom none was introduced,—though the whole most probably were in every sense inferior to her,—had she been aware that the only notice taken of the maiden would be, "Help Emily to the breast of the fowl;" "See that Eliza eats more like a lady;" or "You do not, governess, attend to Charles,"—she herself, in the midst of the ravages committed on flesh and fowl having to rise from her comfortless dinner hungry;—had she been forewarned of all this, surely she would not even have put herself to the trouble of wending her way to the vicinity of Kensington Gardens on the day in question, either in search of a situation of the advertised kind, or to exercise her critical and satirical acumen.

Lady Gorewell differed very widely from Mrs. Puffendorff in history, attainments, and character; for she could boast of gentle blood being in her veins, drawn, she boasted, from the old Norman source. But then she had no fortune, nor even any beauty of person; her only recommendation for a wedded partner being the political interest which her family possessed, and which had not only procured a government situation for him who was mean enough to marry her on account of the advancement in office which an alliance with her would command; but who, to the astonishment of the Dutchman's widow, was dubbed a knight, rendering his spouse a veritable lady by title, independently of her descent. Still, the Gorewells were poor, not merely because the husband's salary was not extravagantly large, but on account of his improvident and gay habits. He cared not much for his wife or for his home. The consequence was that the lady, who was one of your extremely clever women, and a wondrous manager,—a person of great intellectual pretension, and assuredly pre-eminent in respect of self-esteem and effrontery,—lost no opportunity to ingratiate herself with such ignorant and vulgar neighbours, as were able and willing to repay her condescension in associating with them, and her services in the way of counsel, by splendid entertainments, handsome loans, and generous gifts.

It remains, for the present chapter, to say a very few words in relation to Widow Puffendorff's other visitor, Lady Lymington. This fair one, although the mother of several children, was still very beautiful in person; while as to her nature, she was, upon the whole, good-tempered and kind-hearted; excepting, perhaps, when she had an opportunity of contradicting and teazing Lady Gorewell, whom she cordially hated, and whom, from both having their residences at Kensington, at times she would meet in company, Like her antagonist, though also of good family, she was, in her own right, penniless; and having been not only indolent, but without any high moral principle,—being even but poorly educated in all that was not merely superficial and showy,—she had made little scruple in wedding a fox-hunting baronet, who was double her years, even at the date to which our story has been brought, and who, but for the amount of these years and their concomitant evils, would still have lived, for six months in the year, in a red coat, kept his wife awake by the noise which seems to constitute the chief pleasure of a follower of wide-mouthed hounds, and retarded dinner every day.

At length, in order to benefit by metropolitan medical aid, he took up his residence in the courtly suburb where the Dutchman's opulent widow so conspicuously figured in her peculiar way. To become bedridden soon after retiring to Kensington, was a natural consequence of a dissipated lifetime, during which, besides, he had squandered away the best portion of his inheritance. Accordingly, being far from rich, and poorer in respect of character than of purse, what better had his indolent, ill-informed, and unreflecting lady,—one of those characters, in whom it is difficult to say whether the good or the bad predominates, the former having been least cultivated,—what better had such a spouse to do than frequently seek the society of the vulgar, but wealthy and lavishing Mrs. Puffendorff, although in her soul the old baronet's beautiful partner despised the *vrouw* as cordially as she hated the *managing* Lady Gorewell.

CHAPTER X.

THE LAW OF NECESSITY.

MISS NEVILLE, having been required to appear before the trio of mothers, followed the glittering page to the gorgeous drawing-room where they were seated in conclave, and where each of them expected that some young creature would enter who should be overwhelmed at the sight of the grandeur which her eyes were to encounter, and the august presences before her. The maiden entered the gaudily-splendid apartment, but without evincing the slightest surprise at what she beheld, or seeming to quail before the assembled three; even although a pair of them were titled dames, and the third a portly personage, who could command, at any time, thousands, and who was almost smothered in silks. On the contrary, instead of shrinking or being overpowered, she stepped forward with that air of self-possession and conscious grace, which told to the better-born ones of the trio that she was no stranger to courteous life, and to the Dutchman's widow that she had not either a mere milkmaid to deal with, nor an imitative pretender to polish into politeness. Lady Lymington, especially, started from a reclining posture, which the languishing beauty was accustomed to adopt, and had carefully studied; for, sufficiently sensible of her own charms as she, of course, was, and disbelieving that she was, on that occasion, at least, to contemplate features and a figure with which her own could never have been compared, it made her gasp and shake to behold so much radiance of loveliness, with such intimations of mental superiority and pensive gravity of deportment, as the candidate-governess displayed and manifested. As for Mrs. Puffendorff, she looked to her associates, —first the one, and then the other,—to help her out of the confusion into which she was thrown, not only by the looks and bearing of the young lady, but the unmistakable surprise of the titled pair.

"Be seated," said Lady Gorewell, directing, by a pointed finger, the maiden to a chair near to the door at which she had entered. "We, fortunately for you, are ready to be occupied concerning certain of the terms of the advertisement which appeared in the 'Morning Post' in relation to a governess for the charming children of my especial friend here, Mrs. Puffendorff,—which public paragraph, I presume, you are responding to, by coming to Puffendorff House, as this princely mansion is designated."

"I come as an applicant for the situation of governess, which I understood to be open, at least no further back than yesterday morning, at this residence," answered the damsel, in a richly musical voice,—feeling that the appeal made to her was conveyed with the expectation that she would offer a reply. "And yet, if I am to understand you precisely, there must be some mistake; for, instead of reading a single paragraph, the advertisement was broken into several,—occupying a considerable portion of a column of the newspaper; while, as respects the many matters mentioned in the article, these were numerous, and large enough to occupy a much larger space. Oh, there must be some mistake; and, if it be on my side, I ought to solicit your pardon for giving you the trouble I have done;" the young lady rising from her seat as she pronounced the last words, not unpleased at the opportunity which had been afforded her of having a fling at the trio, as Mrs. Puffendorff afterwards characterized her retort.

"There is no mistake on either side," coldly, and with a toss of the head, observed the individual who had taken the initiative in the conversation; "for I, Lady Gorewell, myself drew up the advertisement, and it was perused, and also approved of, by my distinguished friend, Lady Lymington, whom you see before you, as well as by the excellent personage still nearer me, who has the deepest interest in the appointment,—she being the parent of the proposed pupils."

"Then I am lucky in having come hither when you all three happen to be together," calmly returned the beautiful girl, although there was a leer in her mind at the moment; "presuming that you are wishful to put me upon my trials at once, and perhaps upon points in the order followed in the advertisement. Most probably, the excellent lady who has the deepest interest in the appointment of a governess of her beloved children, is anxious to commence the examination. If I remember aright, proficiency in our own proper language was the thing first insisted on."

While Lady Gorewell bit her lip, and the other titled dame seemed tickled and amused, the Dutchman's widow not only looked utterly blank, but felt obliged again to throw herself upon the good offices of her visitors.

"No, girl, we shall not exact any further display with respect to our mother tongue," cried Lady Gorewell, evidently nettled. "We have had ample specimen of your glibness in that department," continued the wonderful *manager*, not merely of her own affairs, but the affairs of all others who had the mind and the means to recompense her temptingly for her trouble; she flattering herself at the moment that she had made a palpable hit, and looking round with an air of triumph. "No, candidate-governess, we do not further insist on a display of your skill in our vernacular, in respect of which every boy and girl who have had any schooling at all is sufficiently educated, and equally, I daresay, with yourself. Let us rather hear something from you about your knowledge of the French and Italian tongues, to go no further for a few minutes."

"Why, as to both, I am as fluent in speech as were they my own mother tongues, having spent several years in Paris, and been familiar with some of the best teachers of Italian in that city," responded the young lady. "I should like you to put me to the test; or, if you be not conversant, say with the French language, the medium of intercourse and high-bred politeness throughout Europe, perhaps you would be pleased to hear me read or recite, —I care not which,—one or two passages from some of the most celebrated authors of that country, and next to listen to my English version of the same. I think I could render the opportunity both entertaining and instructive to you. What say you to a snatch from Montesquieu, Rousseau, Racine, and also Rabelais,— the last being a most amazing classic. Or should you choose to have me tested in the Italian, I will do my best in singing a stave of one of Rossini's pieces, and next read or recite to you, as easily as I can do Pope or Milton, specimens from Tasso, Petrarch, Dante, and so forth;" all this being said with consummate self-command, and a gravity which even staggered as well as out-witted the maiden's preposterous examiner.

"It will have to be at some other time, young woman, that we shall have to witness the *exhibitions* which you offer to make," replied Lady Gorewell, still resolute on subduing the young lady, and having a triumph; but who knew as little nearly of the French tongue and of the Italian as did the Dutchman's marvellously wealthy widow. However, she fancied that she knew something about flowers and certain of the technical terms in the botanical branch of natural history; and therefore she expressed a wish to hear what the maiden could say for herself relative to the "circle," spoken of in the advertisement.

"If I am at once to go to botany," returned Miss Neville, "it will be requisite for you, Lady Gorewell, to say whether I am to abide by the natural or the artificial system. The Linnæan, you must know, is nearly exploded."

The preposterous *manager* looked more surprised and blank than ever; a confusion which Adelaide affected not to observe; for she proceeded, after a slight pause, as follows:—

"Perhaps you would be gratified were I to *exhibit* myself in the exact sciences," softly said she, placing an emphasis on a word to which Lady Gorewell had given a sarcastic pith; "and, as all moderately educated people are fully aware of the mathematics being the instrument, so to speak, by which these sciences are manipulated, I'll give you a proof, if you choose, that I have got over the *Pons Assinorum*."

"What outlandish and break-neck words the young woman speaks," exclaimed Mrs. Puffendorff; "she'd wholly *bamboozle* my charming children. What do you mean, girl, by these queer sounds?" added the *vrouw*, thinking that it was time for her to show off.

"Yes, make yourself intelligible, Miss," chimed in the Lady Gorewell. "What tongue are you making use of in your heathenish jargon now? I long to be instructed, Miss;" the woman of title being really as far at sea about the matter, as ever the vulgar and illiterate mistress of the gaudy mansion was in all her life.

"You spake not far wide of the truth, Lady Gorewell," quietly remarked the maiden, "when you used the term *heathenish*, although not so judiciously in the application of *jargon;* for the words are pure Latin, which was the language of the Roman Empire, and which has ever since the fall of that gigantic power been the common tongue of the scientific world."

"You are trifling with us, Miss," cried the *managing* lady with a superlative air of haughtiness. "Translate to us the terms of science you so pedantically, as it appears to me, have employed."

"Why, *Pons Assinorum*," answered the maiden meekly again,—without appearing to be conscious of having an opportunity to make her response tell,—"literally means the *Asses' Bridge;*" a reply which smote the *managing* lady, as also the Dutchman's relict, as pithily as a pistol-shot would have done; putting a sudden stop to the examination of the candidate, —the issue being accelerated by the loud and prolonged laughter of Lady Lymington, whom nothing could more entertain than to see the individual of her sex whom she most hated, and the *vrouw* whom she most despised, writhing under the quiet chastisement dealt by an exquisitely interesting young person, who appeared unconscious of the skill with which she could wield the lash.

"Let us have a visit from you to-morrow," hurriedly said the abashed Lady Gorewell. "I understand that Mrs. Puffendorff will then be in a condition to offer you terms; which, of course, as you are to be treated just as one of the family, will not be exorbitant, especially as the daughters are little more than children, and the son is still younger. He, in fact, little more than knows the alphabet, and the others are not greatly in advance of him."

"And we have been talking all the while concerning branches which are topics only for the really erudite, and the professors of science at our colleges and universities!" exclaimed Miss Neville, whose name not one of the astonished trio had possessed the presence of mind to inquire after,—the maiden affecting marvel and surprise. "Surely there has been an extraordinary want of common sense in some quarter, when we have been made to waste so much of precious time in treading, if not beyond the depth of yourselves, ladies, at least beyond that into which I ever expected to be led, or pushed, when children who have hardly mastered the letters of a horn-book are the intended pupils. In such a case, and for such an end, I should have composed a simpler advertisement."

Adelaide took her departure with the same grace and dignity that she manifested on presenting herself before the three, astonished at herself for having dealt so unceremoniously with such stately ladies, and also with the resolution never again to practise a course which would thereby become habitual to her, and which she felt was unworthy of the ingenuousness for which she not seldom got credit. Before she retired to rest for another night, she had reason still more deeply to repent having exhibited before people, especially when it was to have the laugh at them, who, she was conscious, were, in every way that was worthy, her inferiors.

She hurried from the neighbourhood of Puffendorff House,—she struck into Kensington Gardens, and soon had her thoughts diverted by the summer beauties of that courtly scene; among which might chiefly be observed the swarms of children and young people, many of them evidently under the care of governesses. The show captivated Adelaide; she fancied that it was the neighbourhood in which she would be most happy, so that she in a measure forgot the disgust, and the temptations to play a satirical part, she had experienced at Puffendorff House. What a display of broad, undulating leghorns! Such flowered flounces! Such sandals! How gleeful the swarm! And, having a natural yearning to form some intimacies, she thought that better opportunities could not occur, for a person in her isolated position, for increasing at any time her circle of acquaintance, than were offered in the immediate vicinity of the courtly suburb of Kensington. Then there was Hyde Park, hard by, with its endless display of equipages, and its other attractions, of which she had heard and read so much. In short, Miss Neville's spirits were exhilarated; she felt herself already as forming one of the numerous young ladies who accompanied juveniles of her sex, and who were on every side of her.

The day was sultry, and why not throw herself upon one of the many benches that were planted beneath the umbrageous growths, to scan at leisure and perfect ease the beautiful and the living scene? No ceremony was required; so that wherever there was seat-room she might plant herself upon the backed bench, —no matter though among the ever-shifting occupants there might happen to be of the first of the land. She was pleased; she was happier than for many days,—even from the period of the Cauldron Cliff affair,—she had been. She chatted with the young people who sat nearest to her, although it might be only for a few moments. With the tact of French ease, she engaged the attention of some of the superintendent ladies, amongst whom she met with two or three mothers who really charmed her. Nay, there were not a few of the sturdier sex in the vast crowds,—tutors as well as fathers,— ay, and dashing gentlemen, — whom it was pleasing to observe. More than once a youth of fashion, apparently, would cast a glance towards her, and then for a few seconds be her next neighbour on the handsome bench, whose respectful address was not the slightest of the agreeable things which occurred to Adelaide in Kensington Gardens on that charming summer's day, in spite of all the paltry hauteur and positive vulgarity she had encountered at Puffendorff House.

The stranger-maiden at length arose from her delightfully shaded seat to pursue her way towards her temporary abode in the City, feeling herself hardly a novice any longer in the courtly suburb where she had spent the last hours. She was nimble of foot, and an expert pedestrian. She had reached Apsley House, and had just struck into Piccadilly, when she was put in mind of not having tasted food since the breakfast-meal. A confectioner's shop, she had observed on going westward, was at no great distance. She bent her steps smartly thither, calling for a jelly and cake. But why the start and unmistakable dismay of the young lady, as she puts her hand to the quarter in her handsome dress where she had stowed her money? Ah! poor Adelaide, ye have much to learn,—ye know not, ye suspect not, half the villanies of the bustling world; otherwise the bulk of your money, which you had converted into a Bank of England note, would never have been placed about your person when you went abroad on the day in question. Alas! the precious piece of paper was clean gone, and with the exception of some five or six sovereigns which she had in her little box at the inn, she was penniless.

What now of the young lady's gratulations in the gardens? How measured she, upon the distressing discovery, her bearings and exhibitings at Puffendorff House? Where was her disgust on account of the nauseating hauteur and palpable vulgarity which she had witnessed within the mansion of the Dutchman's widow? The maiden was receiving another severe lesson; and well will it be for her if she can view it not only as a piece of important teaching, for rendering her more humble than her display before the trio of ladies indicated, but for causing her to fall back more entirely, when in difficulties, than she had ever yet done, upon her virtuous resolves, with a practical energy, and to regard a heartfelt sense of cherishing an earnest desire to perform her duty, wherever that might be, with singleness of purpose and also without repining. Happily, poor Adelaide was gradually, through every new trial, growing both wiser and more conscious of power, if put forth honestly and in a right direction; and, striving to school herself to sustain the great loss she had suffered with some degree of equanimity, she prepared next day to return to Puffendorff House; a necessity, and indeed, a step, she little contemplated on leaving the porch of the gorgeous residence.

Meanwhile the candidate-governess had been the theme of speculation on the part of the astonished trio; Lady Gorewell, in perfect accordance with her habits and natural character, disparaging the young creature with all uncharitableness, and returning to her great preference of some poor, unmannerly drudge, to persons of genteel upbringing and self-appreciation, as the most useful for such purposes as the Dutchman's relict contemplated in advertising for a help to her children and in her household.

"My woman and daily-comer, Martyn, may not be all that I could wish," observed she "Her manners and breeding are a little defective, owing to the fact of her having been much

in a tallow-chandler's shop, somewhere not far off; her father's business being in that line. She could not fulfil all that is mentioned as being expected of the applicants for Mrs. Puffendorff's situation. But then she has the most serviceable ways with her in other respects, as I mentioned before. She does not trouble me with requiring a bed-room, as she sleeps at home. She has no followers of any sort,—a matter of moment, I assure you; and indeed I should like to know what business a mere governess can have for friends or followers,— she, the most of whose life should be spent in the school-room, and whose pleasure should consist in serving and obeying implicitly the party who pays her the salary agreed on at the starting. Martyn is quite satisfied with two guineas per month, and I would not give a shilling more for the pedantic minx who figured in such an exhibiting fashion before

No. 7.—THE GOVERNESS.

us a little while ago. True, she is somewhat prettier than my help; and were it not that she is but a governess, she could not be looked at without being admired. But then, considering her position and calling, her beauty would be the very gravest objection to her, in my mind, especially when united to pertness and pretension. Had you a husband, or a grown-up son, my dear Mrs. Puffendorff, I would most strenuously and decidedly object to her being taken into your splendid establishment upon any terms."

"Children so easily imbibe vulgar habits," breathed the languishing Lady Lymington, "that I would rather see my daughters in their winding-sheets than have them subjected to the manners and example of your tallow-chandler-bred women. As for the young person we are talking of, I hold that she is not only very beautiful, but highly accomplished.

Nor was it so much for her actual loveliness that I admired her, as the sweet gentleness of her countenance,—the purity of her complexion,—the open, truthful out-looking of her fine eyes,—and the easy gracefulness of her movements. She would be my immediate choice, were I in Mrs. Puffendorff's position, on account of those features, quite independently of the fact of her vastly transcending my gifted and accomplished friend, Lady Gorewell, as much in the solid as in the ornamental."

Such was the advocacy of the beautiful spouse of the old fox-hunting and bedridden baronet, in favour of Adelaide Neville; an advocacy by one in whom the seeds of such goodness as might have fructified, even in a sterile soil of mind, were sown, had it not been suffered to remain uncultivated, whilst prejudice and pride, indolence of habit, and ignorance of mankind, found a ready nurture. As for the Dutchman's relict, her inclinations usually fell in more with the views of the poorly-provided mind of the languishing beauty, rather than of the less gainly and more peremptory Lady Gorewell, who, however, was not to be driven from her position, either by taunts or truthful representations. She accordingly returned to her doctrine in favour of the serviceable, however unmannerly or poorly accomplished, in preference to the high-toned pretenders to gentility, and lady-like people : and, knowing how niggardly the Dutchman's relict was in the treatment of her subordinates, the talker assailed in that direction.

"And what may you contemplate as a remuneration for the services of such a governess to your children, as the girl that figured so pedantically before us a little while ago?" inquired Lady Gorewell, with her wonted toss of the head. "Remember she will be at best but a domestic, whose ministry you pay for, and that it will be absolutely necessary to keep such a pert pretender humble and within bounds. Besides, you ought to set an example, my dear Mrs. Puffendorff; for, with your wealth and name, you have great power within your reach. It concerns people of station that the teaching-girls or women whom we admit under our roofs, should not be encouraged in any way to usurp the sway of those who support them, or to supplant their superiors."

"You have told us, Lady Gorewell, that two guineas a month would satisfy Martyn, your help," observed the upstart mistress of Puffendorff House, 'and this without her asking to have a bed in your residence."

"Yes, and without washing," impatiently interjected the economizing lady.

"Well, then, in these circumstances, I will act liberally," continued the *vrouw*, "if I say twenty-five guineas a-year for the young woman, which is almost as much as I afford to one of my footmen."

"And this to a young lady of manifestly superior breeding and parts !" cried Lady Lymington. "One to whom not one of us can hold a candle for five minutes together! Really, I should be ashamed to make the offer, although I set no great value upon severe studies, or your learned women as such, were it for no-

thing else than that my children should not, after they have grown up, be informed that the persons to whom they owed most for polishing them, received smaller remuneration than a bedizened lacquey, or a low-bred fellow who groomed my husband's horse."

"It is all very fair to talk largely amongst ourselves," said Lady Gorewell; "but neither you nor I, Lymington, will like to have our helps made discontented by learning that the schoolmistress of Puffendorff House receives higher wages than we can afford. This is the practical and material point, say what you will; and I press it home upon the consideration of our excellent and distinguished friend, as being worthy of her notice, both as one of our most influential neighbours, and one whose modes of distributing her wealth should become a guide to others."

"You know, Gorewell, that my girls have no governess for the present, and perhaps may not again be benefited by one," replied Lady Lymington. "At any rate, I will for ever dispense with such a teacher and guide for them, unless I can secure the services of some person whose parts and acquirements I estimate at a higher figure than those of a groom or a footman, or even the drudge daughter of a tallow-chandler."

"I'll say thirty pounds a-year, and not a farthing more," interjected the *vrouw*, "and, if the young woman will accept of my terms, I'll make trial of her; taking precious good care to keep her in her due place."

"That is, to be treated as one of the family !" observed Lady Lymington. "Upon my word, if the candidate accepts of your offer, you not only get, at a marvellous cheap rate, a creature of unsurpassed beauty into your house, Mrs. Puffendorff, but of rare manners and accomplishments; and therefore I think you are again one of the luckiest ladies in the world, if you can only feel so, and be content."

CHAPTER XI.

THE HIGHEST OF WOMAN'S VOCATIONS.

ALTHOUGH Miss Neville, from circumstances mentioned early in our story of her, had grown up to girlhood and the state of a young woman, with a pensive turn, and noiseless, if not positively grave, habits, she was yet not without a capacity for humour and a perception of the ridiculous; which, when combined with the advantages of quick parts improved by a good education,—so far as knowledge and accomplishments went, and also with gentleness of manners and great self-command,—rendered her more than a match for such clever people as Lady Gorewell. The young lady's superiority, however, had hitherto belonged more to theory and system than practice and actual experience. But now the heart had begun to receive lessons, and reality to become more lastingly impressive than the lessons of books, or the teachings of any instructor under whom she had ever studied and been trained. It is pleasant to record that she was growing wiser and more self-acquainted, rather than more knowing in the technical sense of the word; even that which she had done, and that which had occurred to her, on the day when she first repaired to Puffendorff House, having served to discipline the damsel in a permanent manner.

We have seen how she chided herself, immediately after figuring before the trio of ladies, on account of her exhibitings and the indulgence of a satirical, contemptuous spirit, which, on reflection, could not be approved of; and we have also learnt some of the particulars of the disaster that soon after befell the friendless creature in the loss of her purse. Well was it that the trains of thought and the resolves which ere long succeeded, in a settled form, the reflections and the plunder referred to, took largely the shape of an ability and readiness to face and bear any hardships which might be appointed for her to pass through, as likewise to perform well her part therein; and with such impressions upon her mind, and such determinations it was, that she repaired a second time to the grand residence of the Dutchman's opulent widow in the courtly suburb of Kensington; serious reflection, almost as much as necessity, counselling her to encounter difficulties and things repulsive to her, were it only as a salutary ordeal. Accordingly, prepared to accept of Mrs. Puffendorff's offer, if made to her, almost on any terms, she set forth to present herself at the dame's conspicuous mansion; happening again also to make her appearance there while the same pair, who had been with the wealthy widow on the preceding day, were in conclave with her, one on either hand, as if they had been her heraldic supporters.

"Thirty pounds a-year, and you may have your washing done at my expense, Miss, at my laundress's," said Mrs. Puffendorff, "is the utmost I can think of giving to any person who is to teach my children at the starting of their education; I promising, however, the farther they advance beyond the A, B, C, that I will keep pace by an increase of salary. Somehow or other, the charming creatures have never yet been able to make much progress; the governesses which they have had having so many different ways with them, and my own time having been so much occupied otherwise, that they have been spoilt or neglected in their reading. Now, however, young woman, I shall look to your having them make up for lost time, should you agree to my terms, which, you know, include being treated as one of the family."

In accordance with poor Adelaide's previous reflections and resolutions, she at once accepted the offer, having however not lost sight of announcing along with her name,—and also with the fact of being obliged by sudden reverses of fortune to have recourse to some honest means of earning her bread,—that the promised remuneration must bear reference rather to the very low elementary teaching which the young people were susceptible of, than the attainments and pretensions of the teacher, much less the exactions of the advertisement set forth in the "Morning Post."

"And yet," added the young lady, "your children, Mrs. Puffendorff, are far enough advanced in years to be susceptible of, and, also, imperatively to require, much more important lessons than any which are contained in mere school-books; and should it so turn out that I prove myself in some measure equal to the higher kinds of teaching to which I refer, and that your young ones improve in such branches and directions, I trust that you will deal equally with me, were it but in according to me, and for the hearing of those who may make inquiries relative to my services, such praise as may be my due."

"What other branches do you refer to, Neville, Miss Neville, I mean,—although I never call the governess of my daughters otherwise than by her surname, Martyn?" inquired Lady Gorewell.

"Branches which were not noticed in the advertisement," answered Adelaide. "Not to say a word for the present about so high a department or theme as that of religion, relative to which, I must confess, I ought to speak with the greatest mistrust and diffidence of myself, there was not a single allusion made to the training of the moral sensibilities and capacities,—not even of such things as pertain to the amiabilities of disposition, the culture of the temper, and of those constant interchanges which render social life either happy or unhappy, profitable or prejudicial."

"Why, young woman, all these things are understood by everybody to be included, though not expressed," returned the lady. "Even as regards religion, which you, so conveniently for yourself, put aside, I am strict and conscientious. My daughters are made to go to church regularly, and give every 'amen,' &c., with scrupulous precision, accuracy, and solemnity. They have, from frequent repetition, most of the Prayer Book by heart; and when they are naughty, I oblige them, or rather the governess as my substitute obliges them, to read chapters out of the Church Service volume,—the length or continuance of the reading being in proportion to the demerit which has to be punished."

"Punishing people into religion! Making young persons pious, and conversant with Christianity, by tasking them to the study of these sacred things as chastisements! Recommending by means of repulsion!" exclaimed the young governess, in a low but tense tone, as if with irrepressible surprise.

"Then what is it you would have, girl? what is it you mean, Miss Neville?" somewhat indignantly demanded the government-official's spouse. "You are wondrously new-fangled, Miss. You would have my excellent friends here suppose that you know more than your betters do,—than I myself do."

"She proved it yesterday, and, I expect, will do as much to-day," was the languishing Lady Lymington's whisper to her associates, which however did not escape the hearing of the maiden.

"There can be little difficulty, Lady Gorewell," replied the young governess, "in explaining what it is which the best authorities mean on the subject of female education, when they speak of its chief and highest branches; asserting, at the same time, that children, even before they may be acquainted with the alphabet, are susceptible, and imperatively require to be trained therein. Yet, for the present, I hope you will not press me farther upon points in relation to which I am a novice myself. I take much blame to me for having talked so long about matters beyond my depth yesterday, especially as I was mainly repeating what had been driven into me by much patient and varied teaching, rather than what I have had the merit to make my own. Should you again urge me beyond my proper level, I'll have also again to betake myself to the tested doctrines of others,—to the discoveries of eminent individuals who have made the human mind and its culture their patient study, without having a single thing to state as the result of my own experience or as a leader of persons younger than myself. I think, Mrs. Puffendorff, you would rather wish me immediately to address myself to my duties towards your young people, and in that sphere endeavour to demonstrate the views I have imbibed, by actual fruits, than run the chance, as I did yesterday, and again am doing, of being petulant and pedantic,— things unseemly in one of my years, when in the presence of those who are older." And as she concluded, the damsel rose from her seat, her modesty of manner, and something like a look of self-upbraiding, especially catching the observation of Lady Lymington.

"No, no; you must not withdraw, Miss Neville," said the fox-hunting baronet's spouse, quickly rising from her reclining posture on the downy article of furniture which she occupied. " I wish to hear you out, and so ought Lady Gorewell. As for Mrs. Puffendorff, she has an immediate and still closer interest in being made acquainted with what you know and what you mean to do."

"Yes, by all means, go on, Miss," was echoed by the economic member of the trio, with a repulsive accent. " I suppose that I must allow myself to be instructed by a juvenile schoolmistress, along with Lady Lymington."

"Never mind, for the present, what is said by uneasy folks, but speak what you know, think, and feel," said the languishing lady. "I, for one, will not be offended should you make me to understand something to which I never before paid heed, or may have thought myself, in my ignorance, too wise to learn. Proceed. But first let *me* propound one question,—only one at a time; I have not as yet put myself very much forward, and therein have so far evinced my prudence. How will you begin with your pupils at Puffendorff House? You have heard how deficient they are in regard to the matter of reading, being however about as far advanced as I myself was at the age of the oldest of them,—a disadvantage of which I am not altogether insensible now, whatever others may think or say. I have, you see, Miss Neville, given you some sort of reason for my putting the question,—namely, what is the first thing you will set about with the three young people— the boisterous boy, as well as the dull Emily, and the perverse Eliza? You see I am not afraid to speak my mind, especially when I know myself to be right. Now take time, and answer me as you best can, Miss Neville."

Adelaide thus pressed had retaken her seat, and looked as composed as ever. She paused before uttering a syllable of any kind, and with her eyes fixed on the floor, the lovely creature cogitated for a few seconds with a steadiness of aspect such as a marble statue would have presented, had the sculptor made the young governess at the instant the subject of his art. And a beautiful study would the maiden have been; so graceful was her attitude, so intellectual the contour of her countenance, so penetrating and intense her gaze. She lifted her head,—a light broke from her radiant face, intermingled with such a smile as an angel may be supposed to wear when on an embassy of peace and gladness,—her organs of sight telling not only her delight, but seeming to exclaim with rapture, "I have found it !"

"Lady Lymington, permit the novice-governess," sweetly said poor Adelaide, "to throw herself upon her recollections, and to deal in the experienced learning and language of another. I once heard a tried and admirable gentlewoman, under whom I for years was placed, in Paris, say, that she never could manage a child, or a girl, who had not yet taken to self-reflection, until she obtained its affections; and, she added, the affections of the young are generally ductile. Now, as for me, it shall be my study, my earnest, faithful, and persevering effort, to gain in the very first place the affections of Mrs. Puffendorff's young people, concomitantly and partly through the necessary book-lessons which they receive. The same practised authority added, that, as soon as the dullest, the most perverse, or turbulent pupil could be made to taste the pleasure of success in any worthy pursuit, little more was required to animate her or him to a docile or creditable continuance in the opened course."

"Admirable !" ejaculated the fox-hunter's partner, clapping her hands in her delight. "You have had many advantages, Miss Neville; but, above all, you have possessed a taste, a judgment, a remarkable ability to profit from and by them."

"But you have not drawn from the young governess what she means when she speaks of the chief and highest branches of education, my Lady Lymington," impatiently observed the other titled dame; "yes, the *chief* and the *highest*, and yet suited to the *youngest*, after the mere age of babyhood is gone, as was confidently laid down."

"You hear the challenge, young lady," smilingly said the old baronet's better half. "I doubt not of your being on the instant ready with an answer."

"I am ready," returned the maiden, "but only by again recollecting what the wise and experienced have promulgated; so that it should be left for me, and the like of me, to act up to the best of our ability and opportunities in accordance with their instructions. Now, an excellent authority has said, that education resolves itself into two great branches,—the one being the acquisition of knowledge, such as of language, numbers, natural history, &c, and skill or accomplishments in a variety of ways, such as in the mechanical, as well as in the fine arts. Secondly, and pre-eminently, education, to be suited for rational and immortal beings, who have to pass through a life in such a state as that in which we are placed on earth, includes the teachings and processes which go to the formation of character and habits. A celebrated writer of our sex——"

But here the young creature paused, manifesting feelings which Lady Lymington construed to be those of modesty or timidity, and therefore she broke out into words of pressure and encouragement; courteously bidding poor Adelaide to proceed, and saying that she was sure to acquit herself in a way beyond all the praise which any one present would be able to bestow, with due discrimination, upon the youthful speaker.

"A celebrated writer of our own sex," resumed the governess, "has said, that although some have maintained that the great aim of female education should be to render the pupils fit for becoming good wives and mothers, yet that this is too narrow an object and purpose, high and broad as it is; for that the true purpose of education in all cases, is not what may fit a person for being that which he or she may never be, but its aim and grasp should never be less nor lower than to cherish and unfold the seed of immortality already sown within the youngest of our species; to develope, to their fullest extent, in the best way, the capacities of every kind, with which an all-wise and all-powerful Being has endowed us."

"But what is the best way, Adelaide Neville?" inquired the fox-hunter's lady, with an eagerness which the other dames had never witnessed, and of which they, probably, deemed her to be incapable.

"I must again task my memory, Lady Lymington,—not draw from my personal practice, or actual discovery," mildly responded our heroine. She paused for a short time as before, looking exactly the same too, excepting being a little more animated and brilliant. "The best way!" Adelaide at length muttered, as she slowly lifted her head. "Why, to speak in general terms, it must be by seconding nature in her efforts; for if this be not done, assuredly she will work out her own course, and it may be, her revenge; punishing most signally those who transgress her laws, which she has obviously, in most cases, established for the government of her creatures. Now, human nature, good authorities say, cannot safely or wisely be treated with cruelty of any sort, nor even by coercion,—such as the brutalizing *fag-system*. The teacher, on the contrary, is to win and to stimulate, as a kind friend and intelligent adviser, as well as willing assistant will ever do,—ever acting in a spirit of cheerfulness and sympathy; virtue, for its own sake, and for the happiness to be found in its path, being held forth and made to be experienced as the chief incentive; this necessarily occupying our best faculties in the most rational as well as profitable and delectable manner."

"You advance, or rather rehearse, things, Miss, as if all people were born alike, and with one and the same capacities," interjected Lady Gorewell, more at random than as one who docilely attended to what the young creature's memory, with some helps from her just perceptions and reflecting habits, supplied; the objector having, however, struck not far wide of an important consideration.

"In my rehearsals or recollections of what others have said and written," replied the young governess, "I can only alight upon, or cull some general, perhaps, very vague things, being, besides, much disjointed or apart one from another. Still, I think that no one can resist the doctrine, for instance, that the regulation of the moral feelings is vastly more important than the acquisition of a foreign or ancient language, or any branch of mere secular knowledge. And in very many cases, perhaps in most school-rooms and seminaries, this paramount matter is altogether overlooked. Then, as to the diversity of disposition, tastes, and talent, nothing surely can be more absurd than to pay no real attention to the inherent peculiarities of the intellectual and moral character of a pupil; or, when the bent is discovered,—a thing which, by care and patience, I have been told, can always be done,—to overlook giving a profitable, which will also generally be a pleasurable, direction to that bent."

"Excellent, dear Adelaide, according to my following of you in the delivery of your recollections, as you modestly characterise the statements," spiritedly again spoke out Lady Lymington. "Let me inform you now, that although I took the liberty to pronounce Emily Puffendorff, that is, Miss Puffendorff, dull, I went only by what several others have said, yet all of whom, I knew, judged of her by some one standard, and as they attempted to test her, this being only in one direction,— namely, the acquisition of her mother-tongue as it is set down in a book, or has to be read. This, however, I know, that she speaks prettily, and, I think, with uncommon accuracy; being guided by an ear of great quickness and sensibility, combined with a most melodious and rich voice. She has even taught herself to play certain airs, not amiss on the piano, from which, however, all the governesses she has yet had have stupidly, in my judgment, withheld her; alleging it was soon enough for the young lady to take to a musical instrument after she could read the words of the piece to which the airs have been set. I should think, and I do hope, that Miss Puffendorff's remarkable capacity in the direction I have mentioned, may not only serve to open up for her a fine field for the exercise of her particular gifts, but become, in such hands as your's, Miss Neville, the key to the evoking of other tastes and talents."

"I think and hope as your ladyship does," eagerly subjoined the young governess. "You have done me no small service in pointing out Miss Puffendorff's natural bent; and it will prove me to be an incompetent teacher, if I do not render good assistance in directing it."

"Ay, but not wholly to music, I trust," energetically cried the dame who had been wont to indulge in languishing indolence. "It is good as an accomplishment to have skill upon a stringed instrument; but I, to my painful experience, know that there are more important things than music to be taught."

"Many sound thinkers declaim powerfully," observed the governess, "against the aim of fashionable female education, in these days, being showy accomplishments rather than solid acquirements,—gilding rather than gold. They say that it is to *accomplish* matrimony that these are so exclusively pursued; although after such an event they are not more useful to their owner than the lease of a house after the term has expired. Medical men have also said that a mania for music injures the health of females, in consequence of the sedentary habits thereby engendered. Some have even gone the length to maintain, that an inordinate passion in the direction alluded to, injuriously affects the nervous system; that, as a galvanic fluid of harmony, it vibrates on the tympanum, electrifies the soul, and thrills through every fine fibre of the body; that it is a potent excitant, which, when applied daily, for a number of hours, to the sensitive system of female youth, who are keenly alive to the power of sweet and arousing sounds, the nerves must become shattered; so that they say, visit the ball-room and the bazaar, the park and the concert, the theatre and the temple,—and among the myriads of the young and beautiful whom you see dancing or dressing, driving or chanting, laughing or praying, few are found in the actual enjoyment of full health; an extravagant devotion to music being one of the causes of the alleged melancholy facts. 'No wonder,' exclaims one physician, 'that the doctors, dentists, and druggists multiply almost as rapidly as the pianos, the harps, and the guitars.'"

"Instead of too much music for dear Emily, what think you, Miss Neville, of showing her what treasures of melody there are in our English poetry,—ay, and many prose works, united to, or, rather, made the vehicle of, the noblest moral instruction. Even our literature for juveniles is not without exquisite things in this way."

"Yes," echoed poor Adelaide; "there are numerous specimens of pure and improving reading, quite suited to the ages of Mrs. Puffendorff's young ladies and son; things by no means written in that good-girl or good-boy style, which scarcely impose upon the simplest understanding; on the contrary, abounding with pleasing and natural incident, lucid and harmonious expression, and that gentleness and affectionateness of tone, which best befits the intercourse of an adult with the rising generation."

"Why these two have quite taken *the shine* out of you to-day," whispered the widow to the Lady Gorewell. She might, also, very fitly have added something about her own lameness in regard to being able to keep up with the discourse, or to catch more than an idea here and there, and this only as if by the heels, when flying out of the window, so to speak.

"Better have an eye that the pert and pedantic girl does not practice upon your *shiners*, my good Mrs. Puffendorff," retorted the nettled dame, directing the widow by the silly play upon her vulgar word to an idea and a suspecting principle which the uncharitable speaker knew prevailed, with regard to her de-pendants, in the *vrouw's* breast. "Look, I counsel you,—look in time to your substantial interests: they will not, I can assure you, be found in listening to the fluency and flippancy of such a mere doll, such a chattering parrot, as has taken somebody's fancy."

"Shame!" was the whisper of Lady Lymington; the trio, one and all, fancying that what was sounded at a considerable distance from the young governess, and under breath, reached not her ear. A quick eye, together with an acute sense of hearing, however, made poor Adelaide clearly to understand what was passing, and particularly to watch how the portly mistress of the house sided on the occasion. The discovery was anything but encouraging; for while a look of ill-nature and offence was given out by the one titled lady, and of sympathy by the other, that of the coarse dame of the mansion was of manifest distrust and bullying confidence.

"Down, poor cowardly tears,—those waters of a troubled heart!" was the mental ejaculation of the young lady. "I'll have enough to contend with, do what I can, and buttress myself as I best may, with the Gorewell and the obviously most vulgar and exceedingly ignorant mistress of this tasteless establishment. And yet the ordeal may be for my training and eventual advantage. Heaven help me!"

While these thoughts and impressions were within poor Adelaide's mind, the trio, especially the economic dame of quality and the Dutchman's *vrouw*, had laid their heads together, apparently to determine some point for the guidance of the governess. It was soon settled, the widow becoming the spokeswoman.

"Your service at Puffendorff House, Miss, and, of course, your salary," said the portly dame, with a grand authoritative air, "will commence to-morrow. You will require till then to prepare yourself for coming into a mansion of this description. My housekeeper, who has been long under me, and who knows my ways and pleasure in most things, will introduce my dear children to you, Miss, showing you your sleeping-apartment as well as the school-room, &c. I am to have a very large party to dine with me to-morrow, so that I shall have no time to see you and give further directions myself. This only for the present I must add: be on your guard on all occasions, never to use any undue familiarities with my children, such as kissing and slobbering when you want anything out of them. Now, you may go," the *vrouw* breathing more freely, and looking triumphantly around, after having, at the close of all, acquitted herself so vigorously.

CHAPTER XII.

THE DIVIDED HOUSE.

"I'LL do it, just to spite him. He dare to put me in a dark place as a prisoner, or to chastise me with stripes, as he threatened! I should like him to try it—the blockhead, as I heard mamma name him behind his back. But she told him to his face, that whatever he did to me in the way of punishment, it would be held the same as if it were done to herself. So let Sir Vaux have a care, for he is no father of mine."

Thus talked the son of Lady Waldgrave by her first husband,—for the reader, having now to revisit Wartham Hall, will have to recal to memory our last scene at that place,—the mischievous, perverse urchin and spoilt boy, addressing his sister at the time, and glorying in his past success, as well as anticipated triumph over the ponderous baronet.

Lady Clementina had not merely caused a large importation to be made to Yorkshire of people of her own and children's suite, but had resolved that they should be maintained at her stupid spouse's expense, whether he was pleased or displeased with the arrangement. At the same time she clearly enough foresaw, as the reader must have done, that her injudicious and extravagant determination was calculated to become a cause of disagreement and contention between her and her wedded partner, as also to result in such misunderstandings, recriminations, and quarrels, as would amount to a division of the house in the most emphatic sense of the word. Accordingly, while our heroine, the governess, was quietly and firmly fulfilling her vocation at Puffendorff House,—her exemplary conduct and persevering efforts being in the face of many trying discouragements,—there were occurring at Wartham Hall breaches and broils between those who seemed to be dandled in the lap of good fortune, which rendered their real condition far less desirable than was that of the young lady in her grinding servitude, bred although she had been latterly in the hopes of inheriting vast wealth and a large territorial possession.

Adelaide Neville was sustained not only by an earnest desire to perform her important duties, —itself an ennobling support;—but she simultaneously enjoyed a sense of elevation of feeling and intellectual strength,—gradually growing, too,—which greatly helped to make her hold on in her admirable course. The very reverse of these honourable and delectable experiences were those of the great and pampered folks who were daily striving one against another under the spacious roof which she had at one period looked upon as destined to spread over her in her exaltation. It naturally happened besides, that while the poor girl's difficulties and drawbacks afforded her impulses as well as opportunities for achieving triumphs over herself and in other conflicts,—lending an elevation you would have said, to her very countenance as well as manners, and such a style of expression to her thoughts as can never belong to a narrow or ungenerous spirit;—that while all this was the attainment of the patent, faithful, and rightly-toned maiden, there were amongst the actors in the other quarter mentioned direct contrasts to all this beautiful display, developments of quite an opposite character, and results which entailed conscious degradation, along with shame and disgust.

The mischievous disposition cherished, and the threat uttered by Master Villiers in relation to his step-father, he well knew, would meet with no heartfelt opposition or displeasure on the part of his mother or those of her side of the house, so to speak. But even had the little fellow in some measure dreaded giving serious offence to his parent, so much stronger was the desire to annoy the over-bearing baronet, that he would not have been withheld from gratifying his propensity. Indeed, so perverse had the urchin grown that the mere circumstance of his knowing what Sir Vaux's will might be, was no small motive for him going much out of his way to show his despite of it, and how heartily he went towards its violation.

It was not long before Master Villiers proved that his menaces were not mere talk, and that he had the hardihood as well as the heedlessness of a very bad boy. He knew that Sir Vaux took an especial interest in his nursery, being noted not only for the variety of foreign trees and shrubs which beautified his grounds, but for the healthiness of the plants he raised from preserved and imported seeds; so that the demand for his growths was extensive,—a pleasant tribute to the man and a source of praiseworthy self-approval. Little Frederick, —the urchin being diminutive for his actual years in all respects, but that of disobedience and evil contrivance,—bethought him accordingly of stealthily damaging certain of the most cherished objects of culture reared within the special enclosure. And, by the bye, the enclosure itself had been an erection of very considerable expense and anxiety; having been not only intended to exclude all idle feet, but to prove a highly ornamental feature in the gardened landscape. It consisted chiefly of trellis-work, which by means of green paint of various shades, as well as of branched pillars and multifarious parisital festoonings,— the frame-work being formed of iron and wire,— presented at some little distance not anything of the character of an artificial fence, but of healthy growths of different kinds.

Now, to surmount such a hedge, and to get by climbing within its range, necessarily did the wire interlacing-work serious injury,— a consequence, however, which affected Master Fred in no other way than pleasurably, although his main object was to uproot certain much admired plants, and to strew them about, provided all this could be done, without it being possible to prove—no matter what the suspicions—that he was the guilty party. He had even been at pains to arm himself with a tiny rake that he might obliterate the prints of his footsteps; choosing also an hour when he felt positively sure that the baronet would be engaged elsewhere.

Thus resolved and prepared, the little rascal, by means of sundry cunning wiles and misleading shifts, at last found himself by the side of the admired enclosure, the gate of which was, of course, locked; the proud and peremptory owner hardly ever losing sight of the key, or allowing it to be out of his immediate possession. To climb the iron-work, with rake in hand, was directly set about,—the blackguard creature having made himself sure that no human eye was upon him. Nor had he any difficulty in nearing the top of the interlacing fence, halting there for a moment not only to take a survey around as far as scope was allowed in the richly furnished grounds, to see that he was still unwitnessed, but also to toss the little rake into the nursery before him, as the possession of the article in his hand was incommoding. All these being accomplished, the thing next to be done was to surmount the topmost of the artificial work,—a proceeding which was conducted with incaution and injudicious haste; for on vaulting in a manner over the summit, he calculated not sufficiently on the slender and limber nature of the artificial frame, which certain parasital plants served to conceal, so that the topmost constructions suddenly bent down under him, continuing, too, from the elastic character of the materials to give way further and further; causing the scoundrel, now terrified at the havoc he was doing, to fling himself off from what he clung to. The consequence was that he dropped from a considerable height into the heart of a beautiful bed of plants, crushing and sadly damaging a number of tiny growths of exotic origin. But this was not the whole of the breakage done; for retributively, in consequence of the fall being from a considerable height, and his coming in contact with the solid earth, being in an awkward manner, the heinous transgressor sustained a fracture of one of his legs, which effectually held him a captive where he fell. Thus, assuredly, was this child of depravity not only made to meet with immediate punishment as part of a fitting return for his guilt, but rendered the subject of a lesson, if rightly turned to account, which would make him a new creature for ever afterwards. On the contrary, if the retribution was to become an incentive to mere vexation and slavish fear, in regard to his wickedness, rather than of real contrition and genuine repentance, the great probability was, that should he recover from the effects of his most wanton transgression, he would return to his evil practices with revenge in his soul, and a more malignantly perverse spirit than before, till at last he might be fatally caught in his villany, never again to be permitted to prove a pest on the face of the earth.

The imp having come to the ground and got his limb fractured, there lay bawling and shrieking till he could hardly find strength to raise his voice to its wonted childish squeak. But no one heard him; no chance passer-by came to his rescue and relief; not a creature, in short, until the baronet himself, in the course of his usual rounds in fine weather, approached to cast, as he hoped, a gratified eye towards his nursery.

It is needless to attempt a description of what occurred when the ponderous Sir Vaux, not only got a sight of the havoc that had been wrought upon his beautiful nursery-fence and the bed of rare exotic seedlings, but discovered who the havoc-worker was. His rage was not properly that of pure fire, either quickly piercing or brightly flashing, but rather resembling the fury of the volcano, which keeps boiling and struggling in vain to get vent from beneath the mighty shouldering mountain that prisons it, quake to its very bowels, although the earth may. He panted and puffed, he ran as he best could, lumbering hither and thither. In his wrath which could not find relief in a proper, hearty burst, he was so surged as to

seem forgetful where the locked inlet to the nursery was situated. He looked at moments as half inclined to pull down a portion of the very carefully and cunningly constructed iron and wire-work, in order to obtain direct access to the prostrated and groaning transgressor. He brandished his gold-headed cane, swung it around him, and flagellated whatever came within his reach. At length the key of the gate did its office, and allowed its master to rush upon his step-son, who escaped not a stroke or two in the rounds of the polished staff, which evoked by each salute renewed bellowings.

"You are murdering Lady Clementina's darling son, Sir Vaux Waldgrave, and we must forthwith deal with you as the child-killer," cried a pair of her ladyship's men-servants, who had been sent in search of the little scoundrel. "Hold, sir, or we must master you," continued the fellows, by this time exerting all their strength upon the artificial fence, to effect access to the scene of flagellation, and actually forcing themselves through, to the greater injury of the iron and wire-work than had before been wrought by the diminutive imp and the maddened master of the place.

"You have fractured our young master's leg, Sir Vaux Waldgrave, with your monstrous blows,—we witnessed your doing it!" exclaimed the servile men, on lifting the agonized urchin and seeing the limb dangling between them. "If you have any compassion, any wish to avert the charge and punishment of manslaughter, hasten to order a doctor to be sent for, while we carry dear Master Villiers to his doating mother."

"Carry him to—to perdition, if you like; I'll incontinently rid myself both of her and him, and you to the bargain, ye greedy hounds. Off with you, or by—by my honour, I'll let each of you feel the weight of my gold-headed cane until ye vanish from this *sanctum sanctorum* of mine;" the gyrations which the polished and stout staff was meanwhile made to perform, advertising the fellows that the threat would not be a mere windy one. The boy, however, heeded it not, for he had fainted away, and seemed dying fast, if not already dead; so the men made speed to quit the baronet's *holy of holies*, who began to calm himself on observing some tokens of obedience, and by calling out "Serve him right, had he broken his neck, instead of his leg, the imp of a place which I never name. I'll see to my darling enclosure, though."

The bad boy was carried to his weak-minded, foolish, and pampered parent to be the occasion of another scene, though of a different kind, of extraordinary excitement; this taking place within doors, in the lady's favourite chamber; and instead of flagellation, weeping, anguish, and vows of revenge, forming the noise. As soon as the little rascal came to himself and could speak distinctly, his story was, that while he had, without any evil intention, climbed a little way up the artificial work, forming the fence, having so far done it no harm, Sir Vaux came suddenly upon him, and by his threatenings and the action of his cane so terrified the climber that he was glad to go higher and higher up, in order to get entirely out of the lusty man's way,—"Knowing," as the *little in-*

nocent, with apparent guilelessness said, "that such a big man could not, or durst not, go aloft after him." Having hastened towards the top of the wire-work, it began to bend away from the adventurer, and in a few moments to let him down quietly in the nursery, without any more damage having been done to the fence, than a little pains at bending back the yielding materials would have cured. But the step-father would not be content with this. On the contrary, he rushed into the nursery like a lion or a bear, having opened the gate with his key; nor sooner had he got to the trembler, who implored for pity and for mercy, than he struck him to the ground,—the very same blow which knocked him down breaking the leg. The innocent could not say how many more strokes he received, for he became senseless through the pain of the fracture.

"But we were witnesses of several monstrous blows being inflicted on our dear young master," cried the footmen; "and had we not broken through the gingerbread affair of a fence, Sir Vaux would, beyond all doubt, have killed the darling clean out then and there. In fact, while most anxiously caring for our young master and having him between us,— his poor leg dangling and showing beyond all mistake the frightful state in which it was,— the great baronet hardly refrained from breaking our heads with his heavy cane in order to get to the dear child, who was by this time insensible, and apparently dying fast, if not already dead. We declare to your ladyship, and will swear to it before any magistrate or judge, that we never saw a human being so transported with rage as was Sir Vaux Waldgrave while doing all he could to slay your son; but more especially was he infuriated when he found he could no longer get at the unhappy

No. 8.—THE GOVERNESS.

:hild because of our interference and protection."

Whilst all this was going on within the Hall, Sir Vaux was growing cooler as he perambulated his pleasure-grounds, reflecting on what had just happened; also beginning to have some misgivings as to the consequences of the scene in which he had figured so conspicuously. By and bye, he came to have something like a correct conception of the case, and to perceive that it was rather unfortunate for him that he had no one to witness on his side, whilst the boy's story and that of the two footmen would most assuredly be strained in order to go wholly against him. He was conscious that he had not broken the imp's limb; neither had the blows with his cane been one tithe so heavy as they effected to be. In fact, the strokes had not hurt the urchin's person at all. Yet what if he should fever and die, or even from the nature of the fracture be necessitated to submit to amputation! In this latter case he would be a living monument in the eyes of the world daily,—the patrician world,—of Sir Vaux Waldgrave's brutal cruelty, the savage barbarity of one who had ever before been regarded as a model of proprieties. What a stupid thing was it for him to get married to a widow, and of London training, who had children under the years of discretion! What a thoughtless proceeding to get wedded at all for a man of his years and habits! But these latter were reflections which he had often of late indulged in, even although they carried with them the confession of want of foresight and self-accusings,—this condition of mind being novel in the history of the Yorkshire baronet.

But Sir Vaux went farther in his cogitation, as he perambulated his gardened-grounds; for he came to something like a sudden sense, from the pressure of circumstances from within as well as from without, that it was unwise of him, for the sake of his own importance and peace, to be so troubled about who was to be his successor as he had been.

"I'm getting to be an old man," thought he, " a very old man. I am already three score and ten, or so; and should my lease of life be extended ten years longer,—a reprieve that I can hardly expect, considering the tear and wear I have gone through within these few last months,—why, it is as much as I can expect. Ten years more!—ha! it is but a speck, an *iota*, an infinitesimal unit, in the lapse of time, not to speak of the boundlessness of eternity. Then what although that profligate nephew of mine should be master at Wartham Hall when I am gone? What odds will it make to me? I'm sure to die ere long,—to be carried to the tomb by people who don't care the value of a fig for me, and who will only have a carousal of gratulation at my decease. I'll moulder into dust like any other piece of human flesh and bones, and be forgotten wholly in less time than one of my farm's term of lease. There will be no remembrance of me for great things done,—good or evil; and when the resurrection comes, —and I have been taught to believe it will come, —a doctrine, however, which I never for a moment considered,—I have no reason to expect that I shall be restored to the possession of dear Wartham Hall, or that I will be acknowledged either as a man of title, of great property, or of long lineage. Nay, I am not at all sure how it may stand with me in comparison with persons of far less pretensions, fewer opportunities to do good, and yet larger real services for the benefit of mankind,—less pride and greater virtue. There is to be a class on the right hand, and another on the left. Where shall the rich Sir Vaux Waldgrave's station be on that great day? Surely not amongst the deliberate slayers of his kind! no: but amongst those who for certain fleeting most unimportant family matters, has made shipwreck of his immortal soul during eternity, and been a laughing-stock even before he reached the everlasting shore, because of his folly, his silly pretensions, and his drivelling life!"

Sir Vaux had never cogitated and reflected with half the soundness and depth that he did now. And such were the stings of conscience on account of misused opportunities; such the true views of his demerits, errings, and wrongdoings, when tasking himself in the eye of reason and humanity, of morals and religion, that he would have disposed of his all for a mess of potage, provided that along with that mess he could have made sure of a comfortable deathbed.

"What will it be to me, destined at last, as I am, to find myself a childless old man," he audibly exclaimed, "whether Ludlow Chesters succeeds me, or an impostor, or some usurious Jew? He, my ungrateful and licentious nephew, will, ere long, have to go to his fitting place, just as I will have to go to mine; and perhaps we shall have to consort together, which will make no heaven to either, unless there be a great change on the part of both."

It happened that the baronet, just as he had come to this stage in his soliloquy, found himself alongside of his cherished nursery with its remarkable fence of iron and trellis-work; the locality and the sight, however, no longer affecting him as it had been wont to do as a sort of *sanctum sanctorum*, but rather now as a remembrance of the recent scene of violence, rage, and suffering, which had been witnessed there.

"The imp,—the boy, my step-son, I should rather say,—may die," ejaculated the arrested Sir Vaux. "He may already have breathed his last, and who knows how perjured fellows may represent the real facts? Liberty, equality, and radicalism, have of late years made great advances with their doctrines. Levelling is the order of the day; and even the law-oracles have the audacity to preach from the bench, that in the eyes of English jurisprudence and English juries there is no respect of persons. In fact, the degenerate and unchivalrous era has arrived when knighthood and *noblehood* are no more reverenced by our reasoners and frequently by our rulers than servitude and the basely born. I may be tried for manslaughter, peradventure for murder. I may be found guilty, and be condemned to die an ignominious death! It would be a fine opportunity for reformers to have me figuring alongside of the hangman on the scaffold of York. Oh dear! I never was in such trouble in all my life. I dread for the first time to approach my stately mansion. And yet if I stay longer aloof from my threshold, my ungrateful, evil-disposed wife,—the partner of my foolish old days,—will think and give it out that from a sense of guilt and blood-spilling, I dare not show my face at my own porch, or within my own saloons. I must and will face the peril and the punishment."

The footsteps of the sorely-troubled man were now directed towards his lordly mansion, but yet by a circuitous course, indicating to himself, had he been candid enough to confess the truth to his own bosom, how strong and serious were his misgivings and fears. As he approached the Hall, and had a sort of stealthy sight of its porch, as viewed through certain luxuriant growths, he descried the doctor of the district issuing from the house, and that next moment he mounted his horse in order to return home. Sir Vaux's heart was at his mouth in an instant, although somewhat relieved on thinking that the worst might be learned from the surgeon immediately, without the necessity of making inquiry of any of his own servants. The baronet accordingly made haste by a near cut to throw himself in the way of the professional man.

"How report you, doctor, concerning the hurt of the boy?" was Sir Vaux's impatient inquiry, on meeting the surgeon; the anxiety of the speaker at the moment, together with the speed to which he had put himself in order to intercept the professional party, giving rise to a degree of agitation which the ponderous personage strove in vain to keep under control.

"Oh! as well as can be expected,—indeed a great deal better than I had been led to look for, from the exaggerated account which was first delivered to me," answered the surgeon. "The little fellow has had an awkward fall, and has snapped his limb. It is merely a simple and very clean fracture, which, in all probability, will be got over in a few weeks. There is no occasion for much alarm, Sir Vaux."

"A fall!—an awkward fall, and not a blow!" ejaculated the baronet, mightily relieved by the tone as well as statement of the surgeon. "Why, the little lying scoundrel, and the servants who carried him from the spot where he met with his mishap, were intent on charging me with misusing the mischievous urchin; but you know better, my skilful and considerate friend."

"I was gravely told that the boy had been belaboured by your cane, Sir Vaux," replied the surgeon, "to the breaking of his bones and the most imminent danger of his life. Yet a very slight inspection of the little fellow's person disproved the representation; for there is not the mark of a blow upon him from head to foot; while as regards the fractured leg, it is quite manifest to me that it is the result of a fall. Indeed, deeming it of importance that the exact truth should be known relative to this circumstance, I took occasion to let the little fellow understand that if he made the slightest intentional mistake in his account of his manner of meeting with the injury, and were to die of the same, he would have to encounter the Almighty's displeasure and punishment. The boy was at the moment enduring

much pain, and was alarmed. He had not the hardihood to persist in a mis-statement, but plainly admitted that it was from the fall he got his hurt, and not otherwise."

"Thank heaven!" cried the baronet, taking the doctor by the hand and shaking it till the entire arm participated in the gratulation. "You are an excellent person, surgeon, as well as a most skilful practitioner and sensible gentleman. You will henceforward be Sir Vaux Waldgrave's family physician. Look to the boy, and cure him as quickly as you can. This done, he shall be bundled off from the Hall, and others with him, for good and all, unless they take warning from what has this day happened to me and to them."

On again most cordially shaking the surgeon's hand, and lavishing hearty praise upon him, the baronet made for the Hall, but by a more direct route and assured pace than he had maintained a little time before. He repaired to his private parlour, where he pompously ordered dinner to be served to him, not deigning to make the slightest inquiry after the health of the imp who had so mightily annoyed and disturbed him.

"The mother of the pestilent thing shall be made to understand as well as the spoiled brat itself," said the baronet within his own breast, now restored to his wonted self-complacency, "that Sir Vaux Waldgrave is not to be driven from his propriety for naught, and that he will uphold his dignity with a firmness that grows in greatness with the magnitude and exactions of the occasion. My rightful authority shall be made known to Lady Clementina immediately, as also what it amounts to when my high displeasure is incurred. She and her importations shall have their apportioned domain at Wartham both outside and inside the Hall, and to the promulgation of my law shall my wits be presently applied."

According to this magnanimous resolve, Sir Vaux set himself to work, conveying to paper for her ladyship's perusal and study his determination and commands for the guidance of her children and people, so long as they might be permitted to domicile under his ancestral roof and have the privilege of enjoying the happiness of being his guest. It was, in fact, just as the lady was looking for apologies and concessions from her husband,—whose interview with the doctor she had not calculated upon,—or at least for the baronet making, personally or otherwise, anxious and sympathetic inquiries relative to her darling boy's condition, that she received a very different kind of communication.

"Your ladyship's people are henceforward to understand," thus wrote Sir Vaux, "that the left wing of my mansion is to be appropriated to their sole use, with a peremptory forbiddance of any one of them upon any pretence whatever trespassing within the quarters which I reserve for myself and my people. A corresponding line of demarkation shall be observed outside the Hall; my masons and carpenters being ordered to dyke off your importation, so as that there may be no mistake as to the division; the same line having my watchmen day and night established to preserve my choicest grounds from such injury as the senseless or the wicked may wish to do me. Let it be kept in mind, that this arrangement is to be as binding and peremptory towards your children, Lady Clementina, as upon your humblest servant; and that the slightest infraction of my commands shall instantly be followed by the dismissal of the offending parties from my habitation and lands, by forcible deportation, if gentler means do not suffice."

CHAPTER XIII.

THE INTERLOPER'S STRATEGY.

WE do not attempt to describe the disappointment and rage which Lady Waldgrave manifested on receiving and reading her husband's peremptory piece of penmanship. She had been confidently expecting, if not a humble visit in her apartment from him, a meek solicitation for her to repair to his favourite and private chamber, in order that he might apologise to her for the severity and violence he displayed towards her son; the opportunity being impatiently waited for on her part, that she might terrify more deeply the baronet by a continuance of misrepresentations about her boy, and the manner in which he came by his hurt. But instead of finding a lever-power wherewith to act to the discomfiture of her lumbering lord, she was forced to the discovery that he was as obstinate and as pompous as ever; and that, in place of her obtaining a triumph over him, he was resolute on letting her feel how dependent she and her people were upon himself.

Her first impulse had been to declare a determination of leaving the Hall for ever, as soon as it might be safe for her boy to undergo a removal. Some doubts, however, about a claim for aliment began to arise in her mind, should she voluntarily withdraw from her husband's home; so that although she meant to hold out the threat of abandoning him, she perceived that it was so far fortunate that her son's illness would allow her a few weeks for considering of some less absolute a step. Meantime, to send back Sir Vaux a most indignant answer to his mandates as regarded the scope to be allowed her children and people within the walls and the territory of the baronet's residence, was her actual proceeding; coupled with the threat that unless each item of a list of her demands was complied with, she would as soon as possible turn her back upon him, and never cease to proclaim to the world his absurdities and cruelty to her and hers. But the ill-advised language being treated with indignation as well as derision,—after having led to a scene of vulgarly-conducted altercation and mutual recrimination,—only served to make the lady and the imported members of her suite understand that by each rash display she was losing ground; her growing error being to constitute every little matter of annoyance to her, and serve the purpose of a fierce quarrel; just as a spark applied to a magazine of gunpowder will do the business of an earthquake. The threatenings of separation were almost daily repeated, and ever with increased bitterness. The lady asseverated that she would go, and the baronet would not stoop to ask her to stay. True, Sir Vaux was a man of such propriety, and was so ambitious of standing well in the estimation of the aristocracy, that he would have been the last to have turned his wife and her children from his house so long as it was possible to keep them within bounds. He accordingly experienced annoyance at hearing or learning the nature of her frequent declaration. Still, he was too proud and highly wrapped up in his good opinion of himself to betray his feelings, or to make the slightest concession.

Matters had continued in this unhappy posture for several weeks posterior to the occurrence of the accident to the mischievous Fred, and with growing virulence whilst he was recovering; a recovery, by the by, which was unaccompanied with any resolve on his part to make amendment. On the contrary, the little rascal only studied how he might most surely be avenged upon his step-father, being stung to the wicked determination, not only by the unceasing recollections of how he had been worsted and exposed on the occasion of his fall at Sir Vaux's much admired nursery, but by his mother's complaints of her husband's overbearing government of his house and all that were within it of the lady's suite. Nothing, however, so irritated the urchin as to find himself prevented from scampering through the baronet's grounds as he had a mind, especially as he, as well as every member of his parent's suite, was confined to the least attractive portions of the noble park, as also the bleakest and most plainly furnished section of the capacious mansion. To meditate evil and retaliation against Sir Vaux was the imp's daily mental occupation as soon as he could make use of his nether limbs as before; not only a greater degree of cunning, as he assured himself, being studied for the perpetration of the intended evil, but a fiercer spirit swaying the perverse creature.

"It is not climbing that I shall think of doing, lest I get a fall again," thought the pestilent Fred; "but to an exploit that will allow me to keep on level ground, and have the use of my heels. What an ado Sir Vaux makes about his hives of bees,—his *wonderful apiary*, as he calls his strange-looking and most curious house for the honey-makers. The building has been brought all the way from Germany; the extraordinary contrivance being to save the bees while you take their sweet produce from them, and thus not to destroy the busy labourers, but allow them to increase at a great rate every year. How I should like to bring their houses to the ground, smashing the buildings, scattering the creatures, and destroying their works and honey. The big baronet spites us by having the hives placed close to the division by which he has dyked us off from his principal and prettiest grounds; but we'll see who'll spite best. Ha! ha! what a demolishing there will be; sending adrift tens of thousands of inhabitants in an instant, and showing what a clever boy like me can do to vex and punish those who dare to rule over me and my mother!"

Now, the boy's contrivance was, after much evil meditation, to throw a sort of lasso around one or more of the Gothic-like pinnacles of the curious wooden structure in which were several hives, and by pulling the whole from its considerably elevated position to the ground in a moment, to demolish the entire fabric, with its valuable contents, in a twinkling of time. As the apiary happened to be placed in a cozy corner, admirably sheltered from cold and storms on all sides but the south,— this screened corner being within a few yards of the spiked paling which formed the fence against the encroachments of the little rascal upon the baronet's more specially cared-for grounds,—no great difficulty seemed to interpose itself against the completion of the meditated evil.

Having, with his wonted low cunning, not only selected a period of the day when he felt sure no particular eye would be upon his motions, he commenced the following out his impish scheme,—with various blinding acts, —and repaired to the neighbourhood of the apiary as nearly as the paled boundary would permit, and boldly flung from him the noosed end of the rope with which he had armed himself. It was not until after the tackle had been thrown out and drawn in again three or four times that the loop caught a turret or branching ornament of the fantastic erection under whose general roof the hives were kept. But, to the wicked creature's astonishment and regret, instead of this ornament being strong enough to bring along with it, in obedience to the strenuously exerted power of Fred's arms, the entire fabric, it gave way and broke off, and thus the intended evil was not at the moment achieved, although sufficient evidence was left to show that vile mischief had been attempted upon the curious property.

"As well to complete the thing at once, as to leave it in this damaged and unfinished state," thought the urchin. "It will be just as safe for me; while, as to my mother, what need she care, when she is at any rate going to quit the Hall and have no more to do with the brute, as she herself is constantly calling the big baronet. Having so bravely begun my work of revenge, I'll bring it to a close in style."

Having thus magnanimously resolved and fortified his mischievous intents, the imp began to climb and stride over the fence, consisting of a high range of close-barred paling, with a series of iron spikes on the top of the whole. It was not many moments before he found himself on the forbidden ground and close to the apiary. To lend all the strength of hand, shoulder, and body which he could muster to the work of demolition was his prompt proceeding; when down came the curious wooden fabric with its complement of hives, all crushing and crushed, to the alarm and fierce indignation of the housed swarms, that, with instinctive certitude, sped on their nimble, tiny wing to wreak their wrath out upon their wanton enemy.

Ah! they were too fleet in their pursuit for the imp. The paling, too, has to be scaled, and this occupies a few moments ere he can reach the summit; when, lo! another unthought of obstruction mars his progress; for, in his hurry, he has got entangled upon the sharp spikes, and is held fast, to be literally stung to death before the dreadful predicament in which he is placed reaches the knowledge of mother or stepfather.

It was a dreadful termination to the wicked boy's life, and it should have been viewed as in some measure retributive upon the parent who had served to spoil him, not only by her ill-judged indulgence but positive example. Instead of taking blame to herself, however, her complaints were wreaked out with redoubled fury against her husband; charging him as having intentionally had his bees so near to the boundary of her darling boy's exercise and play-ground as would expose the young creature to mortal dangers. But although the accusation was too absurd and far too intemperate to merit being listened to, it helped to steel the baronet's mind against the lady, and make him even desire a final and complete separation from her; the hopelessness of her ever adding a branch or sprout to Sir Vaux's family tree having its weight to the production of the wish. And yet another influence was brought to work upon the contemplated arrangement, the nature of which requires that we retrace our steps to an earlier period of our story than what we have recently been engaged upon, and also to something like a renewed acquaintance with a character of whom we have not lately taken any notice,—namely, the Hon. Ludlow Chesters, the gay and profligate Life-Guardsman.

The reader will remember how very sudden were the changes and complete the transitions which took place in the circumstances of several of our characters soon after the commencement of the story, and that Chesters was amongst the first to be affected in the course of these unlooked-for revolutions. Nor, for him, were the variations of prospect confined to one or two strange changes; for not more completely did his hopes of inheriting Wartham Hall at first die within his breast, when his uncle furiously dismissed and repudiated him, than these revived and re-awoke on his becoming acquainted with the discovery which was made relative to the widowed Mrs. Waldgrave's alleged daughter, through the appearance of the ruffian Jobson. But then, again, came the tidings of Sir Vaux's purpose of marriage, that he might have offspring of his own, and next of the solemnization of such a union with the Lady Clementina Villiers, to the prostration of the captain's sanguine views a second time; including his exposure to the Jewish harpies, upon whose usurious mercies he had been pursuing his gallantries. At length has arisen the report, that not merely Sir Vaux and his lady have been at touch-and-go for many a day,—the severance growing from less to more, and from bad to worse,— but that the pedigree-tree remains stationary meanwhile, in respect of increase.

"Let them be separated,—and a vengeance to them,—before they bring a brat to occupy my place," is the prayer of the Life-Guardsman, as he trembles between hope and fear, on learning the recriminating and unhappy terms on which his uncle and the lady live; backed by this mischief-working determination—"I₁ they will not fly asunder of their own accord, and this without waste of time, I shall do the separating business for them, and be, ere long, the lord of Wartham Hall, in spite of fate. Deep-schemed strategy shall be my policy, and the boldness of a daring interloper my conduct. It requires, at the starting, but to open a correspondence with the blundering baronet's joyless spouse, through the medium of her deceased boy's late tutor, who sues for my countenance in London here. This done, the vicinity of Wartham, and perhaps the Hall itself, will have my society. What next? Why, bestirred jealousy; separation to the end of the chapter from bed and board, as, in fact, for months it has already been. In a word, every alienation between the wedded pair,—between the old pompous fool, and the ambitious, soulless dame,—short of a complete and final divorce; and then my triumph is sure, to the spiting and astonishment of the altar-bound yet wifeless and childless Sir Vaux."

"In a sailor's garb! by means of a rope-ladder! And has climbed by such villanous means into Lady Waldgrave's wing of my house!" were Sir Vaux's hurried exclamations, on one of his men-servants reporting to the baronet as he sat, after nightfall, indulging in a brown study, or half-dreaming reverie, in his favourite secluded apartment by himself. "A case of *crim. con.!* a clear ground for suing out a divorce of the wanton, I swear! Where are my pistols? the double-barrelled spitfires, I mean? Was it that she might carry on her amours in secrecy and seclusion that I apportioned to Lady Clementina and her importations a wing of my noble mansion, which never, to the best of my knowledge, was polluted before? I'll blow out the brains of both the guilty ones, were it not that I would thus lose the opportunity of having a more fitting revenge. Hither with me, Thomas, and summon others of my servants with sledge-hammer and crowbar. We'll pounce upon them all at once, and thus shall Sir Vaux rid himself of the baggage that has been the bane of his life from the first day she and her importations crossed the threshold of Wartham Hall."

While the maddened baronet was running on in this way, the man Thomas—sly fellow, and the accomplice in the strategy of the still slyer interloping Captain Chesters,—was getting the pistols ready, yet minus any leaden contents, and also bringing to the aid of Sir Vaux and himself several of the other servants of the house, who, however, were not in the secret of the plot any more than their master or even Lady Waldgrave herself, silly dupe as she also had been kept of the Life-Guardsman's plot. At length, away sallied the party, proceeding as stealthily as possible to the quarter of the capacious dwelling into which the sailor-clad individual had ascended. It took not many minutes for the armed party to near the chamber in which the lady and the interloper were supposed to be planted; Sir Vaux as well as the others having divested themselves of such sounding leather gear as had encased their feet, and approaching most gingerly the door of the suspected apartment. It is but to listen for a few seconds, and overhear that there is more than one speaker within, in order for the baronet to give a signal for forcible action to his men. Swing goes, and down comes the sledge-hammer, driving the door from its hinges; the horrid violence being accompanied by numerous shrieks from within. Forward rushes Sir Vaux, with a double-barrelled pistol in each hand, breathless with passion, and all but foaming at the mouth from sheer fury; a condition which is in no degree mitigated on his nephew being revealed to him in the costume of a tar. Nay, it seems but to exasperate him the more, on finding that, besides his wife and the captain, there are present his stepdaughter, Lucy Villiers, and the girl's French governess. And yet his rage has not yet reached its climax, for his spouse being by this time aroused from her astonishment and alarm, and having also acquired addition to her party by the accession of her servants from adjoining rooms, breaks out in fierce accusation against the man whom she declares to have a design upon her life, and the life also of her surviving child; not being content with having planted snares for the destruction of her darling boy, as, she avers, was too fatally accomplished.

"Who will side with the wronged wife?" indignantly cried the excited dame, "for her protection against a fool and a monster of cruelty? First, he in a sense incarcerates me and mine in a wing of his bastile, with some space of ground for our airing, as if we were convicted felons. He peremptorily forbids the highest of us to encroach on his hedged-in domain, whether it be within or beyond the walls of his mansion; thereby virtually, and in all justice, authorizing his wife, who is better than every way his equal, to preserve to herself and those whose society she may need and court, a like exclusive privilege in her own sphere, or, rather, consecrated quarter. Denied the counsel and commiseration of my husband, what else could I do than seek the advice and countenance of his heir-apparent, who adopted his own method of reaching me and mine, having learnt how senselessly and vilely I am guarded and watched. Answer, Sir Vaux, or let some one of your myrmidons there do the poor service for you. How dared you to approach my presence and abode in the ruffian manner you have this evening done? Out upon you, I say, for your audacity and brutal behaviour. But you are but a trembling caitiff and drivelling fool at the best, as I shall instantly prove to the conviction of every person present, whether my friend or foe."

As the aroused lady uttered these latter words, and finding that she had the sympathy of the majority of her auditors on her side, she sprang forward in quite a virago-style, snatching the pistols from the blundering baronet's grasp, who stood as a person paralysed between rage and consternation; the unexpected deed serving to confound him the more, as also some of his people who stood behind him; thinking, as they began to do, that it was not judicious to be forward in interference between man and wife. Nor did they cease to shrink, or at least to take a sort of refuge, behind the back of the bulky individual who had allowed himself to be so easily disarmed, on beholding with what resolution the enraged dame levelled the weapons at her astounded husband, accompanying the formidable movement with horrid threatenings that if he did not instantly quit her chamber and her quarter of the house, he should not live to commit an outrage upon her privacy a second time.

"Begone, you idiot!" cried she, as the bulky man withdrew, followed by her ladyship and her suite, but without numbering amongst them the mischievous and unprincipled Life-Guardsman; he having adroitly taken to his ladder, and being entirely out of sight before the lady and her party returned to the vacated chamber. "Begone! and rid me of a sight of you, for good and all. I and my people are not only ready to make oath, but to adduce the most irrefragable proof, of being in terror of our lives,—your outrage of to-night's perpetration crowning your monstrous aims. Forthwith, we shall seek shelter from your cruelty, and thereafter let the law of the land and my steady friends in high places look to the assertion of my rights. Begone!"

The repeated word of indignant command was uttered by the lady for the last time, as the confounded Sir Vaux, who brought up the rear of his party, made his exit at the last door belonging to his spouse's division of the spacious residence, as named and appointed by himself. Prompt and imperative were her next proceedings, satisfied as she was that she and hers had been virtually turned out of doors by her blundering husband, and that her claim for a separate maintenance would be easily established, also that the legal allowance would be ample, having a fitting relation to the baronet's great wealth. Nor was Sir Vaux, in his heart, sorry on being delivered from the constant worry which his lady and her people occasioned him; although vexed in having violently burst in upon her at a time when the proof of guilty conduct on her part was by no means supplied. Indeed, on discovering that it was his libertine nephew who had gained in a most irregular manner access to the dame's presence, the baronet set it down in his own mind as a matter which admitted of no moral doubt,—however difficult it might be to establish the point in a court of law or the House of Peers,—that she was a faithless and guilty spouse.

Such being his convictions, with more philosophy than might have been expected from him,—unless it was mere obtuseness of feeling, which grew duller and duller the longer he lived,—Sir Vaux proceeded to recommend to his lawyers that they should have the question as to the amount of maintenance or aliment to be granted to his wife amicably settled; for that domestic peace, and the undisturbed government of his own affairs, just as these might suit his caprices or tastes, were more prized by him than thousands annually of his accumulated as well as hereditary wealth. Accordingly, while Lady Waldgrave had London once more for her sphere of gaiety, with an income much greater than she had ever been mistress of before, the baronet was himself again, although in a great measure cured of sundry of his crotchets; one of the truths taught him being, that his riches would not avail him in the grave.

Then, as for Captain Chesters, his was the satisfaction of a villain who found his wicked contrivance succeed beyond his expectations. He once more, together with the usurious money-lenders, could hardly anticipate the occurrence of any obstacle to his inheriting the splendid property of Wartham Hall, with its noble park, sloping pastures, and many other admired features, provided he survived his uncle. Then there was the system of life-assurances, these being made to serve for providing against his earlier decease than that of the baronet, who was so far advanced in years that his obstruction to the nephew could not be looked for as proving very permanent.

"Fortunate it is, after all, that I escaped wedding the damsel who made such an awkward slip over the Cauldron Cliff," thought he; "and that I have weathered the storms with which the Jews have beset me till now. Lady Waldgrave, meanwhile, must be kept to her indignant purpose of never more returning to her blundering husband. The pretty French governess, who looks after the daughter's training, shall be made to repay my visits to the dame's town residence, which I find is in the vicinity of courtly Kensington,—the scene of many of my most successful intrigues. Would that I could fall in with the still lovelier Adelaide, as the girl was named, and with whom I narrowly escaped being inveigled; for I owe her a sweet revenge, could I but alight upon her, since her descent into a life of dependence and penury,—the consequence of the imposture she was unwittingly made to practise. I marvel what Montague Mildmay, the canting fellow, would say to the girl now, were he to see her, in russet gown, and scrubbing a floor; unless indeed she have already betaken herself to a more flaunting career, to which I could effectually initiate her, if not by this time trained. But there may be a good time coming, and I shall bide its arrival."

———

CHAPTER XIV.

THE CONTESTED ELECTION.

VERY various, truly, are the motives by which people are swayed, as might have been demonstrated at the period, and by sundry of the persons, mentioned in these chapters. Captain Chesters' great ambition, for example, after making himself sure of being the heir-at-law to the splendid property possessed by his uncle, had nothing, apparently, nearer his heart than to be thought a man of surpassing gallantry, and also of such resistless arts and attractions as hardly any woman could be proof against.

With Sir Vaux Waldgrave it had long been a principle of action never to depart from aristocratic rules, except on the occasion of a contested election for a representative to sit in the Commons House of Parliament; and then he would beg of his lady friends, and others with whom he had influence, that they should be particularly liberal in their purchases, and gracious in their smiles, at whatever miserable shop of the town or borough whose people he was anxious to propitiate, and which a political friend might desire to have the honour of representing; the baronet uniformly telling such canvassers that their smiles would not be needed, nor their money expected, after the day of chairing, until a change of ministry, or a new return of a member to the legislature was wanted. Not a particle did the blundering baronet feel about the traditions of our parliamentary annals. He had no high or pure notions concerning the importance of having the concentrated mind and virtue of the United Kingdom for the legislation and government of Great Britain. He was a person whose poodle only jumped for lords and for ladies of high degree. Nomination, not representation, was his principle and practice, as far as his influence could extend. He perceived not that the day was approaching when boroughmongery would have to be cut up by the roots, though it might be to the extinction of the privileged orders; for that it was a far greater danger and evil to run the risk of driving to despair a high-minded, generous, and fearless people, than to encroach upon the unreasonable and long-abused trusts enjoyed by a few, and a great portion of these irresponsible, parties, as regarded being amenable to the vast majority's tribunal. Nor, as is here worthy of notice, had the stupid, obstructive Sir Vaux ever evinced greater ardour and effort for the maintenance of a bad cause, than when radicalism and the pressure for parliamentary reform were making such strides, as that even he could not remain blind to the resistless progress of public opinion; when too many sanguine people imagined that the period had arrived when a dividing line must be made between the old history of England and the new.

Then there was Peter Plumtree, with his eccentricity and his cynicism,—whose professed liberalism, as compared with that of many reformers, was as the ocean compared with the Lake of Geneva, or any other lake; and who took more from the fable which was told of a certain worthy woman than the reported arguments of many of the parliamentary orators, as set forth in the ample columns of the "Times" newspaper.

"Pay heed to me, Sir Vaux Waldgrave," said the recluse to the baronet, during the ponderous man's zealous canvass on behalf of a rabid Tory at the period alluded to above, "and hear what I have to repeat to you, as I delight to do to myself, and when I have only the deaf and dumb negress, Black Martha, for my companion; for I am going to tell you, whether you like it or no, of the excellent Mrs. Partington, and of her conduct on the occasion of the great storm of Sidmouth, said by a clever fellow to have taken place in the winter of 1824. At that date there was a mighty flood upon the town I have named; the tide rising to an incredible height; the waves rushing in upon the houses, everything being threatened with destruction. In the midst of this sublime and terrible storm, Dame Partington, who lived upon the beach, was seen at the door of her house with mop and pattens, trundling her mop, squeezing out the sea-water, and vigorously pushing away the Atlantic waves. The Atlantic was roused;

Mrs. Partington's spirit was up; but I need not inform you that the contest was unequal. The Atlantic Ocean beat Mrs. Partington hollow. She was excellent at a slop or a puddle, but she should not have meddled with the tempest. We will beat Mrs. Partington, to a certainty."

But how did Sir Vaux happen to be discussing politics with the recluse of the Red Cot, and this, too, within the walls of the sort of Hottentot's kraal of that name? The general answer to these questions is, that both of the old men had come to be swayed to this specimen of apparently good neighbourhood by motives new to them; the feeling and indulgence of which afford us grounds of greater complacency than the reader may have been inclined always to entertain towards either of the veterans. They were growing more humanized; and their sharp and intolerable points, long so prominent, had begun to be smoothed down, so that the pair were able to come into some measure of contact, without either of them sustaining injury from the other; and, in fact, to the amelioration and taming of both.

To this salutary and agreeable result, it is pleasant to record, that the consideration of our heroine, the governess's misfortunes, together with the benign influence which her sweetness exerted upon the ruggedness of the two, had worked to this end; there being also other feelings and ideas associated with the maiden's history and brief appearance before them which operated to a like issue. Of a vision that was so beautiful, so gentle, and ingenuous, yet so remarkably the victim of misfortune and wrong, who could think without such tenderness, sympathy, and affection, as must have softened the heart, and been to those who experienced the emotions a source of conscious improvement and self-approbation? Upon the eccentric and often misanthropic owner of the Red Cot, the poor girl's conjectured antecedents and ascertained vicissitudes had a most manifest effect; producing deeper impressions the longer he pondered on the past, especially after she had vanished from his sight, perhaps never again to gladden his eyes with her presence, or to fill his ears with sounds which spoke to his very soul of her innocence, sufferings, and dangers.

So marked was the change in the old man's manner, that no longer was he the growling and laconic Plumtree,—harsh and sour,—but frequently communicative and companionable; not only conversing freely with those persons that repaired to him from the neighbouring town with such articles as his necessities and tastes required, but sometimes walking thither, as if to enjoy some measure of society. On all such occasions, however, the fate and misfortunes of the homeless young lady, to whom he had so opportunely and humanely afforded an asylum, were the principal themes of his discourse and fervently-expressed anxieties; one of his objects in thus conducting himself appearing to be the hope that the publicity of such a monied man's interest and concern in her behalf might lead to a discovery of her; after which he was resolved that she should not readily be allowed again to fling herself upon

CAPTAIN CHESTERS.

the cold world. Frequently, on these communicative occasions, did he speak with fairness and indulgence of Sir Vaux Waldgrave's conduct towards the young lady; remembering how candid and exculpatory her representations had been relative to the baronet; nor often did he fail to express a desire that the owner of Wartham Hall should afford him an opportunity to have a talk concerning the maiden, in whose history and descent he, Peter Plumtree, believed himself to have a deeply endeared concern.

At length this unlooked-for revolution in the manner and sentiments of him who had hitherto been generally regarded as the misanthropic and bitter-hearted recluse of the Red Cot, came to be reported to his neighbour, Sir Vaux, whose electioneering condescension had brought him into the periodical fit of familiarity with the owners of the adjacent town and district. The

opportunity was too precious to be lost upon the baronet, who trusted, if his eloquence could not win over to the Tory and borough-mongering cause the cynical Plumtree, that it might at least neutralize his vote; believing that, as a thorough-going Radical, Peter would be nearly as hostile to a Whig candidate as to a more openly-confessed Conservative. Or, if the baronet could not thus far succeed as to restrain the recluse from voting at all, his hope was that a chance would be afforded for cultivating an acquaintanceship with the owner of the Red Cot as should terminate in such a disposal of his intrusive wedge of land, as would, after his decease, render it an integral portion of the Wartham estate.

We have already obtained some knowledge of the turn which Peter Plumtree's political doctrine took in his discourse to the condescending Sir Vaux, who had walked over to his eccentric neighbour to talk with him concerning certain of the great questions of the day; the owner of the Red Cot receiving the frothy baronet with a courtesy and communicativeness, which went considerably beyond the great man's most sanguine expectations. However, the recluse was as staunch in his liberalism as ever; only going so far to please Sir Vaux as to declare that since the Whig candidate would not, any more than a Tory one, pledge himself to advocate the cause of the ballot, and the other radical alterations generally insisted upon by those who went to the root of the evils of our political system, by a process of extirpation rather than half-and-half reforms, he would keep wholly aloof from both, and not vote at all.

"Thus," cried the cynic, "I'll keep my hands clean from both factions, who to me are but as six and half-a-dozen; leaving it to those who are their supporters to answer to their consciences, to their country for the time being, and to posterity, for having incurred the guilt of upholding with their eyes open the grossest of anomalies and the most shameless of evils. But," continued the old man, after a short pause, "as we, Sir Vaux, are not likely to agree on this subject, let me direct you to another of a very different character, on which I have recently grown more interested than concerning the several demerits of Whiggism and Toryism. You can do me a service, without any very serious sacrifice being made on your part; nor shall I be slow to make you an adequate return for the kindness."

"Speak but the word, Mr. Plumtree," answered the baronet, "and you will have, I doubt not, what you desire. What a pity it is that we have lived so long, almost within the hearing of one another's voices, without having any just and proper mutual understanding! But the anomaly must no longer be allowed an existence. Speak, neighbour, and I will lend respectful heed."

"Not very many months back, Sir Vaux Waldgrave,"—thus courteously, yet gravely, commenced the recluse,—"I earned from the generous and ingenuous gratitude of a homeless wanderer the title of the good or rather eccentric Samaritan, although the benefit I reaped in return, and the revolution which was the consequence of my conduct on that occasion in my feelings and prospects, has far exceeded any stretch of humanity I made or could have testified to the poor, but dear creature. In fact, it was a tender, gentle, but destitute young female whom I took in and fostered; a voluntary fugitive from Wartham Hall, on finding that its hospitalities were no longer tenable by or due to her."

"What! the lovely and distracted Adelaide? Was it she who obtained shelter and kindness in your Cot, Mr. Plumtree?" exclaimed and eagerly inquired the baronet. "I thought that a worthy young kinsman of mine made diligent search for the misused damsel in these woods, far and near, and even at your very door, Mr. Plumtree; but, to his great grief, he received no tidings of the beautiful maiden, and went to a highly responsible and lucrative situation in India, fearing that she was lost to him, and perhaps as respected herself, for ever."

"The dark and bitter spirit to you and yours, Sir Vaux, was within me when the young gentleman approached my threshold," replied the recluse with a deep sigh. "I drove him angrily away, but have deeply regretted my rudeness ever since; the young lady having revealed to me how Mr. Mildmay rushed to her deliverance at the Cauldron Cliff,—of which exploit I was an eye-witness,—but without knowing who the noble adventurer was, or having the power to recognise him at any future period."

"Ah! then you know the unfortunate Adelaide's entire story," observed the baronet, "to which, however, I have but lately come to pay sufficient heed, or about which to experience due sympathy. There has been another of the sex, of a different age and stamp, who, with her importunities to Wartham Hall, give me occupation enough, and not always of the most pleasant sort. Since ridding myself of the plague, however, I have thought not seldom or slightly of the poor fugitive. Would she not be a great accession to me now, so sensible and quiet was the innocent? I would make her my gentle secretary; and, perhaps, along with Montague Mildmay, excellent boy, she might yet inherit all that I possess which can be at my free disposal."

"I urged upon the dear, unhappy maiden that she would consent to become my adopted," fervently cried the recluse, impatient at the colder and more selfish tone of the baronet. "But the heroine answered that it was necessary, in order to merit the good opinion and love of others, as also to securing her own self-approval, that one so suddenly pitched from an elevated station to a state of poverty and disclaimed relationship, should prove her readiness to encounter trials and toil, that she might be worthily reinstated in the estimation of those with whom she had imagined herself born to associate by a hereditary right. Oh! Sir Vaux, it was beautiful and touching to find with what self-devotion and bravery she insisted on my letting her powers and resolves be put to the test,—most willing and magnanimous to me, at least,—who have found reason to believe that her claims upon my innermost and permanent affections are of the tenderest kind."

"Why, she is not your real daughter, legitimate or otherwise, Mr. Plumtree?" bluntly said the bulky neighbour of the recluse.

"No, neither, Sir Vaux; but endeared to me by recollections belonging to a period far prior to the date of her birth, and to a person who could not possibly be her parent," was the earnest answer returned by the mysterious Samaritan.

"Then I am quite out with my guessings. Mr. Plumtree," replied the baronet. "Be so good as to inform me how it is that I may do you service, according to your wish expressed a little ago."

"It is still in relation to the interesting young lady of whom we have been speaking that I have to talk," said the recluse, "of all whose conversations, whilst she was an inmate of this Cot, I have a lively recollection. In the course of these conversations, she several times mentioned that, on hastily quitting Wartham Hall, even as if she had been a guilty and hunted thing, she in her haste and alarm left behind her certain little property in the shape of clothing and dress, of which, Sir Vaux, I should like to become the keeper, I being in some hope that I may yet be able to restore the same to the poor girl."

"And is this all you have to solicit, neighbour, from Sir Vaux Waldgrave, in behalf of the ill-fated and beautiful damsel?" inquired the baronet, as if astonished at the smallness and simplicity of the request.

"Not exactly all, sir," returned old Peter; "for the young lady stated there was a miniature portrait in the bundle of some one which she was said to resemble, and upon which she set a value far beyond what it was really worth, —having intended to carry it off with her from her chamber at the Hall,—a sort of heir-loom, she added with a modest smile, as she was led to believe; and this is the article, above all others, the custody of which I covet."

"I regret to think, Mr. Plumtree," Sir Vaux observed, "that your delicacy should have prevented you, long ere this, from making known to me your mind in respect of the things mentioned. You shall have them this very day, through the hands of one of my servants, or, if you prefer it, send your speechless domestic with me to the Hall, and I shall see that she receives the bundle just as it was left by the young owner; for so pointed and particular am I, that I locked, by the application of my own fingers, the door of the chamber referred to, the moment that I was informed its distracted inmate had hurriedly deserted it; resolved that no human creature for a time still to come should touch the articles therein found without my authority and directions. I am a man of punctilio and propriety, good neighbour; and have often had occasion to be pleased with the orderly habits which I uniformly enforce among my servants and dependants."

"Your care and delicacy in relation to the fair fugitive's little property," said the recluse, "command my thanks and admiration. With what impatience and agitation shall I await the arrival of the portrait!" the old man ejaculated, as if unaware of any one being witness of his deep excitement. "There is a strong presentiment within me that I am about to behold the perfect likeness of one who in her bloom I loved as few have ever done, I am persuaded,—of one, whose very image the forlorn innocent we have been speaking of showed to me an exquisite living copy. You wonder and perhaps laugh at hearing an old uncouth man thus talk, Sir Vaux; but the indelible idea is within me, which has coloured my life, even to the day that now is, serving to make me much of that which I really am, nor can I belie myself."

The baronet wondered that any person of years could be thus faithful to early memories, —he whose enthusiasm had never gone beyond dulness and self-love. And yet he could not but be in a measure struck on witnessing such devotedness of principle and constancy of affection, especially when expressed in a manner that was manly and polished; the exhibition raising the recluse in his favour an additional degree to what he had yet attained. But there was a point to which Sir Vaux was wish-

ful to bring his neighbour before they separated, yet how to go about the delicate subject the clumsy thinker and circuitous talker did not well know, unless he betook himself to a little insincerity. At last, he drove towards the matter in contemplation.

"The interest, Mr. Plumtree, which you have taken, and do still take, in the beautiful creature of whom we have been speaking for some time," said Sir Vaux, "is most praiseworthy and probative of your humanity. When she again casts up, as I doubt not she will, I trust, if I am then still your neighbour, that you will bring her and me together, in order that I may testify my regard towards her by some substantial tokens, although I am aware that, as your adopted daughter, she will be far above my charitable intentions. However, my young kinsman, Montague Mildmay, of Mildmay Park, may be within our ready reach at the time; nay, what is more, the partiality, the warm admiration, which he at a first glance entertained for the beauty, may, by the contemplated period, have ripened into an ardent fancy and eager attachment; for, unlike some, he regards a rationally founded love rather than aristocratic descent or lineage. What if he should propose for the damsel's hand! What if I should make him my successor and heir in respect of all I can dispose of! What if, by my unworthy nephew's prior decease to mine, Montague should legally lay claim to Wartham Hall, as in the case of his survival of me and Ludlow Chesters,—both dying childless,—he would rightfully do! Why, in these circumstances, having united himself to your adopted daughter, Mr. Plumtree, your property would become united to what I own in the shape of houses and land, under one owner. The acres which we now look upon would become an integral portion of the almost enclosing ancestral estate of the Waldgraves. The children of Montague and Adelaide would represent yourself as well as me; nor longer could there be an obstacle to the good neighbourhood of the owner of the Red Cot and the lord of Wartham Hall, for they would be identical."

"Just so," returned the recluse courteously, unwilling to display his repugnance to the idea of his wedge of land ever becoming an integral portion of the adjacent grand estate, unless it were under one and the same head-proprietor; "just so, should all the contingencies occur as you fondly picture them, Sir Vaux. Meanwhile, it is to the immediate and tangible that we have to look, which will naturally become the surer the oftener that you and I meet and carry ourselves as we have this day done. The sorely-tried innocent of whom we have been talking, will, I sincerely hope, be yet the mistress of the Red Cot and the few adjacent acres belonging thereto; Mildmay, I trust, will wed her some day; and then there may not, perhaps, be many obstacles to their inheriting, in harmony and union, one of the noblest estates which serve to give renown to Yorkshire."

The baronet now departed for his home, not clearly seeing whether he should be pleased or disappointed with regard to what had passed between him and the owner of the Red Cot.

He could not, upon reflection, but find that any benefit or advantage he had obtained was slender in a worldly sense, however much the recluse had risen in his estimation, as a man of intelligence, right-heartedness, and courteous bearing. He could not but respect the neighbour who had been so long regarded as a cynic and misanthropist; and having at length consigned to the keeping of mute Martha the bundle already repeatedly alluded to, he resolved on cultivating to some extent the intimacy of his eccentric neighbour in future.

"It is well," said the recluse to himself, as his eager eye caught the first glimpse of the negress, on her return from the lordly Hall, with a large bundle under her sable arm,—"it is well that she has neither ears to hear, nor a mouth to speak; otherwise how might she report of the behaviour of the old man to whom she is bringing the gear;" the soliloquist trembling from head to foot as he spoke.

"Oh! not here; not in the open field, must the things be opened out," continued he, as he began to withdraw to the privacy of his home and favourite chamber. "Should it prove to be *the portrait*, I shall be torn between sweet and woful memories,—I shall never be able to forgive myself for letting the image, the perfect likeness, of the long and sorrowfully remembered one depart from my loving care. Strange! that this old heart of mine will never freeze wholly over, or become icy throughout. It still would cling to my kind,—the gentle, the confiding,—even after having been seared by the faithless one, and embittered by disappointment. But why rave about the past, when so much promises to be coming near? Hither, at your utmost speed, Martha," he next shouted, when near to his porch, as if the docile, obedient creature heard every syllable her master uttered. But to the deaf and dumb one the sounds of Peter Plumtree's voice were not needed. The swing of his arm, the pointed finger, the lip's motion,—nay, the very posture of the body and the glance of the eye,—conveyed a language. She hurried forward; with an anxious smile and a humble curtsey she put the bulky parcel in the old man's hands; and as he rushed with it into his room, and shut the door behind him, the negress believed there was to be borne within that domestic sanctuary such trouble of mind as she had undergone when sold into slavery, and also such hopes and joys experienced, as when her rugged master made her free.

CHAPTER XV.

THE NATIONAL CONTRAST.

FEW things are more difficult and rare in the world than for the self-seeking to comprehend the motives of the ingenuous and generous. The devotedness of the high-principled and the good to known duty, because it is duty, and their zeal in the culture of virtue for its own sake, are little appreciated by the mass of mankind, whose general standard of conduct is not at all lofty or greatly enlightened. To

execute the offices of a teacher of the young, —assuredly a noble as well as an exacting mission,—and to do this with a main eye to the fullest lasting benefit possible of the taught, must be an exalting vocation. To surmount the slowness of the dull, and to stimulate the backward or indolent; to overcome and cure the crossness of the perverse; and to encounter triumphantly the rudeness of the robust and mischievous, must require no small measure of patience and judgment. Indeed, one can hardly conceive that a young and sensitive creature of Miss Neville's education and refinement could have conducted these several processes of training, at one and the same time, as in truth was her task at Puffendorff House, month after month, unless she had been supported in the course of her harassing efforts both by a conviction that she was making some progress in the earnest and benign work, and also by the consciousness that her mind was acquiring firmness and enlightenment meanwhile, so as to fit her for meeting, with composure, greater exactions, perhaps, at some future period. And yet, when it is said that she had to contend with the dulness of Emily, the perversity of Eliza, and the boisterous, often the malicious, coarseness of Charles, the youngest of her pupils, at the gorgeous and gaudy mansion of the Dutchman's widow,— the whole, and perhaps the most teazing, of her annoyances have not been specified; for the vulgar tyranny and ignorance of the mother, the still more intolerable overbearing of her deputy,—the all but brutal housekeeper,—and the disparagement of the ever ill-speaking Gorewell, have not been mentioned.

Better than six months had gone, during which the young lady had to maintain a calm conflict on her side with all these complicated evils and multiplied contrarieties. To this ordeal were also added the misrepresentations and detractions of such of the domestics as wished to gain by base means the favour of housekeeper and mistress; the exemplary conduct of the beautiful governess being a continual reproof to the envious servants. During the six months the young people had made most indifferent advancement in the plainest branches of school education, and still less in respect of their moral improvement. How could they, when the mother almost daily pronounced in a fault-finding tone, in presence of her children, too, that she would not have her Emily goaded forward beyond her powers,—nor her Eliza crossed and contradicted out of season, which included all seasons,—nor have the noble spirit of her boy broken? And yet amelioration was about to set in amongst these spoiled and till now ill-bred pupils. The gentleness, the perseverance, and the earnestness of the teacher, could not always escape the notice of the girls, nor of the robust boy. They began to feel that they made surest of their own inward approbation when they studied to earn that of the governess.

"I will do my best, were it but to please you, Miss Neville," cried Emily, the elder girl, one day, throwing her arms around the young lady's neck, and shedding a soft tear at the time.

"I have wounded your feelings many a day,"

ejaculated Eliza, a week or two after she had witnessed what joy it communicated to the governess when the sister affectionately embraced her, and avowed her docile resolution. "Oh! it has cut me to the heart to see your fair young face have traces of tears upon it, well aware sometimes that these had been shed on my account. Yet so perverse would I continue that rather than own my pain and grief, I persisted in my wickedness, just as if some wicked being had chained me to it, and kept me in a horrid bondage. Now, however, I feel as if I were free, and I am resolved to continue so. Neither shall Charles be allowed to be rebellious, otherwise sister and I will shun him, as we should do bad company and wicked boys anywhere."

"I'll not taste the good wine, but the sour gooseberry along with Miss Neville, mamma, if ye continue to poison her with such stuff," cried Charlie, some month or so after Eliza's striking confession,—the mother, her young people, and the governess being the only persons at the dinner-table on the occasion. "Why should I not stand up bravely for her, when most others are so hard on the other side? Yes, I'll be her champion, because she has striven to do so much for me without complaining, and because she is so delicate and helpless."

Could sweeter incense have been poured into the ear of the anxious governess than what came from the candour of the awakened boy? And did she not on the instant say to herself, "I have now something fit to be communicated to the eccentric Samaritan of the Red Cot?" Yet the night of the day on which Charles Puffendorff talked so gallantly was not allowed to darken down without the vulgar mother finding occasion to have her pitiful revenge upon the young lady, in order, as she expressed herself to the backbiting and vituperative Lady Gorewell, "that the proud wench might not be lifted higher in her own esteem by the young people's idle chatter."

Poor Adelaide forbore to drop a line to the true-hearted Peter Plumtree, having nothing to record, on second thoughts, upon which she could very warmly congratulate herself; although from this date her satisfaction in contemplating the progress and amended manners of her pupils continued to increase, affording her a never-failing antidote to much of the pain she was otherwise made to endure. Little happiness, indeed, did she experience, save while in the school-room and actively engaged in her efforts to advance them in their education, or in aiding the development of the nascent minds with the tenderest care. The elder girl had at length become an expert scholar on the pianoforte, and her practisings afforded pleasure to the often fatigued teacher; while the tacit, if not always expressed, approbation of the female visitors, who sometimes listened to the pupils' performance, yielded additional encouragement. Lady Lymington was the warmest, the most frequent and discriminating of such parties; and although Adelaide felt that it would not be safe to repose in her any particular confidence, yet she was always rejoiced to see her in the school-room, for then the tongues of the vulgar, ignorant mother, and of the bitter-spirited Gorewell, were mostly hushed.

Miss Neville had no friends, no companions at any time within Puffendorff House, unless, indeed, her female pupils were to be excepted, who were gradually growing more and more worthy of her. Seldom was she ever formally introduced to any of the feasting people who patronised the table of the Dutchman's *vrouw*; not often, indeed, was she deemed fit either for dining or drawing-room on these gourmandizing occasions, being consigned to the school or her sleeping apartment, where an unsavoury and sometimes meagre meal would be put before her. She had no followers; for had she wished for any such, they would have been peremptorily forbidden to approach the mansion; Lady Gorewell having haughtily put the question, "What need or right had a governess for friends or associates, seeing that her proper place is the school-room, unless she make herself useful in her mistress's dressing-closet, or at times in the laundry and kitchen?" Need it be wondered at, in these circumstances, that her health began to give way through the toil, the anxiety, and the positive misusage to which she was subjected,—counting the almost hermetical confinement within doors amongst her hardships?

"You will lose, by absolutely killing her, that almost unparalleled young lady, the governess of your children, Mrs. Puffendorff," indignantly said Lady Lymington to the uncultivated tyrant, and also in the hearing of Gorewell; "unless you allow her abundance of relaxation during the kindly weather that is coming on. And by killing her, independently of the guilt you will incur for the cruelty, your young people will lose the best directress, and the most affectionately-considerate friend, they probably will ever meet with. For shame's sake, immure her not longer as you have been doing; there are people in whose good opinion you desire to stand well, and who have feasted sumptuously at your board, who already have taken note of the declining girl. Think you that the charming, gifted young creature does not love life, and some of its most innocent enjoyments? Rather than see her die a slow, consumptive death, I'll take her to my own home, and have the pride and honour, perhaps, of assisting in her restoration to health—ay, and to the rank to which she properly belongs; unless, indeed, as she has ever hitherto done, when I attempted an advance in her confidence, she positively refuse, from sheer prostration of spirit, my proffered good offices. You have my warning; it may not be too late to act in conformity with it."

The lady had spoken with much more than her usual candour and firmness. Fortunately, it happened also that her two auditors were not without some fears of the kind expressed by her. They were startled; at least the alarm came home with some force to the convictions of the Dutchman's widow. She promised relaxation and daily exercise in the neighbouring park and gardens for her young people and the oppressed governess, to whom there was thus opened out a new phase, peradventure, in her diversified history.

It was as a young bird loves to poise upon its feeble pinions that poor Adelaide found herself almost daily among the sweets of nature and the beauties of early summer. Her health mended apace, her spirit acquired much of its wonted sedate vigour, and her face assumed its proper bloom,—her figure its perfect gracefulness. She remained not long a total stranger to one especially, who was of her own sex, in whom she began to take a lively interest, as well as in the increasing attachment of her girlish pupils; the new acquaintance occupying also the position of governess to one young lady.

Charlotte Vernet was French, not only in respect of birthplace and upbringing, but by descent, she could not tell how far back. Nor could there be well conceived anywhere a more striking national contrast than existed between the manner and appearance of these two governesses; she of whom we have hitherto been hearing so much being cast apparently in as perfect an English mould as the other was Gallican. The deportment of her who was of pure British origin,—as would readily have been pronounced,—was at once quiet, grave, and graceful; while the bearing and air of her who was of foreign family were animated, tripping, and as if carefully careless. The contrast extended to the very cut and colours of their dress; that of Adelaide being chastely neat, with few differences of shade, and nothing of what was dazzling; Charlotte's, on the other hand, having the gaiety, in fact, much of the splendour, of the tulip; yet, in spite of the diversity, there being a striking harmony throughout the complete array. The qualities of our heroine have been sufficiently indicated in preceding chapters; and to the delineation of the French damsel it may be enough here to add, that although volatile, she was kind-hearted, and also that she was a pretty, light-feathered thing, from whom all strong emotions trickled off like rain-drops from a duck's back and wings,—a creature that paid heed to nothing but what was uppermost at the time, and as regulated either by convenience or conventionalities.

It was not alone that Charlotte Vernet was a sprightly vivid girl, by the side of whom it was impossible, in a public garden, to be seated many minutes without entering into conversation with her, or even that the ease and accuracy with which Miss Neville spoke French to her pupils, as they frolicked around, caught the attention of the foreign maiden. Something was said and passed on the part of the more volatile damsel, in one of her addresses to the lady who was the subject of her immediate care, which powerfully arrested the notice of poor Adelaide, rendering her forward to enter into discourse with the lively stranger.

"Vat vill Lady Waldgrave say, should you, Miss Villiers, be prisoned for pulling de flowers of Kensington Garden?" cried Mademoiselle Vernet to her pupil, as the joyous girl came up to her governess with a nosegay plucked from certain neighbouring shrubs. "As vell be at Vartam Hall altogeder, as do damage here. Yonder green-coated keepers vill be no better dan de horrid Sair Vaux himself."

There was enough in these few utterances to excite our heroine's closest attention, and to

prompt her to inquiry; she taking care, however, neither to betray her throbbing anxiety, or in any way to discover herself as the young individual whose strange vicissitude at Wartham Hall, her flight, and disappearance, must have been, she doubted not, standard themes of gossip and speculation at the bulky baronet's provincial seat.

The rapidity and accuracy with which the light-hearted Charlotte went over whatever she knew or imagined relative to the people and the more remarkable occurrences in Yorkshire already mentioned in these chapters,—the girl being the very individual whom Lady Clementina imported to Wartham as French governess to her daughter,—soon put Miss Neville in full possession of all with which the reader of our story is yet acquainted, down to the departure and legal separation of Sir Vaux and his spouse,—the latter, as told above, having established herself in a handsome villa near to Kensington Gardens. The scene in which Captain Chesters so adroitly figured, and which led immediately to the severance of the wedded fools,—with all its curious details,—was admirably depicted by Mademoiselle Vernet; her glee being stirred the more in consequence of Lady Waldgrave having grown far happier in herself, and much more tolerant to those under her, ever since she had withdrawn herself from the blundering Sir Vaux.

"I be joyous now," cried Charlotte, as a pendant to her spirited, and, in many parts, satirical rehearsal. "I've got clean away from de horrid Yorkshire Monsieur, and have only to valk into Kensington Gardens, or de park, ven de day is bright and fine, to see de company dat be dere,—de sweet ladies and fine gentlemans. Yet I'd never be downcast as some,—ay, most of de English governesses be, —ven got into bad place. Mope, mope, cry, cry, look solemn and sorrowful—dat be your mode, and foolish, ma chere. Bah! it not my manner,—not de French mode. I make joy in spite of sorrow,—am mostly gay,—but happier the kindlier treated. If unkindly, I kick back; am not in reason called to kill myself to please anybody. Do moche as I can for de good,—as little as possible for de bad. Fag, fag, vont do for Charlotte. Meet gratitude for your good teaching wid gratitude, but de ignorant and vulgar wid contempt; and de less done for such de better."

" 'Tis an easy system, young lady, which you profess to follow," quietly observed poor Adelaide; "but it does not fulfil, I think, the calls of duty, at least to one's pupils; neither, certainly, as regards the doctrine that we are not to return evil for evil, a forbiddance which applies in all cases,—to our conduct towards unreasonable and harsh parents of pupils, as well as to provoking pupils themselves. In a word, your theory appears to me, sister-labourer, to be objectionable."

"Very vell,—all people to deir own vays," gaily replied Mademoiselle Vernet. "Fag, fag; cry, and look pale; kill yourself for de senseless, after feeding deir children wid de very best parts of yourself,—de knowledge of your head, and de emotions of your heart; kill yourself, and be put into de noisome grave before your time,—before you have half enjoyed de;

and vat man or voman is de better for your being de worse? Der be no tanks in de end from anybody. Bah! I do de best dat I can, according to circumstances, or as most oder people do; never forgetting to be gay, to make myself happy, to laugh rader than cry, and to grow fat, as you see, *ma chere*, that I am. But ha! vat do I behold? De handsome Captain Chesters, dat climbed by rope-ladder into my Lady Valdgrave's room under cloud of night, comes our way. Proud am I dat I figure in silk, muslin, and blonde, wid my bijouterie about me, and vinaigrette to de bargain."

While the lively young Frenchwoman ran on in this latter fashion, Miss Neville, not slightly agitated, had called her pupils to her, and was off with them as quickly as a smart walk could conduct her. But she could not outstep Mademoiselle Vernet's pace, who, with a mingled love for adventure and perfect modesty, was calling after the fugitive; blending her cries with a charge of ungraciousness, and also an assurance that their routes must be one and the same.

It was of no avail that poor Adelaide attempted to increase her speed, in order to escape the pursuit of the livelier governess. It equally failed of outwitting or distancing the quick-eyed and striding Life-Guardsman, that the French girl affected to pull the English one behind a clump of shrubs, as if to have themselves screened from their handsome and dashingly-attired follower. A few minutes, or rather moments, served to bring the gentleman to where they stood; Miss Neville's only resource and kind of refuge now being a veil which she drew over her face, at the same time bounding away, with one of her pupils on each side, whom she held by their hands, as if they had been her only protectors against impending, direful danger. But the joyous Charlotte, with her charge, was again at her heels, venting smart and half-upbraiding sentences, thrown at the alarmed one, interlarded with assurances that it was only the gallant Captain Chesters, "the friend and indeed the admirer of Lady Waldgrave," she added.

"Yes, the friend and admirer of Lady Waldgrave, and of all the sex," was the Life-Guardsman's first uttered observation, taking up the shouted words of the pertinacious Charlotte;—"all the sex of a surety," he added, "but of none half so much as of Mademoiselle Vernet, the unparalleled little French brunette, who won his heart at Wartham Hall."

By this time the Honourable Ludlow was abreast of the sprightly governess, saying pretty things to her pupil as well as to herself; his visits to Lady Waldgrave at her suburban residence having put him on terms almost of familiarity with the young people. His eye, however, restricted not its glances to those he verbally addressed, but was eagerly cast forward, scanning the figure and gait of her with the throbbing brow, who was doing her utmost to escape attentions which, without daring to throw a look behind, she felt assured were keenly directed towards her. Indeed, the sounds which reached her ear, almost instantly on his coming up to the gay Charlotte, left our heroine no room for doubt; these

sounds consisting not only of his tread upon the ground close to her heels, but of questions pointedly put to the breezy-voiced brunette concerning her adult companion.

"A sister-governess, of de English breed, yet speaks French as vell as I myself do," was the answer.

"Speaks French as well as you do, Mademoiselle, and yet a countrywoman of my own fatherland!" returned the Life-Guardsman, in a tone of some surprise. "The accomplishment is not common with English people; and yet no doubt you have correctly reported, my charmer, for you must be a competent judge in relation to the matter. I wish you would, my dear, introduce me to the young lady."

"Vy, dat is de ting you ought to do for yourself, Captain Chesters, just as I did for myself, a little time back," replied the brunette. "It is a very easy business, at least I find it soche, ven I desire to learn anyting about anybody from deir own lips. I made friends in a moment; and told her soche a long and clever story about your own honourable self, ven you climbed into my Lady Valdgrave's room at Vartham Hall, dat she vas delighted. In fact, she seemed vonderfully interested on de subject, and had many questions to put to me."

"Perhaps the young lady is acquainted with the place, and also with sundry of the people of whom you must have talked, Mademoiselle," the captain remarked with increasing earnestness, judging from the tones of his voice. "I must accost her, and become more assured of her identity than I yet am, although my first conjectures have been fast gathering strength."

Having thus spoken, he began to step forward at such a pace as would in a few moments bring him in advance of the young lady. At the same instant, however, poor Adelaide had gained the gate which led to the parterre in front of Puffendorff House. Hurriedly she flung the iron-work open; but yet not so speedily as to prevent the audacious Life-Guardsman from lifting up her veil, and discovering to a certainty who was its wearer.

"My lovely Adelaide, after all; I made sure of some day falling in with you in the course of my rounds amongst the beauties of the metropolis," said he, and in a voice so loud and gratified, that the words reached the ears of the Dutchman's overbearing widow, and also of Lady Gorewell, both of whom happened to be seated at an open window of the gorgeous mansion that commanded a near view of the gate at which the libertine's rudeness had exercised itself.

"Witnessed you ever the like of that?" cried Lady Gorewell, on perceiving how the captain had conducted himself, drinking greedily in every syllable he uttered. "I always thought the damsel could be no better than she ought, in spite of all her wondrous modesty and patience. It was clear to me as the light of noonday, that she would never have allowed her superior accomplishments,—as hers in truth must be regarded,—to be employed upon young folks in the circumstances of your's, my dear Mrs. Puffendorff, and for the salary you allow her, unless there were some fatal flaw in her character,—some bygone breaking down of a nameless character. Oh, the minx!"

"And my Adelaide, too!" exclaimed the Dutchman's widow. "She has, depend upon it, been the kept mistress of the handsome gentleman who so freely yet gracefully lifted her veil, or at least of some one of his companions. What a cheek must the wench have had to put her nose into a house like mine, and to be with her pollutions so near to my dear and spotless young folks. But I'll cheek and nose her; for this minute shall she be arraigned and condemned by me, who well can do both, I trow, when my spirit is up."

"Better not let the spirit be up too quickly, lest it be a wicked one; or, if ye care not whether it be of evil or good and honest birth, bethink you, Mrs. Puffendorff, that it is possible ye may come off second best," were the terms of advice and caution which Lady Lymington interposed, she having entered the apartment where the abusive pair were seated without their noticing her approach, and having heard what was said by the frothy *vrouw*.

"What!" exclaimed the Lady Gorewell; "would you have, Lymington?"—the speaker thinking she had now an excellent opportunity of achieving a triumph over her titled acquaintance,—"would you have our excellent and distinguished friend here to become the subject of all Kensington's talk,—to be mocked on account of alleged gullibility,—to have her splendid mansion represented as the receptacle for gentlemen's cast-off mistresses? Impossible! you cannot wish or intend all this, my Lady Lymington!"

"No; but I do intend to speak within the bounds of reason," returned the other; "and should you two do so rashly as to act in the way threatened, then my wish is to be present when you arraign Miss Neville, that I may enjoy your more thorough discomfiture by the remarkable young lady, than I have ever yet known you to sustain at her hands."

CHAPTER XVI.

THE MINIATURE'S MYSTERY.

"A word with you, if you please, Captain Chesters. Where and when will you give me an opportunity of talking with your honour on a matter of great importance to you?" were the terms in which a rough, weather-beaten fellow addressed the Life-Guardsman, as he was about to enter his club-house, on returning in a highly gleeful mood from Kensington, immediately after offering the insult to the young governess described at the close of the last chapter.

"Who are you? I know nothing of you," was the captain's returned salute.

"You may never have noticed me, sir, although I have frequently of late had my eyes upon and towards you. I dare say, however, that you have oftener thought of my services in your favour than of some better dressed people," replied the fellow. "My name is Jobson,—Jared Jobson, as I call myself,—who, when I was hard up, as I happen to be just now, did

a clever thing at Wartham Hall, to the confusion of certain folks, whom you would remember at once, were they as close to you as I am at this moment; a certain pretty young girl being of the number."

"The same that you robbed, and have incurred the penalty of hanging for so doing, as old Peter Plumtree has at length made notorious,—a fact I learned when last in the neighbourhood of Wartham Hall," said Chesters, offended at the tone and manner of the ruffian. "If you consult your interest you will make yourself scarce, for I know where to find the girl you fleeced of her money and trinkets; and I should think she will not be backward to appear against you."

"You know where to find the girl I fleeced of her money and jewels? and so do I," with imperturbable audacity answered the fellow. "I have even been the witness of your rudely lifting her veil a little while ago, for I have had my peepers upon you ever since you started to prowl for game in Kensington Gardens. Nay, more, I was not many yards away from you when you did what you thought was safe, in order to have her brains dashed out at the Cauldron Cliff. I have watched you at times, since then, when you supposed you were unmarked; as, for example, when you rope-laddered your handsome self into Lady Waldgrave's apartment, in order to hurry forward the sundering of the old stupid baronet and his weak wanton wife,—the pair of idiots that they are. You were too clever for them, but are no match for me. You see, now, that I know something of your movements and tricks; for, just like myself, you have to live mostly upon your wits. Nevertheless, this is not the point for the present. I ask when and where I can have a little quiet talk with you, about a matter of the utmost importance to yourself? The sooner the better, for your interests, I assure you. Now, in a quiet corner of your club-room would be the best and wisest plan for you."

"Come this way, then," impatiently returned the Life-Guardsman, finding that the scoundrel was not readily to be shaken off, but moved chiefly by the impression that he not only had the advantage of him in certain delicate respects, but might possibly have something of moment to reveal. The gleesomeness of the Honourable Ludlow had quickly passed away; even his cheeks, which had been enlivened by his forenoon's exercise and disgraceful exploit, paled,—his heart at the same time beating in response to a very different impulse to that which a little while before lent it excitement. His embarrassment and tremor were enhanced by his unavoidable conviction that his tormentor had a perfect perception of how he was affected, looking through him, as it were, with keen and practised eyes. So annoyed and startled was the gallant Life-Guardsman at the manner in which Jobson kept his visual organs upon him, that a revengeful feeling was the result by the time they were seated in the small apartment to which they had repaired, and which was appropriated for interviews of a private nature.

"Would it not be the safest thing for me to give the villain at once into the custody of the police, and compass his hanging?" the rumi-

nating Ludlow asked himself, meeting the sharp and eager scrutiny of the ruffian with a scowl.

"Save yourself the pains, *honourable* sir, of meditating my destruction," quickly said Jobson, putting a significant emphasis upon the distinctive term, which the Life-Guardsman perfectly understood; the fellow not even speaking with a lowered voice, but rather seeming to court the hearing of third parties, to the cowing of his opposite, as the captain, with renewed embarrassment, again perceived he was clearly noted. "Save yourself the pains of meditating my destruction, by instantly having me taken up for highway, or *hedge-way*, robbery, if you like the latter better, in order to the having me hanged, and put beyond troubling you any more; for, though you were at this moment to murder me, as swiftly and surely as you made the attempt on Adelaide

No. 10.—The Governess.

Waldgrave, which I saw you actually do, it would only hurry on your ruin, which I have it in my power to accomplish or to prevent at any time, as it may suit my views; there being sealed papers, consigned by me to certain safe hands, that would unavoidably accomplish the very end which you may render it unwise for me to do. I have provided, I am kind enough to inform you, against the occurrence of any such stop being put to my *splitting*, as you were just now considering of," added the scoundrel, with the most provoking coolness, signifying by a contortion of the mouth, and a peculiar squeak, as well as a sort of circular motion of his hand round his throat, the precise and ugly kind of termination to his breathing to which his allusion was made.

Jobson felt his power over the other increasing every moment, and that now they were in a condition to proceed at once to the particular point of business he had immediately in view. In fact, the Life-Guardsman, with a different impatience than what had swayed him a few minutes earlier, urged the scoundrel towards the subject, by requesting him in a low tone of voice to state what he had to say, without any further preliminaries; making the request, also, that he would moderate his speech in respect of the key upon which it was pitched.

"Oh! very well, then, Captain Chesters; quiet as a mouse and soft as yourself, will Jared Jobson be," replied the villain. "The thing is very easily told, just as what I want can be very quickly done, I have no doubt. As to the first, the short and long is, I can either make or unmake you,—that is, heir or un-heir you, in respect of Wartham Hall, as my interest advises; secondly, I am in need of a little *blunt*, just at this particular epoch. Not a great deal, however; for I am a fellow of moderate views. You understand me. What have you to say in reply?"

"I have to say this, that I defy you; so do your worst. I am the legitimate nephew of Sir Vaux Waldgrave, and the next of kin to the childless old man; so that in spite of all the powers and villains of England I must and shall inherit his ancestral estate if I survive him. You have my answer to your first particular. In regard to the second, I suppose you will not now require any observation from me; so that your business with me is ended."

Such was Chesters' prompt and explicit answer, he rising from his chair as he pronounced the last words, intending to pull the bell, that a waiter might see to the going out of the insolent obtrusionist.

"Not so fast, captain, if you wish to avoid rashly doing the most foolish thing you ever attempted, and that is saying a great deal," quietly yet firmly said Jobson. "I do not put out my hand, however, as you see, to stop you; half-a-dozen words will do for that purpose more surely than any force of arm that I can use. You are not the nearest of living kin, in the eye of the law, to your old uncle. I am not the father of the charming Adelaide. Wilford Waldgrave's widow was an ass for what she did, when she chimed in with my story, and a still greater idiot when she poisoned herself. And yet she was not the mother of the girl you wished to murder."

"What signifies any testimony that such a fellow as Jared Jobson can advance, who, on his own showing, is capable of saying and unsaying anything any day?" observed the Life-Guardsman, resuming his seat, and thereby testifying that he was somewhat staggered by the scoundrel's statement.

"Very true and correct, captain," composedly replied Jobson. "No man, no judge, or juror, who knows anything very particularly of you or me, would believe a word that we utter, though backed by as many oaths as you and I have ever blasphemously mouthed. But it so happens facts are such very stubborn proofs, that even the villany of such fellows as Jared Jobson,—for so I name myself,—ha! ha! ha!—and the *Honourable* Ludlow Chesters, of the *noble* family of Chesters, cannot over-

come them. I have an army of such gear ready for production, in the shape of the testimony of credibly witnessed documentary exhibitions, and even of trinkets, pictures, and clothing, that belong to the person who does stand between you and Wartham Hall. A Jew creditor of your's has a considerable amount of these evidences in his hands at this moment. I seek not to terrify and torment you, for the present, about the way in which I could probably ruin you, even as to the matter of attempting to murder Adelaide, or your hitherto successful trick and strategem of sundering your stupid uncle and his giddy wife, whom a very little pains of mine might reconcile, to the production of a direct heir to the blundering baronet. I have stronger tackle to handle. Listen! Let me pour into your ear a fact on the quiet."

The fellow rose from his chair, and went round the little table that had been between the pair hitherto, and, stooping, whispered something into the auditory organ of the already alarmed Life-Guardsman. It took not half-a-dozen of seconds to communicate the matter which Jobson had to convey, but it was electrical. Up started Chesters; he smote his brow, and reseated himself again. He panted, and actually began to shed tears.

"There now; I told you that there was a way, that is, with half-a-dozen of words, to bring you to your senses," provokingly said Jared. "Woo her honourably and win her, or get her out of the way the best manner you can, to which issue I could be of service to you. The Jew knows something, but not much as yet, of what I am possessed of, and of which a part has been told to you, honourable sir. He is ready to advance you a cool five hundred or so, without much ado. Promise to let me have the half, as soon as it is forthcoming, which will be to-night, if you go hand-in-hand with me in the entire affair, and I'll leave you. Remember, that to woo and to win are important points; for Adelaide, as sure as fate, will have all old Peter Plumtree's property,— she has a right to it; and then what a complete and compact estate will Wartham Hall be, when the Red House is down, and the wedge of obtruding land that shoots to the very bottom of the memorable Cauldron Cliff, forms an integral part of one of the most enviable and lordly estates in all Yorkshire!"

"Have it in your own way, and as speedily as possible," muttered the Life-Guardsman, to whom the idea of immediately getting some two hundred and fifty pounds sterling, in hard cash, was far from disagreeable. "Come here, if possible, to-night, with Moses; I'll not quit the Club till bed-time. You'll have the best and the most that you can swallow. Good-bye, Jared; shake hands, and let us be friends."

It was nearly identical with the time at which these two unprincipled fellows were engaged in the manner just described,—the one doing all that in him lay to confound, circumvent, and mislead the other, whose consciousness of guilty deeds and depraved sentiments seem to have blunted his faculties, and rendered him the dupe of a more gifted villain,— that a very different person from either of them was not only profoundly moved in relation to the misused one who occupied the situation of governess at Puffendorff House, but resolved on steps to see her righted and restored to him, that she might enjoy all the wealth he possessed, and be unto him as a very daughter.

"It is the exact miniature of her whose image is hardly ever absent from me,—the precisely same picture that I gave to her whose sweetness and infidelity have so irrevocably transfixed my heart," groaned old Peter Plumtree, the moment he shut himself up in what to him was a sanctuary within the Red Cot, and burst open the bundle which the mute Martha brought him. "And it is scarcely less the exact portrait of the forlorn Adelaide, who has left and gone, whither I know not, that she—heroic thing—may prove herself in the judgment of the worthy who may ever be made acquainted with her story, that she was in merit equal to the rank which she seemed destined to occupy and adorn, not many hours before I did myself the truest good in taking her in to eat of my bread, and to have my roof to shelter her. Ah! precious inmate!— the very likeness,—the descendant, I am now sure beyond the shadow of a doubt, of her whom I was fated to adore, and to think of the more tenderly, the deeper she wounded me, and the longer I lamented her degradation! I must forth, and set to work, old as I am, in behalf of the living copy of her who, no doubt, has been long the tenant of the grave, in order that the mystery of this miniature finding its way to the unfortunate Adelaide may be cleared up. Yes, unfortunate still, otherwise she would have relieved my heart and her own likewise, of a burden of anxiety, by dropping me a word to say that her lines had fallen in pleasant places, and that her spirit was not dead nor dying within her."

Old Peter Plumtree was for a time to relinquish even the recently moderated habits of a recluse, and what appeared to most who knew him a still greater sacrifice and stretch, was to abandon and desert his loved Red Cot. To dispose considerately of mute Martha, was one of his preliminary proceedings, by having her removed to the society and care of a worthy family in the neighbouring small town, until his hoped-for settling down again, after having carried out some contemplated enterprise, which, although people conjectured not its precise nature or exactions, was regarded as in some way wildly romantic.

"It was remarkable enough," said the gossips, "for the old cynic to qualify his misanthropy so far as to take to travelling beyond the bounds of the Red Cot, and to seeking the society of a few ordinary folks. But to think of him quitting his home altogether upon some wild goose-chase expedition—no one can guess whither—is stranger still, and seems incredible, were it not that people are aware the eccentric man does things as no other body would think of doing; that he is not like any one else, and that among his whimsicalities, the love of mystery, and of mystifying people, is not the least prominent. We know that his late exhibitions and his new start are connected in some singular manner with the girl whose

change of position and prospects at Wartham Hall was so sudden and extraordinary; but why he should quit his home to recover her and restore her to the Red Cot, if he is acquainted with the fact as to where she is to be found,—for surely she would be but too proud to become the adopted of a veteran who is rich as a Jew; or, if he has no such knowledge of her whereabouts, why he should undertake such a toil and uncertainty of wandering at his advanced years, as to seek for her in the wide world,—even such worlds as London and Paris present to the adventurer, can only be accounted for, by supposing that either a wondrous deal of importance attaches to having the girl, or rather the young lady, brought back to the neighbourhood from which she so distractedly fled on the exposure which wrought such commotion and changes at Wartham Hall; or that Peter is growing absolutely crazy at last."

Thus did people speculate concerning old Peter Plumtree's resolves and movements, without, however, in the least disturbing the determination of one who was as self-willed as he was eccentric, and as fond of enveloping himself in mystery after mystery, as he was singularly situated. A feature in his talk, be it told, about the forlorn Adelaide, as upon other subjects relative to which he wished to keep his actual knowledge and fixed intents in a haze to the apprehension of others, was by only revealing lesser points and indulging in bewildering allusions to send their imaginations in a wrong direction, and leave them floundering into deeper and deeper perplexity the longer they strove to wade through the darkness.

And the uncouth owner of the Red Cot is off and away; nor does a soul in Yorkshire know the route he has taken. Yet, might it not reasonably be expected by the reader, that the British Babylon, the mighty metropolis of our empire, would be the vast field for his searchings and the exercise of his intense anxieties? But he had learnt from the maiden's own lips that Paris was the place of her birth and rearing, and that therefore the language of France was as familiar to her as the mother-tongue of those who stood in the position of her parents. Then, what more likely than that she had betaken herself to the city and scenes where she had spent her childish and girlish years?

Or, again, how probable that one who was to lay herself out as a governess,—being skilled in the language which is the passport to the whole of continental Europe,—what more likely than that her vocation might be in some foreign part with a travelling family, the place of whose sojourn it would be utterly idle to grope for? How far these considerations weighed with old Plumtree we do not undertake to state, neither do we say what was the amount of toil, solicitude, and expense to which he put himself while in London,—for to this centre, after all, was his face bent at the first. However, we have to record, that he never thought of exploring the courtly suburb of Kensington,—never once betook himself to its princely gardens, in the course of a wild goose-chase, and what we must here state, in our opinion, to have been as romantic an enterprise as any man of threescore and ten years of age ever undertook. It will not lessen in the mind of the reader the striking character of the veteran's adventure, when it is added that the miniature portrait which had fifty years before been painted at his request, in testimony of his love and homage to the beautiful creature who sat to the artist while the gem was produced, never was allowed to quit being close to his bosom; the crimson velvet-covered case, with its treasure, being regarded by the eccentric Peter as fondly and prized as highly as misers have done their heaps of gold.

Never once did the late recluse of the Red Cot dream of bending his anxious steps towards the quarter in which his darling Adelaide was housed. Had he, however, entertained the most distant conjecture, the slightest idea of the probability, that she was an inmate of Puffendorff House at the moment of his arrival in London; still more had he been informed that on that same day she had not only been insulted by Captain Chesters, but was the object of the gross abuse and fierce attack of the vulgar, ignorant widow in whose employment she had been for twelve months, together with the sneers and vile insinuations of the *vrouw's toady*, Lady Gorewell, we may be sure that no weariness and fatigue, no timidity or feeling of strangeness in the place and circumstances, would have hindered the eccentric Samaritan from hurrying to her defence, succour, and rescue; to the production perhaps of a scene as characteristic as any in which the old man had ever figured. Yet a drawing-room of the Dutchman's widow was not on that same day to be unconnected with certain domestic passages and incidents in the life of a governess, a record of which must serve for the completion of the present chapter.

"You wish to be present, Lady Lymington," cried the Lady Gorewell, with a toss of the head, indicating her sense of the triumphant position which she and the merchant's widow now held in relation to our heroine, immediately after they had witnessed the conduct and heard the few words of the insolent Chesters to the young lady at the gate in front of the mansion where the trio were once more met. "You wish to be present when we arraign the governess-girl, —the light-o'-love, I should rather name her, I judge,—for that your ladyship will have an opportunity of enjoying our more thorough discomfiture by the minx than you have ever yet known us to sustain at her hands. Now, not to speak a word at present respecting your taste, my lady, as respects the source and occasion of your enjoyments, I must say this, that I for one do not hold you to be a good or impartial judge concerning the said discomfitures; remembering that you have not merely always on the occasions to which you refer ranged yourself against us along with the wench, but really taken the burden of such of her arguments and fluency upon yourself as these might be on your side of the discussion. You cannot, any more than others, be impartial in our case when assuming the function of the bench. It would be wiser, I think, to abstain from arraying yourself on the side of a stranger, whose conduct and circumstances at least appear questionable, than to come to her rescue always when such well-tried personages and familiar acquaintances as Mrs. Puffendorff and myself, are sought to be outwitted or discomfited."

"I roundly contradict you, Gorewell, in regard to several things you have asserted, and also the entire tone of your statement," returned the other titled dame. "But not to trouble you for the present with anything more about your mistakes and misrepresentations in regard to myself, let me suggest a thing:—You arraign the young lady forthwith, while I conceal myself behind the sweeping drapery of the window there. I'll merely be an auditor, an unseen and unsuspected one, too, as far as regards Miss Neville's knowledge, and then I shall learn how the examination, the charge, and the trial terminate without having shared in a conflict, where it is two to one; each of the two,— to go by age and experience,—having double the strength of the single combatant. Now for it; you find that I am behind the arras."

The command at once went forth for poor Adelaide to make her appearance, the summons being conveyed by one of the widow's most obsequious and time-serving lacqueys. Only a few minutes elapsed before she made her appearance; there being no small amount of curiosity manifested by the pair to whose tribunal the young lady was cited in regard to the manner in which she would bear herself; a curiosity participated in by the concealed party who contrived to keep the others within range of her vision, although with sufficient secrecy as respected the governess.

A cloud of the deepest depression which a few moments before she entered the drawing-room had nearly overshadowed and engulfed her spirit, was, apparently in consequence of a strenuous effort and a recalled self-reliance, passing off from her lovely young face, upon which the traces of very recently dashed away tears were visible. Quickly was the gracefulness of deportment as perfect as ever, but with something added to her usual sedateness and gravity; a dignified displeasure and an immoveable resolve conferring upon her looks and air something of austerity and sense of power.

The reader will remember that when she for the first time in her life appeared before the trio, they were each more or less struck mute in presence of her faultless beauty, but still more in consequence of her high-bred mien. Now, however, the effect of manner and carriage was not only in a measure different but more commanding, making her would-be censors and judges if not to quail, at least to bethink themselves a second time how they were to address the damsel. There was accordingly a pause, and of such length, too, accompanied with obvious embarrassment, even on the part of Lady Gorewell, that she not only exchanged a look of some confusion with the big widow, but glanced in rather a curious way towards the mass of drapery which shrouded the other dame; the governess observing and construing correctly enough the perplexity of the pair who shortly before had felt themselves so competent to arraign her.

"It may be a relief to you, ladies, if I speak first, although from the reported tone in which I was cited to come hither, I expected you would not have looked to me for such a proceeding," said the young lady, in a voice that at once freed itself of all tremulousness. "Nor do I regret that you have accorded me the opportunity to take the initiative; for had you not sent for me at the moment you did, few more seconds would have been allowed to escape before I should have requested of Mrs. Puffendorff,—to whom I am alone responsible, and to whom alone I shall for the present stoop to address myself,—nay, demand of her, to grant me an audience. Yes, a brief audience, in order to require of her to fulfil her bargain with me,—that is, to pay the last quarter's amount of the thirty pounds salary, due a fortnight ago,—to pay it on the instant, for not another night shall her roof be over my head."

"There's impudence for you, from a mere governess!" cried Mrs. Puffendorff;—"a dependant, that under the pretence of bad health, contrives to get me to indulge her with daily exercise in the gardens and park, that she may go about flirting and philandering with any fellow who chooses to stoop to notice her;" the *vrouw* on thus delivering herself appearing to rise several inches in her seat, and making the large pendent snow-white feather that alternately nodded from her head and swept her coarse, empurpled cheek, do more service in these ways, than it happened to have had occasion to perform for weeks before.

Lady Gorewell bent herself towards the widow, and whispered something in her ear; but whether it was in the way of flattery and warm laudation, or of bitter suggestion, the governess could not say. However, with the view of shortening the scene and preventing the officious visitor having an opportunity of rendering it more perplexed, the resolute and aroused maiden forced the dame of the house to lend her the next hearing.

"It is, perhaps, hardly worthy of me, Mrs. Puffendorff, considering what is due from me towards myself," replied the governess, "that I should do more than repeat my demand for the overdue quarter of my year's salary, the amount of which is seven pounds ten shillings sterling; and having thus made known my determination, to retire until you have time to send me the sum, after which we shall for ever cease to be eyesores to one another, I trust. And yet, finding the superior and commanding position which I at this moment am felt to possess over you, it may not be altogether idle if I not only advance a word of self-defence, but something in the way of advice, as well as complaint and reproval. You have taunted me, Mrs. Puffendorff, and thrown out insinuations, in your characteristic manner," continued the maiden, "about my behaviour when enjoying relaxation in the open air, and also about other things which I do not condescend further to notice. This only will I say in self-defence, that the person who so insultingly treated me at your gate is of high rank by birth, is an *Honourable*, is of a noble family."

"I thought he was such, from his style and carriage," exclaimed Lady Gorewell, clapping her hands in her transport. "The case is clear; the truth will out."

"The person who so insultingly treated me at your gate, Mrs. Puffendorff, is of high rank, is an *Honourable*, is of a noble family by the paternal side," proceeded the governess, in her former quiet but decisive tone, without evinc-

ing the slightest heed to what had fallen from the meddler, or even that she so much as heard the dame's speech. "Yes, an *Honourable!* and yet a villain, who, after having aspired to make me his bride, because my prospects in life were higher and far more promising than his own,—after doing this,—he believing that his suit would be in vain, and, besides, that unless I became his wife, I should stand for ever in the way of his longed-for greatness,—the miscreant, after all this, made a deliberate and cowardly attempt upon my life, and almost succeeded in murdering me in the most appalling manner. Alas! other misfortunes soon after overtook me, one of the bitterest of which has been to find myself for more than twelve months the object of ignorant and heartless ill-treatment in this house, from persons each of them twice my age."

Tears for a moment stood in the maiden's eye, on uttering the last sentence; and a choking sensation prevented her from saying more for a few seconds. But she soon recovered her self-command, when she thus continued:—

"So much for the party whose style and carriage were so prepossessing when he grossly insulted an unoffending young creature, thereby exposing her to your merciless and uncharitable constructions. And yet I am much mistaken if the day does not come, when, heartless as you are, you will shed tears on account of your many acts of injustice heaped upon my innocent head. You have daughters of your own; and remember my words, when I tell you that, unless they fall into more considerate hands than those of yourself and your most mischievous visitor, and also of more competent as well as conscientious teachers than those that preceded me in your establishment, there is too great reason for fearing that, young as the dear girls are,—dear, I assure you, to my heart, and daily growing more akin to my otherwise unbefriended spirit, by any inmate of your house,—they will relapse into the condition, or worse, in which I at first found them. What other can be expected, when you allow yourself to be principally led by a woman whose every visit here has been felt by me, although my vision might have been lucky enough to escape beholding her, immediately after her departure, through the abuse you were at pains to heap upon me, even in the presence of your children,—abuse and wrong-doing, which, from its peculiar tenour and turn the cruelty took, I knew did not wholly emanate from your own head and heart."

"Are such insolence and shamelessness to be borne?" cried Lady Gorewell, rising from her chair in a terrible fury, and appearing inclined to apply her talons to the governess, in return for her fearless and well-grounded accusations. "Can you sit and listen to more of the wanton's effrontery?" continued the dame, appearing the next moment to think better of it than to proceed to personal violence, knowing that Lady Lymington was witness of all that passed. "It is for you, dear and insulted Mrs. Puffendorff, to act vigorously in the present predicament; let the baggage be forthwith turned out of doors, or given into the hands of an officer,"—these latter words keeping time with helping the *vrouw* from her seat to put the threatening into execution.

The effort and the advice, however, only added to the confusion of the scene; for the widow's two daughters, overhearing something of what was said by the mischievous visitor, and of what was passing, burst into the room, and throwing their arms around the governess, declared they would not only defend her with their lives, but accompany her wherever she went, if she was turned out of the house. Charles,—the once boisterous, but now tamed and docile boy,—was also there with his aroused spirit; and who, having imbibed his sisters' notions concerning the pernicious influence of the almost daily visitor, whose ill-will to our heroine was so bitter, broke out in vehement terms towards the dame; declaring that she was the plague of the family, and only came to get from his silly mother what she could not obtain at home.

The result of the interference and strenuous bearing of the young people in behalf of Miss Neville,—who retired from the scene to her own room as expeditiously as possible,—presented, on the part of the widow and her counsellor, a suitable *finale* for such characters. Both fell into strong hysterics at the same instant,—tears being testimonies of too weak a nature and semblance for ladies of feeling,—calling into requisition the services of the dame who had ensconced herself behind the arras.

CHAPTER XVII

THE EDUCATION OF GOVERNESSES.

THE governess's servitude in the mansion of the, to her, grovelling and sordid Mrs. Puffendorff, had been a period of painful experience and severe probation. Youth, with its keen feelings and soaring hopes, is the season, of all others, when afflictions fall most heavily upon the spirit. Wisely and mercifully ordained is it, that these trials should usually leave behind them, when their wounds are healed, and their sting is taken out, lessons which ripen the mind and develop the character more effectually and wholesomely, than the fortunate occurrences of many years of prosperity might have done. It was sad for our heroine to relinquish the hopes of her girlhood, and have to yield to the ungenial, the harsh and cruel authority of strangers. Yet it is doubtful that she would have been a better or more enlightened young woman had she still remained at Wartham Hall, without any obstacles having been thrown in the way of the grand prospects of her most promising and prosperous time, than she was now, on indignantly withdrawing from the roof of the ignorant and preposterous widow of the rich Dutch merchant. The presumption at least is that she would not in the apparently far more favourable position, have acquired so much practical knowledge either of herself, or of the character of others, as well as of the principles which should regulate a systematic education of females, as she felt she had done while an inmate of Puffendorff House.

It was no mean source of gratification to experience the assurance, that during the time of her residence there, she had conferred more lasting service upon the young people entrusted to her tuition, thwarted and curbed though she had been, than they ever received before. She had sown healthful and generating seed. She had striven to make her pupils acquainted with the tenderest and noblest emotions of her heart, as well as the knowledge of her head. It was a constant and pleasurable office for her, to deal more with realities than fancies,—things than mere words. Not content with lessons only as found in books, she, on all available occasions, made whatever struck the attention of the young people the subject of instructive communication; thus throwing light upon a flower, interest around a pebble, and so hallowing very many objects to them, until even they in a measure felt as if a new existence had dawned upon their minds.

Another source of poor Adelaide's solid gratification was the consciousness of making discoveries in the systematic education of her own sex, and of being, as she flattered herself,—now driven back upon her own mental resources and sagacity,—in a fair way of doing essential service to society. Her plan had begun to be formed on principles which were suggested to a naturally vigorous and well disposed mind, by a course of reflection on the attributes of the female character,—the proper position and vocation of woman in life. It contemplated the inculcation of simple and sincere piety, and the practice of the purest and soundest morality; nor did it by any means overlook the beauty and importance of the performance of all domestic duties. The sufferings experienced by herself lent a perceptible turn to her views; for she sought as one leading object, to prepare her pupils to act with energy and fortitude, in the event of their being exposed to reverses and calamity.

The profession of female teachers is nearly singular in this, that external and accidental circumstances are very generally the cause of its being adopted, while natural and acquired qualifications may or may not be present. The means which even a clever young lady possessed, at the period of our story, of fitting herself for the situation of governess,—even supposing her to have had the advantages of what is understood by a good education for a gentlewoman,—were deplorably defective.

In fact, as regarded the methods of communicating her own acquirements to others, or, in other words, the art of teaching, she was left without any recognised guide, and entirely to own ingenuity, good sense, and persevering energy. No person of right feeling could ever think of charging this against a body of females, who for the most part have proved an honour to their sex, and whose labours, in a majority of cases, take their rise in misfortune; yet the fact certainly furnishes a powerful reason why peculiar efforts should have been made long ago, for qualifying these females for the due performance of their singularly important functions.*

Heaven, in the crowning work of creation, gave woman; making weakness her strength, modesty her citadel, grace and gentleness her attributes, affection her dower, and the heart of man her throne. With her, toil rises into pleasure, joy fills the heart with a larger benediction, and sorrow, losing half its bitterness, is transmuted into an element of power, a discipline of goodness. Even in the coarsest life, and the most depressing circumstances, woman hath the gift of hallowing all things with the sunshine of her presence. But never does it unfold itself so finely and potently as when education, instinct with religion, has accomplished its most successful work.

If woman can mould the characters and habits of men to an indefinite extent, what may not be effected by those females who are marked out by circumstances to form the minds of those of their sex, and to direct their energies, —the minds and energies, too, of such as move in superior circles of society, and are looked up to by those in humble positions? Truly, the enlightened and competent governess may rejoice in her high calling, when she reflects on the incalculable benefits she may be the instrument of imparting to others,—to those who are yet to occupy the high places of the earth,— statesmen, philanthropists, and the noble spirits of progress,—many of whom may have kindled at the spark communicated to them by her pupils, which she first let fall; nations glorying in what they receive from those good and great men, who yet may never have heard of or seen the humble individual who was the cause of their energies being thus well directed.

Adelaide Neville had reflected, often and vigorously, in accordance with these views, during her residence at Puffendorff House; being acquainted with the history of sundry governesses as well as their duties,—including their trials, difficulties, and false positions,—their not holding a defined place in society, but one which varied according to the character, habits, and convenience of the family where they might happen to be employed. The situation which she occupied at the very first starting of her teaching career, had been one of severe discipline, in which she learnt not only a good deal of what she might have to contend with from without, but from within herself. To overhear a single striking observation, in the course of her airings with her pupils, let fall from a stranger, if bearing upon the condition of such as she, would set her most serious thoughts to work, and to a process of self-examination.

"Spare me from a fallen gentlewoman, as governess to my daughters; I shall be for ever wounding her feelings," were words that struck upon Miss Neville's ear one day, uttered by a lady-looking person, addressed to a gentleman who seemed to be her husband. Nor often had the young creature more eagerly listened to catch the remark of any one than of the presumed father of the daughters alluded to.

"You speak as many mothers have done, I believe, my dear," said the gentleman. "And yet, if you receive such a one into your family, you give your children many advantages they would otherwise be deprived of. When the mother is a person like yourself, of considerate judgment and right sympathies, it will lie much with her to mould the character and direct the innate feelings, as well as the actual behaviour, of the teacher of her children; just as is generally the case with the employer and the employed in any sphere of life, always supposing that reasonable pains have been taken on both sides for each to know something of the other. I have much faith in the power of well-directed kindness upon any nature that is not greatly vitiated; and from none can this benign influence come with such effect as from one who, in a worldly sense, is more advantageously placed than is the object of her confidence and favour."

"Still I should fear that a fallen gentlewoman,—the terms I used before, without intending anything at all offensive,—if introduced into such a house as ours, and as a governess to our daughters," replied the lady, "will be exceedingly apt to feel herself slighted, when nothing of the sort has been meant. Once slighted, or thinking that such has been the case, she will be always perceiving instances of neglect, and be therefore ever living on the defensive. She will be on the outlook for manifestations of what she feels to be the habitual plan of conduct towards her; and she will think, unless she arm herself from the first against the supposed plan, it will be too late to do so afterwards."

"My dear, you are conjuring up a great deal of dangers and difficulties which are conceivable, and which no doubt have occurred in many instances," observed the gentleman; "nor, in fact, as regards the reception of any female as tutoress to our little girls,—be she of gentle breeding or the opposite,—could one be at any loss for possible misunderstandings and annoyances, if anxious to find such things; although I at the same time feel that a vulgarly bred woman, however good-hearted she may be, would be far more apt to irritate and vex me than the other with the like cordial principles. Have better hopes of your own power and habits of pleasing, my dear, than to despair of a fallen gentlewoman's sympathies for you, and her genial reciprocations; having also much faith in the natural law of considerate kindness, especially when the manifestation of the softening, winning influence comes strikingly first from the more advantageously to the less fortunately placed in external circumstances. Indeed, my heart's sympathies will ever, I trust, go with the woman who labours for herself. Through all the difficulties, the prejudices, and the disadvantages of pushing on in her own course through life,—she who yet does it bravely and sincerely, —such a woman is a heroine. Yet of all these heroines, none, I think, will ever so command my forbearance and my admiration as

* Public establishments have of late years been instituted, in which ladies destined to become governesses, receive such education and training as are deemed best calculated to qualify them to fulfil their exacting vocation. Queen's College, founded by royal charter, at 67, Harley Street, Cavendish Square, is of this number, and from the comprehensiveness of its plan and objects, is worthy of the British metropolis.

a fallen gentlewoman,—to keep to the terms,
—who betakes herself to the really noble as
well as most serviceable vocation of imparting
the best that is in her head and heart to others
of her own sex who are younger than she."

The couple rose from the bench in the gardens, where they had been seated alongside of
Adelaide, at the conclusion of the husband's
last observations, so that our heroine heard
no more of the discourse. She had, however,
drank in a sufficiency, as she felt, for that day,
and took to turning the whole to solid account; being one instance among many of how
ready she was to profit by whatever came to
her knowledge or touched her feelings relative
to the career she had entered upon. Accordingly, although it was with a light purse that
her departure from Puffendorff House had to
be taken, it was neither with unformed judg-
ments concerning her profession, nor despairing views. On the contrary, it was with no
small degree of enthusiasm that she looked
forward,—an enthusiasm with much of a sound
basis, not only belonging to her self-reliance,
but to the consciousness of being a wiser person than twelve months before she had been;
her strength of purpose being sustained both
by the hope of making further advances in
self-improvement, and of establishing a claim
to respect which could never have been due to
her had she accepted of the extraordinary
bounty and urgent offers of the eccentric Samaritan of the Red Cot.

"Montague Mildmay, I trust," she often
mentally exclaimed, "should he ever learn
anything further of me than what he so scantily
gathered while at Wartham Hall, will not have
cause to accuse me with cherishing a sordid
and grovelling spirit, or even such as was at a
first disaster to be quenched and crushed."

For the hundredth time such were the maiden's
strenuous breathings to herself, as she hurriedly went to work packing her little property,
after the scene in the drawing-room, where she
had left the mistress of the house and the evil
counsellor in the ridiculous condition already
described. The glimpse, however, which the
governess had received of Lady Lymington,
as that dame sprang from her place of concealment to the assistance of the hysterical
pair, served to diversify our heroine's cogitations; for the very individual of whom she had
been thinking somewhat distrustfully a short
time before was beside her, ready to afford a
clearer insight into her heart than she had ever
furnished to a mortal being, old or young.

"Here, Miss Neville, is your quarter's pit-
tance,—shame to them!—and also some allowance for the over-time, which I have wrung
from the vulgarest of our sex," cried Lady
Lymington, as soon as she could command
breath to speak, after her exertions in the
drawing-room, and her race to the governess's
apartment. "A few months ago, it would
have seemed miraculous to many had I been
found capable of one-tenth of the exertion to
which I have within the last half-hour subjected myself; while, as to any such heartfelt interest as I can now experience on behalf
of another, I was still more deficient and use-
less. But it is all owing to you, Adelaide, my
dear girl, who have been the instrument of

working a greater change upon me, than you
have actually produced upon the young Puffen-
dorffs, who have been growing more and more
favourites with me every time I came here
latterly, but who never won so greatly upon
my liking all the while as they one and all did
in the recent scene below, when clinging to
you, and defending you; for I was an eye
and ear-witness of the whole."

Her ladyship rapidly ran over all that had
occurred between her and the other dames, immediately prior to the citation of the governess. She explained why she had concealed
herself; and with manifest feeling as well as
perfect simplicity declared, that whereas her
motives for so often repairing to Puffendorff
House, prior to the coming of the young lady,
had been unworthy and discreditable,—namely,
either to kill time, to have her laugh at the
vulgar and ignorant widow, as well as at the pretensions of her evil counsellor,—or to partake,
like any other spiritless toady, of the wealthy
widow's lavish hospitality to such people as
she courted,—she had at length, or rather almost all at once, on the arrival of our heroine,
found herself arrested, as it were, in her frivolous career. She had been aroused to think,
and to think honestly was to sympathize with
the unfortunate.

"You won me much, Miss Neville, by your
first appearance before us,—namely, the trio
of idlers and backbiters," said her ladyship
fervently. "You gained me over still further
at your second coming, and more and more
from all I have seen of you ever since. I began sometimes not only to be ashamed of repairing as I had been wont to do in my
thoughtlessness to the gaudy mansion, but to
resolve on closing my intercourse altogether
with the vulgar mistress of the house and her
principal adviser as well as associate, who is a
woman of faded character. But then the question arose, what was to become of the unhappy governess—of poor Miss Neville? for
poor and ill-fated you might well be called on
becoming subject to the miseries I knew were
awaiting you here; miseries, let me add, which
would have been still greater had I not strenuously exerted myself to alleviate your wrongs.
But, see! a carriage is at the gate, which I
sent for prior to visiting you, as I have now
done. Let me assist you with your boxes and
bundles to the vehicle. I perceive we shall
not be much overloaded,—the more's the pity.
I quit Puffendorff House with a mind never
to be seen within its outer gate again. Once
escaped so far, we will have leisure to consider
of other matters."

So greatly neglected and perverted had Lady
Lymington been in her girlhood and youth by
her aristocratic mother especially, that she was
really as much an object of pity as of censure
during that large portion of her life which had
elapsed between the date of her marriage and
the period at which we first met with her.
When the mother paid attention to the fox-
hunting baronet for her daughter's sake, and
the daughter,—under the mother's instructions,
—for her own sake, the usual process in con-
nubial preliminaries was reversed. Being much
in want of a wife, to superintend his household,
as Sir Mathew gave it out,—he being at the

time generally understood a man of great wealth,—he happened to be rather pleased than otherwise that the trouble and exertion of choosing for himself should be in no small measure dispensed with.

The young lady was handsome, graceful, and sufficiently accomplished for his tastes and mental acquirements, in that she could converse fluently and with vivacity when her spirit was stirred; she could draw creditably, sing sweetly, and dance most fascinatingly. She was of a good family, in the fashionable sense of the term; while, as for riches, the regular repletion of the baronet's coffers at the epoch of their marriage, amply made up for any lack of gold that was on her part. A proposal in due form for the young lady's hand was therefore made by Sir Mathew; and she, then about eighteen, became the spouse of an

NO. 11.—THE GOVERNESS.

individual who was more than old enough to have been her father.

And yet the manœuvred and badly brought up young creature had a mind in many respects naturally superior to mercenary traffic in the heart's best sympathies; although still a mind about as susceptible of improper impressions as of such as were good. She was capable of loving both truly and deeply, and of admiring virtue for its own sake, as well as of rejoicing in the consciousness of high aspirations after noble ends. But the exclusiveness of her mother's creed and example,—she being at the same time an ambitious and imperious woman,—as also her extreme poverty as regarded intellectual culture and a true knowledge of human character and human destinies, descended to, or were made to fashion, her offspring; so that what other could be expected of the young partner of the gray-headed fox-hunter, but a void in her bosom from the day of her nuptials, even greater and more deplorable than the weakness and the vacuity which had characterized the doll-like creature during her maidenhood? She had resigned herself to modes of thinking and enervating influences, which gradually gained upon a nature susceptible of being spoiled as well as of being bettered. A sorry sight, indeed, it was for one to look upon her after she had been a wife for something more than half the number of her years, as she indolently languished upon an ottoman, or yielded herself up to a sort of luxurious reverie, dealing in mere fantasies instead of anything in the shape of stern reality; while the thin yet handsome face would frequently have upon it a dignified calmness, a collected intellectual expression.

Her vapid exercises and abandonment to luxurious dreaming,—why, these very processes and habits were sure to destroy anything like healthful fervour of fancy and ardour of imagination. Accordingly, she had ever lacked the enthusiastic truthfulness and single-mindedness of such a being as our governess; at least these had long lain wholly dormant, never, in fact, having been cultured or warmly cherished.

We have said that Lady Lymington was naturally capable of loving both truly and deeply; so that had she found at the period of her marriage, even after having been greatly spoiled, an object to call forth the hidden stores of a true woman, the heart's finest and most holy sympathies would have been manifested in her life,—they, the dearest endowments of humanity. Such had been, and such was, the haplessly conditioned wife of the old bedridden fox-hunting baronet,—now much reduced in worldly circumstances,—at the period when our heroine first beheld her. But it seemed no longer the same was the middle-aged lady. She said, though late in the day, she had awoke —to the astonishment of herself as well as of all those who took note of her. Her ambition, a quality of which she was by no means devoid, appeared directed in a new channel; while her vanity, which was also not slight, contemplated the culture of higher adornments than she felt that she had ever possessed.

"Admiration I have long courted in the feeblest way," she began to say to herself; "and have never yet won incense from a single soul whose good opinion was worth a moment's study. Why should I not command homage, and devotion by the spirited exercise of that which I feel is still within me, just as the poor and ill-fated, but gifted young governess at Puffendorff House cannot hinder herself from doing, her powers being not yet spoiled and squandered as mine have been? I'll enter upon another career than any that has ever till now tempted me; and let my amazement, my dismay on the review of my past folly, hold me firmly for the future to my swelling purpose!"

In this way it was that the lady came at first to be stirred to activity of thought and intention; her vanity and ambition being acutely touched on beholding our heroine and witnessing her displays. By and by, however, her views took a more genial and affectionate turn;

whatever of jealousy or envy might have been in them, seemed transmuted into sympathy and a cordial desire not only to befriend the maiden, but to have her own spirit a participator in all which served to render poor Adelaide so loveable and truly noble.

"What are your immediate plans, my sterling benefactor, who, though so late in the day, has awoke me at last to a sight and to some knowledge of myself?" were Lady Lymington's first words to the young governess on the two being seated in the carriage at the gate of the mansion which neither of them ever intended, they said, again to enter; orders meanwhile having been given the driver to afford them an airing in Hyde Park. "But do not answer me," she continued, tears now gushing from her eyes, as of grateful affection and tender sympathy, "until you have some idea of what is now, and has been often, passing in my mind concerning you for months and months. I could not but foresee that your stay in the situation, from which you have at last for ever released yourself, would not long endure. But you never afforded me an opportunity,—rather, on the contrary, seeming to shun so doing,— of talking to you about the probably not distant change. Now, however, I can no longer maintain any reserve. What, then, are your immediate views or plans? and will you consent to make my home yours until a better is opened for you?"

"Your kindness and generosity are akin to what I have long ere now most unexpectedly experienced from a very different quarter in respect of everything but the true heart-fountain," responded the young lady, much moved; "nor will I affect to treat your beneficent offer with shyness or reluctance; although, until within the last half-hour, I dreamt not that such undeserved hospitality was intended me. I accept of your affectionate invitation, with this understanding, that I shall not consider your home is to be mine until a better is open for me, but only until I have a new teaching engagement; my fixed views and plans being not only to devote, but studiously to qualify, myself, in such a manner as I may hope will continually yield me a measure of self-satisfaction, and secure at length some considerable share of approval in discerning quarters on account of my perhaps not unenlightened as well as conscientious efforts to be useful to individuals of our own sex who are younger than myself. I had, Lady Lymington, till within a period of something more than a year ago, looked forward to a sphere of life very different from that of a governess; although it might have turned out neither to be so profitable for others, nor so happy for myself as that upon which I have entered. I am what is understood by the phrase 'a fallen gentlewoman.' But no more of this for the present, nor during the future, until I may perhaps find it consistent with my views and position to confide to you the whole of my history. As for the office of tutoress to which I have set myself, my desire is to pursue its duties with earnestness and ardour,— with enthusiasm,—nay, heroism, if it be within me to maintain my strength of purpose,—and to look steadfastly to the true greatness which may be achieved by persevering and honest efforts in a really noble, though often despised, vocation."

"What a child, what a spendthrift of time and a fair portion of gifts, have I hitherto been!" ejaculated Lady Lymington, in the tone of one that was keenly conscience-stricken, at the close of the governess's statement, without, however, addressing the young lady directly, or for the moment seeming aware of her being near; so intense and sudden were the self-accusations of the speaker. She sighed deeply; she sobbed, shook her head despairingly, and smote her breast. It was as if with a thorough self-loathing and unalleviable remorse, that she carried herself for some moments. Then, after a pause, she added, turning to Adelaide, "What a pigmy you make me! you outstrip me the farther each time I anew strive to keep pace with you! Monstrous! my youth and girlhood,—the best years of my womanhood,—have been utterly wasted; nay, worse, they have been perniciously squandered away as respects maxim and example to others! I see it all. My short-comings and wrong-goings, they stand out in dreadful array to my vision at this instant! What might I not have been! what not have done! for I perceive that even the humblest in station may be the most magnanimous,—the least pretending, the most enthusiastic,—the most depressed, the noblest of the land."

CHAPTER XVIII.

THE CONSPIRATORS.

OUR heroine having found a home in the meantime at the villa occupied by the Lymingtons, and in the old baronet's lady a daily-improving and more and more valuable friend, as she trusted, we must turn to another character in our story,—to him, in a word, who, of all the men in England, had the strongest claims upon her gratitude and affectionate recollections,—the eccentric Samaritan of the Red Cot.

The veteran, Peter Plumtree, did not suddenly withdraw himself from London, having been nearly a fortnight a sojourner there when the young governess quitted Puffendorff House; nor did he appear to be resolved on a departure for at least some days to come, to judge by his talk to the landlord of the inn where he stayed. Whether or not he intended to pass over to the Continent, and to visit certain of the principal capitals of Europe, in anxious search for her whom he longed to embrace as his adopted daughter and to take to his own birthplace, in order to establish her there, no one could learn from his lips or his motions. Nay, whether or not, he either, by any personal attempts, or through the agency of others, conducted an eager and rigid inquiry in relation to the maiden within the bounds of England's metropolis, must not for a moment or two be told. Something, however, it cannot be doubted, which was considered by the eccentric individual of importance enough to detain him, there must have been; for his was neither the time of life nor the disposition to linger looking at such gewgaws or novelties as amuse tens of thousands in Babylon the Great. Whether or not his motives and reason for the procrastination would have appeared to any one else sufficient, or merely capricious, has yet to be judged of. One thing is certain, the miniature portrait of the object of his youthful devotion was never by day absent from his bosom, nor by night, when a-bed, from below the pillow upon which his head rested. Equally true is it that he had a taste for enveloping himself and his ways as much as possible in the folds of mystery.

It would be easier to conjecture rightly concerning what Lady Lymington would have been, had she on her marriage-day found herself transplanted to a genial and fertile soil, than to do a similar thing in relation to Peter Plumtree, had he been wedded when a young man to her towards whom he cherished a most profound and undying love. It is impossible to say how far the unhewn diamond that he at first was, and that he still continued, would have been re-shaped and smoothed, or polished. A family of sons and daughters would, of course, have not slightly worked upon his nature,—improving, not spoiling it, there can be little doubt, seeing of what a sturdy and substantial character it was. The continuance too, probably, in the case supposed, to the end of his days, of the condition of poverty, or the being obliged to labour in some shape for the maintenance of himself and of others who were felt to have a claim upon his affection and industry, must have operated very happily upon such a sound subject.

But there Peter was, in his old age, a rugged and often a hardened man; having had a great sorrow to endure in early life, and met with not a few instances of the world's heartlessness, so that he was rendered suspicious, sometimes sour, and hardly less frequently, half-savage. Jilted by the woman he loved, and tried for a number of years afterwards by deceptions and adversity, he seemed, and often professed, to have lost all belief in moral excellence; and where there is not at least faith in virtue, the mind must narrow and wither. He strove to have his thoughts, which had been disappointed in love, absorbed by the world; yet how often were new trials and losses tempting him to be avenged upon it! And yet the stream of grief and misfortune was ever turning back into his own heart with melting influences,—preserving him on humanity's side; so that he would at times think in strains of exalted and beautiful sentiment, and act with the cordiality and tenderness of one sent, as if specially from heaven, on some most gracious errand; although his style of clothing his meaning in words, was now and then so truly that of plain-speaking as to amount to rudeness. As to his beneficence, it had a language which could not be mistaken, for it was uttered in the most tangible shapes, whenever his liberality had its exercise.

In short, after enduring many years' anguish of spirit,—after long toil, and in spite of many reverses, Peter Plumtree, as if at one stroke, had become a minor Crœsus. But then it was with no tie of affection, and no hope of ever forming one,—he seeming not to be linked in the chain of a common humanity at all,—that his great wealth existed. The very heaps of silver and gold which he could command, often appeared to form for the recluse of the Red Cot an encrusting dross, that literally confined him within his own narrow shell, and only for himself alone. Yet where have once been kindly feelings and strong impulses of love known to exist, it is possible that some chord will be found, upon the stir of which these or kindred emotions will be re-awakened; a thing most effectually done by the vision of the hapless, the youthful, and the wise damsel, whom the cynic hailed as the perfect picture or copy of the image that for half a century had occupied the innermost recesses of his heart. From this moment something like a new light and life began to reach his blighted heart with their restoring influences, commencing with her becoming an inmate of his little sanctuary. Her resolute withdrawal, and heroic purpose in so doing, with the view of proving herself equal to her trials; and, still further, the securing of her little property, with the much-prized miniature, appeared to crown him with hope. It seemed now, likewise, to be revealed to him that he had but to live to make her his own by the tenderest bonds of a fatherly affection. He also not only at length accounted himself a warm-hearted member of the human family, but his trust was not slight in relation of what had looked to him, for a number of years, as idle and embarrassing pelf, believing that it would, in the hands of a discreet and amiable successor, find fitting channels for its distribution,—for its sowing, and re-fructifying. Now, a man of the recluse's stamp, when he had once come to cogitate and resolve in these indicated ways, was not likely to be spending time in London, without entertaining the prospect that he was making progress towards the attainment of ends, which were to him all important. He was impatient of delay, but he also studied caution. He had known a good deal of the world, and was much on his guard. But he was neither omniscient, nor even equal to contend from the first with certain conspirators, who held him within their toils almost from the hour he had alighted in the metropolis. Listen, reader.

"Would you believe it, Captain Chesters, the old Crabtree of the Red Cot,—that eyesore to your uncle, Sir Vaux, has just arrived at the Blue Boar, Holborn, direct from Yorkshire. I had notice of the move yesterday, from an acquaintance of mine in the Riding; for you must know, captain, that I have not skulked and prowled for days and days together at a time in the neighbourhood of Wartham Hall, without worming myself into the confidence of sundry easy folks,—sly and slippery ones amongst the lot. It is in this way that I make myself handy in every quarter I may be, or condition placed. Misanthropic old Peter was often within pistol-shot of me of nights; but I was wary, and always am studying to bide my time. However, this is wide of the main matter in hand at present. Here he is, in London, and on what his late neighbours look upon as a wild-goose chase;

for it is neither more nor less than to ferret out the pretty girl,—my daughter that was,—in order to carry her home with him and make her his adopted. I told you all about the young lady having got a roof over her at the Red Cot, after my affair with her in the woods, and also that it wholly lies with yourself whether or not she is to come between you and the mighty inheritance which is to be your heaven, if you can get it. But in the meantime, old Crabtree, as I name him, may be most cleverly worked upon, and sovereigns plentifully got, I expect, without much other trouble than telling a bagful of lies, with a grain of truth among the chaff. What say you, honourable sir? Will you back me? go halves? or any other way we can most hopefully fall upon?—you being the furnisher of the needful meanwhile, I of the brains, and the trouble of fulfilling the scheme, without the necessity of your ever stepping a hundred paces from the Horse Guards or your club-house."

Such was the strain in which the ruffian, Jared Jobson, addressed the *gallant* Life-Guardsman; mingling truths with falsehoods and intentionally mis-stating dates, as seemed best to suit his purpose. For instance, the eccentric Peter had already been considerably more than a fortnight in London, before the ruffian communicated the fact to Chesters, and had from the first been more or less the dupe of the once pretended father of our heroine. The villain, besides, had been cognizant for better than a month of the young lady's place of residence, and the special hardships as well as general nature of her situation at Puffendorff House. However, it was in consistency with such a scoundrel's policy that he should reveal of his multifarious knowledge, even to his most serviceable colleagues, only so much as fitted his ends, and also only at such times, or on such occasions, as fell most fully in with his interests and necessities.

We say multifarious knowledge, meaning thereby principally a very extensive and varied familiarity with villany and crime, including almost every species of such, as practised in different countries. Not that he was destitute of information of a better order; for he had received a fair school education, and had made himself acquainted both with men and books to a wider range than most people have opportunities of doing; advantages which, when enjoyed by a person of good natural parts, such as he was endowed with, must render him more than a match for most men.

Now forty years of age,—the half of which had been devoted to lawlessness,—he was an adept in his way. Commencing life as a sailor, he at length became a seaman, and next the owner in part of a smuggling vessel,—the crew of which was of the most desperate order. On being in the course of a short time ruined as an adventurer in the conveyance of contraband goods from one state to another, by an easy transition he passed into a slaver, and became conversant with the horrors of the Middle Passage; the great market for their merchandize in human beings being certain portions of the American Union.

Piracy was another stage in his maritime history, from which horrid pursuit he was driven by most narrowly escaping a summary death in a romantic manner. And now it was that the land was to become the theatre of his depredations, his frauds, and his infamies. A thief, a burglar, a highwayman, a deliberate foreswearer of himself for hire was he, with other crimes of equal turpitude, perpetrated in continual succession by him and his accomplices, at all of which he was a singularly dexterous performer; the British islands, France, and other continental states, tasting, often in rapid sequence, of his adroitness and daring. In Ireland, by the bye, he made at one time an excellent thing of it, according to his principles of reckoning, by acting as spy and informer in cases of political offence, under the auspices of the imperial government.

"He was, in short," to quote the precise words of the Hon. Ludlow Chesters, uttered on a confidential occasion by the Life-Guardsman, "a monstrous villain and hideous miscreant, steeped over head and ears in infamy of every class and dye, and had so long been habituated to his execrable courses, that they not only became the element of his existence, like unto the air he breathed, but he had such a relish for them that they were loved for their own sake. So congenial, indeed, had they grown with his tastes, that when he found it safe to speak out, his highest gratification appeared to consist in boasting of his darkest doings, and in encouraging or polluting those less experienced in crime than himself, so as that they should tread in his steps, and attempt to rival him in his revolting career."

And yet the *gallant* captain's principles had become so vitiated, and his necessities, as he construed them, so urgent and overpowering,—perpetrating them with his eyes open, and in evil pursuits,—that he was fain to employ the unmitigated miscreant in furtherance of his,—the Life-Guardsman's,—own flagitious schemes, looking upon the ruffian as his tool and instrument; whereas, the more skilful scoundrel of the two was dexterously working with Sir Vaux Waldgrave's *hopeful* nephew for his own evil ends all the while.

The eccentric Samaritan of the Red Cot had been considerably beyond a fortnight a sojourner in London when Jobson, as a wondrous piece of news, informed Chesters that the old recluse had just arrived. From the first of Peter's appearance at the Blue Boar, the ruffian had pretty constantly kept his eye upon the veteran. In the guise of a gentleman, the manners of whom the scoundrel could well personate, with handsome clothes and a sufficiency of pocket-money, he threw himself in the way of the anxious visitor, on the morning after his arrival from Yorkshire, by calling for breakfast in the travellers' room of the very inn at which the old gentleman put up. Jobson had not for a number of years made himself directly notorious in London, although he had always been biding his time, as he called it; so that he was regarded at the Blue Boar,—judging from his appearance and behaviour,—as a highly respectable personage.

Knowing Plumtree's radical tenets, and that he was a great reader of the "Times" news-paper at the period, Jobson anticipated that the cynic would be pretty early in the public-room, in order to obtain a glance of what had last been going forward in the Houses of Parliament. Nor was he out in his calculation, neither unprepared for ingratiating himself with the old gentleman; having taken care to arm himself with the *Thunderer* on his first entrance, and having also ordered a sumptuous breakfast for two. It was not long before the ungainly Peter came hobbling into the as yet scantily occupied apartment, for he was of early habits; his dress as well as his bearing and outward modes being calculated to arrest attention. Jobson, however, took good care not to bestow upon him anything like an impertinent gaze,—not even that of the slightest curiosity, keeping assiduously to the paper. In fact, it was not until the old gentleman advanced to the fellow,—observing from the size and form of the sheet at some distance that it was the very thing he was mainly after,—and courteously inquired whether anything had occurred in Parliament during the preceding night of special importance,—it was not till now that the reader seemed to withdraw his attention from the closely-printed columns, and to observe the querist.

"I cannot yet say, sir, what transpired in the Houses last night, being eager to discover if there be any news from quite a different quarter," answered the villain. "You shall have the paper, sir, in a minute or two," at the same instant with apparent politeness moving the chair next to himself, so as to invite the veteran to be seated. "The fact is," continued he, "though I am deeply interested in regard to the progress of liberal views, being a keen Whig and something more, I have yet at present deeper matters of concern on my mind: I was eagerly looking if there were any tidings from the West Indies,—from Jamaica, this morning."

"From the West Indies! from Jamaica! said you, friend?" Plumtree cried, pricking up his ears as he spoke. "Are you acquainted in those parts?"

"Oh yes, sir, I having several years ago resided a great deal in those parts, especially in Jamaica," replied Jobson. "I did a good stroke in the tobacco line, but nothing compared with what some of my countrymen transacted; and what is worse, not with one tenth of the good luck of one or two of them."

"One or two of them! can you remember the name of any of the fortunate parties," more eagerly inquired the old gentleman than he had yet put his questions; "I mean in the tobacco line. You'll excuse me, sir, for my inquisitiveness when I inform you that I spent the best part of my days in Jamaica."

"You did, sir!" exclaimed Jobson in a tone of some surprise; an emotion, however, which was not strongly manifested, until bending himself back in his chair, he took a deliberate and apparently searching look at the old gentleman; after which,—the party gazed at giving him evidently a prideful opportunity of satisfying himself,—he added, "If I am not greatly mistaken you are the very gentleman to whom I mainly alluded, when mentioning the good luck of certain individuals. Can it be that I am in the presence of,—that I am really addressing myself to,—the famous Mr. Plumtree, one of the most highly spoken of gentlemen that ever adorned the annals of one of England's noblest colonies?"

"I am the person you name, sir," returned Peter accompanying his pleased response with a bend forward of his uncouth body. "A remarkable thing to be sure it is that the very first morning I am in London for a good many years, I find the very first gentleman I meet in this public room recognises me and with kindly recollections. Like yourself, I feel even more interest in regard to news at this moment from the tropics than from either Lords or Commons. Can't we breakfast together, while we talk on the same subject for half-an-hour?"

"With all my heart, Mr. Plumtree," said Jobson, displaying a sufficiently polished alacrity to chime in with the tobacco speculator. "I have been waiting for the last half-hour, in expectation of a friend meeting me here, and had ordered a breakfast for two," taking out a gold watch from his pocket as he spoke, and consulting its dial. "Something, however, must have come in the gentleman's way, so that I'll have to look for him elsewhere. He is from Scotland, and as I know,—for I am of Scottish descent myself,—that the better sort of people of that country pride themselves about the amplitude of their morning meal, I have given directions that we should have a rather sumptuous supply, so that there will be no lack of good things upon the table the moment we call for them. Yes, Mr. Plumtree, I am of a Scotch race,—a Livingstone,—Henry Livingstone, sir."

"What! one of that family to some of whom the great Livingstone estate in Jamaica belonged, and still belongs, as far as I know, —one of the finest sugar plantations in the whole island?" cried Peter.

"Yes, Mr. Plumtree, one of that race," responded the double-dyed villain; "although unhappily without any profitable interest, in a pecuniary sense, in the splendid possession of which you speak, sir."

"Give me your hand, Mr. Livingstone," cordially said Mr. Plumtree, his eccentricities being brushed away on a sudden, partly by the genius of the place in which he found himself, as is not uncommon in the case of old stagers when they find themselves all at once pitched from their rural retirement into the heart of such bustle as years back was as the breath of life to them. "Give me your hand, Mr. Livingstone; we must become better acquainted. Lucky thing, that an old fellow like me should at the first meet with a gentleman, though not much more than half my age, who can yet discourse of places and matters far distant from this, that still readily awaken within me a deep interest. I came from York shire yesterday."

"I have heard that you resided in great retirement, Mr. Plumtree, somewhere in Yorkshire," observed Jobson, "which, however, is a wide word, and upon your own property. But whether the estate is large or small, I do not remember to have been informed."

"Why, as to size, the Red Cot, as I call both my dwelling and the few acres attached to it, it is but a mere patch,—a stripe of ground, which belonged to my forefathers. And yet it would bring a great deal more money from a certain party than it is worth; my neighbour, Sir Vaux Waldgrave, looking upon the sort of sharp wedge, cutting into, as it does, the very border of his pleasure grounds, as nothing better than a thorn in the flesh." Such was the old gentleman's prompt statement, his communicativeness appearing to be stimulated by the abundance and variety of savoury things which the waiter was putting upon the breakfast table.

"Sir Vaux Waldgrave! of——of——; the name of the place, I mean," said Jobson, appearing to bring something to memory.

"Of Wartham Hall," interjected Mr. Plumtree.

"The same, sir," quickly returned the other, as one who had been readily relieved. "If I am not mistaken, there were certain particulars in the newspapers, some twelvemonths or more ago, in relation to the baronet and his Hall, that struck my attention at the time; the matters being kept in my mind the more freshly in consequence of my having some knowledge concerning individuals that were in a measure related to, or connected with, the strange things reported in the daily prints. I happen, for instance, to have some acquaintance with Lady Waldgrave, who, you must be aware, Mr. Plumtree, lives now apart from her husband,—her second husband, for she was a widow when Sir Vaux, out of spite, married her. But it seems that they did not long live very happily together, for she now resides in the vicinity of Kensington, and, to judge from appearances, in no way unhappy in consequence of the separation. However, I believe her ladyship had nothing directly to do with certain more romantic, not to say tragical, occurrences to which I more particularly refer. There was a young woman,—why should I not call her a young lady?—closely concerned in the melancholy family affair, as it was given out, whose case deeply moved me, and of whom, by a remarkable coincidence, I lately happened to obtain some further knowledge. Poor thing! she had found her way to this great Babylon, being in search of a governess's situation, in order honestly to earn her daily bread. At length she got an appointment, but at a miserable low rate as to remuneration, although this was not her only misfortune; for she came to be most cruelly used by the purse-proud, upstart, and ignorant dame, into whose establishment she entered. It helps to arouse one's deepest sympathy for this innocent,— who seems to have become the sport of fortune, or rather of misfortune,—that a considerable sum of money, of which it appears she was mistress on her arrival in London, was stolen from her person in open day, and when she was taking an airing on foot in some one of the public gardens. These are particulars which I learned from an intelligent person who was for a short time butler in the family where the young lady was so unhappily placed. Of this man, however, I have lost all traces, and also, for the present, of the unfortunate governess,—she having quitted her oppressive situation,—although I think it probable that a clue might be found to her whereabouts, without much difficulty, by an individual, for instance, like myself, who am minutely acquainted with all parts of the town."

It would not be easy to picture to the reader the degree and kinds of attention with which the old gentleman listened to this statement; his joy on thinking he was on the eve of recovering the object of his intense anxiety blending with his wonder at what appeared to him the universality of the narrator's acquaintanceship with individual history. Had the eccentric Samaritan known, however, that the person to whom he gave ear continued to be a prowler in the vicinity of Wartham Hall and the Red Cot so long as the young creature of whom he affected to speak so sympathetically was under the roof of the latter dwelling, his surprise would have been turned into hot indignation.

Had he, besides, been aware that the ruffian had much more recently visited the neighbourhood, in order to render himself as conversant as possible, not only with Sir Vaux Waldgrave's circumstances, but with the feelings and intentions of the person he was so deceptively addressing,—in that case, he would not only have marvelled far less at the fellow's particularity of information, but have been led to do more than surmise that he was the audacious miscreant at whose hands the young lady had suffered so deeply. Nay, to surmise, by such a man as Peter Plumtree, would have been speedily thereafter to act with vigour,—a course which must soon have resulted in having Jobson in the hands of justice; when, most probably, it would have been discovered that it was at the scoundrel's instigation, and by one of his associates in crime, the maiden had been fleeced of her money in Kensington Gardens.

But old Peter had no suspicion of these things and facts at the time; his amazement, pained feelings, and eagerness for further information, serving to render him more completely the dupe of the infamous one to whom he listened, and to hold him more firmly affixed to the tenter-hooks which had already caught him than before. His desire to be avenged upon the villains who had so deeply wronged the object of his tenderest solicitude, his vexation and distress on her account, led him into declarations and avowals which laid him the more open to imposition; at the same time certain of his expressions in the excitement of the moment having the power to startle the scoundrel who discoursed with him, and whose designs were so diabolical, as if some scintillations of the truth had nearly reached him.

"A thousand guineas," cried the perturbed old gentleman, "to the person that can and will bring my dear adopted Adelaide forthwith to me, safe and sound. An equal sum to the person or persons who shall enable me to lay my clutches upon the ruffian who had the daring first to lay claim to her as a daughter at Wartham Hall, and soon thereafter to rob her in the neighbouring woods."

The eccentric owner of the Red Cot had risen from his seat while he thus spoke; his eye being kindled, and his gesticulations vehement and menacing, although directed to vacancy. But a new thought seemed to have entered his head just as he concluded his words about the robbery in the woods; for he suddenly resumed his chair and began to address both his language and his looks towards the individual near him.

"No," said he, "I am too fast and lavish in my talk about the second thousand golden coins; for, trust my word, let me but once have dear Adelaide beside me,—a pleasure and blessing which would be cheaply purchased by the sum I named for her safe bringing,—and then it should not be many days, something tells me, before, with her help, I should have the ruffian, Jared Jobson,—as he named himself,—under lock and key, and on the direct road to the gallows. More than this, there is nothing likelier than that it was an associate of that villain who took her little purse of money from the poor thing in Kensington Gardens; so that the securing of the one inhuman vagabond would probably be the catching of the other monster."

Peter again paused, and appeared, by the guilty scoundrel who listened to him, to be taking a more particular and penetrating look at his auditor than he had yet done. It required the practised deception of the villain to remain visibly unmoved; his inner uneasiness increasing for a time, as the old gentleman proceeded.

"Nay, when I think a little more leisurely," continued the cynic, "the possibility is, that even without the immediate actual recovery to my arms, or casting up, of my adopted child, and without her direct assistance beyond that which I obtained from her at the Red Cot, I may get hold of her pretended parent and real plunderer; so close and particular was the description she repeatedly gave me of the person, the visage, and the carriage of the ruthless blackguard. She besides furnished me with as near a portrait of him as memory could supply her clever pencil with. I have it up-stairs in my trunk, resolved to make the best possible use of the likeness whilst I am here in London, where, no doubt, the cruel wretch has practised, and may be at this very moment practising, his villanies. Excellent!" continued the old gentleman, after another brief halting; "what more likely than that the getting hold of the person of Jobson, and the publicity which I should take care to give to the longed-for event, would be the means of instantly sending my adopted girl to me, when the thousand guineas I first spoke of should be thrown into her lap, instead of being given to any base informer or thief-catcher? Do you know, Mr. Livingstone, that while I have been thus confidently and hopefully talking, I could hardly avoid being impressed with the idea of your very closely answering to dear Adelaide's oral description and pencil delineation of the perjured scoundrel and dastardly robber, Jared Jobson. But it is not the first time that I have been struck on witnessing fortuitous resemblances. You will forgive me, Mr. Livingstone, for what I have just said. But I am a blunt speaking member of the old school, and will take my way."

"Forgive you! why, there has been no offence offered or taken, I assure you, Mr. Plumtree," cried the impostor, whose heart had leapt, as it were, a moment before to his mouth, and his thought had been to make a sudden bolt from the Blue Boar, and as speedy an escape as possible from its neighbourhood. The turn, however, which the eccentric Samaritan's speech had taken towards its close, reassured the villain. Once more he breathed with freedom; at the same time perceiving that it would require his best wits, as well as sometimes the boldest daring, to maintain his hold for any considerable period of the wealthy and credulous yet resolute owner of the Red Cot.

In fact, the audacious fellow did not take his leave of the old gentleman on that particular morning, without affording him hopes that the governess might be in a short time restored to him; employing care for his own sinister and base ends to blind the duped one still more effectually, by inviting and persuading him to act as a constant companion, whenever he, the deceiver, set out on a "voyage of discovery," as he afterwards termed each of the then contemplated explorations. And such a voyage took place, sometimes twice or thrice in the course of twenty-four hours; the night, on occasions, being partly occupied by the pair in this way. Of course, the pretended Livingstone had nothing farther from his thoughts than to bring his companion in these researches an inch nearer to the young lady. Nay, in order that there might be the least possible chance of the eccentric Samaritan's eyes alighting upon her, or of her becoming cognizant that her generous benefactor was in London, the scoundrel was at pains, through some one or other of his multifarious and intricate channels of information, to make himself acquainted with the girl's movements, so that he might the longer and the more surely keep Plumtree on the tenter hooks. And profitable to the villain did this game prove, seeing that the rich cynic not only paid all expenses, but was liberal, if not lavish, in his rewards, in proportion as he witnessed the apparently disinterested, patient, yet arduous efforts of the other to serve him,—that other being a *Livingstone* of the ancient family of Livingstone, and moreover a *gentleman* of large expectations in connexion with the West Indies,—the quarter of the world, too, with which so many of the old gentleman's recollections were associated.

"Any good news, Mr. Livingstone, from the tobacco-planters?" was the question which Peter put to the pretender, one morning, on his calling as usual at the Blue Boar. A considerable length of time had now elapsed, every day of which had seen the pair upon their "voyages of discovery," but hitherto all in vain; the invention of the impostor having been not slightly taxed in order to keep up his deceptions, these being ever sustained by fresh representations and novel falsehoods. Indeed, he found that the game could not last much longer, owing to the old gentleman's growing convictions, that after their patient and elaborate efforts to find the maiden, without ever having got any knowledge of what had become of her, she must have quitted the English metropolis altogether, most probably, he imagined, for a foreign country, and perhaps along with a foreign family. "Any good news for yourself, my friend, from the tobacco quarter?" was the cynic's inquiry, on the morning alluded to. "As for me, I wholly despair of glad tidings in the direction you understand me to signify, so long as I remain in London at this turn,—no fault of yours, kind sir. I do not mean that; far from it; quite reverse. Indeed, I feel that I am not a little indebted to you."

No, there were no good news for Mr. Livingstone from the West Indies. In fact, as he had frequently with sighs mentioned to the old tobacco speculator, he answered that his prospects were daily growing the more gloomy, and that he knew not what was to become of him, unless he could find means of returning to Jamaica and pursuing, when on the spot, the important claims which he had in that noble island.

"But," continued the pretender, his countenance lighting up on changing the topic, "it is not with my paltry troubles that I would willingly pester a gentleman of your consideration,—one, too, who has not only treated me with extreme liberality and favour, but who has upon his mind an ample load of anxiety and disappointment of his own, on account of an innocent who is as dear to him as if she were of his very flesh and blood. Yet, at length I am in better hopes than ever of being able to assist my benefactor in releasing him of that grievous burden. Last night a letter was put into my hand by an unknown person. but from an individual whom I have been employing in order to serve you, Mr. Plumtree; which communication I have upon me for your perusal, sir. The hand-writing and the name of the writer are, of course, strange to you, although not at all to me. In short, the penman is he who was butler for a short time to the vulgar, upstart dame to whose children your adopted unhappily became governess shortly after her arrival in this overgrown metropolis. Read for yourself, dear sir, and then you will the more confidently judge of the nature and value of the things alleged and stated. I only have at present to say further, that in my opinion there are fair hopes, if not a certainty, that the lovely Adelaide will be at the Italian Opera this very evening in the King's Theatre,—and that if we two take to the pit of the splendid house, we shall not only get a sight of her, but that without much difficulty I shall be able to bring you face to face, or, in other words, to throw you into one another's arms."

"I am much of the same mind," cried the old gentleman, rising from his seat in a transport of hope, after having perused the writing. "This is, besides, a most lucky piece of tidings as concerns your interests, Mr. Livingstone,— the promise of happiness to me shall be the immediate forerunner of real benefit to yourself. You may have guessed, from what you before heard me state, that I did not intend going hence without my leaving some substantial mark of my sense of your services for me. I will immediately, according to my purpose, hand you the means of proceeding to the West Indies, and also of living there for some time independently as a gentleman; these means being otherwise increased on account of the

fresh and bright hopes ye have this morning roused within me. Should I get a sight, this evening, at the playhouse, of my darling,—much more, if I can obtain conversation with her through your agency, Mr. Livingstone, you may look for additional expressions of my sense of obligation to you."

The old man, whom so many good people long accounted a misanthrope, and who was wont to display repulsive manners and to speak the language of coarseness and of a soured, hardened, and dark spirit, had been, ever since the fascinating but unhappy Adelaide found an asylum in his house, gradually growing less unkindly to himself, and less austere to others. The visit of Sir Vaux Waldgrave to the Red Cot, and contemporaneous circumstances, had helped on with the change,—that change never ceasing to have its advancement, any more than its origin, in connexion with the

No. 12.—THE GOVERNESS.

fate of the young lady; so that at length, on his making his sojourn in London, he seemed a man of courtesies, having most of the conventional forms of polite life in his speech and carriage.

To be sure, both his dress and manners, which he brought from the country, were not exactly suited to the region of the King's Theatre, and the refinements of the Italian Opera. But it was not to enjoy or study these that he purposed to make his visit, or that he allowed himself to be guided as to certain forms and observances on the occasion by the impostor. It was simply for the attainment of an end which was of the last importance to him that he acted; believing from what he had seen of the object of his growing sympathies and absorbing affection, that her happiness would be like to his the moment they were in one another's presence. Of her truth and ele-

vation of principle, and also of the resoluteness of her character, as well as of her perfect
delicacy, he formed the stronger opinion, from
the mere circumstance of her never, to his
knowledge, having sought a renewal of his aid,
or even given him notice of any one of the
discouraging things which had occurred to her
since last he beheld her beautiful face, and
took note of her winning modesty of demeanour; these being favourable conclusions which
the contents of the letter that the impostor
placed before him helped to fortify.

CHAPTER XIX.

THE GLASS AT FAULT.

THE morning meeting of the pretending villain and his entangled dupe, of which mention
has just been made, took place, as has also
been stated, when the former found that he
could not much longer practise upon the old
gentleman's credulity. The interview, besides,
occurred almost immediately after the impostor
had announced to Ludlow Chesters, — the
honourable Life-Guardsman,—the fact of Plumtree being in town; the crisis to which the
ruffian's duplicity and villanous contrivance
had been brought, impelling him to new stra-
tegems and schemes, from which he was determined the titled captain should not escape
free. Nor did Jobson judge too confidently
when he calculated, by his new dodge, as he
characterized the further working of his
schemes, on making the nobly-descended
officer a victim, as he had done all others
with whom he had ever leagued, or over whom
he had at any period obtained a power. The
reader has some time ago been told to what
extent he succeeded with the captain, and by
what means he got his ascendancy and influence in that quarter. It will also be remembered
that the latter acts of the scoundrel's audacity
were very nearly contemporaneous with the
young governess's quitting Mrs. Puffendorff's
house, and her repairing to Lady Lymington's.

Now, all these movements of the maiden
were made known to the ruffian-plotter through
his peculiar channels of *backstairs* information,
influence, and espionage; together with a number of other family particulars in relation to
whatever place or position our heroine might
occupy at any time. Accordingly, Lady Lymington's had become the object of the miscreant's especial vigilance and inquiries. Hence
the fact of his learning that this titled dame
had not only resolved on a visit to the Opera
House on a particular night, but that the
lovely governess had allowed herself to be persuaded to become one of the party, at the
theatrical entertainment. He had even gone the
length to make himself certain as to the box
which her ladyship and her friends were to
occupy; it being easy for him, after all these
preliminaries, to fix on a place or seat in the
pit, whence he should be enabled to see the
individuals of the particular party. The depth,
subtlety, and number of his other plots for the

night in question, will to some extent be learnt
in the course of the present chapter.

The contents of the regularly written, folded,
and sealed sheet of paper, which Jobson declared was every way genuine, that had been
put into his hand, as a letter from his au-
thentic and trusty acquaintance, the butler,
"who, unfortunately, is out of place," were in
effect these :—He had, but a few minutes before penning the epistle, discovered that the
young lady,—after quitting the house of the
vulgar, upstart dame, to whose daughters she
had been acting as governess, and at whose
hands she had endured great ill-usage,—had,
with a broken spirit, withdrawn to an obscure
suburb of the metropolis, and there, in a sense,
shut herself up, as if she had been a voluntary
prisoner, or a poor creature that in her despondency and distress invoked death. By
what means her melancholy condition had
been made known to a lady of quality and
opulence, the writer for the present could not
tell with any degree of particularity. This, however, he could vouch for, that the distinguished
and most humane, as well as intelligent personage,—into whose service the butler was
most anxious to get,—had the young lady immediately conveyed to her own mansion, and
in whose family there was every prospect of
the lovely maiden not only becoming a permanent governess to the younger branches of the
house, but of being adopted as the companion
of the discerning mother. As a proof of the
favour, with which the—till very recently—
unhappy Adelaide was held by her excellent
patroness, the fact of her being urged to grace
a party to the Opera, spoke more than any
verbal testimony could do.

There were some other things in the lying
forgery, which tended to blind and mislead
Mr. Plumtree, but which we pass over. One
further statement we alone call attention to.
It was to this purpose :—that having been
lately insulted by the Hon. Ludlow Chesters,
in broad daylight and while walking in the
courtly suburb of Kensington,—while, too, her
pupils were by her side,—she not only had resolved on avoiding that neighbourhood for the
future, but keeping it a secret, so far as it could
for a time be done, where she had found her
present enviable situation.

"You must excuse me, Mr. Livingstone,"
said the lying writing, "for not committing
to paper the secret to which I have alluded. I
must see you privately, and whisper it into your
ear alone, instead of perilling my prospects of
being on an early day taken into the service
of Lady B——, a danger I might run by any
more explicit and tangible written information.
Besides, I have communicated the above to
enable you and your anxious friend from Yorkshire to act forthwith for yourselves; and, considering the friendship I am bound to entertain towards you, and consequently the good
wishes I must naturally cherish for all in whom
you feel an interest, I trust you will not let
the opportunity at the theatre pass unim-
proved."

The owner of the Red Cot never for a moment
appeared to doubt the truth and genuineness
of the writing. He read and re-read it several
times in the course of the day, commenting

on several parts of its contents; for example, with deepest commiseration and strong emotion concerning Adelaide's despondency and sufferings,—with admiration and gratitude in relation to the distinguished lady's conduct towards his adopted one,—and, again, with hottest indignation and a vehement spirit of revenge in relation to Chesters. With these various bursts, and the most hopeful anticipations prior to the important hour of repairing to the Opera House, the old gentleman got through what appeared to him an unusually long day, not a little enlivened by having the diabolical Jobson with him, with all that scoundrel's glossings and perversions for his entertainment and encouragement.

"Won't I be a proud man," old Peter would suddenly call out, "the moment I have the opportunity of tossing into Adelaide's lap or keeping, a heavier purse than could have been taken from her in Kensington Gardens, or than the value of all that was plundered so cruelly and vilely from her by the cowardly Jobson in my own neighbourhood, when she was broken-hearted, houseless, and helpless. Perdition to the monster that did it! I hope I shall not be gathered to my fathers until I hear of his swinging from some gallows-tree or another. But as for my adopted one, it will be her own fault, should I get a word of her on the evening of this day, if she goes to bed empty-handed. I would not even have her to be dependent on the distinguished personage,—heaven bless her ladyship, whoever she may be, and whatever her name,—for a coin, after I get alongside of the darling."

It was in this way that the eccentric Samaritan would run on; his auditor, delighted with the intimation of his not parting with the young lady without furnishing her with a well-filled purse; a resolve which of course implied that the old gentleman would not go with empty pockets to the playhouse. That the villain should speak in warmest approval of Peter's generous intentions was natural for such a fellow, as was also the various methods he took to sustain and enlarge the old gentleman's declared purpose.

Indeed, Jobson had not a few matters to attend to on the day in question, and which seemed to promise becoming memorable to his Yorkshire dupe. The impostor, for instance, could not but admire the manner in which the lying letter had worked for him; and therefore he thought of trying the effect of another writing of the same sort, to be delivered very shortly before his dupe and he were to start for the theatre. Accordingly, hardly an entire hour prior to their ordering a vehicle to carry them thither, a person, apparently in great haste, brought a communication to the Blue Boar, addressed to the pretended Livingstone; and, of course, purporting to come from the butler. It ran thus:—

"Important things have come to my knowledge since I wrote to you yesterday afternoon, and which I lose not a moment in forwarding to you. You will excuse me for beginning with what mainly concerns myself:—I have got an engagement in the establishment of the excellent and generous Lady B——. Indeed she had no further time to lose in coming to a decision relative to hiring a butler; for it now turns out that she is on the very eve of going over to the Continent, but to what particular part, in the first place, I cannot possibly at present say. Yes, her ladyship, who is a widow with a vast income, goes immediately abroad, accompanied by a large and splendid establishment, in which a new butler is to form a part, although of a very inferior order to that of the young lady concerning whom you and your noble-hearted friend from Yorkshire take so extraordinary an interest. The charming maiden's knowledge of certain continental languages has had its share, it seems, in recommending her to her present patroness's good graces. I am all bustle, but this is nothing to what is going on at the mansion of Lady B——, seeing that we are all actually to start for the foreign quarter to-morrow forenoon, or rather morning; the gentry of the family betaking themselves to the Opera this evening, with the view of getting out of the confusion at home.

"From what I have hurriedly stated, you will see, Mr. Livingstone, that the only chance you can for the present have of getting access to the young governess must be limited to the evening or night of this same day on which I write this communication,—which is confining you to most narrow bounds. By the bye, it appears that Lady B——, with all her benevolence and generosity, is not without an eye to her own interests in the choice of persons who are to be subordinate to her in her fine establishment. As for me, she has had the best of characters and first-rate recommendations; while, to ascend higher, the young governess's acquaintanceship with French, and even with the German and Italian tongues, has, I am told, been taken into special account. I trust, should anything happen to her ladyship while we are abroad,—so as for ever to remove her,—I do trust that she will have made some proper provision for her servants; otherwise, in such a melancholy event, it will go hard with poor me, before I can return to old England and get a new engagement. A like hardship, I fear, would be experienced by the charming governess; unless she have the good fortune to have an interview with your excellent friend this evening."

Such were the contents of a writing which, had it been with any degree of closeness examined,—especially if examined in connexion with the prior document of the same order,—must have opened the eyes even of Peter Plumtree to a sense of there being a species of overstepping design and cunning in the entire affair. But the old gentleman had been at the first so much taken with the pretended Livingstone, had been so borne up and carried along by the impostor, and was now so dazzled and excited by the assurance and certainty, as he imagined, of beholding, if not of recovering, his adopted one, that there was no critical acumen within him. Instead of this, he took all that was said in the second writing, as in the first, to be truth itself, precise and exact; so that in place of questioning the style and consistency of the butler, he launched out into severe surmises, to the disparagement of persons with whom in any case he had no very immediate concern. In this way it was that the Lady B—— came in for her share of lowering remark, to the keeping of his attention quite removed from more obvious and pressing considerations, until the very moment that he found himself stepping into the vehicle which was to whirl him in a few minutes to the theatre.

There were sundry rather comical features connected with old Peter Plumtree, the cynic's, operatic speculation, these becoming, in certain lights, the more amusing from being in close relationship to grave and sadly moving particulars. The contrasts, in fact, were strong and manifest, producing striking effects; the simple circumstance alone of the eccentric, but, upon the whole, sterling man, falling into the hands and leadership of such a deeply dyed and consummate villain as Jobson, being grievous, and yet, in a manner, grotesque. To find him, who had been for a train of years a recluse and a reputed misanthropist in a rural quarter of the country, all of a sudden transported to London, and yielding himself up to the dictation of a scoundrel who was acquainted with every turn, condition, and vice of the overgrown British metropolis, was a melancholy as well as a remarkable occurrence, which yet had its picturesque points.

Think of the vagabond Jobson getting old Peter to submit his ungainly person to a fashionable tailor of St. James's Street, in order that the duped party might appear in the pit of the King's Theatre in a style of proper keeping with the regulations and the fashion of that aristocratic place of amusement! But this was not the extent of the length to which the owner of the Red Cot permitted himself to be carried.

"His Majesty's Theatre," said the pretended Mr. Livingstone, of the ancient Scottish line of the Livingstones, "is a vast as well as a most magnificent edifice, gorgeously fitted up. It has a number of rows or tiers of boxes, one above another, which are generally crammed full of the wealthiest and noblest of the land, including crowned heads, princes and princesses of the blood-royal, foreigners of the highest distinction, and, in fact, such grandees of the world as resort to this centre of civilization. Now, as you are not likely ever again, Mr. Plumtree, to pay another visit to this celebrated scene, and as you must needs desire to look for once upon the faces of not a few of the most notable persons in existence of either sex, it is absolutely necessary that you have an opera-glass, to aid your vision as you gaze around and aloft towards the galaxies of beauty and grandeur that we are about to contemplate. But this is not all, nor the main thing to be considered; for without the optician's admirably contrived instrument, we may, throughout the splendid entertainment of the entire evening, search with our unaided eyes in vain, for the singling out of your adopted daughter, among the thousands of dazzling beauties that will encompass us."

"Ay, now you come to the point at last, Mr. Livingstone," said the cynic; "I'll do anything,—pay frankly for anything, that will help me to get a good sight of my darling, and consequently tend to bring us together. As for a view of the crowned heads, the blood-royal people, and so forth, you must understand, my friend, that, as a Radical Reformer, I cannot pay any homage to such like, not even that of gazing at the grandeur of the dress of these drones, who fatten and grow rich upon the hard earnings of the mass of the people. No, no; no helping glass in order to gaze upon the bloodsuckers of the land; but anything that will aid me in relation to my Adelaide. Therefore get an opera-glass, by all means. You will attend to procuring such an article; and let it be anything but a trashy one, for it shall of course go to my adopted child."

"You will not grudge, Mr. Plumtree, five guineas for an instrument of the kind," insinuatingly observed the impostor.

"Grudge! assuredly not, my friend,—here's the money," was the readily acquiescent reply; and away went the scoundrel to procure at a second-hand shop an old and glassless instrument of the sort spoken of, for a few shillings,—a trifle more getting a poor spectacle-maker to shape, out of a broken window-pane, a piece which, by an exceedingly simple expedient, applied to the inside surface, was rendered utterly impervious to human sight, whether the aged or the young.

Clad in a costly new suit, and armed with his opera-glass, the uncouth eccentric of the Red Cot proceeded to the theatre, accompanied and guided in everything by the villain who had so completely imposed upon the old man ever since his coming to town, and who would not have scrupled for a moment to take the credulous one's life, or to reduce him in the evening of his days to absolute beggary, if thereby the miscreant could have profited himself in regard to securing the possession of the perishable dross, gold, which yet would have a much longer existence than that of the criminal's career. The pair went early to the playhouse, for Jobson had an object in so doing; this being to have a choice of the position in the pit that should best suit his vile purposes for the evening.

The theatre became gradually the scene of great bustle, not only by the influx into the pit, but the filling of the boxes; old Peter's amazement on witnessing what might be characterized as the regularly conducted confusion of a scene, the like of which he had never before beheld, affording a well-concealed amount of merriment to his companion. In the meantime the curtain rose, and soon after, between the caperings of dancers, the declamation of actors, the—to him—unintelligible execution of vocalists, and the crashes of the orchestra, he was kept in mute wonderment; a multitude of other novelties and splendours combining to bewilder him. In fact, he seemed for a considerable time to lose all self-command of thought,—the exercise of his memory, the very understanding of the end he had in view in coming to the place in which he was seated. At length, however, he began to rally, and to withdraw his gaze from the business that was transacting on the stage. Having no idea of what was there doing and there meant, he could not very long be kept enchained by the performances even of the highest paid of those before him. He took to looking around and aloft; not only the pit by this time being crammed full almost to suffocation, but the boxes, so far as he could see into them, being densely filled.

"Where is she? I shall never be able to discover the darling among such swarms of men and women as I see around and above me. Where is the opera-glass?"

Such were the first utterances of the rallying Samaritan after more than an hour's length of gaping silence on his part, during which his attention had been transfixed to the proceedings on the stage, and the accompanying scenery. Nor had Jobson once attempted to awaken his companion from the bewilderment; it being no part of the villain's policy, either to have the merits and capabilities of the optical instrument put to the test very early in the evening, or the possibility of discovery whether the object of the old man's deepest anxieties was present or absent. The main thing for the impostor in the meantime to ascertain was, whether the duped one had brought a well-filled purse with him or not,—the discovery being pretty early in the evening in the affirmative. Next to this, his interest was to prevent Peter from getting a glimpse of his darling to the very last; when, —while the glance and the assurance of her identity would save him, Jobson, from the suspicion of being thought a misleader,—the bustle and tumult of departure from all parts of the crowded house would most effectually prevent his companion enjoying a longer or nearer view of his adopted daughter, than might be obtained between a central part of the pit and a box of the second tier.

"I wish the old fool to get one unmistakable sight of the wench," said the pretended Livingstone to himself, when he beheld Lady Lymington enter, along with her young friend, their appointed box,—this having been accorded her ladyship and party on that particular night, by a dowager-countess, who was a great Opera House goer. "But this clear and convincing view must take place at the moment which is most fitted for serving my purposes, and not for the uncouth idiot's satisfaction."

Plumtree had at length asked for the opera-glass, and to this reasonable demand Jobson was too plausible a strategist to offer anything like a flat refusal. He therefore delayed his acquiescence in the request, by mildly asking the duped one to allow him, as a person to whom the theatre was not altogether strange, to take the first survey. The fellow then pretended to make a patient and deliberate inspection, going from box to box with great regularity, and also from tier to tier, till he had exhausted the scrutiny.

"I have not yet got a sight of the young lady," he whispered to his companion, "although I have taken a minute and leisurely survey; her peculiar loveliness being of a character which, if once beheld,—and I have several times, at no remote date, been arrested by her beauty,—it cannot soon be forgotten. You will, however, observe, sir, that the boxes are of such retiring depth, and the fronts of a

number of them are so curtained, that half-a-dozen of persons may in almost each such division of the theatre be stationed, and yet we in the pit here prevented from getting a glimpse of them. Still, the difficulty and inconvenience to us will be removed in the course of the night, I trust, by not only the screens being wholly pushed aside, but by the farthest from the scope of our view, in each and every box, coming more prominently forward as the interest of the performances increases. It is not fashionable to those who carry their heads so high as the great majority do who are at this moment in these dress circles, to evince too early or too eager a curiosity. They hold that it is only the vulgar, the nobodies, or the clodpoles from the country, that do so."

"Ay! just like the worthless, burdensome, and contemning set," returned old Peter; "I must have Adelaide delivered from their contamination. Now let me have the glass, in order that I may take a survey; believing, as I do, Mr. Livingstone, notwithstanding all your quickness, your remembered impressions of the dear girl's beauty, and your great familiarity with theatres, that my recognition of her, if she but for an instant come within the range of my eyesight, will be still truer than yours. It is not once or twice that I have dwelt upon her attractions of face and figure, but very many times, and on some occasions for hours together."

Old Peter took the optical instrument, and with a good deal of assurance, evinced by his manner, proceeded to put the glass to his visual organs; following as nearly as such a clumsy-handed and unused being could do the manner of many he saw around him who were armed with a similar article. He somewhat superciliously, at the same time, made an observation to the effect that he was tired of the nonsense and the wantonness which were going forward on the stage, and therefore would devote himself to his proper business in such a place.

It was a proof of Jobson's self-command that he did not even smile, try to turn his face from his companion, or evince the slightest merriment when the old man applied the glass to his sight. On the contrary, he was composed, showing, if any emotion, that of anxiety to learn what was the result of his dupe's survey, and next, a sympathy with his disappointment, or rather surprise. The villain actually had the power of thus preserving his gravity, when the other, time after time, took out his silk handkerchief to wipe the outer surface of that which was dimmed and smeared within, using his breath vigorously too, in order to yield a dampness for the cleansing and polishing purpose.

"You do not see very clearly, I fear, through your opera-glass, Mr. Plumtree," said Jobson, with an apparently kind solicitude, after witnessing the unavailing efforts of his dupe with the instrument.

"See through it!" returned the old man. "No, nothing like seeing, I declare, Mr. Livingstone. The thing would not enable one to get a sight of a haystack, were it within half-a-dozen yards of him, nor even of my own Red

Cot, were it standing on that stage before me there. I behold nothing but darkness, and this, far from being decidedly visible, strains my eyes to their uttermost, and till they are like to jump out of my head. You have been greatly taken in, my friend," added Peter, rather peevishly; "taken in to the extent of five guineas. Not that in a case of need and useful serving I care about expending a few pounds. But I never liked, in all my life, either to throw money away myself, or to see others throwing it away for that which is naught. Here, take the trash; I do not wonder you could not find out Adelaide by its means, and yet you were, Mr. Livingstone, looking all the time of your long survey, as if it had been serving you to your mind's content."

"Strange, that our eye-sight should be so differently structured!" softly said the impostor, as he took the article into his hand, and then consigned it to one of his pockets. "I never was more satisfied with any opera-glass I have used than this; by its means I could this moment minutely describe the features, dress, and ornaments of any one in the dimmest distance from us in this vast edifice upon whom the naked eye's vision can alight."

"Let the gentleman on my right hand here try the thing, sir, and then it may be decided which of us two has the best constructed organs," quickly subjoined the cynic, and with increasing disbelief.

Jobson cursed and blasphemed in his heart, wishing the piece of trash at the bottom of the sea, or anywhere but within the reach of Peter Plumtree; seeing that not only through the worthless article his over-reaching and dishonesty might be detected in one transaction, but his entire imposture brought to light. He now felt that he whom he had so recently looked upon as an old fool, must not be too far trifled with; and that if for a time duped, once let him get his eyes opened to the villany, and then his retaliation would be dreadful. While these things were passing through the scoundrel's mind, he was yet ready with a pacifying reply to his companion's suggestion about submitting the glass to a third party's judgment.

"It would not be seemly in such a place as this," said he, "to do what you propose, Mr. Plumtree. There's a better way. The person from whom I purchased the article has as fair a reputation as any tradesman at the West End. I'll go to him to-morrow morning, and have the money back for the thing, or bring him to an accounting for his imposition, if really such has been his conduct. At any rate, you shall not lose a farthing through it. Indeed, it so happens that I have an equal amount upon me at this moment, with the sum I advanced for it. I agree with you, sir, that five guineas are not to be thrown away,—especially to be wasted on a grasping shopkeeper. Here is the cash mentioned, and it will relieve me, Mr. Plumtree, my benefactor, the moment you pocket the amount."

"No, no!—not that either," returned the cynic, suddenly mollified. "Go you to the unworthy tradesman to-morrow, as soon as he can be seen, and try what you can do with

him, for I cannot endure imposition of any sort or from any quarter. As for you, Mr. Livingstone, you shall not be a loser to the extent of a farthing, in consequence of having been cheated in the purchase of an opera-glass; although, let me add,"—and this the eccentric Samaritan uttered very good-naturedly,—"I begin to see that you are not yourself perfect in everything."

A considerable portion of the evening had gone during the species of misunderstanding and wrangling which had so unexpectedly on both sides arisen between the impostor and his dupe in relation to the opera-glass. This lapse and loss of themselves was no subject of regret on the part of Jobson. As for old Peter, he resumed his survey with his naked eyes, with all the eagerness and anxiety to be looked for from him in the given circumstances. The other affected to do the same; nay, he even went so far as to borrow, more than once, the glass of a person that sat near to him,—going over the house with the same apparent patience and minuteness as at first; at the same time taking care that his companion should know the pains he took to serve him, and also his delicacy in refraining to make a second use of the purchased instrument, lest a sight of it might offend and lead again to hard words.

CHAPTER XX.

THE SUDDEN SALUTE.

THE old gentleman concealed not that he appreciated the services, the anxieties, and the delicacy of the other, after the manifestations we have just mentioned. His convictions in this way helped to soothe him for a time beyond what would have been his condition, had there been no reconciliation between the pair after the jarring about the glass. Still, it was impossible for Plumtree to sit out the performances, and near to the midnight hour, without seeing his adopted one, or having the assurance that she was really in the theatre, and not to lose all patience,—nay, nearly all self-control, even as respected the employment of postures, gestures, and voice. He was continually taking out his watch to see how the hours sped. He would jump up to his feet as with a jerk, sometimes looking wistfully and mournfully all around him, on other occasions, angrily and menacingly, to the no small disturbance of those in his immediate neighbourhood, and not without hisses and indignant complaints being directed towards him. Even while seated, his head, hands, and arms performed strange antics, as if he had been in a measure convulsed. He talked to himself, sighed and groaned like to one who carried within him a wounded spirit; frequently, as he talked to himself, comparing his present misery and anguish to what had coloured and burdened his existence ever since the discovery of the infidelity of the loved one of his young manhood. The hardened Jobson came to be alarmed, and to feel that he had been carrying his infamous game too far with such a character as the stern as well as eccentric owner of the Red Cot.

If such were the convictions and alarms of the villain as the night waxed later and later, and whilst the cynic was self-absorbed or abstractedly surged, what must have been the fellow's dismay when his victim turned directly towards him, and began plainly to accuse him with acting falsely and treacherously.

"These letters from the alleged butler," demanded the cynic, "were they genuine, or were they vile forgeries concocted by yourself and some accomplice or another? Is your name veritably Henry Livingstone, or are ye a member of the *swell mob*? Perhaps ye are Jared Jobson, disguised as a gentleman; and if so, this will account for much of your information and your acquaintance with my affairs as well as with those of others for whom I entertain an interest. Speak and be honest, for no subterfuge shall avail you this night; there is no escape for you if ye be the villain I more than surmise."

By this time the old gentleman's conduct had grown too vehement to allow it to be longer tolerated by the audience, had the conclusion of the performances of the evening not happened at the same moment that the aroused Peter accompanied his last cited words with a clutch at the breast-clothing of the villain, in order that he might not escape him. The curtain had been let drop, and every one in the densely crowded house was looking to himself or herself with the view of making their exit as expeditiously and safely as possible, excepting such as were near witnesses of the scene between the impostor and his victim; the wonder being to see the younger one of the pair taking so quietly the threatenings and the handling he was subjected to. The on-lookers did not know how necessary it was for the fellow to be submissive in such a place, at such a time, and when in the hands of the rugged individual whose conduct had made some of them set him down to be a maniac, but who began now to imagine he had some grievous wrong to complain of. Neither were these amazed persons aware how quickly and simply the roughly-handled party could rid himself of the enraged one's grasp. All had risen from their seats, the clutcher and the clutched as well as the rest.

"You cruelly wrong me," cried the latter. "Look there, and tell me who it is you behold. Said I not that by the time the entertainments came near to a close, there was every probability of her coming within the range of our sight. It was but this moment that my eyes caught a glimpse of the young lady; nor might this have been my good fortune, had I not at the very same time experienced the misfortune of being the object of such false accusations and ungenerous surmises being hurled at me by yourself as brought her to look steadily at the scene between us. Look, sir, and satisfy yourself," added the scoundrel, now released from the other's hold, who, like one for the moment stunned and stupified, had neither the power to move nor to speak. But the transfixture was brief.

"You say truly, sir, I have wronged you, but I will make ample amends," were the first words suggested by the revulsed sentiments of the old man, whose innate sense of justice was too strong to allow him to be consciously untrue or cruel to any one. "Adelaide! Adelaide!" were his next utterances upon a still louder key, as he violently fought forward in the direction where she bent over, to make herself sure that it was indeed the recluse to whom she felt herself everlastingly bound, and towards whom, since her withdrawal from the shelter of his roof, her gratitude and affections had been taking a more growing hold of her heart. Ah! little did she know the strength and intensity to which the old cynic's love and admiration of her had reached.

"My wondrous benefactor! wait for me below there, till I come to you," was the response which the transported maiden shot down to the old man, to the consternation of Lady Lymington and the other members of her ladyship's party, on hearing what was exclaimed by the young and beautiful creature, whose character it was to acknowledge openly her joy the instant she recognised the being towards whom her inmost soul cherished yearnings that were filial. "I cannot forgive myself for my silence to, and apparent neglect of, him,—acting on a false principle as I have been doing. At great risk and toil he has come to look for, and after, me. He cannot have received my late letter which I directed to the Red Cot;" these being of the number of her excited expressions, as she hurried hither and thither to get access to the Samaritan.

It was in one of these half distracted races that she entered a box of the lowest tier, when she wildly looked athwart the sea of heads and faces which the yet not half emptied pit presented; a stoppage, in fact, having been somewhat occasioned at the outlets in consequence of the very scene in which old Peter had enacted such a prominent part, together with Adelaide herself. See looked athwart the heaving, the suffocating, and crushing ocean, getting at length a glimpse of the object of her intense search. He was hatless; he was all but insensible from the pressure which was upon him; and yet he was within reach of her hand, two or three feet below where she stretched down her arms, if he could but upraise his.

"My wondrous benefactor! cannot you see me? cannot you speak to me?" cried she, as she strained herself to the uttermost to touch were it but the crown of his head.

The well-remembered accents reached the hearing and soul of the half dead old man. He opened his eyes; he looked up in the direction whence the sound came; an arm was next raised by him, which reached the maiden's; and this was the sudden and brief salute which alone blessed their interview that night, Peter's feeble ejaculation of "Adelaide! my Adelaide!" being the only expressions he had the power to make use of for hallowing the transient and remarkable scene. The outlets lent vent; the dense mass swept on, carrying the wonted recluse with it, as a swollen river would bear the slenderest twig within its bosom, after the confining bank has given way. The ecstatic grasp was loosened. The young one could not follow the old, nor the old return to the young. They were severed.

"Jared Jobson is on your heels, wondrous benefactor! Abide for me outside, dear old man, or but respond where you can be found," were the maiden's only other excited words at that crisis.

But Peter Plumtree heard them not, being beyond their reach, in the drowning hubbub of the moment. The villain, whom she clearly descried, and who was nearer to her when she spoke, was not so dull nor so exhausted as the older man; a scowl of revenge being the return he gave to her recognition and announcement. The remembrance and look of the diabolical monster were too powerful for her to withstand. She hastened back in search of Lady Lymington; but the dame and her party were not to be found,—they had gone,—whether in displeasure at the part which the governess had performed, or through some misunderstanding of her conduct and intentions, she could not say.

"No matter, or rather it is the better result, that I am left and allowed my freedom to tarry and search for my noble-hearted benefactor," said the young lady to herself, as soon as she was in the open air in front of the theatre. "Their carriage and their company will be nothing to me, compared with a conversation with him who has adopted me in his heart. I will tarry here till daylight, if I thought that then I should have the privilege of clasping the knees of the rugged but sterling recluse of the Red Cot."

But old Peter had also quitted the playhouse and its vicinity; for no sooner had he got into the ample lobby of the pit than speedy relief came to him from the purer air which he breathed, and in consequence of the deliverance from the suffocating, crushing pressure. A few minutes more, and he is in a street-vehicle on his way to the Blue Boar, being now considerably lighter, in respect of weight, than when he last left that hospitable inn; for not only was he minus his hat and a great portion of his new outer-garment, but his gold watch was gone,—which had been a sort of heir-loom in the family for an hundred years,—as also the well-filled purse which he had hoped being able to throw into the keeping of his adopted one.

"I care not much for these mishaps," sobbed the old man to the landlord of the hostelry, from whom he had temporarily to borrow the sum to pay the fare of the vehicle which brought him home; "I mean the mishaps of lost and torn clothing, and will include also whatever of gold I had upon me, although I should give five times its original price or worth to have the watch back again. But what of these losses and sorrows to my being torn away from my darling, my adopted daughter,—she who recognised me at last, and cried out to me in the most affectionate terms, in the crowded theatre, too,—nay, who was grasping this coarse hand of mine, and passionately clinging to it, when, alas! I became insensible, and was swept beyond her reach? This will prove my killing loss, my continual sorrow, while I breathe,—a sorrow only to be equalled or surpassed by a far earlier one."

But Peter could say no more for some minutes, filling up the intervals with such sighs, groans, and weeping as some old, strong men will do in their utmost extremity.

"There is another thing which distresses me," he at length said, having recovered something of his usual composure: "I have wronged and misused Mr. Livingstone, whilst in the theatre, by my impatient vehemence."

The old man here related what had occurred between him and the other towards the close of the performances, leaving out, however, any reference to the opera-glass and other particulars, the statement of which, perhaps, might have helped the landlord to come to some positive conclusion in his own mind relative to the character of Mr. Plumtree's theatrical associate. At the same time, he who was at the head of the Blue Boar establishment happened to be a person of a grave and well-bred disposition, who would have in any case been exceedingly slow to express any opinion that would run the risk of compromising him with a customer, and such he looked upon the worthy of whom the Yorkshire eccentric had been speaking, as having ill-used. Boniface, therefore, politely acquiesced in most of the old gentleman's conclusions, with a simple bend of the head, or a "Very true, sir;" only quietly volunteering an observation to the effect that it was not to be recommended to country gentlemen, who had the appearance of *warmth* about them, to go to a London playhouse with watches in their fobs or heavy purses in their pockets,—a remark in which the lightened listener entirely concurred.

The hour had by the end of this discourse waxed considerably beyond that of midnight, and the old gentleman was about to withdraw to his bed, to see what repose he might there obtain, and whether a nap would in any way restore him to his wonted self. But just as he was very slowly rising up out of his chair, like a greatly tired, and, indeed, an unwell person, who should, at that unseasonable time, in ordinary circumstances, rush into the room, but the pretended Livingstone. The circumstances, however, were not of an ordinary character, for sober and regular people, at least; for, not to say anything about the very unusual incidents of that night, in the course of which he had somewhat figured, the fellow now had the aspect of having been a chief actor, and this, too, in what looked like a tragical affray.

It was not alone that the impostor entered apparently in a condition of most violent excitement, or that his dress was in great disorder,—being in parts torn and also smeared with mud,—or that blood trickled from his mouth and nose, as if it were slow to be stemmed, after having dyed his face and other portions of his person,—one of his arms being slung in his pocket-handkerchief,—these were not the only remarkable things about him, and what he had to tell. As soon as he was able to articulate distinctly and consecutively, as the tumult of his breast subsided,—the whole being very cleverly simulated,—he began to unfold a tale of adventure and disaster which deeply moved and astounded the Yorkshire eccentric.

The trumped-up story was this: that he had been robbed not only of the few pounds sterling that were upon him, and also of the opera-

glass, which had already been the occasion of misunderstanding and uneasiness, but he had at the time of suffering the loss a distinct idea of the person who perpetrated the felony, as he persuaded himself. The thing, however, having taken place while terribly squeezed in the pit,—the stoppage to the usually free egress of the company having been no doubt caused, the scoundrel said, by a combination of swell-mobsmen for their own particular ends,—he had no opportunity to lay hold of the thief, and it would have been folly to charge an individual in the existing circumstances of the moment upon suspicion. However, he kept his eye upon the supposed criminal, holding also, by means of extraordinary exertions, near to him,—in this way losing proximity to Mr. Plumtree, and indeed, at last, all sight of him. At length he got into the lobby, and next into the street,—he having by this time a hold of

No. 13.—THE GOVERNESS.

the supposed robber, amid the still swarming crowds, as well as a wilderness of carriages, when he found himself surrounded by, no doubt, a party of the perpetrator's accomplices, all of whom instantly "pitched" into him; so that after fighting for a few moments manfully, he was completely mastered, and left sprawling in the street. However, he was lifted up by some humane persons, otherwise he might certainly have been crushed to death by the hurrying vehicles all around. Even as it was, he had sustained a severe contusion in one of his arms. As was to be looked for, the suspected thief and his party were nowhere to be seen when he was brought to himself. This, however, was not for a considerable time, if his ability to walk, and otherwise have any tolerable command of his powers, were to be taken into account. In fact, it was not till after having been conveyed to a surgeon's, and there for some space kindly attended to, that he was in a state to get to the Blue Boar; his anxiety about his friend Mr. Plumtree, and his strong presentiment that evil might also have befallen the old gentleman, serving to increase his agitation as he approached the inn.

"What has greatly added, besides," said the impostor, " to augment my distress and fears is this, that I could see from the eager and strenuous movements of your adopted daughter, Mr. Plumtree, that she wished to meet you somewhere outside of the pit,—a thing which might have been accomplished had I been enabled to keep by your side, and then to station you at some one point, whilst I flew to bring her to where you remained. But I fear, sir, that you had not the happiness of speaking to the young lady when you felt yourself at any degree of liberty. Indeed, I need not conjecture; for the depression and disappointment of your looks tell me of deep sorrow;" the scoundrel hereupon affecting to sympathize profoundly with the old man, as well as to endure a great deal of mental pain on his own account.

The eccentric cynic reciprocated the sympathy with anything but a simulated feeling, and with as unabated a confidence in the false fellow, as if not a doubt regarding him had shot into the man's mind. He next related his own mishaps at the theatre, dwelling, with a species of rapture, upon the circumstances of the sudden and transient salute between him and his adopted, so far as these were known to him, and next, with a corresponding anguish and despair, about her being lost to him for ever, as he said. As a minor grievance—which, however, would have been regarded a very serious one, had it not been transcended greatly by the idea of having looked upon his adopted daughter for the last time—the loss of the heirloom watch was a disaster which came in for a share of the lament; the robbing him of his well-filled purse —careful money-hoarder though he had been, and still mainly was—troubling him far less than having been deprived of his old-fashioned gold keepsake, which, in the regular market, would have been worth little.

"There are ways, without difficulty, of filling up the silk-bag again which held the gold pieces," said the cynic; "but I see of no chance or probability of getting the ancient tenant of my fob back to its wonted place. As to the few scores of coins that were in the purse, what does it signify to me their passing into the hands of such a cut-throat and mean scoundrel as some Jared Jobson or another, seeing that there is no likelihood of my ever having my darling girl to bequeath them to? Truly, in my old age I am an unhappy man, and one that finds his miseries growing upon him every day."

It must have been a hard heart that was not moved on witnessing how deeply afflicted this genuine man of years really was as he thus talked; an individual, too, who, in accordance with his recluse habits for years—with mute Martha for his only domestic—had kept his griefs to himself, or growled them to the solitude around the Red Cot. But the impostor had no pity for, or upon, the eccentric Samaritan; the wretch had no bowels of compassion for a soul on earth. On the contrary, his

designs upon his dupe had been **growing** more fiendish and fell, the longer he preyed upon the old man's credulity; and now that the recollections of how Peter turned upon him in the theatre were uppermost, his revenge towards his victim burned in his breast with something of a volcanic fury, producing after all whatsoever of that tumult was genuine, which he manifested that night on entering the Blue Boar.

It was not an unnaturally made arrangement for the impostor to take up his abode under the same roof, on the night in question, with him who had been his companion and dupe at the Opera House. It was not a less obvious course for the infamous plotter to tell the old gentleman, as they parted to take to their different dormitories, that he would, before they met at the breakfast-table, have, probably, certain things matured in his own mind, not only with regard to the recovery of the watch, but as concerned the circumstances and condition of the adopted damsel. With respect to the little silk-bag, and its golden contents, the scoundrel could suggest no hopes of restoration; although he evinced much anxious curiosity to learn what the old gentleman remembered or thought about the manner of this particular loss; the refraining from building up his dupe with reference to the coins, being thus far consistent with his guilty belief that he knew they had got into his own keeping, before he left the side of his victim, early in the squeeze of the company's departure from the pit of the playhouse.

Morning came, when the impostor and his dupe met once more,—after a series of such social interviews at the breakfast table, Mr. Plumtree, ever since the first day of his stay at the Blue Boar, having been induced, by the representations of Jobson, to have a parlour for his own exclusive occupation, instead of allowing himself to mingle with the nondescripts, as the cunning pretender characterized them, who frequented the travellers' room. After the usual salutations, befitting the first meeting of the day, the anxious and confiding Peter eagerly inquired of the other if what he had alluded to when they last parted, to go to their beds, had in any measure ripened in his mind; and, if so, he begged to have the suggestions. The villain, who by this time had got his raiment brushed, and the slight fractures of the same mended, and also the blood washed from him which had issued from his gums and nostrils, in consequence of a few self-inflicted scratches—his uninjured arm, however, being still in a sling, and his complaints of the bruises he had sustained not less indicative of felt injuries—proceeded to explain himself.

"My suggestions, to which you allude, Mr. Plumtree," answered the impostor, " of course, have had for their subject, first of all, the young lady towards whom your own principal anxieties have their exercise. Now, there can be little doubt that we may, with comparatively small trouble, after what we have undergone, learn this much, whether the Lady B——, whom the butler represented as being on the eve of passing over to the Continent—whether she has really gone off this morning or not.

The ascertainment of how this fact may stand will, no question of it, be the discovery whether the young lady accompanies the titled dame or not. If they have both taken their flight, then your further pursuit and search in England, for the present, my good sir, must prove unavailing."

Just as the villain had got to this point of his talk, old Peter evinced symptoms of being taken suddenly ill; a mental spasm, even more than the physical crushing which he had sustained on the bygone night, denying him for a little while the power of speech. At length he requested the other to proceed, adding that he felt and feared whatever was to be quickly executed, must be seen to without his presence and personal exertions, for that he had been more injured the night before than he was aware of at the time; a confession and statement which were highly acceptable to the plotter.

"Obviously, the primary step," continued the pretended Livingstone, "will be for me to proceed, the moment we have completed our morning meal, to the Opera House, in order that I may learn who was the principal occupant last night of the particular box, in which we got the first glimpse—although at the close of the performances—of the young lady we so long looked for in vain. If the matron of the party for the evening was a Lady B——, surely the name will in full be at once announced to me. This done, what hinders but that I forthwith make all haste to ascertain in what quarter she resides or has been residing? My course is plain, and the discoveries we are so eager about, may all, I should think, be made in a few hours. The other subject of my sleepless hours' reflections, Mr. Plumtree, has been the possibility of recovering your much-prized watch."

"Never speak of the watch for the present," impatiently cried the unwell old man; "it is not to be named in the same hour, much less in the same breath, with my darling jewel, who, like ourselves, has an immortal soul to care for. I slept but little since last going to bed, I assure you, Mr. Livingstone, and that little far from soundly; my startled dreams being fearful. Somehow, in the visions of the night, it was strongly and strangely borne in upon my distracted mind that ruffians had run off with her from the theatre; nay, that you yourself were a mover in the enormity, having set on others to do the deed; nay, more frightful still, Jared Jobson was in the conspiracy, I thought, and that it was by his as also by your counsel and help mainly that she was taken to a den of infamy, there to be sacrificed in a manner more woful than I can name. But these were only dreams," added the old man, relapsing into the sort of mental spasm which had seized him a little while before; being merely able to add, "Away upon your mission at once; I'll stir not from the inn until I see you again."

The impostor was too glad to see and hear this, to remain a moment longer at the time in the presence of the old gentleman, whose nocturnal visions no doubt took their shape and complexion from certain surmises which he had entertained against the pretended Liv-

ingstone whilst in the playhouse, and also in part from his over-wrought solicitudes about the damsel. Once beyond the precincts of the Blue Boar, the impostor's arm passed out of the sling, and he who had been walking gingerly, and bearing himself as if he had been bruised from head to foot, was off with nimbleness to some one of his haunts, to dispose of, as he found it most convenient for him, the contents of the stolen purse, and also to take further counsel with certain of his accomplices in crime, of what was next to be done. One, and the chief of these villains, was a fellow of the name of Ned Norland,—the same individual in fact who had been seated at the right hand of their victim in the theatre, —and who took the watch, while Jobson hemmed in the old gentleman on the left.

Six or eight hours,—long hours truly to Peter Plumtree,—elapsed before the return of the pretended Livingstone to the Blue Boar. Nor could the lugubriousness of his countenance fail of at once intimating to the old man that he came laden with doleful tidings.

"I have nothing to learn but the worst," cried the dupe, who was pacing athwart his parlour in an agony of anxiety, unable to hold himself in a posture of stillness and comparative ease throughout the latter part of the dreary interval.

"No, no,—not the worst," returned the impostor, with a show of impatient sympathy. "I know not, indeed, whether we ought not to conclude that the information which I bring should enliven us, Mr. Plumtree, although I fear, the gloom which was in my own mind, as I came into the room just now, arising from other reflections than any that immediately concerned your adopted darling, must have looked an evil herald. The truth is, that she has not been run off with by ruffians; that Henry Livingstone has had no hand in any such enormity,"—this being said with a well-feigned air of hurt innocence; "and that as concerns Jared Jobson, I have not been told of his having the remotest knowledge of, or connexion with, her, since her coming to London. The short and long are these:—that, as the butler's letter informed us, she is off for the Continent with Lady Barrington, the extremely wealthy widow of an Irish baronet, and who is going to spend a twelvemonth of travel on the Continent, then to return to reside mainly at her suburban mansion in the vicinity of Hammersmith. No doubt she'll bring back with her the young governess, unless, indeed, the beauty find a partner for life abroad; all of which circumstances, should we live another year or so, will be easily and minutely ascertained by us, and when, too, I trust, we shall be in a better state of spirit as well as of body than we are now to enjoy meeting with her, or at least of hearing of her wedded happiness, as, I think, is more likely than that such a charming creature should be long allowed to remain single."

"No, no—I will not have her to settle abroad, nor to wed a foreigner," cried Peter, thus changing the ground of his fears and anxiety, and necessarily at the same time taking a more hopeful and gladdening footing than he had immediately before been holding. "She has a noble youth already in her eye, and who shall be my adopted son-in-law, if I have anything to say in her arrangements for life. But why did she not contrive to seek me out, after what she saw and knew of me last night? Perhaps a few hours might have sufficed for this purpose; and what considerable difference would it have made to Lady Barrington, if she, for the sake of one she is said to have taken such a liking to, had put off their departure so short a time? Adelaide must have told the titled one of what she might expect from me, and she must be a selfish, tyrannical woman if she would not accommodate the governess of her children to the extent I mention."

"Mr. Plumtree, you'll forgive me for saying," replied the impostor, "that you are forgetting yourself when you thus speak, or rather you are overlooking the exingencies of business as well as the ways of the world. What! after all Lady Barrington's luggage was shipped, and the hour as well as day determined on when she and her retinue were to sail from Father Thames in a particular vessel, which, for anything I know, carries the mail to some foreign port,—were every one of these arrangements to be marred for any private individual's interests,—which interests, after all, might not seem to a neutral party of extreme importance? However, all I can speak positively to is this, that, having received the necessary preliminary information at the Opera House, I proceeded direct to Hammersmith, in whose vicinity I found a splendid mansion, to which has lately been given a name after that of the opulent widow who purchased it, and that at Barrington Lodge a matronly housekeeper told me the particulars I have mentioned. She stated, at the same time, that Lady Barrington and suite were to take up their abode from yesterday till this morning at some hotel in the West End, the title of which she did not know, and that thence they were early to proceed to their ship."

Old Peter had nothing left for it but silently to console himself in the best way he could for his harrassing disappointments; having, however, his spirit manifestly lightened by the turn the information brought him, such as it was, had taken; although he might not at the time have acknowledged to any consciousness of the relief. As a proof of his recovery from the torture of his mental anxieties, he passed on to the subject of his watch, saying that he should be pleased to hear what his counsellor had to say as respected the possibility of recovering the heir-loom.

CHAPTER XXI.

THE SWELL-MOBSMEN.

THE villain, Ned Norland, was of quite a different stamp from Jared Jobson, as might be expected, were it owing to nothing but this—that he was a purely London-bred criminal. We have, a long way back, been told something of the general and the variedly eventful history of the latter pest of the world,—a wretch who was steeped to the lips in every species of infamous enormity, and who with good natural parts, and a fair amount of edution, had an extraordinary extent of villany's experience.

Accordingly, he could occupy positions, fulfil parts, and personate characters of the most opposite kinds; the greatest drawback to his assumption of the gentleman being that sort of weather-beaten aspect, both of figure and of face, that indicated the endurance of great hardships, perhaps as much as the having lived under different climates. At the same time he could dress and carry himself with a fitness and regard to fashion with as much self-possession in the drawing-room, or at the genteel dining-table, as when in the costume and following the ways of a smuggler or bandit. The brutal footpad and the mounted highwayman seemed to be equally his part; his language and conduct, with a wonderful fertility and elasticity, being suited to all these conditions.

But as for Norland, he was exclusively and purely a London swell-mobsman; or, if there was any diversity in his gifts, his acquirements, and his proficiencies, it was in the ready exchange of the frank, business-like, and accomplished man of trade and commerce of the city of Cockneys, into the tip-top exquisite of the West End. In this latter character indeed it was his principal ambition to figure,—for Ned's tastes were aspiring as well as genteel, to which his handsome figure and originally elegant carriage seemed naturally to fit him. He dressed with good taste; at the gaming-table, where he was a skilful player, as well as a dexterous cheat, and in those masquerading or dancing saloons, where the most aspiring of those females of questionable character and pretensions do congregate in the overgrown Babel, he was a mighty favourite; never by any chance for years having been known to compromise himself by a breach of manners, any more than by an act of real or detected dishonesty. Nay, at times, he had found access to patrician circles in consequence of his connexion with profligate scions of nobility, through his expertness with the dice, and in horse-dealing, and also turf transactions.

Like all swell-mobsmen, however, although Norland looked upon himself as their prince in the British metropolis, he found himself obliged not only to have recourse to the services of accomplices, but such as were of a far inferior class to himself, although he always both felt degradation in the contact and great peril. We should have mentioned that he was a first-rate practitioner at sleight-of-hand tricks; that he might have almost as worthily been styled a Wizard of the North, as he had been named Norland; for in his playful humour with his acquaintances who might be sporting a piece of jewellery in their breast under-clothing, or other articles about their person, he would,—after telling of the wonder he was going to achieve,—do the very thing he promised, without their knowledge of, or belief in, the circumstance, until they saw the taken article in his hand. In this way he far excelled Jared Jobson, who was rather a scoundrel that, by his daring and the multiplicity of his resources, perhaps surpassed all miscreants of his class in this country at the time, than by the polish and expertness of his manual arts, or the fascinations of his eye; this last-mentioned gift being said to belong to Norland to such an extent, together with his art of in-stantly distracting the attention from what he was mainly intent upon, that he often withdrew the ring from a finger without the robbed per-son being aware of the theft.

It was impossible that such fellows as Jobson and Norland could be long in London at one and the same time, without their becoming mutually acquainted, had it been but through the underlings of each other. They had, ever after their first interview, entertained reci-procal fears and jealousies, and, if it may be said, reciprocal respectfulness. Neither of them would confide in or employ the other, when he could help it; yet there were cer-tain times when they both felt it to be their interest to work together as if they had been partners in a particular firm. Old Peter Plum-tree had been the victim solely of the pre-tended Livingstone; but the period arrived when the despicable impostor found it needful for him to call in the aid of others, to accom-plish his vile ends towards not only the York-shire Samaritan, but her whom that worthy man was eager to treat in the same way as if she had been his own daughter. These ends re-quired the participation of still another villain of a different rank from any of the pair we have just been talking of; concerning which third party, and his peculiar doings, in due course. But first, of the suggestions concern-ing the recovery of the heir-loom article.

"What value do you set upon your lost gold watch, Mr. Plumtree," was the impostor's question, " or rather what would you give to have it in your keeping again, being for a long while a much prized family article, I believe? I put these questions to you in the most friendly spirit, which you will allow as soon as you un-derstand that frequently, in the case of stolen property in London, when the person who has been robbed is ready to pay as much to have the thing back as the thief in the course of his nefarious transactions can get for it, an ar-rangement is made by means of a third party, —a sort of *go-between*, as they have it in China in the matter of courtship,—through whom the object is restored without the capture of the stealer. It has occurred to me that I might be of service to you in a business of this kind; and if you think I can probably be so, perhaps you will say how much you would give to have the watch back."

"I would not grudge twenty pounds ster-ling," answered old Peter, "although I could not get five for it were I to offer it for sale. If you think you can manage the exchange you have been speaking of, on these terms, Mr. Livingstone, I'll advance you the sum I have mentioned that you may try your hand with it. If you cannot succeed, it is but returning me the money, I paying you for the trouble you have been at. I have only this further to state that I must know the issue of your efforts the day after to-morrow at the latest. I have got enough of London for the time being, and must turn my face elsewhere."

The pretended Livingstone having stated that he would have to issue a peculiar sort of hand-bills and other advertising forms for his purpose, hastened to set his new piece of black-guardism to work, glad to hear that the old gentleman had got sick of London, and was about to take wing, as the villain despaired of having it in his power to fleece him much fur-ther. Jobson felt, besides, that he was every day running the nearer risk of being pounced upon by some one who had known him in another guise or quarter, if not by old Peter himself.

It was no later than the very next day, about the cynic's dinner-hour, that the impostor came in a hurry to the Blue Boar, apparently in an ecstacy of thankfulness, with the heir-loom watch in his pocket, having given ten pounds to Norland for the exchange, and kept the other ten to himself. And no less delighted, indeed much more really, was the owner at the sight of his old bulky companion, which speedily found its accustomed bed in the old man's unsophisticated fob. In fact, so fully completed did Peter now conceive all the business which could, in the metropolis, be transacted by him on that visit, and so happy was he to find himself master of the family piece again, that he resolved on leaving that very afternoon; stating to the pretended Livingstone that he should start from the Belle Sauvage Inn, Ludgate Hill, for Yorkshire, at a certain hour of the evening, and requesting that the still confided-in impostor would meet him at that spot, that they might bid farewell to one another at the place of his taking a seat to go northwards.

The wonted recluse, like all punctual people, having sent his portmanteau and carpet-bag by the porter of the Blue Boar before him to the office of the four-insided vehicle, by which he was to travel homewards, and having hand-somely cleared his score at his inn, trudged slowly and gravely along for Ludgate. It was twilight,—a slight shower falling at the time, which had the character of a thick mist, in fact, rather than otherwise; but not such as to obscure or hide the features of one person from another, should they be passing narrowly by at the time. It was just as the unsuspecting gentleman had crossed the entire breadth of Farringdon Street, near to certain of its diver-gent lanes, that a person put his hand upon his shoulder, and claimed a sort of acquaint-anceship with him.

"Ha!" exclaimed the obtrusive one, who was dressed most handsomely, and in the first style of fashion, having rings upon his fingers, whose diamonds shed a beauteous light in the obscurity, and a massive guard-chain arranged in proper order upon his waistcoat,—"ha! how has it fared with you since I sat beside you in the Opera House t'other night, and where I witnessed your misunderstanding with your quiet companion. If you'll take a look at me you'll remember I was the person to whom you wished to refer the capabilities of the opera-glass your friend had purchased for your especial use that evening. I regretted that I had not the opportunity of acting umpire between you, for I would assuredly have given my opinion on your side, if with any show of reason it could have been done."

"Curse the opera-glass and your impertinence," said Peter, having come to himself after the abrupt interruption.

"I beg your pardon, sir," quickly returned the other, consulting his own gold watch at the moment. "It is past eight o'clock, I find, to my astonishment, and I had a particular appointment with a young lady at eight, in Fleet Street."

"And my coach starts at eight from the Belle Sauvage," subjoined the old gentleman, hobbling along as fast as he could do while he fumbled for the heir-loom article, and as the exquisite disappeared in the mist. But watch there was not in its accustomed fob, neither again ever should be, for Mr. Ned Norland had a second time got his clutches upon it. As for the robbed one, he felt it would not only be a waste of toil and anxiety for him to cry "catch thief!" but that in all probability this would peril his chance of getting beyond the stratagems of swell-mobsmen that night. He therefore continued to hobble onward and to growl to himself, as he had been accustomed to do at the most misanthropic period of his recluse-days; certain lights at the same instant shooting through his brain, concerning the pretended Livingstone, and these not only as regarded the scoundrel's association with the rascal who had last taken his watch, but the fellow's identity with Jared Jobson. In fact, all the old man's cynicism and his distrust of mankind, as experienced in his most embittered and eccentric days, seemed on the instant to return upon him, chasing away every particle of that courtesy and propriety, if not blandness of language and carriage, which had generally characterized his bearing and discourse since coming within the metropolitan atmosphere.

"Where be you, ye cut-throat,—ye impostor and robber?" cried the suddenly enlightened and enraged old man, on his stepping into the entrance of the yard of the Belle Sauvage, he having ascertained from the right time-keeping clocks of the fully lighted shops which he passed, that he was quite half-an-hour before the necessary moment to be at the coach's starting post. "Shut the gates and keep him inside till I have my paws upon him,—upon the villain, Jared Jobson, by which name he passed when playing the coarse ruffian in Yorkshire, but now a swell-mobsman of the first water, in the guise of a gentleman and under the *alias* of Henry Livingstone," louder howled Peter Plumtree, while he stretched out both arms and stood in the gateway to prevent the egress and escape of the scoundrel, should he happen to be inside, and resolved to attempt flight.

But the impostor and robber was not to be so caught, for he had taken care to be outside, and to keep the opposite path of Ludgate Hill to that on which the inn was, anxious to learn in what humour the old man might be after the loss of the heir-loom for a second and final time. Nor did the trebly-dyed villain remain to learn more than the commencement of the awakened accuser's charge and wild talk, seeing that not only the inn and coach-people of the yard the old man was endeavouring to barricade by means of his pair of arms, were crowding towards him, but that policemen and multitudes of passers-by without kept rushing to the spot, even to the consternation of Peter himself, who began to think it best to back out of the inconvenience. This he did by stating to the officers, who took him into the inn to listen to his story, that he did not think he could identify the fellow who had just taken his watch, but that he believed him to be an associate of a scoundrel who had for some days been imposing upon him at the Blue Boar, and who passed as a gentleman of the name of Mr. Henry Livingstone, at that inn, although he rather suspected that he had before taken the appellation of Jared Jobson.

Peter's excitement, however, as well as his story, appeared to the policeman and others, who listened to him at the time, to be those of a crazed or drunk person, which it would be idle to act upon; and, therefore, as the old gentleman really desired, he was permitted to go off with the coach; although from certain inquiries which were soon made at the Blue Boar, so much transpired, that was more than confirmatory of what he alleged, as would have assuredly detained him for farther examination before some of the chiefs of police in the metropolis. As it was, and indeed as the now embittered cynic anticipated, while he travelled northwards, messengers followed with warrants to bring him to town, in order that the arch villain, who had so terribly and successfully preyed upon him, might be the more surely traced. The owner of the Red Cot, therefore, acting upon his fears, did not even set foot, on this occasion, on his tongue of territory, much less enter his grotesque home; only paying a stealthy and most hasty visit to the quarter of the neighbouring village, where all letters were to be left for him, the people of the particular house never having, since his last leaving them, received the slightest notice where he was to be found. Two of these communications affected him in the tenderest manner, and produced, with regard at least to one individual, another sudden revolution in his sentiments. The epistles were from the adopted girl, and had been written not only after his quitting home and arrived, to make search after her in London and its suburbs, but immediately posterior to her quitting the mansion of Mrs. Puffendorff, and her reception under the roof of Lady Lymington. Each of the writings breathed a most affectionate, grateful spirit to her "wondrous benefactor," as she there styled him, and also a resolute determination to achieve her own independence, without extraneous aid; so that she might stand, perhaps, in the estimation of Montague Mildmay on a more elevated pedestal, as well as in her own, than without trials and adversity she could have ever done, or could have had opportunities of reaching, had she not been put to a governess's ordeal. Not only was her deep resolve clearly and eloquently stated, but her hope was avowed of her being, at no distant period, in a position to tell her "wondrous benefactor" of her rising prosperity; of where and how she was situated; and either to pay him a visit or to solicit one from him. Meanwhile it concerned her, as was slightly hinted, that she worked out her own deliverance and promotion.

"Strangely heroic thing!" ejaculated the

old man, as he stealthily withdrew from his native neighbourhood; not a soul receiving a single hint whither he was going or what he intended to do. "I have, in running homeward after my worse than idle visit to London, and after being fooled and played upon by a cut-throat and the vilest of wretches, like an old idiot as I have shown myself,—I have been charging her with the heartlessness of our race, and beginning to think of relinquishing all care about her; so that had she at any time come within the reach of my eye and voice, I might have scowled and growled at her as at the bulk of our vile kind. But no more of this by and from Peter Plumtree towards the adopted of my heart; and were it that I could but be assured she is safe from the villanies of Jobson and others who may have an evil eye towards the noble creature, I would with a tolerable measure of contentment await her own time and way of blessing me to the uttermost that any one human being can now do; that happiness I do trust, being in conjunction with Montague Mildmay's."

Leaving old Peter to speculate and to hope as he best could relative to the adopted of his heart and the future, and also to pursue certain designs he had been entertaining ever since he obtained possession of the dearly-cherished miniature-portrait which Sir Vaux Waldgrave consigned to his keeping, we must return to the young governess, as she properly might be styled, down to the night of her going to the Opera House, where she so unexpectedly got a glimpse of her benefactor, interchanging with him not merely a few words, but a sudden and transient salute.

While residing under Lady Lymington's roof, and, as the reader will remember, before the girl went there, that dame had manifested and professed towards the young creature a wonderful admiration and affection. She had even gone to the extent of avowing that her own renovation and hope of being exalted to her proper position and influence depended on cherishing such principles as the beautiful but all but friendless damsel seemed to make the rules for her own conduct. Adelaide Neville was at first rather distrustful of the constancy, if not, perhaps, of her ladyship's utter sincerity, she, at least, for a time fearing that she might prove fickle, and relapse into her former indolence and frivolity. But a continuance of strong professions and declared resolute purposes, combined with no slight efforts to obtain for the maiden an enviable situation, overcame all Adelaide's doubts and scruples in a very short time, after having the titled dame's table to sit at; although, had the trusting girl been aware that her ladyship secretly marvelled, nay, was dissatisfied in consequence of the closeness which the governess maintained relative to a variety of circumstances in her brief life,—not even the character and extraordinary acts of generosity on the part of the eccentric Samaritan, having been divulged to the over-curious dame.

"Say what I may, do what I can," Lady Lymington would whisper to others of her acquaintance,—some of the younger ones entertaining a jealousy of Adelaide, on account of her gifts and acquirements as well as her surpassing beauty,—"all is of no avail to that creature whom I so generously patronise. There must, I fear, as Lady Gorewell will have it, be, after all, 'something rotten in the state of Denmark' with her. But I must test her a little longer, and a little more closely: time discloses wonders."

It is clear that any person who would speak and act thus disguisedly to another, especially to one who manifestly entertained no suspicion of the secret doubts and the growing disparagements, was, if not a positively dangerous individual to be near, and one unworthy of any reliance being placed in her honour, at least of such a disposition as might be turned to an innocent and inexperienced creature's hurt with fearful effect at some critical moment or another. In the meanwhile, poor, confiding, and flattered Adelaide had her hopes raised to a high pitch; more than once, as the reader has been told, writing to her strange and "wondrous benefactor," from the fulness of her heart.

In fact, it was not without some sinister curiosity that Lady Lymington, and a few more, looked forward to the evening at the Opera with regard to the manner in which Adelaide might deport herself at that theatre, as if they had anticipated that by some strange incident she would be induced to commit herself, or at least that it would be seen she was not equal to the exactions from people, who were to occupy a dowager-countess's box. They were entirely ignorant that the maiden had been more familiar than she afterwards approved of, or would have chosen in mature years for herself, with the music, the performances, and, in fact, all the technicalities of such places of entertainment, as these are to be met with in gay and giddy Paris. If thus it was that the oldest, as well as the youngest, of the Lymington party speculated on going to the playhouse, they soon found that Miss Neville, with retiring modesty, not only kept back in the box, allowing others to have the benefit of the seats most favourable to hearing and seeing what was going forward on the stage, of scanning the theatre, and of being observed in their turn; but that she could speak of the pieces of entertainment, their authors, and the past history of both, with critical knowledge; that her judgment of the performers, as, for example, of several of the singers as of the instrumental efforts, when she happened to be appealed to, had plainness and obvious propriety in it, putting to conscious shame the gossips of jealousy. Indeed, whoever of them had hoped that the maiden would deport herself to disadvantage on that occasion or as a novice, whatever might be her lovely looks, learnt reluctantly that they were in error regarding the theatrical education of the poor girl; so that Lady Lymington felt herself forced to compliment her aloud time after time on her taste and intimacy as regarded the higher branches of operatic art, and musical science.

"Here, as on all other occasions, my dear," observed her ladyship, "you take *the shine out of us*, as Mrs. Puffendorff would say. I marvel where or how, at your age, you have got all your skill and familiarity in regard to branches that the most accomplished of our sex might well be vain of. You are a strange girl, truly, take you which way I may."

"You will yet, probably, Lady Lymington, hear of and see stranger things of me," quietly replied the governess,—having taken note of the peculiar tone and manner of the *patronising* dame,—"than you have yet dreamt." This was said when the maiden stood forward in the box at the close of the performance,—moved by the extraordinary bustle which was going on in the pit, as already described, between the pretended Livingstone and his victim,—her eye at the instant alighting upon the ungainly old man, with certitude of recognition,—the circumstance suddenly and strangely affecting her.

The reader is acquainted with what immediately after this occurred, not only in the pit of the theatre, but on the part of the poor governess, as she strove to get near to her extraordinary benefactor. The girl appears to have been swayed at the time by some unusually potent impulse, and to have acted as if under a resistless presentiment, that, unless she now could cling to the generous old man, she never again should have the opportunity to secure his protection, and that a fearful doom impending over her should soon be irrevocably sealed. That which would naturally tend to produce these dark forebodings was the discovery that Jared Jobson was in the playhouse, and in contact somehow with the owner of the Red Cot; for the damsel's quick eye had caught a glimpse of the villain at the very first, and just as her recognition of the other took place; although her naturally deep excitement on the discovery made, and the species of opportunity allowed her, afforded only room for exclamations responsive to the eccentric one, and the brief utterance of what was uppermost in her heart.

As to the view which Lady Lymington and her party took of the governess's conduct, there can be little doubt, judging from the circumstance merely of the carriage which took them up, on issuing from the playhouse, being driven as quickly as possible away, the moment they were seated in it, without waiting to see what would become of the poor girl, or the slightest effort being made to ascertain how it fared with her.

"As I somehow irresistibly was forced to surmise," said her ladyship, "I thought our visit to the Opera would open my eyes and be decisive on certain points with regard to that extraordinarily gifted and educated, but unhappy young woman who has just run off from us, and made such a spectacle of herself in His Majesty's Theatre. I do hope and trust that her mad, most indelicate behaviour will not in any way compromise ourselves, as having had her one of our number throughout the preceding parts of the evening. To have remained to take her up when it suited her to look after our carriage, or to have made anxious inquiries in the lobbies about her, would certainly have insured our being exposed to a world of gossip and scandal; and yet, after all, proved of no service to her. She has chosen to act for herself in the most remarkable and indelicate manner in the presence of the aristocracy that at this moment swarm in London, to the great

jeopardy of the reputation of each of us; and she must now shift for herself in the future, at least so far as may concern any anticipated continuance of assistance and protection from me."

In this way it was that the dame talked as the carriage in which she and her party rode whirled along towards Kensington; her ladyship's mode of reasoning showing that however fickle or heartless she might in reality be, it cost her an effort to defend her own present conduct, and that she was not quite at ease with regard to what was to become of the poor governess.

"None of us can say, I believe," continued she, "who the individual was into whose arms the unfortunate girl strove to throw herself, as was the fact, we all know, from even the little we saw and heard in regard to her unprecedented behaviour. Whether the person was old or young, whether of mean or genteel appearance, we are ignorant. So great was the hubbub, and so hideous the noises of the house, especially in the pit, that it was impossible distinctly to discover,—unless we had been infatuated enough to mix ourselves up with the ill-fated creature's immodest doings,—the real facts of the case. We may depend upon it, however, that her motives and proceedings admit not of any such explanation as even she would have the hardihood to offer to me; and that to the cloak of mystery at the best she would, as usual, have to betake herself. And yet, after all, I do commiserate the wretched thing this really cold night, thinly clad as she is, and in full dress,—most of which, by the by, I lent to her,—and having nothing but a shawl to envelope her person. But she shall have her boxes the moment they are sent for, which, of course, will soon be, and not a word from me to the messenger as to what of mine she has upon her. I am sorry that she has not meanwhile, I dare say, a coin upon her; but she'll find a lodging for the night, no doubt, or *somebody* for her—who knows but it may be the party into whose arms she wished to throw herself even in the open theatre? What, indeed, is more likely? The world is coming to a pretty pass."

In this way the old fox-hunting but broken-down baronet's dame strove to excuse herself, as she and her friends sped towards her suburban abode; not one of the party endeavouring to cast in a more favourable word for the beautiful and innocent governess, or to mitigate her ladyship's constructions from any more sympathetic or charitable feelings. Meanwhile, what of the full-dressed, thinly-clad, unattended and unprotected girl, who kept shivering in the cold, under the portico of the playhouse, even after the whole of the company had nearly disappeared, and when she was becoming an object of speculation to all who came near her?

She had said to herself that she would abide at the spot where she was till break of day,—ay, and all alone, if she had assurance of then clasping the knees of her "wondrous benefactor." And this the girl would have done, for her moral resolution was great. But she soon began to be convinced that old Peter had disappeared from that neighbour-

SIR VAUX WALDGRAVE.

hood for the night; conjecturing also that he had been hurt in the crushing of the pit, as indeed his aspect and his manner of speech to her, when she grasped his hand, too plainly told. She perceived that she was becoming an object of amazement on the part of some,—of evil construction on that of others. Her condition was growing intolerable. What was she to do in the peculiar circumstances, and now near the midnight hour? Whither was she to go? To think of walking the miles that intervened between the Opera House and Kensington would have been madness, especially in the garb she found herself, and with the white satin shoes upon her feet; especially as a cold and driving rain had commenced coming down. She was literally penniless at the time; never calculating that there could be the slightest call made upon her by necessity on that occasion of fashionable and patronised

No. 14.—THE GOVERNESS.

entertainment for drawing upon the little savings which lay in a corner of one of her trunks at Lady Lymington's. It was a deplorable position to be placed in, and as the poor girl contemplated it in all its abandonment, destitution, and misery, her stout heart died within her, and she burst into an agony of weeping.

At this very crisis, a handsomely dressed person, in every respect having the appearance and manners of a polite and polished gentleman, came running up to her, as she staggered to one of the pillars of the portico, addressing her in words that sounded most welcome to her sad heart, and affectionately naming her.

"Where can you have been, Miss Neville, all this time?" he softly said. "Lady Lymington, with her other friends, have been waiting round the corner in the carriage for you, ever since they issued from the theatre,—sending everywhere for you, and employing every one who recognised her ladyship in her rather queer position,—halting upon the street,—to look for you. In this way my services have been put into requisition. Take my arm and hurry through the rain: a minute or two will bring us to the carriage, and then all will be well."

"Thank you, sir,—a thousand thanks to you for your goodness," was all that the young governess could articulate at the moment, for her tears required drying.

CHAPTER XXII.

THE OUTCAST'S EXTREMITY.

WHEN one finds the heart suddenly loosened by some unlooked-for agent from a weight of misery which has been utterly sinking it, and released from such dark forebodings in an instant, as were, if possible, more distressing than the immediate and actual sufferings, the rebound is apt to be immoderate, and the confidence in that agent whose ministry has been welcomed with a burst of joy, is in danger of becoming unguardedly entire. The poor governess, in a moment, after she understood the story of the courteous and handsome person who accosted her as she shivered and was ready to drop to the pavement under the portico of the King's Theatre, being transported with the gladdening tale he told,—she, in a moment, clung to his arm without a question put to, or an entertained doubt of, him. On the contrary, she tripped as nimbly along in the direction in which he led her, as it was possible for him to wish; so that in almost as brief a space of time as it took to make himself understood when he addressed her, she was by the side of the vehicle intended to receive her. A moment more, and she had disappeared by means of the let-down carriage accommodation for her footing; nor with less fleetness and alacrity has Ned Norland, the handsome agent who has brought her such unexpected happiness, and another, planted themselves, one on either side.

"Where is Lady Lymington? You have led me to the wrong carriage," were the words which instantly escaped the maiden's lips, uttered with such a voice of misgiving and alarm, as showed that the revulsion of her feelings from those of joy, to a sense of being betrayed, were as sudden and complete as the previous transition had been; her dismay and her conviction of being the victim of treachery not slightly arising from the discovery that there was not a female in the carriage.

"Where is Lady Lymington? you ask, pretty innocent dove," said one of the fellows, who, from his accentuation, she immediately discovered was no other than the Hon. Ludlow Chesters, the *gallant* Life-Guardsman, of former notoriety in the history of her perils. "You could not possibly expect that she would tarry ever since the termination of the

performances in the theatre till now, to suit your convenience, especially as you voluntarily and, I must add, wantonly, deserted her and her party in order to throw yourself into the arms of some other. No, her ladyship lost all patience, and is by this time, I dare say, under her own roof, or very nearly so. In these circumstances, and having an idea of the extent of your destitution as well as folly, I have been delaying my departure from the vicinity of the Opera House, in order to find you a lodging for the night; so that surely, instead of upbraidings, I merit your gratitude."

All this was spoken in a mocking tone, and while the carriage was rattling over the stones at a rapid rate,—the side blinds being let down and all possibility of the poor girl making her cries heard by any person outside, being also as completely precluded as was the power to effect her escape while unaided.

"Jared Jobson is in this conspiracy," were the poor innocent's first words, ejaculated again and again, as the titled miscreant talked. Then, as she became a little more collected, and just as Chesters paused, she added this stinging remark, "My pretended and perjured parent, as he called himself, truly is fit associate for him who aimed to take my life, while affecting to be my wooer and destined husband—the base plunderer and deliberate assassin yoked together for the destruction of a helpless girl! Who this other *manly* accomplice may be, I for the present know not. although I feel as if assured that ere long his name and history will be revealed to me,—my presentiment being strong, besides, that at no distant period I am to be the instrument of bringing to their merited doom the entire three. Shame upon you, and lasting ignominy, ye cowardly villains!"

"Upon mine honour, the wax-doll talks with amazing glibness of conspiracy," exclaimed the captain, "for one who was a principal party to as monstrous and infamous a plot as ever was concocted, in order to supplant me and cheat me out of my family and hereditary rights. Nor was this infamous attempt made on the sudden impulse of a moment, or under an instantaneous temptation, but it was the deliberated contrivance and sustained enormity of a series of years, to the blinding and deception even of my sagacious uncle, Sir Vaux Waldgrave of Wartham Hall, where I had the misfortune first to meet the wench. And then, Norland, to hear her take so readily to prophesying as we have just heard her do, gives an idea of her impudence. For my share, I cannot pretend to any unusual gift in the soothsaying line, and yet I fancy that it has been revealed to me what shall be the condition and fate of this same prophetess before eight days from the present date have gone, and that by the time specified she will be as gentle towards Ludlow Chesters, as you ever saw any other cooing dove."

"Mendacious and despicable wretch!" was the poor innocent's ejaculation.

"The young lady need not be so vindictive towards Ned Norland," observed that worthy; "seeing that I so courteously yielded to her plaintive petition whilst I passed her in front of the Opera House, and was in pursuit of quite another individual. Take my word for it, Captain Chesters, she prayed me to have pity on her, and to see that she was taken to some genteel quarter for the night, for that she was in mortal terror of falling into the hands of any low and moneyless fellow. As to my character,—concerning which she, a total stranger till now to me, appears to entertain some degree of curiosity,—all I shall say for the present is, that I am not unknown at the West End, nor amongst the best houses in that wide region. Meanwhile, she cannot allege that I have put a foul finger upon her, or used towards her a rude expression. Neither is it my intention to do so at any time. I know myself better, I trust, than to interfere with other people's goods."

"Vile trepanner!" was the ensnared innocent's breathed words of contempt.

"A foul finger!" exclaimed Chesters, affecting to be mightily amused at the expression and the idea it conveyed. "I confess that I am a bit of a voluptuary, but then I woo ere I wish to possess, although my style of winning has its peculiarities, as shall be seen in the case of this same little dove who has flown hither of her own accord to nestle in my arms. Nor shall she have cause to repent her choice, if she will be but reasonable, even after all her hatched contrivance to oust me in another direction."

"All that I can say is, Captain Chesters, the young miss was but too happy to accept of your kind offer of protection, and was transported at the idea of having your carriage so near at hand to jump into," observed Norland. "As for what is alleged to have been spoken about Lady Lymington by the girl, or any other titled dame, I am ready to make oath at any time that the notion is quite a mistake. Miss has been dreaming."

It would have been idle for the poor innocent to have attempted making any appeal to such a pair of villains as now sat beside her. She had truly said that they trepanned her, and she as truly felt that they had her wholly in their power. What added to her distress, in no small degree, was the thorough conviction that the monstrous Jared Jobson was in the conspiracy, and also that old Peter Plumtree was in some shape the victim of the same band of plotters. And then, when her thoughts rushed from one circumstance to another, of what had befallen her that night, and of what she had herself done,—done irregularly and strangely to no small extent, she could not but perceive,—her despair and distress grew the more overpowering. She even perceived that the facility with which she believed Norland when he accosted her, and the unwariness with which she seized his proffered arm,—the reckless haste, too, with which she jumped into a carriage which probably one attentive glance would have told her was of a very different shape and colour from the capacious coach which Lady Lymington had hired for the accommodation of her party,—all these things raced through her distracted mind, being interpreted with exaggerated colourings to her own disadvantage every way. It was the natural working of frightfully overtaxed innocence for her to become a severe self-accuser.

"I am, in every sense and direction, entangled beyond recovery," thought she; "but perhaps worst of all, through my own unguardedness, facility, and unhappy fate. Who will believe my story of innocence, were I even at this instant at my own free control, and in a position to enable me to appeal to the first person that might pass me in the street. My dress renders my condition the more deplorable, for besides being such as at this late hour would, to most sober and plain-minded people, appear one of levity and of unfitness for modesty, it also would soon be seen to consist of materials not at all suited to the finances of a young governess. Nay, the greater part of what decks my person has been lent me, and might be set down as stolen property by such as commenced regarding me with suspicion. Oh! I am all-unfortunate; nor can I conceive of the chance of any possibility of escape from degradation the direst, or exposure the most ruinous, even were I this instant released from the merciless villains who have me in their power wholly."

It was some relief for the poor innocent that after what has been given above as the insulting discourse of the Life-Guardsman and Norland, they both for a considerable space kept mute. Meanwhile the carriage was rattling along at a quick rate, but in what direction or in what quarter the maiden could not have told. All she positively knew in these respects was, that, by means of the unscreened front glasses of the chaise,—for such she found the vehicle to be, instead of a double-seated coach,—they had passed along one of the bridges very soon after starting from the vicinity of the Opera House, and that therefore they were travelling to the south of the river. On and on they drove, but whether in a straight line forward, or circuitously, she could not say. After the lapse it might be of an hour, as it seemed to her, the rows of houses ceased to be continuous, and a little later, to be altogether left behind, or with only a dwelling or two at a time, with long intervals. They were not merely therefore in the suburbs, but in a thinly-inhabited quarter, with few lamps to be seen, and never anything of the character of a lighted window.

"Whither can they be carrying me?" was the agonizing question which was constantly rising to the poor innocent's lips. "Can it be to have me murdered in some sequestered and lonely spot? But no; this cannot in any way be contemplated. Chesters meditates a more terrible outrage; preparation and a more studied contrivance having been manifestly employed by the conspirators, otherwise they could never have allowed the carriage to be driven onward mile after mile without even making one stop or issuing fresh orders to the postilion. Ah, Jared Jobson has been making pre-arrangements with them. I cannot guess how numerous may have been his and their snares, or how intricately and well-contrived their combined plottings. All I am assured of is, that unless heaven come to my succour in some signal manner and soon, I am utterly undone."

Alas! how worrying were the poor girl's thoughts. The extremity of her terror and excitement for a time was so complete that she could not even find that sort of relief which the shedding of a flood of tears affords. But just as she came to the conclusion of such cogitations as we have now been recording, she burst into a fit of bitter weeping; her wail being at moments loud, wild, and most heart-rending. Is it not wonderful that there are natures either originally so devoid of all sympathy, or which have grown so hardened through vice, as to remain unmelted by the passionate weeping of the grossly wronged? Yet it is so, and was so in the instance mentioned; for the hapless girl met not with one compassionating response to the utterance of her sore affliction; on the contrary, words of mocking were dropped by the Life-Guardsman, such as "It would do her good to cry," and "a damsel never looked so interesting as after shedding a flood of tears, although these might be, as in most cases, from a crocodile source, or wholly feigned to serve a concealed purpose."

These insults had the effect of stemming the bitter tide; on the discovery of which result the captain again pitilessly spoke.

"I knew, Norland, how to put an end to her tiresome noise," said the barbarian.

"I can but die," ejaculated the maiden, a little after she gained some measure of composure. "I believe in God,—His goodness, and justice. Let me abide His will in silence!"

Hardly had she spoken these words of something like recovering assurance and confidence, as well as of resignation, before the carriage stopped; Chesters having mocked her at the same moment, by saying to the other villain, "She has taken to prayer, always a promising symptom in such pretty doves as this."

"Truly, you are a wooer of a peculiar kind, captain," was Norland's observation.

"I told you so and my duck here, did I not, a little while since," replied the Life-Guardsman. "A person of pleasure, and of the world likewise, must accommodate himself to circumstances, otherwise he is not fit for his calling. There are some hearts that must be broken before they can be won. I cannot afford to throw away wooing; I bide my time. But now, friend, the door of my *sanctum* has been opened, the coast is clear and lighted, I see. Do the amiable, and hand my little dove or duck, as I have just been rather inconsistently calling the wax-doll, to the ground, and next up-stairs. I'll follow, of course."

How the poor girl got out of the carriage, and whether she offered any sort of resistance or not to being led into the house at the door of which they halted, her memory did not retain. However, she soon found herself in a chamber up several flights of steps, she was aware; the room being clean though scantily furnished. She swooned, but it was only for a few moments that her senses left her; nor sooner did she come to herself than Chesters spoke words that afforded her a degree of relief.

"This apartment must be your abode for some days, girl," said he. "Its accommodation is better than you deserve at my hands. But having thrown yourself upon my protection,—having sought for my succour, when, through your own folly, you were reduced to a strange perplexity, I am not the man to turn my compassion away from you, or to harbour a relentless revenge. You'll want for nothing, save the opportunity of gadding about in that dress, till I pay you a visit, which may be some days hence perhaps. A damsel will attend my little duck at fitting times."

The captain and his accomplice withdrew without his saying more; the poor innocent finding that they locked the door of the apartment in which they left her the moment they issued from it. Nor saw she another human face that night. There was a bed in the room, with a table and one chair. A lighted candle was allowed to remain, that enabled her to take a survey of the place at her leisure, which, during day, received its scanty light from a small window in the roof, and therefore she was at the top of the house. But we must leave the poor captive a prisoner here for some time without further knowledge being obtained of her, in order that we may attend those who had conspired against her,— trepanning and kidnapping the poor innocent to her ineffable dismay.

Ludlow Chesters was a voluptuary, and was not ashamed of boasting that he was a man of pleasure, as he called it. He was licentious and a sensualist in the amplest meaning of the terms; and so long had been his practice in his favourite walk, and so frequent and numerous his achievements in his peculiar way, that his moral perceptions had all become perverted, and his sensibilities to whatever was pure, delicate and cultivated, woefully blunted. But his slavery to the most debasing of all passions and pursuits was not the only bondage to which the wretched fellow found himself subjected. The expert and subtle Jobson held him in chains, the most galling and strongly riveted; nor did that unmitigated monster in crime fail of resolving to drive home the iron which was upon his bondsman, to his very vitals, if needful to the ruffian's ends.

The captain's sensual pursuits had been, in fact, without any moral renovation of his character or revolution in his tastes. For a time, at the very period at which we have arrived, he was so mastered by certain fears,—or rather certain dangers and possibilities were so suspended over his head,—that his deepest thoughts were thereby altogether pre-occupied. This enslaved condition had, with all its iron obduracy and power, commenced at the period of that interview between him and the ruffian Jobson, which took place in the Life-Guardsman's club-room, as represented a considerable number of chapters back; the period being identical with the deceit and trickery that were practised upon the eccentric owner of the Red Cot, by the same experienced and many-engined scoundrel who terrified the titled captain into bondage.

"Jobson has my liberty, if not my life, in jeopardy every day we both have being, and the girl together, whom I was to wed, according to my uncle's willing," was a conviction which never quitted Ludlow's bosom. "He was witness, it seems, of my *enterprise* at the Cauldron Cliff, when she *made the slip* and went over the precipice. The fellow would not scruple for a moment to swear in a court of justice, that he saw me give her a direct shove, and no doubt he could contrive to get the girl herself to come forward, with the same sort of criminal charge. Besides, he has not only got me so into his trammels, as to extort money from me at will, but money obtained for such illegal ends and daring criminal enterprises that he is constantly rendering me his accomplice,—thus enchaining me the more irrevocably each day I live. In this way he has made me a participator, I verily believe, in the robbery of old Plumtree; not merely a portion of the gold pieces which were taken from the miserly wretch, having found their way into my otherwise empty pocket at the time, but with my knowledge that they were of the identical number of coins actually taken from the cynic; and also with my acquiescence being obtained to the enterprise of robbing the old goose hours before the commission of the felony. And the old gold watch too, I have been obliged to purchase at last, knowing it to be stolen property. Truly, I am in a pitiable condition of bondage,—of bondage to the most unscrupulous and deeply steeped in villany of all the scoundrels, I believe, that can be found in England."

But the terrors and perplexities of Chesters were not allowed to terminate with uncertainties concerning the continuance of exemption from criminal prosecutions. Jobson had the faculty, if not the well-grounded means, of holding him in constant alarm of his not being, after all that had occurred, the nearest of kin to his uncle, Sir Vaux, even although the baronet should die childless.

"I frankly and truly admit," Jared would say to the captain, who had come to be obliged to lend the ruffian audience daily, or rather nightly, "that the girl whom they named Adelaide Waldgrave is not my child. But it is equally true that one of the strangest and most intricate mysteries attaches to the history of that girl, and that at any time, with very little trouble, I could not only unriddle the whole, but also, by means of bringing together of living witnesses, who for the present know nothing of the existence of each other, I could establish beyond the shadow of any doubt that she is the legitimate offspring of your uncle, Sir Vaux Waldgrave's legitimate brother. Now, it is only for you, gallant sir, to render it worth my while to keep the key for the unlocking the whole of the romantic facts to myself, not only by aids as I may require them while we go along, and your succession to the old baronet is safe and sure."

The captain knew of no other resource than to be at the dictation of his tormentor or enslaver, who had other schemes and intrigues in view for the bondage of his guilty victim than transpired in his last cited speech.

"I cannot part with Adelaide," the villain would daily repeat; "for you, Chesters, see how useful she may be made to me to further my ends with yourself, who, well do I know, have no better liking towards me, than a certain personage that for the present shall be nameless has for holy-water. And yet I am not at all against turning her over to your advantage, provided this can be done consistently with mine at the same time. I tell you she is the rightful heiress to Wartham Hall, although the pretty creature has not the remotest notion of the fact in these her days of adversity. But that you should wear her as your wife after what has happened is an idea that will not be very cordially stomached by either of you. What then? Why, that you get the better of her in some other way, captain; that you debase her, if ye cannot readily seduce her, so as to degrade her in her own estimation, and render her despicable in the eyes of all others. Her life must be spared; but if ye can ensnare or trepan her into your keeping, this may serve your turn nearly as well as if she were put out of the way altogether. I doubt not,—with *gentle* Ned Norland, the accomplished swell-mobsman, for our associate in the affair,—of being able to accomplish her undoing, a thing I am intent on forwarding, were it for nothing else than her way of thinking and talking of myself, and furnishing old Plumtree with a picture of me, to my no small peril, I assure you, captain. The Opera night may be made to develop much. I foresaw how, with my management and agencies, more dogs than one might be felled with a single stone on that promising occasion."

Chesters could not but perceive that any scheme which Jobson would suggest for the injury or ruin of the poor girl would be managed in such a manner as to involve himself criminally in the eye of the laws of the country,—for as to any breach of merely a moral nature he cared not a rush. He saw that his enslaver and tormentor was inveigling him deeper and deeper. But then he was a voluptuary, as he genteelly described himself at times. He gloried in intrigues and conquests where the fair were concerned. He had no objection to resort to violence towards the helpless innocent, especially as his cherished revenge was strong, his hatred deep, in return for what he was pleased to represent as her calumny towards him in relation to the affair at the Cauldron Cliff, and his consequent dismissal by his enraged uncle from Wartham Hall.

"Now's your opportunity for trepanning the unwary girl," said Jobson to Chesters and their accomplice Norland, on the night of the Opera House adventures by the miscreants; the ruffian having so arranged matters that the other two remained in a neighbouring quarter within their vehicle, which had been hired prospectively for the furtherance of their diabolical plot against the poor innocent. "The old fool of the Red Cot is off to the Blue Boar, the theatrical company has dispersed, and she lingers alone, in hopes of still falling in with him who is so forward to behave to her as his adopted daughter; growing wretched, however, at neither seeing him, nor finding that Lady Lymington has tarried to pick her up. Some soft-headed people would pity the *dressed* wretch, as she begins to perceive the strangeness of her condition, her helplessness, and exposure. Lucky thing for us that the night is cold and that the rain has set in. Now off with you, smooth-tongued Ned. By this time she's growing miserable in the extreme, and next to desperate. As for me, whom she would recognise and probably at once denounce, I must shift for myself, after warning you, Captain Chesters, that once having housed her in your *sanctum*, as you call it, in Surrey, you must leave her alone to your manager there to keep the creature under lock and key, without molesting her further until you consult with myself."

The arch-conspirator having thus given his directions, disappeared from the neighbourhood, in order to smear his clothes, and see to certain little self-inflictions, to give a colour to the story he had concocted in his own mind for the ear of old Peter Plumtree at the Blue Boar, whither the scoundrel hied him. The reader is acquainted with the rest, as concerns the misused owner of the Red Cot, and his departure from London. We hasten to the poor imprisoned innocent.

Sleepless we may be sure were the hours that elapsed between the time when Chesters and Norland left her and daybreak, although she had thrown herself upon the bed in the apartment, which, on inspection, seemed fitted to afford satisfactory rest. Two or three hours more escaped, during which, although she heard some stir in the dwelling, not a step was noticed as approaching to her door. At length it was opened, just as a degree of drowsiness was creeping over the maiden; the noise causing the terrified captive to spring from where she had been stretched, and to stand in her satin and richly white-laced robes as a petrified image. The key turned in the lock, and instantly, instead of Chesters or any one of the sterner sex making his appearance, there stood before her a pretty damsel about her own age, with a tray in her hands and the proper materials for a breakfast meal; there being some one immediately behind, who kept outside the door, remaining unseen by the poor governess, and turning the key upon the servant.

"Oh! it is not with meat or drink that I would have you, pretty creature, to come to me," cried the imprisoned one, throwing herself upon her knees and embracing those of the ministering girl. "Tell me rather where I am; what they mean to do with me; and if I am long to be kept a captive here;" the young thing to whom these words were so rapidly put, being so far embarrassed by the clinging innocent, as to prevent her instantly reaching the table where she meant to place the breakfast materials, and hindering her from quickly restoring the other to her feet, which she was eager to do, to save the "glossy satin," as she said, "from being soiled by the uncarpeted floor."

"Glossy satin! said you, sweet creature?" cried Adelaide, as she was obliged to release the girl's knees, and take to her feet. "Would that my raiment were plain and coarse, of inferior and simpler fabric than what clothes yourself so neatly. How much more fondly would I exchange my captivity for freedom, than even this gay display for russet attire. Have pity upon me, pretty one, and great comfort will, I trust, for many years rise within you for having befriended a poor misused sister."

"Do not take it so sorely on, young lady," whispered the girl to the captive, a not unkindly smile playing about the creature's mouth, still more attracting poor Adelaide, while a balm-like influence characterized her accents. "But I must not be heard talking with you, and my crabbed old mistress is coming to let me out. Good bye, just now; most likely I shall see you at the dinner-hour. Captain Chesters is very kind to his young ladies."

CHAPTER XXIII.

THE FORLORN HOPE.

A FIRST, a second, a third day fled of unrelieved imprisonment for poor Miss Neville, and without her ever once beholding another human face besides that of Hannah Nichols, this being the name of the smart girl who regularly brought the captive the victuals ordered. These, it so happened, were neither stinted in quantity, nor unsavoury in regard to quality, thanks to Hannah, whose control in the household, although the cause and fact were all this while a secret to the young governess, had become considerably enlarged in consequence of her cankered mistress being a good deal confined to her bed by rheumatic or some such complaints. Still, every time the girl came to the imprisoning apartment some person was close at her heels to turn the key the moment she got her person in; Hannah peremptorily refusing to say to the outraged innocent who such a jailor was, as well as keeping mute, or only shaking her head in response to such questions as referred to the number of inmates and their character, besides the crabbed landlady and her active help.

It did not seem to be the fact that Hannah withheld the information sought for from any wish to conduct herself harshly to the young lady, but only from fear of evil consequences as respected her own interests; and even what little she communicated was done in whispers, with looks askance towards the door, and always with some degree of trepidation. She felt considerably for Miss Neville, as she often named the captive, and seemed really concerned that the young lady took next to no food. At the same time the innocent could perceive that the creature did not regard her own degraded condition, nor the danger that beset the virtue of the other, as any very serious matter; chiding, in fact, our heroine for "taking on so strongly," and intimating, more than once, that after a few months they might go out into the world, and nobody be the wiser beyond Captain Chesters as to what had befallen them.

"Then, are you, Hannah, a prisoner as well as myself?" inquired Adelaide.

"Not now, although I was much in the same way as yourself, young lady, for the first day or so of my being here," answered the light-headed damsel. "But I am now allowed good wages, and get some presents from the captain and his friends; so that I mean to feather my nest a little before I fly away.

The captain is really very good to me when he has it to give; but he is not constant in his love to any one, and soon takes to some new flame; his fancy going from servant girls to milliners, and from these again to young genteel persons, like yourself, Miss Neville. He'll soon, it is likely, let you alone. I understood from him and his friend Norland that you ran to him for protection, which is not the way to retain his attentions. He is always talking of conquering the shy. I wonder that you should have so soon changed your mind after coming here. I'm sure I do all that is in my poor power to make you comfortable."

As the more than usually communicative Hannah got to this point, she showed an anxiety to be let out, probably pained to find, as she talked in a strain which she hoped might encourage the young lady, that she was only adding to her deep tribulation. There were twenty things which the innocent would fain have asked the other at one breathing, but she could only learn in addition to what she had been told one or two particulars more at that time, each of which added to her misery and dark forebodings.

"The captain is generally here every other day, and sometimes several days and nights at a time," was the answer returned to one question. "It is strange, since you are here, young lady, that he should have kept away so long; but we may depend upon it, he will remain the longer when he comes, and this, I could bet all I have, will be this very evening, perhaps late at night. I'll do all I can that you are not drugged, as I am sure was done to me. I call it a shameful, unmanly trick. Do not you agree with me, Miss?"

But the innocent had no power to utter an acquiescence, or a word of any kind,—resigning herself to despair, as Hannah was let out; this having instantly taken place as the unthinking girl concluded her sensible observation, as she deemed it, and uttered her appeal to the imprisoned one.

It is impossible to convey any adequate idea of the shudderings, the horror, the despair which seized our heroine on that afternoon when she drew so much from Hannah. She had frequently before this searched the bed and room to see if she could discover any article with which she might defend herself against outrage. The investigation was vainly once more renewed. We are not sure that she did not think of ridding herself of existence in this extremity. But even an attempt at self-murder was precluded. A knife or fork she had not from the first been permitted to handle, and as for bed-post, or any point from which she could, by strips of torn sheeting, have been enabled to suspend herself, no such thing was in the room.

Often did she look up to the skylight overhead, and fixed in the high-roofed ceiling of the chamber, as if she could scale the bare walls with her naked fingers, and travel by the same to the central part, where the panes of glass were inserted, and then drive through the brittle material and ascend to the top and exterior of the building; when, to precipitate herself to the paved floor a long way below would not have required half the amount of

dread and despair that was actually, hour after hour, surging her bosom and harrowing her innermost soul.

But she could not, poor maiden, overcome impossibilities, nor perform miracles; so that she had to continue to shudder and to wail,—sometimes, as if unconsciously, making mention of the name of Montague Mildmay,—sometimes, more collected, calling out for her "wondrous benefactor, the aged Samaritan of the Red Cot;" but still more frequently, and with greater self-approval, turning her imploring voice to Heaven, praying that "Providence would sustain her, give a little longer aid, and direct her." It was as she had once again uttered these last cited words, and fancied herself in some degree buttressed and reanimated thereby, that steps heavy as those of a man, and certainly not those of the tripping Hannah, were heard, as if making a steady and direct approach towards the door of her imprisoning room. Night had by this time enveloped the earth, and she was without a candle or light of any kind, unless the twinkling of some stars, far, very far overhead, might be excepted, putting her in mind of regions of liberty and bliss. To thrust back all her misery into her heart, to repress her voice, and to await the issue of the visitation, were the poor innocent's heroic efforts of the moment; the climax of her sufferings having all but absolutely arrived.

With what a straining of the eyeballs did the damsel watch the opening of the door! and what a thrill pierced through her, accompanied by a shriek, which Hannah Nichols, the attendant girl, afterwards declared, shook the house, and sent its echoes into the lanes of the sequestered neighbourhood! Such, in fact, were the vehemence and resistless shrillness of the cry, that even the intruder was startled and transfixed to the spot, where it struck him as if he had been shot through by a supernatural voice, or by an arrow from a celestial quiver. And yet the arrested one was no other than the hardened Jared Jobson, whose heart was steeled against all human appeals, it might well be said.

"Really, girl,—daughter, I should rather call thee,—I'm—that is—thou hast shaken me by that voice of thine," said the fellow, after a pause of a few seconds, uttering his first words with a stutter. "It is foolish, it is unnatural to give a parent such a reception, especially such a parent as has not only the will but the power to succour his child;" the scoundrel advancing into the room, as he spoke the last words, with a lighted candle in his hand, and shutting the door behind him.

The innocent meantime had shrunk back to the corner of the chamber farthest from the intruder, and but for the two walls which formed the angle into which she pressed herself, she would have been unable to stand upright; being bereft of much of her strength,—enfeebled as she was through mental suffering and abstinence,—not only by the terrors that mastered her, but exhausted by the unparalleled shriek she had raised. Jobson had actually to repeat in substance what he had at first said, and to keep declaring that he was anxious to assist her, "upon certain terms," as he uniformly added, before she had power to make him any sort of answer. Nor would she have spoken, it may be stated, at least certainly not in the terms of which she made use, had it not been for his constant employment of the words "parent" or "father," as applied to himself, and "daughter," or "child," in relation to the maiden.

"Save yourself the trouble of mouthing these sacred words of kinship to me, ruffian and robber," replied she with utmost and unmistakable scorn. "My nature recoils from the pollution of being in any way related to such a monster as now insults me. Our several looks, the contrarieties which characterize us, give the deep denial to the presumption; even were there not such contradictions in the enormities to which I have been subjected to by, and through, the hideous agencies of the miscreant, as stamp him to be in league with the father of lies. There is but one office now left you, demon, as relates to me, that can go beyond the wrongs and cruelties thou hast perpetrated already; and this is to be my cold-blooded murderer. Now to thy work."

The maiden advanced a step, as if eager to become the sacrifice she mentioned,—a species of courage actuating the poor creature, and being felt to increase whilst she kept speaking. Besides, although she might not at the moment have been conscious of the fact, certain evils and terrors had passed from her for the time, which a few minutes before had been uppermost in her soul, on becoming assured that it was not Captain Chesters who had paid her a visit. No doubt the sight of Jobson was dreadful and scathing; harrowing her to the uttermost, and drawing from her that shriek which had seemed so superhuman. But there was a change of terror and alarm; a turn was lent to her forebodings; and in this transition and altered state there was a degree of relief, enabling her to carry herself, after a little lapse of time, with some measure of her wonted energy and conscious reliance. Jobson perceived, to his amazement, that she was a creature of far greater self-reliance and strength of character than he had dreamt of; and that mental suffering, brooding alarms, of continuance for days and nights together, and close imprisonment, had not broken her spirit as he had calculated upon. His next speech to her was framed in accordance with the unexpected discovery he had thus made.

"I came, headstrong girl, to talk to thee," said the villain, "as a parent should do, and naturally does, if not cruelly crossed, to his offspring. I was going to assure and to show thee, that but for me, Ludlow Chesters—the *Honourable!* the Life-Guardsman! the voluptuary, and accomplished, resistless man of pleasure, as he delights to think himself—would have been here and proved thy destruction, nights ago. Let me inform thee, that he and I have had a fall out to some extent; and that to baulk his lewd purposes is a thing to which I contemplated having recourse, quite independently of my regard for my child. I meant to offer thee deliverance—nay, to effect it—but only upon certain terms, which, from thy perverse and impracticable tone, I am reluctantly forced to expect thou wilt not accept."

The scoundrel paused for a few seconds to deliberate, within himself, what next he should say, and also to discover if his mode of address, and conditional succour, had produced any change in the girl's feelings towards him. Her scorn, and indignant distrust, however, only appeared on the increase, if such was possible, and therefore he thus resumed his talk:—

"My proposal is," continued the monster, "that in exchange for thy immediate deliverance from this lonesome room, that thou will not only implicitly trust thyself to me, to be conducted, without troubling me with any of thy alarms, to the quarter I choose, which will be forth of England, but that thou at once most deeply swear never to return to this country again, except with my countenance and in my company. Agree to these terms, ay, and on the instant, and thy deliverance from this, with money ready for thee, for thy immediate wants, as soon as thou art upon a foreign shore, shall be thine.

"Terms of any kind by me with such a deep-dyed villain as Jared Jobson!" exclaimed the imprisoned innocent with a recoiling loathing. "Impossible! Waste not words, monster, but to thy deed of blood, here where I stand, and on the instant, rather than in any more frightful spot, or with new and needless enormities."

"Mad girl! bethink thee of the consequences, should I leave thee here," said the fellow, evidently vexed and disappointed. "I seek not thy blood. Knewest thou all, it would not be necessary for me to swear to thee, that thy preservation is indispensable for my own ends, as well as thine own elevation at some future day! Thy life must be spared even for my enrichment; although, the preservation of thy honour and virtue may not be required. Thou understandest me. Contemn and drive me hence, and, anon, Chesters will assail thy innocence. I therefore pray thee to bethink thyself, and to deliberate on my proposals and promises

"To deliberate in such a case, my innate sense at once tells me would be profanity as well as utter folly," returned the maiden. "Begone, then, and spare me from a sight that is in itself killing. Oh! I could not live in proximity to such a fiend, for but a fleeting hour, methinks."

"Then, lost and ruined one, I quit thee," cried the ruffian, "but with this warning and assurance—that if thou dost persist in maligning me, or shouldst even meditate giving me trouble, on account of aught that has passed between us, my severest and deepest revenge will overtake thee, before thy purpose can have its fulfilment. Thou canst not escape me and my agencies. From the past take a lesson;" and having thus threatened and given instructions, the scoundrel withdrew.

The poor innocent never once regretted having refused to listen to any proposal which could come from such a being as he who, after claiming her for a daughter, conducted himself towards her as a merciless plunderer, and who, since that period, she had not the shadow of a doubt was her arch enemy. Still she could not, in a manner clear to herself, discover what could be his motives for offering her the terms

ADELAIDE.

he had done, supposing him to have been speaking his real intention; or, if he wished to visit her with deeper injury than he had yet inflicted upon her, what hindered that such a villain, especially with the accomplices and agents whom he manifestly could call to his aid, did not treat her just as suited his will and designs, without a moment's consultation of her mind, seeing that he had not the slightest compunctions on account of her actual sufferings and wretchedness?

The imprisoned girl, although she conjectured truly enough, so far as she went, concerning the villain, knew not one tittle of his atrocities, of his diabolical schemes, or of his evil resources. Neither was she at all aware of these further particulars; namely, that a misunderstanding had arisen between him and Captain Chesters, and besides that certain presentiments had taken possession even of such a

ruffian's bosom, as rendered him afraid of the poor governess. These forebodings having once taken their hold of him, and being greatly strengthened by the report by Chesters and Norland of the hapless girl's inborn convictions, and her prophesy, on the night the latter trepanned her, that she was yet to be the instrument whereby all three should be brought to encounter public justice, and be brought to an ignominious end, as was represented,—impressed with such dark anticipations, the hardened Jared Jobson became the slave and victim, to a remarkable degree, of the imagined retribution. The predicted things operated upon him with a force that became superstitious, those deepest steeped in crime not being always exempted from harbouring such horrors.

Consistently with his growing fears, the scoundrel became desirous to have our poor heroine,—the captive girl,—removed to some distant quarter, and in another land; although to such a practised hand, such a scheme, after being carried into effect, and backed, too, by the damsel's oath never without his consent to return, one would say could not have appeared to afford any considerable security, even so far as her revenge might extend, and dormant testimony. However this may be, the phantom which now ceased not to haunt the ruffian's soul, together with his harboured notice that he might at some future time render the girl instrumental to his aggrandizement, led him, not only for the period of her captivity which had passed, to screen her from the intrusion and ruinous designs of the Life Guardsman, but to offer the terms to her which he had done, and which she had so scornfully rejected.

This contemptuous and indignant rejection, we have already stated, vexed not slightly the foreboding villain, rendering him also enraged to a degree that made him threaten the poor innocent with an early visit by Chesters. On his descending to the quarter where he met the cankered keeper of the captain's *sanctum*, he began to carry himself like a savage and in his coarsest character, especially as compared with the courtesy which he could assume and had actually maintained for the most part while in the presence of the imprisoned one. He cursed, and raved, and lustily swore that he would have his revenge glutted in sundry quarters, in order that his power might become the better understood; hinting that he should begin with Captain Chesters and all who aided him in his lewd practices. In fact, in his fury, which had ever the phantom of his brain alluded to above in prospect, he conducted himself as a person that had become suddenly demented; menacing, it seemed, without any distinct aim, and proclaiming his thirst for revenge without an assignable end as regarded his own interests, unless it consisted in the indulgence of sheer malignity. To the girl, Hannah Nichols, who ventured to throw in some deprecating word, he returned for answer a cruel blow that sent her reeling to the ground and marked her face for life; the sight of the consequences of this outrage, especially as the crabbed housekeeper, in spite of her rheumatism, made for the door to carry alarm to the nearest quarter where she could hope to find assistance to seize the scoundrel, admonishing him to the effect that it was high time for him to decamp.

Nor sooner had he done so, than the injured Hannah resolved that she would quit the house for ever, in order to be beyond such unprovoked ruffianism as she had encountered, as well as the danger of exposure and punishment as Jobson had threatened to bring upon her and others. Full of this determination, the girl took the first opportunity that occurred of confiding her purpose to our heroine, who of course greatly approved of the resolve.

"But, Hannah Nichols," said Adelaide, "you would not surely run away from such a dangerous place, and leave poor me behind,—for whom I am sure you have some pity,—if ye can help me. The day may come,—nay, it perhaps is not distant,—when I might, were I once at my liberty, prove to you the best friend you ever had, not merely on account of your

having saved me from destruction, but the pleasure it would yield me to be doing good to one who, I believe, is capable of becoming an ornament to her sex."

The captive had become thoroughly aware that the ignorant and light-headed, but not malignantly-disposed girl, liked to be praised, and that she was to be moved by the prospect of profit in a worldly sense. This was a feature of character to which the young governess had not failed to address herself to the uttermost; receiving always for answer, however, that to steal the key of the imprisoning room from the pocket or from below the pillow of her cankered mistress, would be as much as her place was worth,—that she wished to feather her nest a little before she went away, and that it was foolish for our heroine to "take on so strongly, after having willingly thrown herself upon the protection of Captain Chesters, who was a real gentleman, after all."

Hitherto, accordingly, the giddy, ill brought up, and insensible Hannah's interests had been found to oppose too strongly those of the poor and misrepresented captive. But now a sudden change of the light-headed creature's mind had suddenly and most unexpectedly been wrought, of which the dreadfully endangered one was most eager to take advantage, together also of Hannah's avidity for gain, clothes, and such like material objects.

"No, no, dear Hannah, you'll never go away and leave me, if you can help it, behind you," cried Adelaide, throwing her arms around the neck of the girl, and passionately, by words, tone, and action, giving the most touching expression to her implorings. "You will not refuse to run some risk to save a fellow creature from worse than death. Perhaps I may even have it in my power to enrich you ere we take flight;"—for the captive had observed that the damsel frequently threw a longing gaze towards the glossy satin and the rich lace that decked the principal robe,—costly articles which rightfully belonged, however, to Lady Lymington, though by this time considerably wrinkled and soiled. Upon the recollection of such longing looks, the young governess adroitly began to act.

"Yes, ere we take to flight," said the captive; "for though I am aware that the several yards alone of the costly lace that is around and upon my person, would bring at the shop of any of the second-hand dealers in such gear more money than would purchase all tha tis upon you, Hannah, twice over,—not to mention the pearls that were in my head-dress, but which I have hitherto contrived to conceal even from you,—I am willing to exchange the whole for the clothes which you are now wearing, including your shoes and the plainest bonnet you possess."

"Will you do that, Miss Neville, if I obtain for you the means of letting yourself out?" cried the girl, transported at the prospect of having a "real lady's" full evening dress of her own, at the expense merely of parting with a portion of her own most ordinary wearing apparel.

"Do it, and love you while I live, to the bargain!" returned the other, trembling between the prospect of escape which was before her and the fearless Hannah's attempts to assist her might miscarry, the dread lest Chesters might arrive in the meanwhile; being not perfectly sure if she, with whom she was making arrangements in words, was to be relied on in act, should she once get the coveted gear into her hands. However, to expedite these arrangements was manifestly the imprisoned one's interest, so that her proposal to the other to lose no time in supplying her with the articles of exchange was instantly made, in order that Hannah might the sooner have the greedily longed-for things in her possession.

"Let not an hour more of the night speed away, Hannah, without your seeing me in the changed raiment, and also with the means of escape in my hands," beseechingly said poor Adelaide. "Your mistress asleep at the time, as I trust, or at least altogether undisturbed by any noise on our parts, you may have your bundles or boxes in readiness for me to assist you in conveying your clothes to some snug corner outside these walls. This accomplished, we must consider how next we are to bestow of ourselves and of them."

Not to detain the reader with any more details connected with the adventure of the poor captive's escape from the horrid walls which had imprisoned her for not less than an entire week, we go forward to state, that besides Hannah keeping perfect faith with her, so far as their bargainings had gone, and the stealthy abstraction of the key which was to open her door of confinement, and also the keys of other barriers, the avaricious girl surprised the poor innocent with further facilities.

"I shall not need your assistance more, now that I have got all my things out in safety," whispered Hannah, she being fearful that the young lady might wish to keep with her, in order to borrow back some portion of the costly articles she had parted with, so foolishly did the giddy, greedy creature reason within herself. "I'll be able to carry all my own myself, now that we are fairly clear of old crabbed Rheumatism, as I may at last safely call my late mistress. Your way will be in another direction than mine, I guess; so, hoping that we may meet again somewhere, we must each shift for herself. Farewell, Miss Neville, and get out of this dangerous neighbourhood as soon as you can."

The liberated captive was but too happy to take advantage of Hannah's impatience to get rid of her, to require a second bidding to be gone: shaking the giddy creature gratefully by the hand, the young lady flew away in the openest direction that her vision could discover, until she felt confident of being beyond the reach of the laden girl, who only tarried in order to take a different route. As for our heroine, she drove on at a rate which was even more rapid than that which characterzed her morning flight from Wartham Hall; direr horrors being behind than alarmed the poor girl at the period of that first adventurous flight.

"But oh! there is no Red Cot to receive me in all this quarter,—no good Samaritan to extend the hand of wondrous welcome and kindness to the forlorn one, as old Peter Plumtree did," sighed the poor girl, ever and anon, as she ran forward in the darkness,—having found a beaten path in the moonlight, which happened to be fitful, owing to the troubled state of the sky at the particular time. "Alas! I know not even in what direction I am driving." At length, she added to such sad breathings these alleviations:—"Yet it matters little whither I am going, so long as I am making away from the vile and fearful place of my recent captivity. More fitting than to complain and be dissatisfied would it be that I returned fervent thanks to Heaven for my providential deliverance, than that I grudgingly compared my present fortunes with a former homeless and houseless condition."

Having thus admonished herself, the forlorn maiden bent the knee to the ground, and poured out, in the most devout and earnest, though not the loudest accents she could use, the gratitude she felt and owed to the All-good and All-powerful; concluding her sky-directed burst of fervour with these pious expressions:—"God, who does the work, ordains the instrument; let me wait His will humbly and trustingly."

The girl rose from the ground, and this with a start and a strained vision which were not to have been looked for from her immediately preceding utterances of reliance and resignation. Yet, who could charge her with want of faith or of fortitude, when informed that the sound of horses' hoofs upon the path she herself was treading, reached her ear, filling her on the instant with the assurance that Captain Chesters was near, and about to traverse the very ground she had been speeding over, on his route, no question of it, to the very house in which she had been so cruelly and criminally immured. To dive into the thicket which happened to hedge in the rustic road at the particular spot was the innocent's prompt proceeding, the beatings of her bosom being so loud to her own sense, that she dreaded lest the same should be equally audible to passers-by. And hardly had she hid herself in the manner mentioned, when, in consequence of the outshining of the moon at the moment, she discerned a pair of horsemen advancing from the quarter towards which her steps had been bent; the next instant it being clearly revealed to her that not only the Life-Guardsman and Norland were the riders, but that their discourse concerned directly the concealed fugitive herself.

"You'll take back my cattle, Norland, to their own stable, immediately on our getting to the *sanctum*, unless Jobson, the scoundrel, has worked me such mischief there as to prevent me alighting at all," were the words which reached the hearing of the trembling innocent, spoken by one of the horsemen, whom she at once perceived was no other than Ludlow Chesters, the *honourable.*

This discovery, and the various remarkable circumstances of the poor innocent's condition, very nearly extorted a scream from her. Yet, though this was not the immediate consequence of her surprise and alarm, the effort which she made on the impulse of the moment to shrink further into the thicket where she sought to conceal herself than at first, caused such a crackling amongst the bushes as arrested the attention of the riders.

"What sort of game is astir here?" cried Chesters. "Can it be that my little cooing dove, whom I expected to find at the *sanctum*, has taken flight, and happens to be nestling on the very border of our bridle-path. If so, it is in some shape Jobson's doing. However, just for the fun of the thing, let us beat up the cover, the locality being well known to me, and safe for the footing of our cattle. Take you, Norland, to the one side of the still crackling spot, and I'll to the other. There is not a second of time to lose, for the game, whatever it be, is stealing off."

At these words both horsemen plunged into the thicket, the Life-Guardsman's charger entering the copse so exactly at the part where the fair fugitive at the first strove to hide herself, that had she not removed in her alarm from the spot, she must have been trampled upon by the animal's feet. As it was, she had only got a few yards off; and so perilous did she feel her position to be, that her terror wrung from the innocent another such shriek as she gave voice to when Jobson stood before her at the door of her prison-chamber in the *sanctum*,—Chesters having also the remembrance of much the same note and utterance of affright and agony when he helped to hurry her over the appalling precipice at the Cauldron Cliff. The similarity,—the identity of the never-to-be-forgotten shriek was to him proof positive that the same innocent against whose life he had formerly aimed a murderous effort, and whom again he was resolved to assail in a still more villanous manner, if this could be, was almost within reach of his grasp, although in some strange way, unknown as yet, she had all but escaped from his clutches. A mighty oath passed the miscreant's lips as he announced the certitude of his discovery to his associate, and nearly the simultaneous plunging of both in the direction whence the shriek of affright and agony came; the hope of escape from the villains who had conspired to effect her ruin, which she had been cherishing a few minutes before, being now a most forlorn one. But the next chapter has to reveal the particulars of the midnight adventures of the poor maiden and the pair of lewd monsters who were intent on her destruction.

CHAPTER XXIV.

THE HUNTED INNOCENT.

HAD the pair of horsemen who had plunged into the copse, as told immediately above, been on a glorious enterprise, instead of an adventure of infamy, they could not in the darkness of that night have borne themselves with keener ardour. In fact, they went to work with great daring, dashing forward amongst the bushes, as if resolved on driving an invading enemy from their borders, or of taking captive an audacious foe; their steeds obeying the heel and hand as gallantly as had they been charging in the battle-field. And then Chesters not only declared that he was well acquainted with the locality, intimating to his associate, in saying so, that he could safely

conduct him, although under the cloud of night, in the business of "unearthing the fox," as he called it, while shouting his joy on having descried the hiding spot of the fugitive.

Fortunately, however, the Life-Guardsman's knowledge of the thicket was not so minute as to be acquainted with certain inequalities of the covered ground, or to be aware that sundry felled trees which had been allowed to lie on the earth, as well as others which were half laid prostrate by storms from time to time, had for years been giving out sprouts, saplings, and branches that had always seemed to him to be of the nature and origin of the regular copse. While the creature, therefore, was creeping away, at times under large stems, or finding a hollow in the surface of the soil that afforded her a more rapid run, the riders were every now and then meeting with stout and unexpected impediments, or stumbling into unseen ditches, to their great annoyance,—their vexation and disappointment being aggravated by catching glimpses of the hunted one considerably a-head; for the sky had cleared, and the moon shed its unclouded light during the cruel chase.

"We shall lose her after all, at this rate," cried the captain, giving all the emphasis he could to his words by dreadful oaths and curses. "I should not wonder if we got for our pains only torn clothes, scratched limbs, and lamed horses. Perdition to the wench. Ha!" shouted the Life-Guardsman, immediately after having called for a curse upon the hunted innocent,—"ha! I behold her not more than a hundred yards from us, and upon open ground, too. Here's for her!"

And away went the cavalry-officer, on his gallant charger, having got clear of the copse without any difficulty at the moment, being closely followed by Norland. Of course, having level and clear ground to ride over, they at every bound gained upon the affrighted and despairing fugitive, although running for her life, as she considered it. A few seconds served to bring the horsemen very nearly up to where she struggled, though with enfeebled and now all but fainting steps, to escape them.

"To the one side of the wench, and I'll to the other," cried the captain to his associate; "we'll easily pluck her up between us if she holds on; or, should she crouch and lie down, it is but for one of us to alight and take charge of her, while the other keeps hold of the riderless steed. It must be my office to dismount."

This was spoken while both horsemen slackened their pace for an instant, being hard upon the heels of the fugitive, and fully assured that her escape was now impracticable. But again the chargers are prompted to advance, and next moment they are abreast of poor Adelaide, who actually crouches at the instant,—aye, and disappears in a second of time from her base pursuers. Yes, she has crouched, and with the same change of attitude she has thrown herself upon a declivity that leads to a rivulet a good way down; the descent not being so abrupt as to endanger limb or life, especially as the brushwood which feathers the slope arrests her progress before she has got half-a-dozen of yards away from the level surface at the brink at which she stooped and flung herself forward. But the reader will not expect that the mounted miscreants, whose cattle were dashing onward at the same instant that the fugitive changed the manner of her efforts to escape them, had an equal good fortune with the innocent at that turn. Inevitably, the villains, with their spirited animals, went down the declivity with headlong speed and violence, without meeting any such gently arresting abstacles to their descent as saved the young lady from reaching the rivulet, whose channel was rough and broken. In short, they made a dreadful plunge, landing at the termination of their chase at the very bottom of the unlooked-for and unseen deep hollow, to the dreadful damage of man and beast; not one of them escaping without a broken limb, besides severe contusions; results which led to having the pair of quadrupeds shot, and the two bipeds to the occupation of beds of sickness for a number of weeks to come.

The hunted innocent had no mind to ascertain what was the issue of the headlong tumble to her merciless pursuers. Hardly knowing for some time what she did, the poor girl retraced her steps across the open field, very nearly to the part of the copse and bushy quarter from which she had shortly before emerged. On reaching that spot, she began to think of the concealment it afforded her, and also of the stems of prostrate trees under which she had crept. Nor did exhaustion of strength fail to admonish her of the necessity of taking some rest, after the extremity of terror and exertion to which she had been put; and all this in the case of a creature whose bodily strength had been greatly impaired during the preceding week from want of due sustenance and through mental anguish.

She sat her down upon a half-rotten stem that was canopied by the growths which sprang from itself and by surrounding bushes. The night was one of dampness, although not of actual rain; the seat was clammy, and the ground, upon which her delicate feet rested, chilling. And yet the maiden believed she must have slept, supported in her position by the branches and sprouts amongst which she had planted herself. It was after a troubled slumber that she descried the dim dawn beginning to glimmer overhead, and that, stiff and shaking, she essayed to quit her hiding-place; resolved, if it were possible, to put distance between her and the quarter she had been occupying in the thicket before the morning was far spent.

"But whither shall I go?" she once more put to herself, after having striven for some considerable length of time to leave the copse without making almost any progress. "Alas! the future is an awful blank to me," she continued to ejaculate; "it is something like to that which the imagination pictures what the world must have been when the deluge was gone by."

As on the morning flight from Wartham Hall, she began to skirt fields, hedges, and lanes, but at a far more enfeebled rate than when she for the first time found herself houseless and homeless. Yet now and then she went fast and faster, like one who was at such moments delirious. Such exertions could not be continued for many hours. Something like what she fancied was a mortal and last weakness, beginning inwardly, and soon extending to her limbs, seized her, and she fell, poor creature. She fell, and lay on the ground, just in the position in which she had fallen,—her face pressing the wet turf,—these words after a little while escaping her, sounded, too, so as to startle her own hearing:—

"I have some fear, some hope and wish," muttered she, "that here I shall die."

The utterance served to re-animate the creature, and she was up again; being obliged at first to crawl on her hands and knees. Anon she rises to her feet, and for a little while seems not only as determined, but as able as at the commencement of her flight from the neighbourhood of her horrid imprisonment, to speed away from the locality. But it was impossible for one who had endured so much and fasted so long to maintain any pace whatever. The sun had got to a considerable altitude, when the fugitive came to road-crossings, where there was a sign-post, with arms pointing in the different directions which the branching routes took, having lettered announcements on them, stating the main places to which each way led. One of these public and useful intimations of course indicated the nearest road from the particular spot to London,—informing the traveller, besides, that the great metropolis was ten miles distant.

"Here I must linger, and make up my mind," thought the poor girl, "in what direction to bend my weary steps, if ever again I shall be able to travel;" leaning against the sign-post for support, while she thus spoke to herself. "Yet not here must I tarry, for at such a public spot every one who passes will wonder what I am doing, or at once conclude that I am manifestly an objectless and lost wretch,—an inference which I would not even have an utter stranger to me to form."

She withdrew from the road-crossings to some little distance, and to a shaded nook, both as regarded wayfarers and the sun's beams, as well as the sweeping breeze; with pain dragging herself to the comparatively cozy spot. Again she slept; and when she awoke, the day's great luminary was at its height. She felt somewhat refreshed, especially considering that she had effected an escape from immediate outrage of the direst character, although she knew herself to be friendless and utterly destitute.

"What am I to do? where go?" she ejaculated, "now that I have time and solitude to regain some measure of reflection. Want and starvation are approaching me, pale, bare, and scowling. To London I dare not entrust myself, were it but that Jobson haunts the vast Babylon; not to speak of Chesters and Norland, should their mishap on hunting poor me prove but trifling,—the misadventure, in such a case, but exasperating them the deeper against one who never wronged either of the villains."

Lady Lymington, after a lengthened pause, was the personage that drew from the innocent the exclamation, "What says reflection relative to her ladyship? Why, that she was deeply offended and affronted by my behaviour in regard to my wondrous benefactor at the Opera House, and that her hurrying away from the theatre, in order that I might have no chance of being taken into the carriage with her, proves the extent of her displeasure and her resolve to renounce and repudiate me for ever. Besides, how could I account to her for my absence during the interval that has elapsed since last I beheld her? how account so as to be credited,—she having, as I am aware, been previously dissatisfied with what her ladyship considered the mystery in which I enveloped passages of my life? Worse and worse, how account for appearing in the garb in which I now am thankful to find myself? How explain to her the reasons for my parting with her costly articles of dress, which were of more value to her than all the clothes that she will discover in my boxes which are under her own roof, together with the few gold pieces, the savings of my scanty allowance at Puffendorff House? Oh, I am in every way destitute, though happily not in captivity. Truly I am an outcast, and forlorn in the extreme."

The maiden again paused, yielding herself up to a state of aimless abstraction, rather than reflection. Nor was she aroused from the inactive condition until an unfavourable change of the weather,—for it began to rain,—and the gnawings of hunger stirred her.

"I know not," murmured she, "whether or not I am near to any human habitation; and even were I at the porch of such, what have I to say for myself, what appearance to present that would gain belief or excite compassion? I have no claim upon any one, and cold charity will have to be entreated before I can obtain a crust of bread, or the shelter of an outhouse. Reluctant sympathy must be importuned at the best. Almost certain repulse will be incurred, before my tale—had I even the courage to tell it—will be listened to, or one of my wants relieved."

The maiden was perfectly aware, although she had not for an entire week had the opportunity of consulting a mirror, that her looks were haggard, compared with what they once were,—that she was thin, and like one that was bloodless,—in short, worn almost to nothing, as if she had been a spectre. The pangs of famine, besides, were now within her,—the vulture hunger was upon her; while, as regarded her raiment, now soiled and rent, it spoke of anything, she felt assured, rather than of innocence or of misfortunes unincurred by guilt and a life of shame. On reflecting on all these things, a throe of unmitigated despair rent and heaved her heart; she thought there was nothing left for her but to submit unresistingly to the accumulated evils,—the apathy that was engendered by the gnawings of craving nature, clogging more and more soul and limb.

"It is but to die, believing and trusting in God," she ejaculated. "Yes, to give up the ghost where I am, I, who am yet so young, and was formerly so fond of life. Montague Mildmay! knew you but my woe, you would weep, although in a far-off clime. Wondrous bene-factor of the Red Cot, it would almost kill you, were any one to relate to you the sorrows and sufferings which have assailed me since our transient interview took place in the crowded theatre."

The latter portion of this soliloquy was not in harmony with the former, which breathed resignation, if not a longing to die,—a thing unnatural for one so juvenile in respect of years, so conscious of being singularly gifted, and so recently buoyant with hope, as well as heroically resolute. She had subsided from the despairing, into the tender and melting; a fit of weeping accompanied the transient change; and this again having been stemmed,—the bosom being relieved of the pent-up anguish, —a new idea found its way to her lips.

"But I must strive to live, instead of invoking death," breathed the poor girl, as she made to leave the concealed nook which for a series of hours she had occupied. "I must bend to what is appointed me, were it even the meanest species of rustic toil, like so many more of my sisterhood;" and having thus reflected and thus talked to herself,—thrusting away from her, by a mighty effort at the same moment, all her misery,—she quitted the cozy spot, and took to one of the branching roads that went from the above-mentioned signpost.

"Not London-ward be my route," said the maiden, as she slowly approached the highways, "for there my story would find no corroborations upon which I could readily throw myself. No, not towards that wilderness of streets and receptacle of villany, but in quite an opposite direction will I strive to bend my steps."

Wandering on southward, something after the manner of a lost and starving animal,— being struck also with the fact of not meeting for more than a mile with a single wayfarer,— the homeless innocent at length descried what she took to be a straggling village or scattered hamlet, which was still at a considerable distance. The sight of human habitations, where of course, no ruffian hands would be allowed to molest her, gave the girl some encouragement, while the gnawings within her were so keen, that she felt as if resolved and capable of imploring relief in the shape of a morsel of food at the first open door at which she should arrive. With this determination uppermost, and feeling that her condition was such as nothing but a false modesty would prevent her from making it be known, she actually found strength to accelerate her steps a little, trusting that her speedier progress would expedite the reception of such relief as she so sadly stood in need of. On and on the poor creature dragged her limbs, until she came within a few paces of the first house of the village; her heart now palpitating painfully at the thought of begging a crust of bread, and, in fact, her resolution seeming to fail her altogether. A look at her raiment, and her thinned hand drawn down her once most lovely face, helped not slightly to discourage her. She halted; she thought that if she retraced her steps a little way, and re-reasoned the matter over, she would acquire once more the fortitude to seek a little assistance in the shape of food.

But the irresolution appeared but to gain upon her by such a process of leaving and coming back again ; so that finding she could not much longer keep upon her feet, she advanced without any very determinate purpose, and as a person prepared to be guided by the suggestions of the moment, as to what was to be done or not done in the trying circumstances.

The young lady at length reached the house upon which her eye had been so anxiously fixed, descrying as she came near to it, from the fact of a young man carrying within a large board covered with hot, smoking loaves, that it was a baker's shop and residence. She felt herself quicken her pace ; she was at the window, which was well filled, as also the counter of the establishment, with the staff of life, in all sorts of shapes and tempting conditions. Surely never were the steam and scent of bread so savoury to a creature as what issued from this shop to the sense and appetite of poor Adelaide Neville. There were piping dishes of baked meat, too, upon the counter, ready to be carried away to the intended eaters of the same, at the sight of which the teeth of the famishing maiden might be said literally to water. Oh ! how longing, perhaps greedy, must have been the looks of the gnawed creature at the abundant viands ! Yet how could she enter the shop to beg a morsel of the plainest and driest article her eyes rested upon, either from baker or customer,—several persons of the latter character being there ? The famishing one's appearance, looks, and manner must have been remarkable, for she called forth the observations of some of the people who were on business within the shop, —observations of a nature that had the effect of moving the master baker himself, although he was closely engaged in serving the customers, and taking money from them. Yes, he was so far moved as to quit his post, and, this by a round-about course, so as to advance to his shop door, in order to address himself to the starving gazer.

"You had better begone, hussy, from there," said he to the innocent. "Plenty of your sort tramp this way, from St. Giles's and the like in London, to see what they can pick up by their lying and impudence to honest people's faces, and pilfering behind their backs. Begone, I say, ye good-for-nothing ; otherwise I'll take another course than words with you. In fact, the wretch's diseased looks," added the man of loaves, addressing himself to his customers, but so as also to be heard by Adelaide, "are enough to put one out of conceit with his dinner : she might actually poison my bread, I can imagine, though the window be between her and my staff of life."

The poor young lady had not moved away from the spot where she was standing when the baker addressed her ; she being stunned by the assault and the manner of his language. She for a moment or two, on apprehending what he said, and perceiving what an object of curiosity, and indeed of suspicion and disdain, she was on the part of the people in the shop, became unconscious of what she did,—remaining stock-still, and stupified ; her bearing seeming to the rash accuser that of insolent daring and bold defiance. To put his threat of dealing into execution against the transfixed girl was his next step.

"So ye will do as ye like to annoy me and my customers in my own shop, will you, ye base baggage ?" cried the imperious and impetuous man of loaves. "I'll teach you better ;" and having thus spoken and stepped up to the helpless, innocent, and exhausted starveling, he took her by the thinned and delicate arm, and lending her a violent whirl, sent her into the mud of the gutter that was a little way from his door, where she might have long lain, from the want of physical strength and the hurt she had received in the fall, as well as from the iron grasp of the brute, had not some boys, who saw the cruelty done, come to her assistance.

These youngsters took Adelaide out of the puddle, and placed her on a sort of stone settle which was not far off ; kindly also freeing her, as well as they could, from the mud that clung to her clothes. Moreover, one of the urchins, who thought that she looked like a starved and hungry creature, and who had been munching at a lump of stale bread, and another lump of skim-milk cheese, thrust both into her lap. The moment that she beheld the food within her reach and at her service, she ravenously fastened upon it, to the wonderment of some of the boys, and to the excitement of the sympathy of others of them.

"How can the girl gnaw that, Bill ?" bluntly inquired one of the youngsters of the giver of the bread and cheese. "I'll get a basin of milk from mother for the poor thing, which will help to wash the other down, and then I shall be happier for what I thus do than the brute of a baker, who might by his violence have dashed out her brains. But we all know what a savage he is to the poor, and slave to the rich. Father and mother will not taste a bit of his bread, though we have to send a long way for every morsel we eat. It would be serving the big, coarse brute as he deserves, were somebody to give him a sound drubbing for having done what we saw him do to this poor creature, merely because, when starving, she looked through his window at his bread."

Most of this was said by the compassionate and plain-spoken boy, after he had returned with an ample basin filled with good milk ; the reviving maiden being strengthened as she tasted of the wholesome things given her, feeling soothed and refreshed by the sympathy manifested to her. At length, having swallowed the food, and being anxious to quit a quarter where she had met with such a cruel reception at the very first, as well as to escape from the speculation of which she was the subject, Adelaide again took to the highway, resolved, whatever might be her sufferings, never to gaze with longing eyes into a bakery for the future.

The street of the straggling village, if the highway which divided its houses might be so named, having been trodden by the poor, houseless maiden, without ever once again halting, she found herself emerging into what appeared a flat and almost treeless country. Nor did it seem to be dotted with dwellings in any direction her eye could roam. Besides, the hour of twilight was at hand, and night must soon once more envelope her. It was a desolate, destitute condition, especially for one who had been so delicately reared as our heroine : hers was now a dreary prospect, although absolute starvation had been put off. It was fortunate for her, indeed, that indignation and contempt toward the brutal baker took the place of any feeling of affront or disgrace she at first felt, so that her spirit was sustained in a manner she thought very remarkable. ●

The country into which the helpless creature was passing,—the period of the year being well advanced in autumn,—presented almost interminable stretches of what seemed to her to be tall brown, or half-withered grass. This dusky expanse, however, ere long became one of utter darkness; the moon not yet, nor for several hours to come, shedding its light on the region. It was now that the incertitude of the homeless wanderer became again extremely painful; her enfeebled frame and exhausted powers rendering it impossible that she could long hold on as a traveller. In these circumstances, her anxious gaze was to catch a glimpse of some light that might guide her to a solitary country-house, at which, she fondly imagined, she should meet with more sympathy than in town or village. To offer to perform any drudgery to which she might be put, in return for lodging and aliment, until her strength and spirits in a measure were restored, was a thought that constantly occupied her mind, and never without being regarded as a blessed condition compared with that of the horrid captivity in which she had been kept at the *sanctum* of the infamous Ludlow Chesters.

"Might I not obtain the berth of seeing to a child or two in some family, and thus of letting my other qualifications be known in course of time?" she hopefully enough put to herself. "At certain kinds of needle-work I could render myself serviceable, until I obtained some respectable raiment. As a teacher, my education and experience might early become appreciated. I might surprise rustics with what I know of music, and also in the employment of the pencil."

Thus the elastic spirit of the heroic girl, now that the cravings of hunger had been appeased, buoyed her up; and when she at length had discovered a lighted window, as she supposed the shining at a distance to be, she resolved on being guided by the beacon towards it, and of making the proposal of the humblest servitude to those whom she might meet at the place.

"We hold no terms with night-trampers at any time, especially if they be of the women-sort, and not even with strangers at any hour of the day," was the answer which the homeless innocent received at the door of the house to which her toiling steps had conducted her. "It is a wonder that our mastiff has not torn you to pieces, impudent slut, for he is somewhere about; thieves and robbers being rife in this part of the country. Most like ye are, young woman, of some one of the gangs that infest us; so you had better go back to where ye came from, and say that we of this house at least are prepared to give any of the marauding tribe that trouble the district a warm reception, if they come within gun-shot." ·

"Robbers, marauders, and people of violence infesting this lonely region!" were expressions that escaped the innocent, as she reluctantly withdrew from the human habitation. But we shall refrain from going into all the fears and tribulation of this second night of exclusion from a domestic hearth,—a night, which, after having been threatened with a fall of rain, at last became one of tempest and torrents; the poor girl having no other resource than to creep up into a cart which stood under a roof that was open on all sides, affording for the storm of wind which drove and swept through the inviting space a ready passage; the peals of thunder and the forked lightnings being still more terrible to the trembler.

Dawn at last again sent its intimations into the cart-house. The maiden feared the coming, to the place she occupied, of the farm-servants. Besides, she discovered as the light increased that a number of corn-stacks were in an enclosure near to where she had passed the night, and attached to the dwelling at which she had vainly appealed in order to obtain some sort of employment, and secure a shelter.

"It is the time of incendiarism in several districts of England," said the forlorn one to herself, the thought being suggested to her by the sight of the corn-stacks. "If I am discovered in this situation, the suspicion will at once attach to me that I have been upon such a wicked mission as to fire the grain, and that in revenge for being refused lodging in the evening, I no doubt meant to ruin the farmer, and wantonly destroy his precious provender."

The thought put mettle into the maiden; she left the cart with something like nimbleness; and though the road into which she struck was deep from the rain of the night, she slackened not her pace, such as it was, until she was a length of way from the spot where she had spent the dreadful hours of storm and darkness.

The day which had thus commenced was one of unavailing appeal-making, and also of sad exhaustion for the homeless wanderer, as well as of hunger. Not indeed until it was far down in the afternoon did she taste a morsel, being deterred from asking any such relief, until passing a countryman, who had been at work on the way-side, and was treating himself to some bread and beef, she took heart to solicit from him a morsel of the same.

"If thou be'est in earnest," said the rustic, "thou mayest have a half, although it might be as much charity, perhaps, to throw it to the first dog that passes me. I do not like young women of thy stamp, that go about begging, and often doing worse, I trow. They should work for their bread, as honest folks do, instead of such as thou, who hast had a pretty face, I can see, wandering about our hedges, and bringing the sons of farmers and others into disgrace and shame."

The innocent had nothing to say to the countryman after receiving the bread and beef, and listening to the nature of his suspicious speech. To hasten from him and to swallow the victuals, as soon as she came to a pool of what seemed drinkable water, was the maiden's

MRS. PUFFENDORF.

proceeding; the toughness and hardness of the food requiring this accompaniment fully as much as the boy's dried and stale bread, with the skim-milk cheese, needed the more nutritive basin-full which another youngster presented to her.

But, after all, the two instances of succour which the wanderer had received in the course of two entire days,—posterior, moreover, to a week of distaste for solid food and of wasting anguish, together with the toil and fatigue to which she continued to be exposed, besides her protracted mental sufferings,—these two instances of receiving bodily support could not possibly sustain either her physical frame or any measure of hope. She began to feel thoroughly assured that the personal appearance which she presented, and the tale of rivation, as also of eagerness to earn er bread by honest industry, were altoether against her, and that nowhere

No. 16.—THE GOVERNESS.

would she be believed. Fever, she imagined, through unmistakable symptoms, was taking a firm hold of her. The weather continued to be blustering and unpropitious for the homeless creature; and so absolutely convinced was she that another night's exposure to the open air and the stormy elements would find her in the morning a corpse, wherever she might drop down or lay her aching head, that she had all but resolved to struggle no more with her fate, but to let darkness overtake her at the stone she could first meet with on the side of the lonely road she had been travelling which offered anything like a tolerable seat. Such an accommodation did present itself about the time of the sun's setting. She with apathy took possession of it; darkness gathered around; the pitiless rain pelted her; and thinking of nothing very distinctly, she awaited the issue of her direst trials with much of a stupid sort of stoicism.

It might have been expected that nothing should awaken her from this torpor, and that as the exhausted wayfarer throws himself down upon the snow through which he can no longer toil, there to fall asleep, never more to open his eyes upon the earth,—it might have been looked for, had any one been made acquainted with Adelaide Neville's condition at this climax of her sufferings, without being able to succour her, that her mortal doom was inevitably sealed. Yet something awoke and stirred her, even in this sore extremity.

CHAPTER XXV.

THE LAST APPEAL.

"HAVE I been dreaming, and with my eyes open?" breathed the maiden languidly, as of a sudden she seemed to strive to shake off the torpor from her, as well as the drenching wetness. "Or has it been some supernatural light that appeared to my spiritual being, which I so palpably beheld a moment ago, as if it had been within reach of my hand? Ha! there it is again, but further off than I fancied it before. It flits, too, from place to place, and from window to window, unless it be a will-o'-the-wisp, which is said to betray the night-traveller who trusts to its guidance. Be it what it may, I will endeavour to near the spot where it shines."

The homeless and utterly destitute creature had not gone forward in the direction of the light many paces, when she became assured that it was a candle which shone sometimes more distinctly through one of two windows than another, and therefore that she was in the near vicinity of a human habitation. A very slender thrill of hope raced through her, on beholding an index of warmth and shelter; that thrill slightly nerved her stiffened limbs and benumbed body. She advanced as quickly and stealthily as she had power to do, and soon found herself under the projecting roof of what she took to be a neat and commodious cottage. Having planted herself against the wall, between the pair of windows through which the light streamed, and now screened by the sort of canopy which jutted from the eaves of the dwelling, the poor girl set herself to watch what took place in the comfortable-looking apartment, and to gather, if possible, the sense of anything that might be said by the inmates. These consisted of several females; also of a large Newfoundland dog, with two or three sleek cats,—the latter class of inhabitants being luxuriously stretched out upon the hearth-rug, which was warmed and irradiated by an adjacent blazing fire. Oh! how fain would Adelaide Neville have thrown herself down upon the same spot which was occupied by the four-footed creatures, and partaken of the food which, no doubt, fell daily to their share!

The females were four in number; three of them appeared to be one another's sisters, the eldest of whom might be four-and-twenty, and the youngest, perhaps, sixteen, with the mediate one about half-way between these extremes. They were plainly but genteelly attired, the youngest reading aloud, whilst the others plied the all-serviceable needle. The fourth of the number was a matronly enough looking woman, of not less than threescore, who kept bustling about with a candle for her own share, and whose movements or transitions produced the flittings of light which at first puzzled the houseless wanderer. This elderly personage did not appear, either from feature or raiment, to be the parent of the young people; but rather, from her bearing and general aspect, a superintending, a much confided-in and old-established domestic.

The youngest of three sisters, as any person at the first glance would have set them down to be, sometimes stopped when any observation was prompted by what she had been reading, but still more frequently to give place to a remark about the inclemency of the night, and an anxiety for "Frederick and Hector's return,"—these names distinctly reaching the eavesdropper's ear, as well as the word "brothers," especially when spoken by the matronly dame, whose voice was coarse as well as loud, and who fully as oft as all the others expressed her solicitude about "the young gentlemen," as she characterized the absent ones. Never once, during the entire time that poor Adelaide was listening and watching at the windows, looking through a redundancy of festooning growths which garnished the wall, and the openings that admitted the sun's beams, did she overhear the elderly woman make any reference to what was read, except on a single occasion, when all three of the sisters burst out at a certain passage into a hearty laugh.

"Had your father and mother been spared to this stormy night, young ladies," said the old woman, "they would not have laughed so heartily over a book in which there is not a word of truth, but the nonsense of some of your idle novel-writers, when your two brothers are from home, and we know not what may have become of them."

"You are quite wrong, good Dorothy, about what our lamented parents would have said touching the volume that Sarah is reading," gently said the eldest sister. "They were both great admirers of "Ivanhoe," and, indeed, of all or most of the tales written by the popular author of this same beautiful and moving romance. They would not even have approved of our sitting moping here till our brothers come home, knowing where they have gone to, that they are gone together, and that they generally stay to a later hour than has yet arrived before they return from the same place. Ah! Dorothy, there is many a houseless wanderer, this night, who is ten times more to be pitied than our Frederick and Hector, who will only get, perhaps, a wetting, owing to the highness of the wind preventing them from hoisting their umbrellas. They'll have a good supper to come home to, and a warm fire-side; and what would you more, so long as they are in excellent health and doing well in the world?"

"If they have a good supper to come home to, and a warm fire-side," growled Dorothy, "the dear young gentlemen deserve the same. Mr. Hastings has secured from the colonel the handsome church-living which his ability, learning, and piety deserved; and Mr. Hector made a good trip, for his pocket, in the Indiaman, of which he is such a gallant and useful officer. We must think of our own people, before we trouble ourselves about every houseless beggar whom misthrifte, or worse, makes outcasts."

The poor and desolate eavesdropper could have pulled the ear of the old woman on hearing her thus deliver herself; and, on the other hand, knelt before the eldest of the three sisters, and bathed her feet with tears of gratitude and affection, on account of what that young lady had said about the destitute houseless wanderers, in such an inclement night as the innocent was at the very same instant exposed to. The poor maiden, in fact, must have made some movement at the moment, or raised a slight noise, perhaps, of the nature of an irrepressible sigh, or unconscious groan, which reached the hearing of the quick-eared Newfoundland dog; for Neptune, as the sagacious and noble animal was named, instantly sprang towards the window, through which the sound had passed, and set up such a rotund and full-toned barking, as drew echoes from a distance; setting old Dorothy to her best wits' ends, in order most officiously and affectionately to welcome "the young gentlemen," who, she doubted not, had aroused the excellent four-footed housekeeper to the pitch he exhibited.

"Now, for my last appeal," ejaculated the houseless wanderer, knowing that she could no longer conceal herself. "I must creep to the porch of the dwelling, the best way I can, and confront the coarse-featured and surly Dorothy;" the already wofully faint heart of the unhappy maiden utterly sinking within her.

"Who are ye who disturb a peaceful and retired family at this unseasonable hour?" demanded the old yet sturdy woman of threescore, eyeing the wretched applicant from head to foot, and regarding the innocent with indignation.

"I am a destitute, utterly desolate creature, who, through no fault of my own, has been without a shelter from the weather these last two days and nights," feebly answered poor Adelaide, the huskiness of her voice nearly hindering her from being understood. "I am famishing, besides, for want of food; and unless some kind soul take pity upon me this inclement night, and let me have a roof to crawl under, and some warmth as well as sustenance to cherish me, never more shall I look upon the sun."

"A very likely thing, indeed, that I should believe your trumped-up story, young woman, or that of any of your cast and appearance," replied Dorothy, while she not only held the door by the one hand, and angrily eyed the applicant by means of the light which was in the other, but was gradually narrowing the open space through which the innocent had a view of the comfortable quarters within, judging from the snug lobby. "You are modest, truly, at this time of night, girl, to ask for a lodging, for a warm bed and a hearty supper. No, no, you must tramp back to the place you last came from, and where I dare say the people have an acquaintance with your character, that would in no way recommend you to strangers; otherwise they never would have sent you about your business in such a night as this. Now go, for you cannot and shall not be here," Dorothy at the same instant that she spoke the last words, slamming the door in the homeless one's face.

"Then the door of mercy and humanity on earth is for ever and finally barred against innocence and unmerited misfortune," said the poor girl in accents of deepest woe. "Here I must die, upon what I hoped faintly might prove a hospitable threshold. I can no more; I cannot even crawl hence, however anxious I might be to save the inmates from being troubled with my noisome corpse."

The exhausted and shaking girl sunk to the cold stone that floored the porch, and then managed piously to add a few words more.

"It is Heaven's appointment and will that I should thus end my youthful days," breathed she, "though lately my heart was so full of promise, and my prospects almost princely. But, let me bend humbly to the decree of the All-good and the All-powerful; raising my thoughts, so long as they have coherence, to the Everlasting throne, thankful that I have escaped the villany, providentially, which was contrived for my ruin, though it was to die untended and unpitied here."

The poor girl could no more, and fell back upon the unyielding stone, incapable, while unaided, of ever lifting up her head again, although not bereft of sensibility or intelligence. In fact, her ear drank in the accents of sympathy that now were uttered by persons who stood over her, and raised her to their arms.

"You shall not die here, if ye have a few moments to live," said one manly voice; "neither be untended or unpitied," subjoined another speaker; "no, although, poor girl, you were the most worthless outcast which England contains, instead of being, I verily believe, an unfortunate;" it being Hector Hastings who pronounced these words, and his elder brother, Frederick, the clerical personage, who made use of the earliest expressions of sympathy.

It was in vain for old Dorothy now to grumble and frown, muttering that she never before expected that their handsome cottage should be made a receptacle for beggars, and worthless young girls. Poor Adelaide was carried into the parlour, where, although now speechless, she manifested intelligence, as well as a capability of swallowing a few small quantities of warmed wine, administered with great care at intervals. To disrobe her of her drenched and muddy raiment; to bathe her limbs in tepid water, and have her clothed in dry, soft, and clean nightapparel, were the kind and most anxious efforts of the three sisters, who, in turn, kept by the innocent's bed-side throughout the night; they being more and more struck by the poor wanderer's appearance, the longer they looked upon her, and took note of features and circumstances inseparable from the maiden, and ineffaceable.

"How delicate is she!" said one of the sisters. "How unused to coarse work or treatment!"

"Yes, and how beautiful, now that we see her freed from her soiled clothes, and her features unmarred by the blackness and the foreign matter that attached to her countenance," whispered another of the fair sympathizers. "She is nothing less than lovely, in spite of her emaciations; and surpassingly comely and handsome she will assuredly be, should we have the happiness of being instrumental in restoring her to health."

"It is her really lady-like aspect which strikes me most for the present," observed the third of the sisters. "What if her character and accomplishments should harmonize with her looks! Will not we be grateful to our brothers, for having afforded us the opportunity of perhaps succouring the most spotless innocence? Both Frederick and Hector declare that, in her despairing and last ejaculatious in the porch, of having not only been delivered providentially from the contrivance of villany, but of her having been bred to cherish almost princely prospects, there was moral demonstration of her good character. What a romance and what a mystery may belong to our guest's brief history!"

In this way the three sisters speculated concerning poor Adelaide, as she lay speechless before them on the sick bed, although counselled by their brothers, especially the eldest of the two, not to be too hasty in their conjectures and conclusions; declaring besides, that it would be necessary, as soon as the unhappy girl could be questioned, with safety to herself, that she should account satisfactorily for being in the deplorable condition in which she was found at their door, and that she be sent to her proper home.

The threatened questioning, however, did not take place as soon as the clerical brother had hoped and expected; the prostration of their patient, and the reaction to which her exceedingly over-taxed mind and person had been subjected, requiring a series of days for amendment and proper recovery. The young, the terribly outraged and wronged girl, did not absolutely become the victim of violent fever, but was rather, for at least ten days, the helpless and passive creature, all this while, that might be expected in the case of one who had been subjected to a continuous train of cruelty, more or less refined—more or less savage and brutal. It needed time, composure, and the most gentle treatment, rather than the skill and medicine of the physician, to bring about her restoration; the constitutional soundness of the maiden's mental and physical system working its own slow renovation, when aided by the genial care which was taken of her.

The days of indisposition passed away; the young patient was allowed more generous food, and a larger abundance of it, than during the greater period of her confinement to the sick bed had been deemed prudent and safe. She was permitted by the directions of the clerical brother to converse sparingly with his sisters, but enjoined by no means to be impatient to quit the chamber in which she lay, nor in any manner unduly and prematurely to tax her spirit or frame; as a relapse, from injudicious freedom towards herself, would, in all probability, be more perilous than the first illness.

The poor, grateful girl was obedient to all these suggestions, even after she was conscious of being more convalescent than her anxious nurses supposed her to be; allowing them to go about her couch, to prescribe and administer to her, and avoiding discourse with them wholly, unless when she was addressed with the view of obtaining from her some necessary answer. From this self-command on the part of Adelaide, she was made acquainted with many things which the three sisters and their brothers said and thought of her; being informed by the whispered and side-talk of the young ladies as she lay unmoving, and without opening her lips, while the others imagined she was slumbering or insensible to what was passing near her. Amongst other things, she learned what were some of the principal speculations concerning her character, native condition, and antecedents. Wonder was several times expressed as to how, on descending to the parlour and the lower parts of the handsome and commodious cottage, she would bear herself to old Dorothy; it being thought that from her behaviour to the long established one, a fair judgment might be formed of the unhappy young creature's disposition and moral principles. In the manner mentioned, without any eagerness on her side, she gleaned a variety of hints which it required only a moderate discretion duly to profit by some of the matters and points speculated upon; causing her to feel no small share of anxiety, whilst others were truly encouraging and pleasant.

"You know, sisters," more than once in the sick chamber said Charlotte, the eldest of the three, "how particular and exacting the *minister* is,"—thereby meaning their elder brother, Frederick. "He will to a certainty take our patient strictly to task concerning the past years of her life, the circumstances of her family, and the cause of those reverses which had nigh sent her to her last account on the night she providentially was conducted to our door. If she be candid and consistent, then she will gain him wholly over; if otherwise, there will be a speedy end put to our familiarity with her. I really wait the result of his examination of the young and beautiful creature with solicitude and misgivings."

The anxiety which such statements as this was calculated to keep up in Adelaide's breast, were modified by the unfailing tenderness and prepossessing services of the sisters, and by none of them more than the eldest, whose authority on the female side was properly paramount in the family. For instance, days before the convalescent one was supposed to be in a fit state to leave her bed but for a short time, and to have the "run of the room," so to say, she observed that there was a neat and becoming quantity of raiment provided for her, in order that she might appear in the parlour and before the brothers, as the youngest sister, Sarah, said, like the stranger's *proper self*,— a delicate piece of kindness; while the commonplace clothing in which the houseless girl had wandered for days and nights together was washed, mended, and folded for her service, should she wish to keep possession of the articles.

At last the maiden was permitted to descend to the part of the commodious cottage where the family generally met and spent the day; neither of the brothers making their appearance in the restored girl's presence on this first occasion of her being conducted to the parlour after her recovery. By this time her natural beauty and wonted healthiness had nearly altogether returned. Her eye was no longer dimmed, nor her cheek wholly robbed of its charms. Her melodious voice had resumed its sweetness and compass; while as to the language and manners she was mistress of, these could not have been lost by any period of sickness in the case of one to whom an easy and polished politeness were natural, it might be said, as well as constantly habitual.

Our heroine could observe that some time after she had been invited and conducted to the snug and comfortable parlour on the day alluded to, the sisters, one after another, withdrew, leaving her alone, as if by concert, and for some special purpose, as regarded herself. In a little while old Dorothy came into the room, as if to put the furniture to rights, manifesting at the same time considerable uneasiness and perplexity, and hardly seeming to notice the presence of the young and grateful stranger. Now, poor Adelaide's gratitude by this time had been won towards the old woman; for the girl had learned when on her sick bed that the matronly individual was the person who had put the torn and soiled clothes to rights, and had been at no small pains to get in readiness whatever delicate thing was thought fit for the patient during her illness. In these circumstances, the maiden felt that from herself it was looked for to make advances to the housekeeping party; and, accordingly, the damsel, as soon as she caught the eye of the elderly woman, rose and made towards her.

"I am glad to have this early opportunity," said Adelaide, "to acknowledge my obligations to you, good Dorothy, from the hour of my being received under the roof of this most hospitable and delightful dwelling. Accept my thanks, I pray you, and let this kiss be the token of our friendship, and the forgetfulness for ever of anything which at first sight and under forbidding appearances may have been misunderstood between you and me. I have only for the present one other thing to ask of you, Dorothy," added Adelaide, after having saluted the cheek of the sturdy, but, after all, sterling dame,—ignorant and contracted though her notions were,—"that you will let me have something to employ my hands towards assisting you in your household duties; for idleness is not of my choosing, much less the disposition to be burdensome to, or in the way of, any one."

"Dear creature! you overpower me with your gentleness and generosity," said the worthy, but not faultless woman, in a voice that was disturbed by her surprise and emotion. "I am sorry for what I said and did to you, young lady, at the first; for how was I to know that you were what I now believe you to be, the equal every way of the best that is in this house? It was all a mistake of mine, although I was of the mind that I acted for the best towards my master and mistress."

"No more, I beseech you, in this strain or on the subject," cried Adelaide. "Let me rather have something to do, with the needle, if you will. Have you not a handkerchief to mend: I care not whether it be cambric or silk, and you'll see how I learnt in France to fill up a hole and join a rent."

"Well now, just for the sake of amusement, and also that I may get some insight into foreign ways," replied the charmed Dorothy, "I'll let you, miss, have a cambric pocket-handkerchief which belonged to my dear deceased mistress, the mother of all these young people whom ye here meet, and which somehow got torn since coming into my possession."

All was smoothness and reconciliation now between the elderly and the young parties; the former of whom bustled away to her apartment to bring the named article to the poor girl, with the other necessary things for testing the maiden's dexterity. Speedily, the news of the undertaking, together with the particulars of the interesting scene now described between the pair, were communicated to the anxious and expectant parties elsewhere, by the overjoyed and garrulous Dorothy; although neither of the three sisters required a report of the circumstances, they having so planted themselves as to be ear-witnesses of what transpired in the parlour, soon after their concocted leaving of the apartment, as already told.

The young needlewoman in the course of an hour or two acquitted herself to the admiration of all in the cottage, upon the cambric handkerchief; Hector, the younger brother, after examining the performance which had been submitted to his inspection as well as to that of the clerical critic, declaring that it would be worth while burning a hole in his India article, just to see how the expert artist would succeed on a silken fabric. Nor sooner was the word spoken by the frank and free young gentleman, than the deed was done by means of a small red-hot cinder.

"Request of the interesting girl," said he, "that at her leisure she try her handiwork upon this genuine piece. I'll do as much for her at the first fitting opportunity that offers; and yet I am one of the slowest in catching the lucky moment for any such service, being doubly ungraceful in my attempts when feeling that they are out of tune and time."

"The way with people of great parts is not to wait for opportunities,—it is to create them," observed the clerical brother; "but you, Hector, find yourself too often taking hold of the heels of an idea, when it is escaping as if through a window, allowing it to fall into the hands of some readier-witted person."

"Yes, just as a certain young aspirant after church preferment, by his sleek addresses to an exceedingly pious young lady, has contrived to get a handsome living, with an elegant parsonage-house, in the Weald of Kent, when I was treading the deck of an East-Indiaman,' answered the purser. "But I may find myself up-sides with you yet, brother Frederick, after a few more trips to Calcutta and back, when perhaps I shall settle in old England quite a nabob."

"What with being on occasions out of tune, Hector, and at others rash and random-spoken," somewhat reprovingly replied the one who was in holy orders, "I fear you will prove a blur-derer to the end of the chapter of your life."

"Well, it pleases me to think," retorted the seafaring young gentleman,—whose temperament was as frank, open, and fiery, as that of the other was cold, close, and calculating—"that I shall soon be, for at least twelve months, beyond the lecturings of a learned clerk. Meanwhile, I should like to know,—indeed, to see—how the darning of my handkerchief proceeds, which our sisters have put into the hands of the fair stranger."

Before the cautious parson could check his off-hand brother, who, whatever he might say of himself in respect of the seizure of fitting opportunities, was never backward to speak and act according to the uppermost feelings at the instant, Hector had bolted from the room, in which the more learned one was engaged principally with his books, and was next moment in the apartment where the young ladies, his sisters, were eagerly looking on, while the darner was setting herself to fill up the hole in the silk handkerchief which the hot cinder had made. But, however intently the purser meant to watch the sewing operation, his eyes but very briefly were directed to the nimble fingers of the plier of the needle; his gaze becoming riveted upon the artist's countenance, till he not only became in a measure enraptured with her beauty, but felt it impossible to withhold the expression of his admiration from his more circumspect brother.

"We have taken an angel of light under our roof," cried the purser, the moment he ran back to the "minister," as the clerical one was mostly named by the members of the family,—the delighted herald of the tidings paying not the slightest heed to the frown which was upon his brother's face. "Neither you nor I have seen the stranger since that tempestuous night in which we no doubt saved her life, during all her confinement, and when, although we were penetrated by her pious expressions, we could have no idea how much loveliness of form and features were concealed by her wretchedness."

"I really wish, Hector, that you would act and speak with a little more guardedness," impatiently said the minister. "You do not, by your senseless rhapsody and indiscretion, allow a more experienced person than yourself to interpose a check to your course. The truth is, you will to a certainty compromise our sisters and myself by your ridiculous conduct; forcing me, I fear, to turn the young woman sooner out to seek some other asylum than I had intended to do; nay, making me almost regret that we gave her shelter at all."

"Senseless rhapsody! do you call it, brother?" exclaimed the purser in return,—his utterance and manner being more enthusiastic than before. "I call him senseless, whoever he may be, who can behold such charms as I have just been looking on, and not discover that, with the choicest gifts of heaven lavished upon the stranger's person and visage, she is as pure as she is lovely. What gladness do I feel on thinking that you, Frederick, were forward to succour the poor wanderer, when she looked the emaciated, the pallid, and besoiled creature, that was fain to cling to our stony threshold! Oh! brother, you'll never repent having befriended the young lady."

"I am sure I shall have to repent it, and you too, foolish young man, judging from the rate at which you have begun with an utter stranger to whom strong suspicions, on my part, attach,"—the minister now not only speaking loudly and very angrily, but declaring that the girl, without questionings or inquiries of any kind, should trudge next morning to other quarters. "I am too much disgusted and exasperated by you, Hector, at this instant," continued the clerical speaker, "to perform to-day with becoming composure the task I impose upon myself, as now stated. But tomorrow, the girl, whatever may have been the cause of her outcast condition, must take her departure hence, for good and all."

"Then I'll trudge and depart with her!' cried the purser, in a much more vehement tone than his brother could use. "I'll be her honourable support and guardian until I see her placed in some more kindly dwelling, and with some more christianized people than he who now hears my words, a minister of religion though he be; nor do I doubt of saving her from further insult, peril, and strange hardships, before to-morrow's nightfall. I'll to Colonel Pegsworth's with the young lady at the very first: that gallant gentleman's pious daughter will not rashly turn the wanderer away."

There was something in this latter statement that startled the minister,—making him throw himself into the chair from which, in his excitement, he had a few moments before angrily risen; the purser at the same time proudly and indignantly turning to depart to his own chamber.

CHAPTER XXVI.

THE CATECHIZER CAUGHT.

"WHITHER go you, in that mood, Hector? What has happened between my two brothers,—and so suddenly, too?" eagerly and anxiously asked Miss Hastings, as she met the purser leaving the minister's room. "The noise of altercation reached me in the parlour,—my two sisters being equally vexed and alarmed as myself by what they heard. Nay, the stranger young lady,—for I cannot characterize her but as a highly polished and superior person,—was startled by the noise, lifting her eyes with an expression of distress and dismay from what she was most expertly and beautifully executing, to my deep vexation. 'I know,—I feel certain, that I am the cause of discord between your hitherto loving brothers,' exclaimed she, with great and touching emphasis. 'I had begun to entertain a hope that, until I should find some work that is honest, no matter how menial, you would let me stay with you, occupying myself in any way I might be able for your advantage. I thought, if you would but be so kind as to show me what you wished me to do, I might not be greatly burdensome, until I heard of service elsewhere. How I dread the horrors of homeless destitution! Yet, rather than be the occasion of contention or disagreement, however slight, between persons from whom I have received such unspeakable kindness as you, young ladies, and your brothers have lavished upon me, I will at once take my departure, praying for your prosperity and thanking you with my tears.'"

"There had been no altercation, Charlotte," said the elder brother, "had Hector acted with ordinary discretion and caution."

"Yes, and you with less coldness of calculation, learned clerk," observed the sister smiling. "Yet tell me quietly what happened between you," added the thoughtful and benign young lady; "for I feel certain that I shall prove a pacificator in this as in some former instances of your discord."

Hector at once hurried to the recapitulation of everything that had been said on both sides; with his wonted generosity, giving the minister a little more credit for the part he acted than he merited.

"I see exactly how it was," cried the sister, soothingly. "Hector, as I anticipated, and indeed, as I thought at the time, when he paid a visit to the parlour, to see how the darning of the silk handkerchief proceeded, therein acted unguardedly and prematurely. I am sure the stranger, if such I can now call her, felt as I did; and then his bearing and language, as described by himself, seem to have been still more thoughtless and reprehensible towards his senior on coming to this room. But yet, brother Frederick, I feel that I would rather have been chargeable with all these indiscretions, than entertain for a moment the idea of turning the homeless and houseless charmer from enjoying the shelter of my roof, so long as she desires it, or even of uncharitably cherishing suspicions regarding her character."

"Bravo! sister Charlotte," cried the purser, clasping the young lady in his arms, and imprinting a hearty kiss upon her cheek. "You have carried the day, girl,—the minister himself according it to you. Is it not so, learned clerk?"

"I must judge for myself of the strange young *lady*, as you will both have her to be, some day," answered the clerical gentleman. "Let her have another week of the fostering care of my sisters, provided Hector does not compromise himself or any of his family by his absurd forwardness. I shall have to be from home for the greater part of the interval mentioned; so that to your prudence, sister, I must in my absence confide the conduct of the house, and your brother in particular as regards your *protegée*."

"That *protegée*, I feel assured, will, during your absence, Frederick, prove herself to be a perfectly competent guardian of her own character and dignity," returned Miss Hastings. "There is innate power and repelling propriety about her in respect of the indiscreet. Somehow she makes me feel, even when my assiduities have been the most painstaking and tender in her behalf, that I am all the while doing myself the chief kindness and honour. She appears to be above our charity, although I am sure she does not feel in that way, and that there are convictions within her which are nobler than our compassion."

"No more of these generalities, sister of mine," exclaimed Hector. "Our cold and cautious brother will learn more and better things of the stranger, after seeing her and talking with her for the space of ten minutes, than all that we can tell him about the young lady. I shall long for his return. Meanwhile, Charlotte, hasten to the parlour, and assure those you shall find there, that better harmony never existed between your brothers than at present."

Miss Hastings was not slow to obey her younger brother, the very aspect of her countenance, nay, the mere elasticity of her step and the complacency of her bearing, showing to the anxious Adelaide that she came with glad tidings.

The minister's time of absence, during which he had been engaged in preparing for his removal from his native home to the scene of his future clerical labours, passed away, at the close of which period, with considerable anxiety on his mind, he returned to his sisters and brother. In the course of that absence the late houseless young lady had constantly been gaining upon the esteem and admiration of the Misses Hastings, but still more of the warm-hearted purser; although he had not during the interval had an opportunity of conversing with the interesting girl more than twice or thrice,—at any rate, never, except once, when she was by herself, and unaccompanied by one or all of his sisters.

"I know not how or when I shall have an opportunity of testifying my admiration of your exquisite performance upon my handkerchief, Miss Neville," cried the young gentleman, hurrying to accost her in the garden which was attached to the tasteful cottage,—not knowing how otherwise to claim her attention with the most delicate respect. "I suppose, from all I can learn of you, that my best course will be to give you a similar task to perform, were it but to carry the specimen of your handicraft out with me to Calcutta, in order to present the rare piece of needlework to a friend of mine in that far distant part, to whom I owe much, but to whom I will not be allowed by him to present any testimony of my gratitude, except in the shape of something that I prize greatly on account of other than its marketable value."

The purser thought that he had made a remarkably pretty beginning to his wooing, for, in fact, he was by this time deeply love-struck with our heroine, having from morning to evening each day had his eye upon the movements and graces of the young lady, whenever he could get a glimpse of her without incurring the displeasure of his sisters by any indiscreet forwardness. Not small, however, was his surprise, on accosting Adelaide in the garden, to find that she did not seem to perceive the elegance and delicacy of his introductory speech, but at once flew to another topic, such indeed as was suggested by his studied address.

"I, too, have a friend in India,—in Calcutta, at this moment, as I suppose,—to whom I owe much; not less, in fact, than the preservation of my life, when a titled villain intended murdering me," returned the young lady; "and he of all men on the face of the earth is dearest to me, and, I feel assured, ever will be. Had he remained in England till now, I should not, I think, have been an intruder upon the hospitality of entire strangers at this period of my life."

"How similarly you speak, Miss Neville, of a friend, to the way I would wish to do, of the person who has won my most lasting gratitude in Calcutta!" said the purser. "I had an introduction to him by letter from my brother, last time I went to India,—they two having been fellow-students at the University; and one of the results of this introduction was his rescuing me from being drowned. I well remember him telling me that he once had been the instrument of saving from a fearful death a precious fellow-being in England,—one of whom he could never think,—and that was not seldom, he assured me,—but with the deepest solicitude."

"May I ask, Mr. Hector Hastings," eagerly inquired the young lady, "who that friend of your's in the far east is?"

"He is of the suite of the Governor-General of British India,—the private secretary, in fact, of the noble lord," was the purser's reply.

"Montague Mildmay, of Mildmay Park, Yorkshire, is the gentleman, is he not, my friend?" more impatiently inquired the young lady, shaking from head to foot as she spoke.

"The same!—the same in every particular!" responded the young sea-farer; "but the discovery has dashed all my hopes. Oh, Miss Neville, I had begun from that very hour when I obtruded myself upon you and my sisters in the parlour, to witness what you could do merely as a darner of silk,—the occasion when my brother remonstrated angrily with me on account of my impertinence. Yes, matchless young lady, I have been growing madly in love with you ever since. Now, alas for me!—my prospects of happiness are blasted, unless, indeed, I find felicity in contributing to yours and his of whom we have both been so gratefully speaking."

"Ha! look!—yonder is your brother, Mr. Hector, who is nearing your villa, on his return home," cried the heroine of our tale, suddenly changing her tone. "No more of this, I pray you. Indeed, I have broken thoughtlessly through a reserve which I had resolved to maintain to your excellent sisters. Not a word, I entreat it of you, generous young gentleman, concerning what has been passing this instant between us relative to an absent party. Oh! I beseech you, not a syllable on that subject, unless I myself broach it."

The purser was again surprised, wondering what reason the girl could have for so eagerly desiring reserve in relation to a party with whom he felt it would be for the honour of any one to have an intimacy. And yet he was proud of the confidence which the charmer had reposed in him; nay, was delighted to think that she even wished the circumstance of their meeting, by themselves alone, in the garden to be kept from the knowledge of his brother, judging from the sort of alarm she manifested on seeing the minister approach them, and the haste with which she endeavoured to elude his observation. If, however, Adelaide was anxious to escape being seen by the clerical party in earnest conversation with his brother, her solicitude on this point was not only too late in its manifestation, but the speed and course she took to separate herself from the purser were distinctly noted by the parson; lending to his surmises and fears a keener edge than had yet stirred him.

"That fool-brother of mine," muttered the minister to himself on marking, though from a considerable distance, what was passing in the garden,—or at least construing what he beheld according to previous suspicions,—"will bring disgrace upon us, in spite of all my precautions and care. He must no longer have the advocacy of Charlotte in his behalf. I will instantly speak to her decidedly on the subject."

Miss Hastings was painfully surprised, on hastening to welcome her elder brother, to find a scowl upon his countenance; a manifestation which quickly drew from her an inquiry as to what the frown meant. The explanation was instantly afforded, together with a sterner declaration than before, that he would have the stranger-girl at once informed that she must quit their home, unless indeed she afforded them some most satisfactory information or references as to her past life; a thing, so far as he yet knew, she had by no means given.

"She is, it would appear," he said, "no way very forward to lend us such knowledge she has exceedingly little of the volunteering principle about her, unless it be to darn handkerchiefs. Yes the tramper must trudge, and take to the road this same day to the bargain. Some time ago, on my way from my parsonage-house at Sedley hither, I passed a family of gipsies. The wax-doll had better go and litter with them than longer trouble a respectable family, that has quite enough to do for themselves, especially since there is a senseless, headstrong member for the time amongst us, who gives us quite a sufficiency to do, independently of any light-o'-love minx who may throw herself upon our hands. Now go, I command you, Charlotte, and bring the stranger with you into my study. There will not be an hour's harmony in the house till this matter is disposed of, and we are rid of the baggage. You hesitate, and would intercede, sister! Then know if I am to be thwarted on this occasion, I will immediately leave you to yourselves, and go to my new home, which is all but ready for my reception."

The minister was angry,—very indignant indeed,—austere and authoritative even beyond his wont; although since having been appointed to the handsome church-living of Sedley by Colonel Pegsworth, of the Priory, in that parish, he had been observably growing sterner and more pompous, together with evincing a colder and more calculating temperament than ever, noted as he was by those who knew him best, for his pride and ambition.

"You are, brother, a hard as well as an eager man," muttered the distressed Charlotte, yet loud enough to let the minister hear what she said. "Would that you had more of Hector within you. But I submit, the result

MONTAGUE MILDMAY.

of what you are forcing on, Frederick, may be different far from what you anticipate. You are of the mind that your sisters know little of our guest, yet that little must be much compared with what has reached your thoughts of her. Besides, never before did I feel so strongly as now that a woman forms conclusions regarding the characters of those of her own sex from tokens and premises different from such as colleges inculcate."

Miss Hastings withdrew, resolved at once to bring the scene between her elder brother and their guest to a speedy conclusion; for indeed she dreaded considering for any length of time of the certainty of its occurrence, besides being anxious that neither her sisters nor the purser should have any anticipations of its happening. Charlotte immediately signified to our heroine that she wished her presence elsewhere than in the parlour, where the

No. 17.—THE GOVERNESS.

beautiful girl, with kindled hopes, was ruminating alone, thinking of Montague Mildmay, —the excitement of what Hector Hastings had revealed to her concerning the object of her incessant cogitations, lending such a radiance as Charlotte had never in all her life beheld.

"You'll have on the instant to prepare yourself for a scene with the exacting minister, Miss Neville; but I shall be present, and on your side, you may rely on it," said the agitated young lady. "My authoritative brother is in his study; let us repair, as soon as it suits you, to where he awaits our coming."

Adelaide Neville was naturally brave in spirit; and now that her health had been completely restored, and also that she had her hopes revivified, she possessed an affluence of life, which might be read in the expression of her penetrating eye. So greatly different did

MONTAGUE MILDMAY.

of what you are forcing on, Frederick, may
be different far from what you anticipate.
You are of the mind that your sisters know
little of our guest, yet that little must be
much compared with what has reached your
thoughts of her. Besides, never before did I
feel so strongly as now that a woman forms
conclusions regarding the characters of those
of her own sex from tokens and premises
different from such as colleges inculcate."

Miss Hastings withdrew, resolved at once
to bring the scene between her elder brother
and their guest to a speedy conclusion; for indeed she dreaded considering for any length of
time of the certainty of its occurrence, besides being anxious that neither her sisters
nor the purser should have any anticipations
of its happening. Charlotte immediately signified to our heroine that she wished her presence elsewhere than in the parlour, where the

beautiful girl, with kindled hopes, was ruminating alone, thinking of Montague Mildmay,
—the excitement of what Hector Hastings
had revealed to her concerning the object of
her incessant cogitations, lending such a radiance as Charlotte had never in all her life
beheld.

"You'll have on the instant to prepare yourself for a scene with the exacting minister,
Miss Neville; but I shall be present, and on
your side, you may rely on it," said the agitated young lady. "My authoritative brother
is in his study; let us repair, as soon as it suits
you, to where he awaits our coming."

Adelaide Neville was naturally brave in
spirit; and now that her health had been completely restored, and also that she had her
hopes revivified, she possessed an affluence of
life, which might be read in the expression of
her penetrating eye. So greatly different did

she seem now from what was her condition and aspect on the only occasion that the minister had ever beheld her, that he was wholly unprepared to encounter the subduing influence of faultless female beauty, especially when combined with the most expressive tokens of intellectual and moral power.

The young parson was seated at his table, and seemingly so earnestly engaged with a book which he held up before his eyes, that he did not show himself to be cognizant of the entrance of any one into his room; or, at least did not manifest that he had any wish to address them. Both the ladies, nevertheless, were perfectly aware that it was not the pages before him upon which the minister's eyes were mainly bent, but upon the extraordinary vision of grace and loveliness that met his gaze; so extraordinary and unexpected, indeed, that he in a moment regretted having been so rash and peremptory in his conduct and commands to his amiable sister with respect to their guest.

Both ladies stood stock still on entering the room, the moment the door was shut, tacitly agreeing that the first words should come from the minister. However, as he did not seem prepared to utter anything, his sister broke through the taciturnity, embarrassing him siill more by what she said.

"I have, my brother, orought Miss Neville with me to your presence, at your special command," said Charlotte, in a low tone, and not unaccompanied with tremulousness, occasioned by the excess of her emotion.

"True, sister dear," returned the gentleman. "Be seated, ladies,"—the volume being again lifted up, as if he were too much absorbed by its contents to think of the living intelligences near to him.

"We had better come back when you are more at leisure, my brother," said the sister; "and yet we ladies wish to have an end put to the business for which we were summoned hither, as soon as possible."

"Yes, I think you had better come back when I am more at leisure," returned the now almost quailing minister, glad to have an excuse for delaying a scene in which he seemed to anticipate discomfiture. "Meanwhile, it is like my rude absence of mind, that I did not congratulate Miss Neville on her restoration to health; to her proper self. I trust, young lady, that you feel your recovery to be complete."

Having thus spoken the clerical gentleman again held his book before his eyes, indicating, thereby that he wished to be left alone.

"Yes, I feel, Mr. Hastings, that my recovery is complete, in so far as bodily health is concerned," answered Adelaide. "Nay, even as regards my spirits, I experience considerable buoyancy, being naturally, I believe, endowed with a cheerful temperament. But yet, there are upon my mind pains and anxieties which are not, and ought not to be, without their weight. I am oppressed with the sense of the wondrous kindness and hospitality of yourself, sir, of your sisters, and brother," she continued uninterruptedly; "having the conviction, at the same time, that I have no means of testifying my gratitude but by words, which may go for nothing."

"No, words do not go for nothing, when they are manifestly the expression of an overflowing and honest heart, Miss Neville," responded the gentleman; evidently wishing to back out of his awkward predicament as speedily as possible.

The volume had been again dropped, affording the stranger young lady another opportunity of scanning the gentleman with a penetrating eye; for, indeed, Mr. Hastings presented a person and features that might well rivet the attention, being also of a cast that afforded an index to his temperament and character.

"He is manliness itself, according to what we learn of the Grecian model," thought Adelaide; "but yet he does not impress me as being gentle, yielding, or spontaneously generous. It would be worth an ambitious woman's while to contend with that cold and calculating individual; it would also be a victory of no mean kind, did she discomfit him;" these ideas passing through the gifted girl's mind, whilst simultaneously she framed a reply to the minister's last words.

"Had you, Mr. Hastings, afforded me an opportunity of conversing for a few minutes with you a week ago," said the young lady, "I should have expressed myself exactly as I do now, thereby discharging a duty, and freeing myself, to some extent, of matters that weigh within me. I would have told you, not only that I am absolutely homeless except but for your hospitality; that I know of no link, by blood, that can entitle me to the fostering care of any human being; nay, that so great is the mystery which, not many months ago, all at once began to envelope me—so dense the cloud that suddenly over-shadowed me—so impenetrable the darkness, it seems, that broods over the history of my birth, that I do not even know my rightful name."

"Miss Neville, my brother, has not withheld from your sisters these things," interjected Miss Hastings; "only you would not, on your longed-for return, have patience to hear what I could have rehearsed to you. But I interrupt you, dear young lady."

"Yes, I was suddenly hurled from a position of very high worldly expectations," continued Adelaide; "upon which reverse I sought for employment, in order to earn my bread with persevering industry. In my fortunes as a governess I was not happy; but, even in that capacity I might have enjoyed a tolerable share of comfort and contentment, had not villany assailed and persecuted me, until, in self-protection, I was obliged, under the cloud of night, to take to flight, well knowing that slander, foul as false, was ready to track me. Yes, I fled, not knowing well whither or how; hurrying, as best I could, from place to place, in a country where all was strange, until hunger, exhaustion and despair, overwhelmed me utterly at the threshold of your hospitable home."

"Strange it is, I must say, that you, young lady, can afford us no clue by which we might restore you at least to the honourable position of a governess!" exclaimed Mr. Hastings, with a marked, if not an incredulous, emphasis. "Surely there must be sundry individuals, that in your happier and promising days knew you, who would be forward and proud to lend you succour, or at least recommend you to the favour of others."

"Yes, there are such persons," responded the young lady, "although I believe them to be but few, whilst the most friendly of them are beyond my reach, either by known remoteness of position, or the impossibility of my finding them out, or the delicacy which hedges me from them. Besides, there are reasons which are powerful with me that prevent the revealment, even to the inmates of this house, of all that I could actually disclose. My own interests, as also the sense of what I owe to some others, put a seal upon my lips in the meanwhile, which will not easily be broken."

"You do not at all succeed in removing my views concerning the unsatisfactoriness of your statements, Miss Neville, since such is the name you go by," observed the clerical gentleman, relapsing into his coldness and caution, and being again guided by his eager ambition. "As a minister of the Gospel, who is about to enter upon his pastoral functions in a neighbouring parish, and as the head of a family in which there are three unmarried young women, and for the present a wilful brother, you yourself must see how delicate is my position, and how exacting the views which all will entertain concerning me. I lament that you cannot give us a clearer account of yourself, young lady."

"I lament no such thing, and would resist further divulgence were Miss Neville to offer it, before she feels it proper, in duty to herself, to be more explicit," cried Miss Hastings, rising from her chair at the same time, and offering her hand to poor Adelaide.

"Neither do I lament the want of further disclosure, for, in fact, it is not needed," exclaimed the purser, on entering his brother's study at the instant; the impetuous youth having been a listener outside, it must be confessed, for some time. "I have heard you say, Miss Neville, that you are willing—nay, eager, to earn a livelihood in any honest way, however humble, for which you are competent. I have also learnt that you have been a teacher, in your adversity, of young people of your own sex; and to this office I have no doubt you are ready at once to return, however narrow and plain at the starting be the sphere."

"Most willingly, Mr. Hector, and most thankfully," cried Adelaide. "Show me where to get work, or how to seek for work, and gladly shall I this instant enter upon the matter, eager as I am to dispense with charity,—nay, resolved if I can have an opportunity of repaying Mr. Hastings and you all, if not with current money, for your unspeakable kindness to me, at least by showing in my conduct that I am both mindful of what is due to you all and to myself."

"It will be difficult to resist such testimony, such a reference, I judge," said the purser, "however exacting ministers of our church may be;" he and the pair of ladies taking their leave of the young parson, who, chagrined and perplexed, was nigh recalling all three, and confessing that he was in the wrong.

The minister, in fact, was not only of a cold and calculating disposition,—eager and ambitious, but he rated his abilities and influence far too high. He was, after all, a person of very ordinary parts; which parts, however, had he not latterly set his affections on worldly advancement, instead of letting them have the incense shed around them of an originally not altogether sterile heart, might have rendered him an amiable, if not a bright, member of society, and as disinterested a parson as the generality of the sable brotherhood are found to be.

From the moment, however, that he succeeded in working so upon the simple and genuine piety of Miss Pegsworth,—who, the only surviving child of the opulent colonel, was as the apple of the gallant old gentleman's eye,—as to obtain the handsome church-living, with the elegant parsonage-house of Sedley, he had greatly changed to the worse; being now only by starts guided by amiable and humane impulses,—such as when he found the houseless wanderer, apparently at the point of death, at his door; impulses which were gradually growing weaker, and the intervals between them the greater.

It was far from being a good trait in the history of Frederick Hastings, that he had done all that in him lay to supplant his brother in the affections of Paulina; representing Hector, in his absence, when on the wide sea, as a wild, rakish, and reprobate fellow, while he himself affected to be thoroughly imbued with a religious principle, and wholly devoted to heaven and heaven's children. And yet the unscrupulous aspirant discovered that at times he overshot his mark; as, for example, when he anticipated that, as the catechizer of poor Miss Neville,—the dismisser of her from his door, unless she made it clear that she was of superior birth,—upon which his hospitality would be noised abroad, to the enlargement of his fame and interests,—he found that he but gave a handle to his brother to reduce his pious pretensions in the judgment of the colonel's daughter to their proper level.

CHAPTER XXVII.

THE YOUTHFUL SCHOOLMISTRESS.

THE family from which our heroine got her implied dismissal by its clerical member, although far from wealthy, were of ancient descent and well allied, entitling its more ambitious son to aspire to positions and connexions of distinction. To be sure, the young parson's good fortune authorized him, as he thought, to ridicule his brother's sea-faring professional choice, and the rank of a purser; although, having an appointment in a large East-Indiaman, the generous and robust Hector not seldom had a telling answer when at home,—smarting under the lettered scorn of the other, especially when the more warm-hearted and vehement one reflected on the fact that, but for his gains lately, the family's means would have been inconveniently straitened. In short, but for the purser's well-filled pocket when he returned to his native spot, together with his remittances, the sisters must have gone out to some sort of service to, and dependency upon, strangers,—perhaps in the character of governesses, in spite of their aristocratic descent and alliances, and also to the humiliation of the aspirant after a valuable church-living.

Considerations of this kind had their weight with the young ladies as well as with Hector, when they thought of the friendless and outcast condition of poor Miss Neville; they being at the same time aware that from the singularly simple and pious turn of Paulina Pegsworth's disposition, a stronger recommendation of the forlorn wanderer could not be produced than the assurance that she was without a home and yet greatly admired by her late hospitable nurses; except, indeed, that recommendation should be presented in the person and behaviour of our heroine herself.

"Be of good cheer, Miss Neville," cried the purser, shortly after quitting his brother's room with the poor damsel and his sister. "I'm off on an embassy in your behalf,—with a letter in my pocket from Charlotte, to one of her dearest correspondents. Be for the time of humble views and easily contented. Brighter days, I trust, are coming for you. Give me a few hours, and I'll be back again, perhaps ere nightfall, so as to have you under another roof before the supper hour."

In perhaps shorter time than ever Hector travelled the distance between the place of his birth and the Priory,—a fine old Gothic fabric which had been turned into a convenient mansion many years back,—did he on this occasion speed over the four intervening miles. The purser had always been a favourite with the colonel, and this in a great measure because the young gentleman bore a very striking resemblance every way to his father, who had been in the same regiment with Pegsworth. In Paulina's estimation,—this young lady being but a year younger than the sea-farer,—he had been wont to stand higher than his colder and less genial brother, until the aspirant for a rich church-living worked upon her credulity, to the injury of the truer character of the two.

However, not unaware of the young lady's lingering partiality towards him, and especially of the resistlessness of the appeal which he was, together with his sister's letter, to make to the tender-hearted and pious Paulina, Hector gleefully hied him along, every now and then muttering ejaculations to himself.

"Frederick has overshot his mark! He must not think of having everything his own way, although a minister of the established church; at least, unless he can and does pay for the same. May be I'll turn the tables upon him some day yet, in regard to the young lady of the Priory, seeing that my hopes are blasted relative to a still brighter beauty. At all events, if I can be of service in placing Miss Neville above immediate sheer want, and every—even the slightest—frown, I'll be doing a good turn, were it only by my triumph over Frederick; teaching him to be more tolerant and meek."

Such were the terms with which the purser cheered himself, as he strode along to throw his striking story about the outcast Adelaide upon the mild consideration of the ever-beneficent Paulina.

Miss Pegsworth was moved by the purser's account of the houseless wanderer, having faith in what was told her, without a questioning expression, when the representation came from such sources as that of Charlotte and Hector Hastings.

"It is strange that your brother should have been so harsh, so changeful, and at the end so unbelieving," cried the colonel's daughter, "in the case of such suffering, and destitution, as you describe; in the case too of such an interesting fellow-being! He should have remembered that he has sisters of his own, and also that the most high-minded of us all, who shall think that our standing is sure, may be suddenly overwhelmed with calamity, not at all incurred by our own fault. And what if that unhappy creature, that is so unexpectedly arrested and plunged into a sea of difficulties at once, should be a young woman, delicately reared, and the object of villanous persecution! I shudder to contemplate what might be my own condition were I in an instant to be rendered fatherless and fortuneless—thrown upon an unfeeling world—a world whose heart is set on grasping wealth and estate—even the professed ministers of religion being, in not a few instances, the greediest of the cormorants. Tell your brother, Mr. Hector, what I say: he'll not soon regain the position in my mind that he sometime ago held. Above all, see that the unhappy outcast be brought hither directly. John shall go with you, Hector, taking my gig; which, old-fashioned as it is, will hold you all three. Now, be expeditious."

Here was another sudden change in the fortunes of our heroine; one, indeed, which seemed to threaten the young parson of Sedley with something like disaster. Everything, however, appeared to depend on the opinion which Paulina, in the first place, might form of the forlorn one, and, secondly, on the latter's subsequent judicious self-government; the purser having whispered to her, as they drove to the Priory, that Miss Pegsworth's creed insisted greatly on genuine humility and active beneficence as being the tests of virtue and goodness.

"She has it in contemplation, I know," said the young gentleman, "to found a free-school for the female children of the poor peasantry of this rustic and generally uncouth district; but she complains that she cannot find, even through the promise of a fair salary, a female teacher who is at all to her mind. How delighted should I be if you, Miss Neville, could bring your mind to undertake the office; believing as I do that such a temporary sacrifice would eventually be for your lasting good—your eventual advantage."

"I like your counsel, Mr. Hector, and thank you with all my heart for so candidly volunteering it," almost cheerily answered the poor girl. "Do you know, I feel so equal to what in your great kindness you would have me do, that it almost looks as if it were accomplished. How I pant for an opportunity, however obscure—in truth the obscurer the better, in my present peculiar circumstances—to earn my bread and find my self-reliance, when fairly treated, put to the trial."

Favourable as was the prepossession of Paulina Pegsworth concerning our heroine, the feeling was by no means so high as after the two young ladies had spent the evening together; their conversation having been discursive, earnest, and, for the most part, of a practical nature.

"What," at length cried the colonel's daughter, "will you do with your tastes, Miss Neville? What with your sentiments, your accomplishments? Bear in mind that the sphere in the neighbouring poor village is narrow; indeed, to most minds refined and educated as yours has been, it would prove painfully narrowing. What will you do with such insatiate yearnings and continuous aspirations as must be yours? I tremble to think how deeply I may be involved in occasioning the sacrifice of your intellectual gifts and acquirements. I must, and will, find some more suitable situation for you, my dear girl."

"Relinquish not the idea, I beseech you, Miss Pegsworth," responded our heroine. "I wish to prove to myself, yes, and to others, that I am equal to great sacrifices, so long as I remain morally untainted. Besides, it is not clear that in the present instance there will be any sacrifice at all; seeing that but for you, kind lady, should I not be again a houseless, forlorn wanderer, without any sure prospect of ever having a roof under which to lay my head, or that I should be able to say, This crust of bread has been honestly earned by me? I hail the ordeal and discipline that are before me; being determined, in as far as I can, not to look back, but steadily to pursue an onward career, such as in Heaven's wisdom I am appointed to undertake; Providence having given us, I believe, the power in a measure to shape our own destiny."

"Excellent!" exclaimed Pauline; "yet how difficult the fulfilment of our best resolves! You will have ragged, rude, ignorant, and stupid subjects to deal with; and I cannot but be conscience-stricken at the sort of profanity I have been in your case committing."

"At the starting, I doubt not, I shall have trials," returned Adelaide; "encountering disgusts, obduracy, and ingratitude, if not sometimes gross indignity, from parents perhaps as well as children,—the latter being probably grown-up, raw girls. But I have had some experience in teaching the stupid and the refractory before this; having found the faith confirmed upon which I relied—viz., that kindness, perseverance, and a heartfelt anxiety for the advancement of your pupils' interests, are sure at length to be triumphant in the great majority of instances. At the same time, I am not to forget that the coarsely clad peasant-born ones are of flesh and blood as good as the scions of the gentlest genealogy, and also that genius is not confined to families or races. In short, to cultivate the pleasure which is sure to arise from a sense of doing one's duty must be my study; and confident am I, Miss Pegsworth, of success following my efforts."

"How stupid or perverse must the Rev. Frederick Hastings have been to suspect that innocent and rare creature of imposture," muttered Pauline to herself, as soon as Adelaide withdrew to her dormitory. "Assuredly she is richly gifted, and, I should say, hardly less indebted to culture. It looks as if a most happy combination of planets had presided over her birth. She will abide scrutiny; coming out of the trial brighter than on her going to encounter it."

The school was opened in a humble cottage in the hamlet,—for the village was little more, —which spread itself out almost within the shadow of the Priory's turrets. A greater than anticipated number of girls at the very first repaired to see the "pretty youthful mistress" of the seminary; the interesting teacher having her parlour of white-washed walls and sanded floor, with the plainest and most serviceable articles of furniture, on a level with the school-room, while her bed-chamber above was of equally unpretending aspect and internal supply.

Nor did she miscalculate in her anticipations as to the success, any more than as regarded the annoyances,—especially at the starting,— of her obscure undertaking. When four or five months had passed away with her as a schoolmistress, she, however, found flattering proficiency in a number of instances; the branches taught being confined to reading, writing, ciphering, sewing, and knitting. Approval met her in many directions; in fact, she became a favourite in the neighbourhood. When she went forth, she received on all sides cordial salutations from old and young. But it was the colonel's daughter who proved the most constant and warmest of her friends, almost daily paying the youthful schoolmistress a visit, and often taking a part in the business of instructing. Not seldom, too, did Paulina bring her distinguished visitors to bestow their admiration upon our heroine.

There cannot be a doubt that had the Misses Hastings been near neighbours, they would have shown the exemplary girl all possible countenance. Miss Neville herself sometimes travelled to their abode, to which the elder brother still clung, although with considerable regularity performing his ministerial functions at Sedley.

"You must come, Mr. Hastings, and take frequent cognizance of my school-people. I shall always be proud of, and thankful for, your suggestions and superintendence," was Adelaide's smiling address to the clerical gentleman the first time she visited his cottage after her dismissal from it. Nor seldom at length did he pay the humble seminary a visit; this being, some people thought, chiefly intended to ingratiate himself anew with the young lady who founded and supported the school. As to Hector, at an early period of the charitable undertaking, he had to join his ship.

Our heroine's measure of contentment with her obscure position was remarkable. The state of her mind indeed might be read in her looks; for, while a schoolmistress at Sedley, she grew into a more matured beauty than had ever before distinguished the maiden.

Hers had now become a graceful form, without losing its youthful elasticity; being full, yet fine in contour. Her face had all along been considered one of perfect loveliness; but now the pure tints of rose and lily blended more exquisitely than ever,—no other charm of feature being wanting, or without faultless development. There were throughout, in short, the most regular yet delicate lineaments, crowned with the rich and plenteous ornament of tresses, that kissed her cheek and floated to her shoulders.

As the winter waned and genial spring drew near, Colonel Pegsworth's visitors grew more numerous than during the more inclement season; and as the youthful and lovely schoolmistress formed a frequent theme for discourse on the part of Paulina and of her father also, often did she find her humble parlour as well as the apartment in which her pupils assembled crowded with gentry and titled people. Indeed our heroine at times felt uneasy, being afraid lest by possibility she should be recognised as the individual who had at one time passed as Adelaide Waldgrave, and the heiress to a splendid fortune. What rendered the number of guests at the Priory greater than heretofore, was the circumstance of the old colonel and Paulina having spent some two months of the winter in London, when the fact of the young lady's prospects, in respect of wealth, was circulated amongst metropolitan fortune-hunters and others.

One afternoon, just as Adelaide was dismissing her young people, she observed Miss Pegsworth approaching with a bevy of stylish people; the colonel's daughter being no doubt ambitious to show off her pet, as she frequently named our heroine, — naturally, of course, taking a portion of the praise which was bestowed on the beautiful schoolmistress to herself. There seemed to be a predominance, at the first view obtained of the comers, of gentlemen,—these bringing up the rear;—but on a closer inspection, our heroine was rather surprised on observing that some of the more remote persons were in livery,—at least, a pair being in the bedizened costume of lacqueys.

The company approached, three or four ladies being in front, along with Miss Pegsworth, and next two gentlemen, arm-in-arm; these being followed at some distance by the servile members of the party. Yes, the bevy drew nearer and nearer, until Adelaide, who was standing at her door to welcome her patroness, could distinctly note one of the gentlemen as being a person with whose features she was acquainted,—these having been indelibly impressed upon her memory.

"Oh! if it had been Montague Mildmay or the old man of the Red Cot, how should I have exulted," ejaculated the damsel, as if she had become suddenly demented; "but it is the infamous——" the next intended name sticking in her throat, as if she never should have the power to pronounce it,—the lovely and terrified creature at the same time falling to the ground as one who, in the twinkling of an eye, had been bereft of life by a winged arrow.

What immediately after happened she could not tell, but when she came in a measure to herself, Miss Pegsworth and one of that young lady's servant-maids were bending over her, and ministering to the poor girl with all the tenderness and assiduity possible.

"I have sent my visitors away, Miss Neville, that no idle curiosity may further disturb you here," said Paulina. "Compose yourself as quickly as possible; and, when you are suffi-

ciently recovered, you will accompany me to the Priory,—to my own private room; for I know there is some grave reason for one who is so self-possessed as you are, my dear girl, being thus suddenly and frightfully overwhelmed,—even when I, your real friend, was in the van of the visiting party."

Paulina was the more particular and lengthened in her address, thinking thereby the sooner to restore the confidence of the young schoolmistress, who followed the speech with eagerness and intelligence, although scarcely yet able herself to articulate a complete sentence. But Adelaide's eagerness and intelligence were not all the while solely directed to what fell from the lips of the colonel's daughter; for, after her still languid eyes had kept gazing for a few seconds towards the window of her little parlour, into which she had been carried, she again became distracted with terror and alarm.

"See! see!" cried she, as loud as her strength permitted her; falling into a new state of insensibility.

"Some sudden delirium or strange delusion has come over the dear creature," said Paulina, greatly shocked. "Oh! I trust that no permanent frenzy has seized her; and yet, from all that I can learn of her more recent life, she has endured hardships and tribulations sufficient to unhinge her mind,—to unseat her reason."

It took some time before Adelaide was again restored to sensibility and intelligence. But when she did a second time come to herself, and observed how deeply affected the colonel's daughter had become, she made an effort to encourage the sympathizer.

"I am better now, and will, I trust, continue better; so take heart, good Miss Pegsworth," muttered the young schoolmistress, in broken parts. "All will soon be explained, but to your ear alone. Whatever little property I have here, will not be burdensome to your maiden, whom I should wish to gather it for me, and bring it to the Priory. Never again dare I set foot within this cottage, if once I escape from it with you."

"You terrify me anew, Miss Neville," said Paulina, again wringing her hands. "I feared a little ago, that some strange and perhaps permanent frenzy had suddenly seized you, although soon after I felt assured to the contrary, by certain encouraging words you spoke. But now you seem to rave more wildly than ever. Try to let me have conviction that you are in possession of your reason."

"It is neither a fit of frenzy nor raving that has seized me, good Miss Pegsworth," responded the youthful school-mistress; "but the blow that was given my head and heart by the sight of monsters, of whom I live in mortal fear, was, on the instant, too heavy for me. Now, I am composed, and cannot immediately dread danger; but my revelation must take place elsewhere—in your own chamber, dear lady, if you will."

Adelaide and Paulina bent their steps towards the Priory; the former repeating her request that the servant would be so kind as to collect the few articles of clothing to be found in the little bed-room up-stairs; saying also, to the handmaiden, that she would there find her purse and some other small things, of which she should be thankful to keep possession.

"Having done this, lock the door and bring the key to your excellent mistress," added our heroine; "for all that remains belongs to Miss Pegsworth."

"Strange, resolute girl!" ejaculated the colonel's daughter, on hearing these various minute directions.

"I wish to be methodical and accurate," observed the poor maiden, bursting into tears.

The pair of young ladies soon gained the Priory, and next Paulina's chamber, without being accosted, or in any way interrupted by the visitors; although not a little speculation already existed amongst certain of these as to what had happened at the humble school-house, and even posterior to that singular scene. In fact, more than one of the gentlemen had suddenly decamped, without assigning to the old colonel any reason for their hasty departure; he at the time being ignorant of poor Adelaide's predicament.

"Captain Chesters, the *honourable*, the Life-Guardsman," said she as soon as seated in private,—emphasizing the two latter distinctive terms with a loathing contempt,—"is one of your visitors, Miss Pegsworth."

"Yes, dear, he drove hither to spend a few days with us along with his friend, Lieutenant Revel," frankly answered Paulina. "In winter, when in London, the colonel and I got acquainted with the two gentlemen, as well as a good many others; a considerable portion being military characters, towards whom, indeed, my father has a leaning. Not one of them, however, paid so marked attention to us as Chesters. He is of a great family, I believe, and his prospects in Yorkshire, we have been told, on the death of an aged uncle, are almost princely."

"And Chesters, along with Revel, I presume brought two liveried lacqueys with them?" inquiringly said Adelaide.

"I believe they did, or rather the livery of both fellows was that of Captain Chesters," replied Paulina; adding, "I use the term fellows, for they impudently stared through the window of your little parlour, Miss Neville, as I distinctly noted, when you went off in your second swoon, after exclaiming, 'See! see!' as you did."

"True, Miss Pegsworth," returned our heroine, "and I can give the names of these same two fellows, and also assure you that they are fitly in the service of the *honourable* Life-Guardsman. No trio could be more properly yoked together! What is more, knew I how, or where, to find those who would be forward to witness for me, the possibility, if not the probability is, that for their villany towards me, I should make the precious triumvirate be united under the same gallows-tree some bright morning, before the current year was much older."

Paulina stared, being both shocked and incredulous, almost thoroughly convinced that the poor girl was beside herself; the idea at the same time occurring to her, that, perhaps but for some strange perversion of mind, some obliquity of imagination, some wild erratic dis-

position, the lovely creature should never have been reduced to the state of misery and destitution she had experienced, and that she might still have been basking in the bosom of the family where in her childhood and girlhood she had been cherished.

"You are startled,—you disbelieve, Miss Pegsworth," said our heroine, with solemn composure; "but perhaps you will be still more astonished when I declare my hope and trust to be that the day is not far distant when Chesters shall be brought to the bar of criminal justice on the charge of having attempted to murder me by stealth, and this too, when his handsome face was wreathed in smiles, ay, and when he professed, in the language of fulsome flattery, to be wooing me for his bride."

"Fulsome flattery, and wooing you for his bride!" exclaimed Paulina. "Now, Adelaide Neville, I begin to think that it is not delirium or delusion that prompts and sways you, but some grievous truth, knowing as I do that the person you allude to is apt to make modesty blush by his rank adulation; although the fine ladies of London call it the language of gallantry, which I am sure is about the hollowest and most heartless style of speech that exists. He is no favourite of mine, although, as a military character, my father approves of him and affects his society. In short, I know him to be a fortune-hunter from the way he has always talked to me."

"Then, Miss Pegsworth, there is no danger for you in that quarter, I rejoice to learn," subjoined the other. "You speak true; the Life-Guardsman is a fortune-hunter, drowned in debt, as he at present is; one, too, who would not hesitate for an hour to stop the breath of his wife for ever, if by that means he could get unquestioned power over her dowry. Worse still, he is not only a shameless fortune-hunter, but the most heartless of libertines. In short, his life for years has been of the falsest, because the most deceitful in his intercourse with people of quality,—a man of the grossest profligacy, to the ruin of many an innocent creature. He stops at nothing in his villanous pursuits. I would not consider myself safe for an hour after nightfall, if not strongly guarded from him and his ruffian myrmidons, Jobson and Norland, of whom I got a glimpse at my parlour window, for they are scoundrels who would, as his agents, but for a providential interposition, have rendered me loathsome to myself for ever."

"There are footsteps of some one coming hither for me, Miss Neville; they are my father's, and I know from the vehemence of the tread that he is agitated, perhaps in a towering passion," said Paulina, with a new alarm.

"Not a word about what we have been speaking of," whispered Adelaide, "or of what I have now revealed; my happiness, probably my life, depends on your silence and discretion, my dear friend."

"Here's a pretty ado!" exclaimed the colonel, the moment he could accost his daughter, and find language, as well as breath to express himself. "That Captain Chesters is a strange fellow, or rather a great scoundrel, I should say. Why, he is off with Revel and his hukeys, without ever saying 'By your leave!' having got the horses put to the carriage in a twinkling, and then away at the rate of Jehu. Ha! my pretty schoolmistress! so you are here. I understand that the Life-Guardsman was nearly your death a little while ago, although it was only a sight of him that brought you to the ground. But then and next, he and his people appear to have been hardly less frightened, for they have incontinently fled. There must be something extraordinary about all this, and it shall be looked into."

CHAPTER XXVIII.

THE REVISIT.

LEAVING the colonel and his daughter to discourse between themselves of the singular circumstances that had disturbed them, as described at the close of the last chapter, we must accompany Adelaide, who was resolute in her purpose of quitting the Priory and its neighbourhood, and of repairing to some quarter where she might consider herself secure from the villany of Chesters and his agents. Her course was once again, not unnaturally, bent towards that great vortex of life, London, although without the intention of prolonging her stay there for any considerable period.

And yet the enterprising girl did not reach the metropolis without an incident occurring which was not altogether without noticeable results in her career. As Adelaide stepped into the coach by which she was to travel to the capital,—one of the colonel's domestics who carried her boxes to the public conveyance having wished her good-bye and a safe journey,—she found only one inside passenger preoccupying the carriage, who immediately invited conversation, and although not with the most polished tact, with evidently a matronly good-will. In short, before they had got to the termination of their ride,—the destination of both being the City, many of whose merchants and tradesmen are princes, if wealth be taken as the test,—Mrs. Hogson had formed such a favourable opinion of the young creature who was her companion in travel, and began to feel such an interest in her welfare, that it required but a very little additional intimacy between them to make the persecuted one an inmate of the good woman's house, in the capacity of tutoress to her only girl.

Mrs. Hogson's residence, and of course that of her husband,—a little, round, and good-humoured man, with small features, florid complexion, light blue eyes, a flaxen wig, a garrulous tongue, and bustling gait,—was in a small dingy court off Gutter Lane; a spot having on three sides a row of uniformly constructed dark red brick houses, the windows faced with white, and most of them decorated with pots of London-pride and wallflower. The back-front of a small church filled up the greater part of the fourth side; so that what exteriorly met the eye on entering the court was gloomy and airless. But once enter the mansion of the saddler, or harness-maker,—for

such was Mr. Hogson by trade,—a vast and successful contractor in leather with Government besides,—and all was the most scrupulous neatness and cleanliness, in spite of the density and besmearing qualities of London smoke.

Mr. Hogson was noted for one domestic, or rather animal, peculiarity, although he could feel no lack of citizens around his habitation to keep him in countenance as regarded the ruling passion. His gastronomic tastes were nearly the incessant theme of his home discourse; so that while he ambled up and down his small, dull, yet tidy parlour, on the morning of Adelaide's entrance into her new situation upon a month's trial,—the burden of his discourse being addressed to the young lady,—it wholly regarded the excellence of various kinds of eatables; the bustling body's hospitality being at the same time exemplary.

"Have a rump-steak for lunch, Miss,—a veritable London rump-steak; or say a sandwich—a nice ham sandwich," squeaked out the restless creature. "Real Westphalia ham, I assure you, Miss; is it not, Mrs. Hogson? Beautiful sort! bought it myself! Quite a nosegay, ain't it, Mrs. Hogson? Let us, my dear, have a goodly dish of Birch's turtle-soup for starting with at dinner. People from the country, Miss, have no notion of the riches of Birch's article. It goes all round the world, I assure you. And, Mrs. Hogson, I must have Mogg's muffins for tea; I leave the rest to your own admirable providing. Wonderful man was Mogg,—has made already two hundred thousand pounds by his muffins."

Adelaide found that first appearances did not belie the Hogsons; the saddler being a mere good-natured gossiping body, while his spouse was a vulgar, advising, patronising, but yet true-hearted and conscientious dame. As for the girl, there was not a brighter nor a worse point about her than might be expected from such a parentage; so that for the greater part of each day Adelaide was left to the combined wretchedness of loneliness and constraint.

The bustling harness-maker, it has been stated, was noted for gastronomic tastes, his main domestic peculiarity; yet before Adelaide had been for a fortnight an inmate of his house, he seemed to bid fair for becoming distinguished in another way. In a word, his attentions to the lovely and fascinating girl, in spite of all her repelling modesty and considerate conduct, were growing so obtrusive and undisguised as not only to disgust her, but to attract the notice of Mrs. Hogson, whose jealousy of her partner had never till now been stirred. What with the constant and obtrusive pressure upon the maiden of the delicacies of the table, of which the would-be courteous body was every day making purchases himself,—a circumstance which he was continually proclaiming,—his inopportune attempts at gallantry, and his puerile facetiousness, he contrived to render not only his spouse but the governess so extremely uncomfortable that the young lady felt it would be impossible for her to remain longer a member of the family than to the close of the month for which she was engaged. It was just as this specified period

MISS CHARLOTTE HASTINGS.

was about to terminate that an incident led to a sudden severance of the parties.

"La! Miss Neville," cried Mrs. Hogson, shortly before the ordinary hour for dinner, —the saddler keeping up the old-fashioned periods for his meals,—"here come several of my grand visiting folks. Run and put my dear Mary, your gentle pupil, to rights, that she may be fit to be presented to these distinguished people. Bring the darling to the drawing-room when I send for you."

"And this is your daughter's governess, of whom you have been telling us so many fine things, Mrs. Hogson," cried Mrs. Puffendorf, the moment she could command language to express her astonishmennt and horror, on recognising our heroine,—the big widow being accompanied by her never-failing satellites, the Ladies Gorewell and Lymington, each of whom bore herself charac-

teristically, to the production of a scene that will be much more easily conceived than described. "The sooner ye get quit of the loathsome thing the better," added the woman, with a mighty toss of the head; "I tremble for the virtue of your sweet child," something like a hysterical fit putting an end to the personation of wounded feelings.

We do not detain the reader with the particulars of what followed in the drawing-room, further than to state that Adelaide, while insulted and disgusted, carried herself in a manner which made each of the others quail in her presence, and this chiefly by means of the polished dignity and the radiant expression both of conscious innocence and triumphant virtue which marked her conduct and sparing speech. The opulent trades-man's house, in the dingy court of Gutter Lane, was no longer a home for the maiden.

No. 18.—THE GOVERNESS.

"I'll to Yorkshire,—to the vicinity of the scenes of my first experience and tribulation in England,—to Peter Plumtree's cot itself," said the young creature to herself, not only made resolute by the sudden attack made upon her by a parcel of scandal-mongers, but feeling on the instant assured that in no quarter of the world would she be more anxiously avoided by Captain Chesters and his infamous allies than in the neighbourhood of Wartham Hall and of Sir Vaux Waldgrave. "What if I should open a school in the thriving town of Wartham itself, which is not above two miles from either the baronet's stately residence or the fantastic dwelling of the good Samaritan! Who knows but that I may at length find felicity near to where my career of misery had its commencement."

Adelaide was soon on her northern route, and in due time she arrived at the town of Wartham, at an hour, too, which was considerably earlier than that of mid-day. Having bespoken a bed for at least one night at the inn where she alighted, and having put herself in proper trim for taking a solitary walk, the young lady directed her steps towards the Red Cot. It was not long before she found herself upon the tongue of land which the wonted occupant of the fantastic habitation owned; the spot at which she paused happening to be at the bottom of the Cauldron Cliff,—a locality rendered so memorable to her, that the maiden stood as if rooted in the ground from which she obtained the first view,—and it was the most effective of any, as regarded the picturesque yet frightful aspect of the precipice.

"What dost here?" was the angrily-put question by a coarse voice which struck upon the ear of the wrapt gazer at the frowning cliff,—the speaker having come upon the young lady along the grassy path quite unheeded; a smart touch on one of her shoulders with a heavy cane, to the infliction of some pain, serving to lend force to the scream of sudden surprise which she experienced. "What dost here, young woman?" was the repeated inquiry, and put by no less a personage than the ponderous Sir Vaux Waldgrave himself, but in less angry accents than the baronet had at first used,—the maiden having turned her gaze towards him, and in the flush of her excitement,—now doubly aroused,—bending upon him such an indignant and commanding look,—her bearing and attitude being in keeping with the expression of her countenance and the awakened emotions of her spirit,—that the blunderer in some degree quailed,—stepping back a pace or two to make him surer of a sufficiency of room for what might follow.

"You ask, unmannerly man, or rather assailant,—one old enough to be my grandfather," said the now fearless girl, conscious of the strength of her position, "what I do here? My return to your rudeness,—to the salute of your weighty cane is this,—Who are you, and what right have you to question me, standing where I now am?"

"I am Sir Vaux Waldgrave, the most influential personage in this quarter of Yorkshire," answered the baronet. "That cliff which I found you gazing at so strangely, and I doubt not with a mischievous intent, along with some skulking fellow or another for a companion,—both of you ready after nightfall to break into my gardens, orchards, dovecots, poultry-houses, and so forth,—I say that most picturesque of all precipices I have ever yet beheld in this country, or any other, is mine by inheritance, together with a vast range of other beauties and carefully ornamented scenes in this neighbourhood. Learn then, pert minx,—you who have had the shamelessness to talk of Sir Vaux Waldgrave, of Wartham Hall, as an unmannerly clown,—learn, then, that it is my practice, as well as my bounden duty, not only as a large landed proprietor in this Riding of Yorkshire, nay, as the magistrate,—yes, the magistrate, of largest political as well as social sway in the whole county,—it is my practice daily to look to the boundaries of my more properly home territory, to see that no vagrants and vagabonds be prowling about for the purpose of pouncing upon my possessions, and invading my grounds when my back is turned, or night darkens the land."

Sir Vaux very well knew when he thus imperiously talked and wordily bounced, that he had not seen the young person before whom he blundered do any harm to him or anybody else. He also perfectly understood that he himself was as much a trespasser at the moment as she whom he so rudely took to task could be. But sluggish of mind, as he was, yet peremptory and imperious, he thought of frightening the young creature, presuming her to be ignorant not only of a country magistrate's extent of authority, but of the limits of his territorial possessions at the particular point where they stood. Besides, in the protracted absence of the owner of the Red Cot, the avaricious baronet actually began to look upon himself as not merely the guardian, but the proprietor, of the wedge of land which so unceremoniously shot into the very heart almost of his fine pleasure-grounds; and accordingly he talked bigly, as we have heard. Little, therefore, was he prepared for the rebuff and the rebuke which immediately followed his pompous verbosity, and his implied menaces.

"Learn, Sir Vaux Waldgrave, of Wartham Hall," retorted the maiden,—her plain dress and a large, face-enshrouding bonnet concealing from the dull baronet in a great measure her beautiful and peculiar features,—"that from a gentleman of your age and social position, politeness to woman is to be looked for. I would wish you also to understand in the course of your daily practice, that a magistrate of one of the Ridings of Yorkshire,—even though he wear the empty bauble of an hereditary title,—is not above the reach of the laws of the British empire."

The blunderer winced, and thought of withdrawing with some scornful utterance on his lips and contemptuous terms; but he was not allowed to get away so easily.

"Sir, I charge you now, and will persist in charging you," continued our heroine, keeping close to the ponderous baronet, "with being guilty of a most uncourteous address to me,—no matter how young or poor I may be,—nay, with a most unprovoked unmanly attack with your weighty cane,—a salute which pains me at this moment."

"Begone, thou baggage!" growled Sir Vaux. "See, there's a crown-piece for thee, and have a care to abstain from doing aught that will again put thee into my clutches."

"Keep your crown-piece for your heir, Sir Vaux," smartly returned the damsel, scarcely able to conceal her merriment, as she stumbled upon the pert yet seasonable advice. "The adopted daughter of old Peter Plumtree, the owner of the Red Cot, and the wedge of land upon which that dwelling is built, has as little need of your alms, as you have a right to insult and assault her on that gentleman's grounds, when she was but paying a revisit to a scene which will be ever memorable with her."

"The adopted daughter," cried the astounded Sir Vaux, "of Mr. Plumtree, my excellent and respected neighbour, with whom I was growing most sociable and friendly just before he went off,—nobody can tell why or whither, unless it be myself, that have an inkling of his motives and movements! The adopted daughter! Then I owe you, fair lady, ten thousand pardons. I have made the most stupid of blunders. It is myself who trespasses! A strange mystery stares me in the face."

These exclamations were quickly followed by sundry pointed questions put to Adelaide, for there was now no disposition on the baronet's part to get immediately rid of the young lady.

"The adopted!" cried he, apparently both astounded and alarmed; "the heiress to be of my good neighbour, Mr. Peter Plumtree! Then what is your name? When and where did you first fall in with him? Tell me, if ever, fair creature, you looked on my face before. Are you actually the fair Adelaide that once had an ugly tumble over the cliff there?"

"Here comes a mute who, nevertheless, will speedily answer your questions, sir," responded the maiden, having that moment not only descried that old Martha, the deaf and dumb negress,—the faithful domestic of the wonted recluse of the Red Cot,—was hurrying towards her, but with unmistakable signs that the affectionate creature had recognised the young lady. And no sooner had Adelaide thus replied than she sprang away to meet the genuine and singular friend with a burst of gladness that told as much to Sir Vaux about the identity of the damsel he had that day at first so rudely accosted, with her whom he had at one time regarded as his niece, as could well have been done by an articulate explanation. Nor was there anything improbable in the fact of Blackie,—as her master used to name his housekeeper,—traversing the ground nigh to the Cauldron Cliff at the moment; her visits being almost daily paid, in the absence of the old man, to the fantastic fabric under whose roof she had for a number of years dwelt, in order to keep the surrounding garden in some sort of order.

The two met, and say not that on this occasion the deaf one was wholly dumb; for, on coming within a few paces of the fair object of her recognition, she gave utterance to such a species of yell, that though most unmelodious, harsh, and almost frightful, yet when combined with the rapture which mantled her coarse countenance, and the transport which her acts, attitudes, and contortions expressed, offered a spectacle that might well have pleaded the cause of the African race and the sable daughters of slavery, as Martha at one period had been; the eccentric Samaritan having purchased her freedom years before he brought her to England.

To throw herself at the young lady's feet, to clasp her knees, and to kiss the hands which were busy in their efforts to raise the old woman from the ground, were some of the things which characterized the ecstacy of the negress. Nor sooner was she upon her legs again than the exuberance of her exultation made her caper and dance in a manner that was no less significant of her happiness than had been the other tokens of her uncouth and genuine joy. Meanwhile Sir Vaux had drawn near to this scene of rapturous recognition, impelled more by anxiety than curiosity. But his close approach worked a sudden change in the exhibition, of which he had not reckoned; for on perceiving that he came almost alongside of them, Blackie flung herself between him and the maiden; forcibly pushing the latter towards the fantastic cot with one hand, whilst with the other she menaced the ponderous baronet.

The show was now of a mixed nature, yet no less expressive in its parts than before, when it had but one language; the mute woman, after her own mode of acquiring information, reading intimations, and construing facts, appearing at once to have come to nearly as clear an understanding of what had occurred between the old gentleman and the young lady at a bygone time, and of their present relative positions, as if she had not only been an eye-witness of all the particulars, but had make herself acquainted with their preceding and subsequent histories.

The negress stamped angrily with her feet, frowned fiercely, and threw as it were blows with her clenched fist towards Sir Vaux, in the course of her severing process. But when she turned to Miss Neville, urging the maiden the while towards the Red Cot, the change of conduct was no less marked than it was instantaneous. Now the old woman cherished the arm of the younger one, was profuse of curtseys, and every other conceivable indication of welcome, of joy, and a determination to stand by the young lady; so that the baronet felt glad that he could make his retreat without coming into actual collision with the talons of the sable creature.

Not for a long time, perhaps never, had Sir Vaux returned to the Hall, after a forenoon's stroll of inspection, more baffled and rebuked than he did on the day of our heroine's revisit to the vicinity of the Cauldron Cliff; the conjecture, which turned out to be a correct one, that she intended in the meanwhile to take up her residence in the neighbouring town of Wartham, helping to perplex and annoy him exceedingly. But there were certain other matters looming before him, of which more anon, that, in connexion with the existence of the young lady, now troubled him extremely.

It would not have been an easy matter, had Adelaide even wished it, for her to quit Wartham, or, in other words, to get away and free from mute Martha, who, along with Peter Plumtree's wonted canine housekeeper, the sagacious and majestic Cerberus, were boarded at a handsome rate, on his part, with a worthy family in the town. In short, the young lady not only resolved on taking up her residence in that place and there opening a school for the improvement of such daughters of the better class of inhabitants as might repair to her establishment, but to take both the mute negress and the dog under her roof, as associates and servants; an arrangement which transported Blackie nearly beyond all bounds.

Martha fortunately had become an expert discourser by means of the language or signs of the fingers, since her eccentric master quitted the neighbourhood; several of the people who were most friendly towards her acquiring a like conversational skill. Hence it happened that she could communicate to these parties all that she knew and sagaciously conjectured relative to the young lady; her reports and interpretations, the reader may feel sure, being highly favourable and full of promise,—the positive manner in which she not only talked of her good master's having adopted the maiden as his daughter, but the confidence with which she predicted his return to his proper home, — the prophecy by a *dumbie*, and therefore by a mysteriously gifted person,— being circumstances which had no small weight with the townspeople. And then with what hopefulness and pride did the genteel mothers contemplate the happy fortune of having an opportunity to get their young ladies to receive their training,—it might be their finishing polish,—at a cheap rate, under one who had been reared with the highest expectations and in the most admired of styles.

CHAPTER XXIX.

THE MAN IN BLACK.

ONE of the results of Sir Vaux Waldgrave's recent troubles and growing perturbations, was a growing addiction to the bottle, and the habit of solitary drinking; his uniform and constant mental occupation being, during such *sederunts*, to recapitulate his distresses and wrongs,—his troubles and anxieties,—and not seldom his remedies and his contemplated measures of revenge; his feelings and cogitations, when the strong waters in which he indulged, had reached a certain elevation, venting themselves in audible, often in loud and angry utterances. His complaints always ran in one and the same channel, and the several evils in serial order, according to their actual occurrence.

"First, there was that lying relict of my defunct brother," Sir Vaux would mutter to himself, when the wine began to warm his brain, "who brought with her from Paris a prettyish girl,—one of some litter of beggars,—seeking to fool me by *uncling* me to the rubbish. Humph! And what a fine affair was made of the imposture in double quick time! Then, how plainly did Captain Chesters, my petted nephew, show the cloven hoof before the first chapter of the tragedy and my disgraces had well begun!"

Something like a brown study,—a dull rumination over the incipient disasters alluded to, would follow this opening of the rehearsal; several appeals to the cup being required to stimulate the ponderous intellect of the man to a further and more vigorous recapitulation of his sorrows and mishaps.

"Most cruel of all is the threat of disinheritance which hangs over my head,—a tremendous blow that may strike me any hour with the fatal force of a thunderbolt," the huge blunderer would wrathfully exclaim, as he drew himself out of his easy-chair, and staggered away, in order to take from a repository a certain document in the shape of a letter. "Here it is,—a monstrous intimation, which, but that the announcement and menace are too grave and vital to be disposed of by burning,—for the hideous thing would only hereafter confront me in a more ghastly shape,—should long ago have fed my fire. Ah! Jeremy Blight, you know not, though well-meaning you may be, how horribly you have scared me — how awfully alarmed!"

In order that the reader may understand that which constituted what the baronet regarded as the climax of his distresses, we have to state that the letter with the contents of which he had almost daily alarmed and lacerated himself for months, without any alleviation, had been received about the period when Adelaide effected her escape from the horrid den and imprisonment to which she had been consigned in a rustic and sequestered quarter not very distant from London, by Captain Chesters and Norland, on the night when she was beguiled away from the Opera House. The writer, in short, of the communication which proved so astounding to Sir Vaux, was no other than the ruffian who had gone, at least for a time, by the name of Jared Jobson,—a villain of endless expedients, as well as being unscrupulous to the last degree, and who would as readily circumvent an associate as he would be avenged on the bitterest enemy, if there was herein a promised gratification.

Now, the letter which this thrice-dyed miscreant sent to the assured owner of Wartham Hall, having for signature the name Jeremy Blight,—purported to be from an individual who had lately arrived in the British metropolis from the United States of America. The writer also declared that he had met, since coming to London, with an individual with whom he was acquainted in their younger days, but who was now upon a sick, if not a dying bed; and that among other long remembered matters, they talked of the Mr. Waldgrave who had gone over from England to the New World about the period of the War of Independence, in which the gentleman fell when fighting bravely for the interests of his native country.

"Jared Jobson, — for such is my old ac

quaintance's name," said the letter, "by his own showing, has for a number of years led a lawless life; and among other things which in his conscience-stricken condition he confessed to me, was his claiming as his daughter a young lady who, on coming from France, was under your guardianship,—she being regarded at the time as your niece and the heiress to all your wealth. Now, Jobson admits that he perverted the truth by such a story, and that he afterwards behaved badly to the young lady; but this both he and I are in a condition to prove, provided time and opportunity be allowed us, that Adelaide is the legitimate grandchild of your elder brother, and consequently the lawful and rightful owner of the splendid estates to which you honourably became heir, as you supposed, on the decease of your kinsman who fell in battle. I communicate this to you, sir, in confidence and in secrecy. It is not likely that Jobson shall survive to assist me in the revealment of the important truth to which I allude. But, as I am on the eve of departure for my native land,—from which I intend to return to England shortly,—I doubt not of being on that return in a condition to satisfy you completely that what I state concerning the young lady already referred to as being your brother's granddaughter, is as clear as noonday. Still, the discovery will be most religiously confined to my own bosom until I have a personal interview with your honoured self; your character being of so high and celebrated an order, as I learn in London, that my greatest pleasure will consist in saving you from any disturbance to the end of your days."

Such was a portion of the long letter which Sir Vaux had received from one who subscribed himself Jeremy Blight,—a letter which, from the moment it was first perused, never failed most deeply to disturb the repose of the baronet when he thought of it. No wonder then that his anxieties and alarm were rendered doubly distressing when he found that the young lady,—upon the history of whose parentage so much had already depended, and now so much more hinged,—had returned to reside and to be industriously employed in his immediate neighbourhood!

At length a thing occurred which put the baronet in a twinkling to his utmost shifts and highest mettle, even eventually to a daring resoluteness. A second letter from Jeremy Blight reached the Hall, announcing that the writer had just arrived from America once more, having hardly any occasion for recrossing the Atlantic, except on an affair that vitally concerned Sir Vaux. It even named a particular day on which he should be in the city of York, where he hoped the baronet, for his own sake, would meet him. The credulous blunderer was aroused to the very loftiest pitch of anxiety by this notice, instantly determining to meet the unknown writer, and to act with decision, as the things to be disclosed to him might direct.

By the very same post which brought the impostor's epistle, another arrived at Wartham Hall, which, although in all reason entitled to by far the greatest attention, exacted from Sir Vaux comparatively little concern. This notification was to the effect that his spouse, who had been separated from him for a length of time, was suddenly taken ill of what appeared a dangerous malady; the writer—a relative of the sick one,—urging the necessity on divers accounts of his hastening to his lady's bedside. Nor was the baronet dilatory in starting for the metropolis, affecting great solicitude to have an interview with his spouse, before it might be for ever too late, although mainly intent to reach York, in order to converse with Mr. Blight.

"I presume I have the distinguished honour of being visited by Sir Vaux Waldgrave," said the scoundrel, on the big baronet's presenting himself at the Minster Hotel, where the speaker, with an alleged daughter, were impatiently waiting for the arrival of their dupe.

"I am the person you name, sir," returned Sir Vaux; "and you, I believe—indeed, I have been positively informed by the waiter, are Mr. Blight, from America; and that is your daughter, I suppose, of whom you made mention in your last letter to me."

"Yes, Sir Vaux; my only child," answered the deceiver; "Julia Blight. I am a widower, having been bereaved of the best of wives, a year ago. I thought it hard to leave my daughter behind me; hard for myself fully as much as for her."

"The young lady could not be long in finding an enviable partner anywhere," observed the baronet; a complimentary saying which was replied to by a bow and a bland countenance on the part of Mr. Blight; the beautiful Julia, with a show of modesty, withdrawing before the courteous speech had been well uttered.

"I take it, Mr. Blight, that you belong to some denomination of the holy ministry," was the next observation which Sir Vaux let drop; no doubt judging from certain externals of the impostor.

"Your conjecture is correct," responded the other. "I have been an expounder of revelation, and a preacher of the Word for a number of years, under a similar episcopacy to that which obtains in the English establishment. Since the death of my wife, however, indifferent health has made me desist from my sacred functions. Instead thereof, being in circumstances of pecuniary independence, I have travelled a good deal, and this not without being of service, I trust, to the great cause to which I have been consecrated."

The conversation of the pair continued for a few moments quite away from the subject they had both most at heart; the impostor clearly perceiving that the dupe was like to burst with anxiety to hear what the "preacher of the Word," had to disclose relating to the legitimacy of our heroine and her preferable title to the lands which the baronet had so long claimed and held as his rightful property. But Blight had a reason for keeping his stupid victim some time longer in a state of torturing suspense, pretending, that till after the dinner hour, certain pre-engagements would prevent him from enjoying the society of the baronet; an hour which the villain very well knew might be rendered doubly advantageous for his base purposes, through the sot's known addiction to the bottle.

Sir Vaux was obliged to acquiesce in regard to the postponement of business, as he called it; being the more readily reconciled to the arrangement by the other's statement that Julia would, meanwhile, feel greatly flattered in having an opportunity to supply her father's place for a few hours.

"And then we shall all three dine together," cried the baronet, somehow greatly pleased with the substitution; a cheerer or two, as he named his forenoon's potations, helping to put the blunderer in unusually good humour.

The impostor returned at the exact time appointed for dinner to be on the table, perfectly assured that they should have a sumptuous feast. And how it made the villain laugh in his sleeve, when he found the baronet quite cozily seated close by the side of the beautiful and artful Julia, and altogether frisky; an apology, by the crafty scoundrel, for his unceremoniously leaving the old gentleman alone, serving to conceal the fellow's satisfaction at what was passing.

"No apologies, no excuses, I pray," promptly responded the baronet. "I have found a most agreeable substitute in your beautiful, your accomplished daughter. By the bye, I am glad to hear you have been punctually keeping your appointments, were it but that this gives promise your stay will not be long protracted in York. In fact, I have just been saying to Julia —Miss Blight, I mean—I really make a thousand apologies for my premature familiarity— I have just been stating to the young lady that, perhaps, we could all three find it convenient to travel together to London. I have my own roomy and excellent carriage with me, although I employ post-horses from stage to stage. I do not mind delaying my departure, if you will but meet me half-way by expediting yours. What say you, Blight?—I ask pardon again; I mean Mr. Blight."

"Nothing could be more agreeable or flattering to us, than to journey to the British metropolis in company of Sir Vaux Waldgrave, and in his own stately carriage too," answered the man in black. "It will be something for us to boast of at the other side of the Atlantic."

"Oh, you have no baronets in Yankeeland, I believe," said the baronet, laughing immoderately at his own smartness.

In short, it was settled before the trio had well commenced dining that they should start immediately after breakfasting on the morrow; Sir Vaux, the moment this was agreed to, doing ample justice to the good things as these were set down upon the table,—declaring that nothing gave him more pleasure than charming company when he banqueted. He even added, that of late he had felt very lonely at his meals, "taking more of discontent than anything else; not having any Julia Blight to cheer and delight me on those occasions." And the old fool again looked as coaxingly as he could in the girl's face.

"How charming would the novelty be for a person of my years and transatlantic experience only," winningly sighed Julia, "to find myself a sojourner, but for a week, in one of the grand English country mansions! Should not I then be among the noble growths that were planted by statesmen and warriors of the olden time? and should not I behold in the living and latest member of the great heraldic tree all that is necessary to feed young romance in youthful woman's bosom, and to stir to heroic deeds the striplings of the age? Ah! there is not in all America, I am well aware, a seat to be compared with that at which Sir Vaux Waldgrave has been nurtured, and been held in honour for many years; and where, too, dear father, as we learned in London, his splendid hospitality has been unbounded."

The young lady, whose experience on a theatrical stage had been considerable, felt herself taking the old baronet by storm; her fluency and affected enthusiasm charming him above measure, and forcing from him a pressing invitation that the beautiful creature and her parent would honour him with their society as guests during the longest sojourn they could accord to him; unless, indeed, he found matters in a more distressing state at his wife's London residence than he "wished for;" the impostor perfectly well seeing through the ambiguity of the emphatic exception.

The dinner was such as might be expected in a first-rate hotel, when furnished to the order of one of the most substantial men in Yorkshire, and whose fame for hospitality and sumptuous living was widely spread. The liquors were various, and excellent; each one of the three feasters appearing to enjoy the entertainment in the highest possible manner, to the utter forgetfulness of any anxiety they might previously have experienced.

Mr. Blight, to be sure, drank very sparingly, alleging that the state of his health, as well as his cloth, imposed upon him great abstemiousness. As for the baronet, he not only ate at an enormous rate, but during the feeding process drank like a huge fish; the wonder of the others being that even his capacious paunch could hold all he swallowed, while yet he seemed not in the slightest inconvenienced. In fact, by the time the table-cloth was removed, he appeared to be perfectly sobered down, and to have wholly surmounted the intoxication that preceded the dinner,—only a greater flow of animal spirits continuing with him than was his usual manner when unenlivened by means of the cup.

As for the young lady, she did wonders in keeping the stout Yorkshireman in countenance; alleging that since her dear father was in default as a boon companion, it was her part to do her best in his stead; her freedom evoking such sparkling displays as again took the baronet by storm, or as if by a broadside on a sudden. This conquest was in an especial manner and degree achieved, when, after having sung a luscious song, and next recited a scene of romantic, passionate love, from a warm drama, she sprang to the floor, and went through an operatic dance that might have coped with anything of the kind that has been witnessed in the Queen's Theatre by the Court and the hereditary wisdom of the empire, in as far at least as the figurante's attitudes and evolutions bordered on gross indecency.

It was nothing, perhaps, beyond what might have been expected when the old Yorkshire aristocratic bumpkin joined in the chorus of fair Julia's amorous verses; although his voice, —partaking of the coarsest of grunts and the sounds which may be evoked by bellowing into an empty vat,—ill accorded with the lady's melody. Certainly, however, it amounted to the broadest of what is farcical, when the unwieldy Sir Vaux took to the floor, in order to ape the nimbleness of the fair one's light fantastic toe.

And now, too, the spirit of fun was in Miss Blight, as well as that of triumphant exhilaration. Accordingly, before the huge patrician well knew what he was about, she had him linked in what purported to be a waltz. Next, the lithe and animated girl,—having once got the human leviathan into some such continuous motions by means of her fine arms upon his vast rotundity, as to correspond to a certain degree with her glidings, manœuvrings, and whirlings, —so sustained the momentum, that her partner became wholly subject to her will; a will that was determined to be satisfied with nothing short of so dizzying the ungainly lump as to make him believe all the world was wheeling around him as its prodigious centre. In fact, Julia accomplished the feat so well, and brought it to such a pitch, that had it not been for the large chair which the gamesome baronet vacated being near at hand, into which she made him fling himself at the moment he could no longer maintain anything like a perpendicular, he must have gone wholesale to the ground.

Neither the enchantment of the luscious song nor the whirl of the dance could continuously, nor during every one of his waking hours, be made to keep the baronet in a state of delirious enjoyment, or so as to be entirely at the will of the impostors, and influenced by their devices. But then there were other never-failing instrumentalities wherewith they worked upon the blockhead. Wines and other strong drinks, could always be pressed into their service by the artful and really bewitching Julia, who found no difficulty in rendering her society so delightful to the old fool, that he felt lonely and uneasy whenever she was away from his side. In short, by the time they had all three been in London one complete week,—the same hotel at the West End being the place of their sojourn,—the ever-muddled and mystified baronet had got to the length of lamenting that he was not in a condition which rendered it possible for him to enter into a new matrimonial engagement; otherwise, he again and again declared, with all the fervour and solemnity which he could use, that he would speedily and unhesitatingly make Julia his spouse, and then be assured of having offspring of his own to succeed to his large possessions.

The stupefaction induced by continuous recourse to intoxicating drinks and the allurements of the false and frail Julia, were aided in the direction which these influences took by all the representations which the man in black could bring to bear upon the stupid victim. By means of a skilful mixture of truths, perversions of what was real and actual, and unmitigated lying, the villain contrived so completely to overwhelm Sir Vaux with the conviction that our heroine, Adelaide, was the granddaughter of the baronet's elder brother, who fell in battle during the American War, as before told, that the besotted one could think

of no other relief to his despair than was to be found in the bottle and the pernicious society of the artful girl.

And yet the impostor's contrivances and success did not stop here, but went on to embuing the baronet with an equally strong conviction as that on the other point, that he, the man in black, was now the only living person who was cognizant of the facts regarding the direct descent and the legitimacy of the young lady, in relation to Sir Vaux's elder brother. In a word, the villain made it clear to the dupe, that he was the minister of religion who not only officiated in marrying the girl's parents,—her mother, as alleged, being the only child of Reginald Waldgrave,—but also at the christening of their infant, and that he could adduce the most abundant and irrefragable proof that the maiden whose adverse fortunes have been the subject of so many of these pages, was, at the moment he divulged to the baronet the astounding fact, the rightful owner of Wartham Hall. An obvious consequence of this progress of power over Sir Vaux's convictions, was to make the unhappy man feel that unless he made it an object of sufficient importance to Mr. Blight and also to Mr. Blight's daughter, the keeping of such a grand piece of knowledge secret, it would immediately be divulged to the party whose interests were so deeply identified with the disclosure of the truth.

It is not to be supposed that Sir Vaux could be many hours in London, without paying a visit to his sick lady, who, to her praise be it recorded, had during her illness become anxious for a reconciliation with her husband; being at the same time prepared to confess that the misunderstandings that had arisen between them were as much to be attributed to herself as to him. Nor did Blight act otherwise than urge the baronet to maintain at least a show of deep concern for the recovery of the lady; contriving along with all this to persuade the dupe that he had not merely been a thorough student of physic and the medical art, but had frequently practised accordingly, in connexion too with the performance of his sacred functions. What more natural, then, than that the man in black should accompany, as a professional person, the Yorkshire aristocrat to the bed of sickness, or that the big blunderer should recommend his American friend to the lady's confidence, as a physician of the highest transatlantic renown?

Ere concluding this chapter, it has to be added, that the man in black had, amongst his other infamous plans and practices,—amongst his other triumphs over his blundering dupe,— got the conglomerated brains of the facile victim to receive an impress from such hideous and criminal suggestions, as that the spirit of evil may be supposed to have peered over the baronet's shoulder and mockingly laughed on finding how like to others who yield themselves up to guilty thoughts, the white-headed sinner was rushing to perdition. Who could have anticipated, some twelve months prior to the period at which we have arrived, that Sir Vaux Waldgrave,—the man of boasted proprieties,—would ever lend an ear to suggestions which not only involved the idea of foully getting for ever rid of the girl whose rights, as represented by Blight, so direfully threatened him, but also of his ailing spouse,—she whose recovery would so positively stand in the way of his taking to himself a much more youthful partner, with the hope of having children of his own?

CHAPTER XXX.

THE SCENT OF THE SUBTLE ESSENCE.

"I REJOICE to see you, Sir Vaux," was Lady Waldgrave's first exclamation,—on awaking from a prolonged and apparently refreshing sleep,—finding that her husband and the physician were by her bedside. And now with much feeling and earnestness she talked, in order, as she said, to relieve her breast of many things that had long oppressed her. "I feel a sort of certainty," she at length cried, "that my recovery has commenced, and that I shall soon be able to accompany you back to Wartham Hall, where I hope we shall yet have many happy days to spend together. Meanwhile, you and the doctor there will excuse me, when I request that you will for the present be satisfied with my smiles of welcome. I have talked too much since my awaking from a sweet sleep to be able to say more at present. I feel drowsy; but relinquish not my right hand, Sir Vaux, until you find that my slumber is sound. When next you look upon me, we'll have a more important meeting."

Drowsiness, promising and healthful, had already began to weigh down her ladyship's eyelids; and, as they closed, the smile which had predominated upon her countenance from the moment of her last awaking, remained in such a touching manner, that Sir Vaux could not look upon it, knowing the thoughts he had been harbouring concerning her, without deep pangs of conscience and convulsive sobs. He still held his wife's hand with one of his, but his other had to cover his streaming eyes from which scalding tears flowed, blinding him as they raced from their fountain.

"I have not been told to stand forward," murmured the man in black within himself; "but I see not why I should not volunteer my services, seeing that the lady's drowiness is too heavy to allow her to speak to me, and also that the stupid baronet is both, for the present, blind and mute, —being hardly conscious of what he is about or that I am here."

As the villain thus mentally concluded, he glided forward noiselessly to the bedside, passing his hand most gently over the sleeper's visage, hardly touching the marble brow or the pallid cheeks, and only pausing as he reached the nostrils. But what is that tiny thing which he holds within the hollow of his traversing hand? A phial!—and charged with what? Horrible! it is the most potent and deadly of poisons, whose virulence acts with an instantaneous intoxicating and narcotic pungency the moment the olfactory organ inhales the subtle essence.

"What a start was that!" cried the sobbing baronet, as he sprang from his chair, his thoughts recalled by the convulsive movement of the hand he held, when the deadly poison shot its piercing scent into the brain of the murdered one, thrilling her every nerve for the first and last time. "What have you done, Blight? Have you stabbed my dear wife to the heart by means of some hidden dagger?"—terror, blended with anger, being in the looks and language of the not guiltless man.

"What have I done, you ask, Sir Vaux?" responded the impostor. "You plainly see— nothing; for I stand behind you, never having moved from the spot since entering the sick chamber, waiting to receive the command to go nearer, so as but to feel the pulse of the patient. Nay, you angrily inquire if I have stabbed the lady to the heart by means of some concealed dagger? Be judge for yourself, and examine that vital region instantly,—I implore that you do; or, if your trembling unfits you for the office, let me assist, and then be you content."

The insolent wretch stepped forward, and while with the one hand he removed the bed-clothes so as to show that no injury had been done as the baronet supposed, whose dimmed vision followed only the movements of that limb, with the alert fingers of the other the murderer reapplied the subtle scent to the nostril, to make certainty doubly sure. Now, however, there was no response of the former kind which had recalled the husband to himself,—no inhalation, for the spirit had escaped to Him who gave it. And the smile, too, was gone, there being in its stead rigidity and ghastly death.

"You are a widower, Sir Vaux," said the satisfied villain with a well-suppressed mockery. "We had better summon the females of the house to attend to the remains of the late Lady Waldgrave."

But the widowed man was too overpowered to hear, or pay heed to, the demon. He had sank down in the chair as one benumbed and senseless, requiring the help and upholding of his tempter, until other aid arrived, when the ponderous baronet was carried to a separate apartment.

"Let the broken-hearted Sir Vaux have brandy in copious draughts, otherwise he too may sink no more to breathe no more while we gaze upon him," said the false physician. "Look to him, good people, while some of you accompany me to the lady, in order to see if life may be recalled; perhaps it is, after all, but a wondrously heavy slumber that hath come over her."

The murderer led the way to the death-chamber, and once more to hold the phial with its subtle essence to the fixed and motionless nostril, with the pretence that of all reviving scents the one applied was the most effectual restorative. For some little time, with a great display of anxiety, he thus busied himself; but at last pronounced that never should the late sufferer awake from the slumber that was upon her, until the consummation of all earthly things.

The monster withdrew to attend to Sir Vaux, as he professed; an attendance which meant dosing the stupified man with strong

JARED JOBSON.

drink, until he was really unwell. And thus was afforded an excuse for having the miserable sot conveyed to his hotel in a neighbouring street, to be nursed by the artful Julia.

Once under such superintendence, it required no great stretch of ingenuity to keep the victim to his bed-room by intoxicating draughts and such simple drugs as furnished excuses for the remaining aloof from the activities belonging to the sepulture of Lady Waldgrave. Ere many days, the mournful solemnity had its close, with all the pomp usual at such times, where lavish wealth was ready to uphold conventional rank. The tomb closed over the misused dead; the speculation of a circle concerning the cause and mode of death, as also the lengthened severance of the spouses, had hardly a nine days' existence; nor did the world cease to go on as before.

No. 19.—THE GOVERNESS.

"Betake yourself to a suburban villa in the vicinity of London, for a few weeks, Sir Vaux," was the man in black's suggestion, who began to wield mercilessly the hold he had got upon the infatuated baronet. "Neither Julia nor I myself will ever desert you. Shortly, you will return to your noble country-seat, a happier man than ever you have been; neither the owner of the Red Cot, nor the pet whose interests he has so chivalrously espoused, being permitted to molest you, or to impede any one of the great plans or views which you may have in contemplation."

Handsome apartments were procured in a retired suburban quarter, in accordance with the impostor's suggestion; his notoriety being such, and even Julia's history so well known in certain districts of the metropolis, that it was perilous, in relation at least to Sir Vaux's confidence and favour, for them to continue in any public part of the town. All three, therefore, removed to a place of comparative privacy, upon the plea that this was necessary to the health of the widowed baronet; it never seeming to occur to any one of them that they were any more to have separate interests or separate habitations. As for Sir Vaux, he was to all appearance sinking into dotage, and entering upon his second childhood,—a result and calamity which could not but be expedited by the harassment to which he was daily subjected by the artful wretches in whose hands he was held; by the torturing thoughts which sometimes visited him relative to the death of his wife; and, above all, by his habitual intemperance.

"Foully duped! made the sport of the vilest of impostors and of a loathsome girl of infamy!" cried the inveigled baronet, after perusing a second time a letter which had been put into his hand, written by the very clergyman who had, in his ignorance of the strange facts of the case, united the old gentleman a few days before, according to all the regular forms of the marriage contract, to the worthless and polluted Julia. Hardly, in fact, had two months after the decease of his murdered wife elapsed, when the astounding intelligence put an arrest in the meanwhile upon Sir Vaux's growing fatuity, and brought him to something clearer than his wonted senses at best; the prelude to certain extraordinary scenes being the exclamations just cited. "Where have I been? What have I been about?" he shouted aloud, pacing his sitting apartment in the suburban residence to which he had been wiled, in a state of distraction, as a number of recent circumstances flashed their light upon him, to which he, at the moment of their occurrence, had been strangely and wofully blind. "Never was a man so infatuated,—never so cozened, degraded, and ruined, as I, who now all at once perceive the extremity to which I have been carried. To be ejected from dear Wartham Hall as an usurper; to be beggared, made an outcast and a scoff, are nothing to what has overtaken me in my old age, or to the convictions which torture me on account of things to the accomplishment of which I have lent myself. Oh! that Lady Waldgrave had not died! and that I had not harboured guilty forethoughts towards her destruction!"

It was while the baronet was thus surged that Blight and Julia entered the apartment in which with an unwieldy violence he indulged his rage and remorse. The sight of the vile impostors hurried the wretched man into a still greater paroxysm of passion and self-condemnation; a number of incoherent utterances bursting from him, and thus concluding:—

"Fiend!" roared the heart-riven man, feeling as if the weight of the whole earth were crushing him down to another and still more horrible region than that in which he breathed "I'll meet and confront thee in the place eternal torture, hastened thither by thy temptations and snares."

As the torn and distracted man uttered these words, he drove forward towards the door of the apartment in which the extraor-dinary disturbance took place, cleaving his way in spite of every offered obstacle to the stairs, down which he flung with a certitude of step which was remarkable for a person of his years and clumsiness, especially when so surged and transported. To the porch of the residence he hurried, and out and off he ran, with such speed as he for many years had not exercised,— every now and then, as he sped away with outstretched arms, leaping wildly from the ground, the snow-white and lengthened locks of the hatless head streaming behind, and adding much to the frightfulness of the demented wretch. Oh! it was a sad and painful sight to see to what a state the pride and avarice of a weak-minded, credulous, worldly creature had brought him,—being the ready, and not guiltless, dupe of unblushing impudence and matchless imposition.

The maddened baronet could not for any considerable distance drive on at the rate with which he had set out from the place of his temporary residence. Men's hands were ere long upon him, seeing that his conduct was that of a being at the time bereft of reason. Among those who interfered to arrest the unhappy Sir Vaux, who should be foremost but his own nephew, Captain Chesters, the Life-Guardsman, whose interests had drawn him, as on sundry other occasions, to the vicinity of the suburban abode,—anxious and envious as the profligate was relative to the succession to the lands which the old gentleman had long possessed.

"You have made a maniac of my uncle, Jared Jobson," said Chesters, the moment the baronet was taken to the house from which he had so wildly fled,—the impostor little expecting to be in his turn so soon put to confusion as followed the appearance of the Life-Guardsman. "Ten to one but you have rendered him a pitiable idiot to the end of his days. As for this nymph of the *pave*, whom you have palmed off as your daughter,—by an equal trickery foolishly fancying you could *wive* her to the old man, when in his second childhood,—she had better betake herself to her recent haunts and walks, now that her notoriety prevents her from any more treading the boards of a theatre."

"You talk, Chesters, with still more unadvised assurance," retorted the man in black, "than did your drivelling kinsman a little while ago. You forget that Adelaide Waldgrave lives, and you must also learn that not only am I acquainted with her place of abode, but that I'll not flinch, at whatever risk to myself, from bringing her forward against you, having been a witness of your murderous attempt at the Cauldron Cliff, as well as being fully acquainted with your abduction of her from the Opera House."

"Who speaks of the Opera House?" at this moment demanded a voice of some one from among the number of people who had entered the house, assisting in bringing back the demented baronet. "I have something to say to a subject that has connexion with that dangerous theatre."

It was old Peter Plumtree that spoke, the news of Sir Vaux's strange marriage having met the cynic's eyes in a morning print the day before, and guiding him to the present scene of tumult.

"And who is it that so freely talks of the Cauldron Cliff, and the murderous treachery which was practised to the terrible peril of Adelaide Waldgrave, by a villain at that locality, when I myself was near at hand?" demanded another voice,—the speaker, as did also the eccentric Samaritan of the Red Cot, cleaving his way into the now crowded room as he best could.

It was Montague Mildmay who thus questioned; his voice, as had Peter Plumtree's, being recognised in an instant by the fellows who had been a minute earlier dealing in bitter recriminations alternately.

The hints communicated by the eager questions of the two unexpected and unwelcome visitors, both of whom had been guided to the spot,—though unknown to one another,—by one and the same newspaper announcement, were speedily acted upon by the pair of guilty wretches, who shortly before swaggered so confidently. The man in black knew well the turns and contrivances of the house, and glided through a side-door of the apartment which conducted into an adjoining room, instead of making for the more usual and patent way of quitting the villa. Nor did the honourable Life-Guardsman disdain to follow with all nimbleness the coarser miscreant; the activity of their limbs and the opportune seizure of a critical moment saving them for that time.

"The man in black, that has vanished so nimbly by yonder side-door," said a third ejaculatory and surprised speaker, addressing himself to Montague Mildmay, "is the very same villain, I feel assured, of whom you and I have had so much to relate,—the fiend in form of man, who has been the cause of all my miseries and anguish. Hardly any disguise, or any change which the lapse even of twenty years could work on the features of one who so deeply wronged and treacherously used me, as did Jared Jobson,—for such is his name,—can ever conceal from me the identity of the miscreant."

It was a new character in our tale who thus delivered himself; his few observations being of a nature that promised to bring to light certain past events, to the unravelment, more or less, of the story. Newcomb Neville was his name,—a man whose unhappy fortune it had been, while master of an American trading vessel, bending her course in the Mediterranean, to be mutinied against by his crew,— Jared Jobson, the mate, being not only the ringleader of the villains, but the wretch who, with a murderous intent, tossed the captain overboard. The victim of the conspiracy, however, although unknown to his desperate enemies, after having for a time kept himself afloat by means of a spar that came within his reach, while swimming for his life, was picked up by a Barbary coaster, and ere long sold for a slave. At length, having been in bondage for about twenty years, and made to endure the most varied and distressing hardships, he was liberated through the humane agency of Montague Mildmay, on that young gentleman's return from India along with his superior, Lord Rivers, they having taken the overland route, at the termination of that nobleman's governorship of the great British Eastern Empire.

But Neville had other interesting matters to disclose than immediately concerned his miserable and prolonged captivity. Being a native of the seaport town in New England from which he had always sailed on his trading-trips, he had married a young woman about a twelvemonth before undertaking his last voyage, who also belonged to that place, although an orphan from her infancy, and reared at a public institution amongst other parentless children. The name that she went by was Maria Waldgrave, the offspring of an English couple, as was always given out; the father, whom report represented as being of superior birth and rank, having fallen in the war of American Independence when fighting on the side of King George, and the mother, suddenly reduced to destitution, dying soon after of a broken heart.

But Newcomb Neville neither looked towards the acquisition of fortune nor of title when he wooed and wedded the beautiful and amiable Maria. He loved her for her own sake and merits; and so devoted were they to each other, that she accompanied him in his last and disastrous voyage, having given birth to a daughter only a few days prior to his crew having mutinied against him; the infamous conspiracy which led to his being tossed into the deep taking place while they were not many leagues from Marseilles. Of the fate of his young wife and their babe he had necessarily ever since been in ignorance; never ceasing to have been tortured with the deepest anxiety on their account, more especially as he concluded they would be at the mercy of the arch-mutineer, Jared Jobson, who had proved himself a villain of the deepest dye, and most consummate duplicity.

——

CHAPTER XXXI.

THE CROWNING TESTIMONIES.

THUS far did the liberated captive's statement serve, if not entirely to unravel the mystery that brooded over the parentage of Adelaide, at least to direct attention and inquiry into definite channels. In fact, it required but old Peter Plumtree to hear what fell from Newcomb Neville's lips, to put that earnest and energetic individual into a strain which speedily issued in important disclosures. Nor sooner had Sir Vaux Waldgrave been consigned by his young kinsman, Mildmay, into the keeping of proper medical men, than he and Neville afforded the old yet strong-hearted owner of the Red Cot an opportunity to detail such of his recent adventures as bore more immediately upon our heroine's position and prospects. But first, he was most impatient to learn in what way the captive whom Mildmay had enjoyed the opportunity of liberating, received his knowledge of the ruffian Jobson; being also eager to have some account of his birth and fortunes,—the name

Neville having struck Peter's ear with an unusual suggestiveness.

The American went rapidly over his history, the outline of which has been given in a previous chapter; nor had he well got to the close of the account, when the eccentric Samaritan burst as it were upon the narrator with direct interrogatories to the folllowing purpose:—

"Know you this picture? did you ever, Newcomb Neville, look on it before?" cried old Peter, drawing from his bosom the miniature portrait which he had obtained from Wartham Hall, and upon which the cynic set an inestimable value.

"It is the identical picture which my wife possessed," returned the surprised and admiring American. "It was shown me by that lamented possessor at the commencement of my wooing her for my spouse. I never missed being told by Maria that the portrait was that of her mother; while it seemed to be almost the only article the orphan ever inherited. The subject of the picture, I have been given to understand, was from England,—Yorkshire was even particularized; and thence also came her husband, according to the vague reports that reached me."

"That picture was painted according to my orders and at my expense!" cried Plumtree, bounding from his chair, with an energy, and elasticity, that was wonderful in the case of a man of his years and apparent inactivity. "The subject, of whom it is, in my view, a breathing likeness, was the only woman—call her girl—I ever wooed, or thought of making my wife. She was my betrothed; and when I went to foreign parts, in order to better my fortune, or rather that I might be rich enough to make her a lady—for she was of humble birth—we bound ourselves to one another by the strongest of vows and engagements of fidelity.

"Another came in my stead, when I was far away, and stole the heart of my idol. He was handsome, gay, and high-born. He wiled her from her home, and carried her to America; but whether to abide with him in the New World by an honourable or dishonourable tie I knew not till of late. My impression was that the former had been the poor thing's fate; and hence the bitterness which filled my cup to overflowing long after.

"I had many excuses for a confiding, sensitive girl, who had no one near to counsel her, and to show her the sin, the danger, of her infidelity to her first lover. The second, who, as I have said, was gay, handsome, and high-born, had mighty advantages over the poor adventurer,—the rugged and uncouth Peter Plumtree. All this I knew,—all this I set down in Maria's behalf. But when I could hardly suppose that with the loss of her truth to me she had kept her maidenly virtue, sickness came over my heart; I strove to fill it with gall,—endeavouring to convince myself that all mankind were false, treacherous, and impure in their innermost souls. How this diseased sentiment coloured my conduct and shaped my ways after returning, not unladen with riches, from the West Indies, to vegetate at my Red Cot, those in the neighbourhood of that dwelling know something of. My betrothed forgot me, or rather threw me overboard, and then went off with another; but, praise be to Heaven! not to be a wanton, I now know, or to live a life of infamy. No, no! and hence much of my present joy—my present hopes. She was beautiful to look upon—more lovely than this dear picture to the eye; but it was the graces of her immortal part which most charmed me, and which constantly, for some years grew, upon me, making me her slave. Artlessness, and I know not what else to say concerning that which binds heart to heart, were hers. But she became the wife of another, instead of Peter Plumtree. Yes, the wife! I rejoice to proclaim it,—the spouse, the wedded partner of the handsome and gay, the rich and the high-born; who had become enchanted by her fascination, and would have bartered away his birthright rather than lose her."

By this time the old man, as he still stood up, had worked himself into a state of strange transport, surged by a variety of commingling emotions.

"Yes, the wife! the wife!" exclaimed the eccentric Samaritan, after a short pause to recruit himself, having arrived at the point and reached the pitch indicated by his last cited words; a sort of ecstacy swaying him. "The spouse—the wedded partner of Reginald Waldgrave—the elder brother of Sir Vaux, whose grandchild is Adelaide my adopted—the grandchild, too, of her who was my betrothed!"

The old man could proceed no farther; but, falling back into his chair, was so much overwhelmed as to become the subject of hysterical tumult—laughter and weeping apparently being at strife which should have the mastery. As Mildmay and Neville busied themselves, in order to soothe and compose him—being alarmed lest the conflict should prove mortal—he responded to their assiduities by looks and motions which showed that he not only appreciated their efforts, but was anxious to exercise the utmost self-command. He embraced them, one after another, with something like feminine fondness; and, when, at length, his breast became so loosened that he could articulate, these were his remarkable words:—

"The conflict at this turn is over! The transport shall be controlled! Neville, you are the father of my adopted! and Mildmay, it is decreed that you shall be the husband of Adelaide, who is the rightful owner of Wartham Hall,"—the old man winding up his brief and pregnant utterances with an account of the patient investigations which he had pursued on the spot in New England to which the liberated captive belonged by birth; every particular which Peter discovered and now disclosed going to corroborate and enlarge the facts spoken to by Neville.

"I obtrude myself as a self-accuser, together with this unfortunate girl that is with me," hurriedly said Ned Norland, who was closely followed by the frail and fallen Julia, whom Jobson had passed off as his own daughter; the impatient pair in a manner forcing themselves into the presence of the three gentlemen, being eager to reveal everything they knew concerning the infamous conduct of the ruffian and impostor, as also that of Chesters.

in as far as the villanies of those wretches bore upon the history and fate of Adelaide.

It was easy to see through the motives of the pair who volunteered their testimony in the manner mentioned; their purpose being to screen themselves, as approvers and the lesser criminals, in any prosecution which might be instituted on account of the enormities perpetrated by the two absent miscreants with whom Norland and the girl had become allied. The most important thing divulged by these volunteering unprincipled ones related to the fate and fortunes of Neville's young wife and their infant after he had been consigned to the deep; it being positively stated that Jobson afterwards conveyed the supposed widow and fatherless babe to Marseilles, where he temporarily provided for them in a particular hotel of that city, which was specified, and where eventually the mother was taken into the service of Mrs. Wilford Waldgrave, who happened to be sojourning in the same town and dwelling under the same roof at the time. To adopt the babe, and to proclaim it as her own, was a main part of the barren lady's deceitful procedure.

Now here was a key to further and distinct investigation. Not an hour was idly spent before the three eager and anxious gentlemen were on their route to France; never, in a sense, drawing rein until they were within the boundaries of Marseilles. It merits a record, that although, after Captain Chesters, Montague Mildmay was the legal heir to Sir Vaux Waldgrave, supposing Adelaide's claims to be unsubstantial, yet never had there been a more earnest champion towards the establishment of another's interests than was the young gentleman for those of our heroine.

The crowning testimony, as regarded the direct and legitimate descent of Adelaide Neville from the elder brother of Sir Vaux Waldgrave was found at Marseilles. A Madame Latour, who had been in the service of the ambitious and intriguing spouse of the younger brother, Wilford Waldgrave, at the period when the disconsolate Maria Neville and her infant were brought to the hotel in which the unprincipled lady at the time happened to reside, made it clear, by means of her verbal evidence, and also documentary proofs, which the real mother of the child had confided to her fellow-servant, that the beautiful creature, Adelaide, with whose history she was more or less acquainted, until the girl had been removed to England, was secretly ever regarded by Maria Neville as her own and only offspring. This fact, however, the poor mother dared not openly avow, having an undefined dread of Jobson, when allied with Mrs. Wilford Waldgrave; and this the more especially when the fond parent looked forward to the exaltation of her child through the adoption.

The joy of Montague Mildmay and his two friends, on finding every doubt to be cleared away which had hung over the parentage of our heroine, may be more easily imagined than described. But while they were pursuing their inquiries on an absorbing subject to each of them, there were others, who have figured in these chapters, who cannot be supposed to have been less eagerly engaged in their own behalf,

and their peculiar lines. Assuredly the safety of Chesters and Jobson must have become a matter of paramount importance to these miscreants, from the moment of their flight from the temporary suburban residence of Sir Vaux Waldgrave. Indeed, so sensible were the villains of their perilous predicament, that, as they hastened from the neighbourhood of a spot at which, by some unaccountable concert, as they thought, there had in an instant congregated witnesses whose testimonies would hang them, they felt desperate, and prepared to engage in whatever enterprise might seem to promise them a single chance of escape, if not of triumph.

Community of danger seemed, instantly, to reconcile the scoundrels to each other; and also, as they hurried away, side by side, to make them eager to court suggestion; although, in reality, during less exacting times and calmer moments, no two could be less mutually trustful. Jobson's being the more inventive genius, and also the more fertile of evil, it was this runaway that first spoke out, as they stealthily made for one of his haunts.

"The game is all up with us, captain," said he, "unless we are more expert than ever. There was just now your kinsman, Mildmay, the old man of the Red Cot, and another, of whom more hereafter, whose testimonies will gibbet me, should the myrmidoms of the law lay their clutches upon my person. You, yourself, Chesters, are not a bit securer, should Norland act the informing traitor, which, I am sure, he is prepared to do. Observe, I am supposing that the girl, Adelaide—the only being that stands between you and the northern estates—comes also forward, as no doubt she will, under the wing of Mildmay, to the bargain, to bear witness against you. There will be much to tell by these lovers of a certain Life-Guardsman's services at the Cauldron Cliff; while, as to the abduction from the porch of the Opera House, and subsequent captivity, depend upon it, the fair Adelaide has an exceedingly fresh recollection; Norland, at the same time, confirming all that she will accuse you of, in regard to that adventure of yours. In short, you are not, honourable sir, one whit in a better condition than your humble servant, the cut-throat ruffian, Jared Jobson; so that the short and long of it is, we must work more fraternally than ever, combine our interests, and either greatly triumph or ignominiously die together."

"What would you do, Jobson? What counsel give you?" inquired the captain.

"Why, after what we have sometimes attempted, aye, and nearly carried into execution," responded the execrable scoundrel, "the course seems obvious enough. Nay, never were there such motives and inducements, as have unexpectedly arisen to day, for our putting our hands effectually to the deed. Your uncle's sudden and, no doubt, finishing illness, will in all probability, put him out of the way, sending him to his long home, in the course of a few months at most. He has lived years enough —he had become of no use—and I take some credit to myself for helping to rid the world of such lumber."

"What then?"

"Why, there is only the grandchild of Sir Vaux's elder brother in the way; and she must summarily be disposed of. Not only summarily, but suddenly and immediately; for if there be many hours of delay, in effecting this final stroke, we are irretrievably undone. Adelaide keeps a school at Wartham town, in the near neighbourhood of the Hall, as I told you yesterday, captain; and although for the present those who are so anxious for her promotion, and the establishment of her right, may not know where to find her—hiding herself, as she has been, from your tender mercies, *honourable* Life-Guardsman—how long will this ignorance continue? Old Plumtree will be at his cot, perhaps, about as soon as we two can accomplish a journey thither. I cannot promise for Julia's keeping a morsel more true to me than Norland will to you, captain, and she knows well enough where Adelaide is to be found; although, for her own sake, until to-day's discoveries, she has been close as the grave on the subject. You stare and shudder, Chesters!" angrily and threateningly ejaculated Jobson, on observing the condition of the resourceless captain, who well enough understood what the ruffian, who took to himself the title also of cut-throat, was driving at. "But will your silly dandyism and trembling scruples avail you at this pinch? Will your sighing and regrets here keep you from the gallows yonder? Be up and doing, man, or die as a dog; for I swear by all that is unholy"—and here the wretch mouthed terrific words,—"I will not be kept longer in suspense, but shall rather be beforehand of Norland—giving myself into the hands of justice, with the story of our mutual enormities; trusting thereby, after denouncing you, to be the principal witness against you on the day of public trial."

"Do as you will, fiend! I am at your bidding—at your diabolical service!" cried the Life-Guardsman, in an agony of alarm and despair. "Lead me where you will, but meanwhile tell me no more about what you mean."

"As if you did not in reality know and approve of my purpose, viz., that of putting Adelaide as surely out of your way, as Sir Vaux will speedily be," whispered the cruel and triumphant tempter in the other's ear, while they hied them forth, in order, without a moment's loss of time, to reach the vicinity of the young lady's residence; Jobson maliciously rejoicing to see how the weaker villain writhed, and how helpless he had become, in his vile hands.

The cut-throat ruffian's resources seemed endless in every way. Even his purse was full, and at the service of the captain, owing to the facilities which, as the Reverend Jeremy Blight, he had enjoyed in drawing upon the old Yorkshire baronet. Quickly were they whirled along, the more expert and daring of the pair minutely describing his plans as they travelled; although, in the perturbed and confounded condition of the Life-Guardsman, he failed to follow with any degree of clearness the miscreant's details. So stupified and bewildered, in fact, had Chesters been from the moment he fled in haste from the suburban residence of his miserable uncle, that he never seemed to have comprehended how little his personal safety would be secured, even were both Sir Vaux and Adelaide in their graves, so long as Jobson and Norland were alive, not to speak of others who might be forward to accuse him of gravest offences.

As the vile pair travelled along, Jobson affected to be most willing to ease the other of the more exacting part of their murderous enterprise; for to this extremity the cut-throat was now determined to bring their policy; partly instigated to such a course from a spirit of revenge, on account of being seriously foiled in regard to all his efforts, but especially by a calculation of how he might turn to account the accession of Chesters to the Wartham estates, after having made him an accomplice in a capital crime. It is strange with what daringness, and with what reliance on escape from conviction, the fellow argued. He trusted to the want of home-bringing evidence as to the actual perpetrator of the murder. He made himself sure of being able to buy Norland over; and even should he himself and the captain be taken into custody charged with the enormity, he schemed in his own mind how to betray his associate, and thereby effect his own deliverance.

"You'll have to leave to me all the activities of this undertaking, honourable sir, which has become so indispensable to the existence of us both," said Jobson. "I myself must execute the final deed, you keeping apart,—a deed that will be easily transacted in the neighbourhood of old Plumtree's Red Cot; which, as I have taken care to learn, is almost daily visited by Adelaide, often unaccompanied, and never attended but by the old cynic's mute negress. The young lady looks upon herself as already the owner of Peter's property, being his adopted daughter; and takes a wondrous interest in the fantastic place,—the tongue of land that so offensively shoots into the very heart of the splendid grounds of which I intend speedily to make you master. 'For the furtherance of my purpose, I come variously armed; although my chief, and indeed my positive reliance, is upon the application at the first of a most potent and stupifying perfume applied to the nostrils. This done, let a little prussic acid be swallowed with a sip of water, and the business is over, before you can count a score. There will be no bloodshed; nay, not a drop of such an accusing fluid; so that the most that can be concluded, in all probability, will amount to this—that the forlorn girl, in a fit of despondency, made away with herself. Mark me farther, captain! you may keep as far distant from the scene of action as the dense woods, of which you are soon to be the lord, will allow you for the purpose of concealment. I feel assured that I shall not hold you long in suspense. I'll approach or pounce upon the girl as a lurking but rejected lover would do, and, therefore, besides using considerable force, I must appear in a somewhat gayer garb than the methodistical and priestly one I at present wear. We will, captain, exchange coats and small-clothes for an hour or so; and this is all I ask of you, except to accompany me in our departure from the neighbourhood of the Red Cot, and to assist in our further proceedings with your counsel."

It seemed something after the manner of an automaton that the Life-Guardsman accorded with all that was said to, and asked of, him; nor need we retard the progress of the story by any further details, but now, at once, land the villains in the densities of Wartham woods, there to lurk in secrecy till such time as it might best suit the cut-throat ruffian to pounce upon his prey—the forlorn Adelaide.

The forlorn Adelaide! How so? Was she not the teacher of a superior class to what she had found at Sedley? and was she not in a condition of independence, as regarded the comforts of life? She was admired, nay, greatly courted, by the sprightliest in the circle of Wartham; and then she had in mute Martha an ever faithful servant,—no small advantage, considering the love and the antecedents of the negress, when compared with the condition of the young lady on more occasions than one. Nay, let us not forget to mention another being of extraordinary intelligence and fidelity for his kind, that might well have served to gladden the heart of the maiden. This was no other than the ecentric Samaritan's sagacious yet stern housekeeper of the canine order—a creature which, at the first sight of Adelaide, on her return to the Hall, recognised her with more than human promptitude, lavishing upon her all the fondness which the animal could manifest.

Why should the maiden feel forlorn, were it but in having the negress and Cerberus for friends; the latter never being absent from her side when she was abroad, especially when the Red Cot and its neighbourhood were the scenes of her little evening excursions? Great was the young lady's reliance upon her canine attendant. Indeed, so confident grew she in the protection of the animal that she called him her guardian; all fear, though the shades of night were gathering around, at length leaving the maiden, even when she might be distant from human society, provided Cerberus was at her heels.

And yet the youthful schoolmistress was not happy,—not half so happy as when at Sedley; for she had no Paulina Pegsworth to associate with, after the hours of teaching; there being also absent,—perhaps, never to return,—those with whom her immediate neighbourhood was constantly associated in a touching manner.

The highest circle of society which the town of Wartham supplied was composed of commonplace, vulgar persons, who were full of the paltry gossip and petty details of the narrow sphere in which they moved. Amid this little coterie, it is true, there was no lack of interchangings of visits. But what were all these but tea-drinkings and small tattle; or, at most,—which were still worse,—things they called "evening parties," including cards and cake,—music, lemonade, and ennui. The mutes,—Martha and Cerberus,—were preferable society, in the estimation of Adelaide, to any that was furnished by the aristocracy of Wartham.

There had been, during the months that the damsel dwelt in this gossiping place, but one stranger that had ever won upon her affections and sympathies. This was an orphan of some seventeen years,—of the name of Betsy Bay-

ley, whom the youthful schoolmistress took much pleasure in giving lessons to gratuitously; for the girl had been left with but a very small sum for her annual support; and, being of a delicate constitution, and almost constantly ailing, the poor thing could do little in the way of eking out her means of livelihood, not to speak of paying for education. As she boarded with, or rather lived in the cottage of, a sordid couple, her condition was far from enviable. To add to her misfortunes, perhaps, it might be added, she was endowed not only with the finest sensibilities, but superior intellectual powers and aspirations. Let it not be deemed out of place to state that she was nearly as beautiful as our heroine; indeed, there was much that seemed akin between them.

For about two weeks Adelaide had not seen Betsy, neither heard of the amiable girl,—having been led to believe that she was on a visit to a distant relative a good way off. Her regular home was fully two miles from Wartham; and, in these circumstances, the youthful schoolmistress had made no inquiries concerning her interesting friend. But the tidings came that Betsy had returned to her wonted abode, ailing, as was not unusual with her. A week elapsed, and then it was reported that she was suffering from small-pox. A few days after this, our heroine resolved on going to see the patient. But what was her horror! what her indignant disgust, on reaching the desolate-looking chamber in which her favourite had spent years; its bare and clammy walls being alone sufficient to send sickness to the heart, and illness to the body! More woful still and lamentable, there lay the corpse of the lately lovely girl, disfigured beyond conception by the fell disease which had preyed upon her.

But in this there was nothing extraordinary. Here was the horrid thing,—the matchless enormity! By the side of the dead body stood a brutish-looking man,—an unlicensed country practitioner in surgery and various other branches, who was about to obey the mandate of the sordid cottagers. From the poverty of the deceased, and to save expenses, they had purchased a ready-made coffin, but being too short for the lifeless frame,—a tabernacle which had been sanctified by one of the sweetest spirits,—the order had gone forth that the head should be severed from the body, to suit the size of man's carpentry; the arm of the butcher being actually uplifted to perform the revolting process of mutilation.

Adelaide rushed from such a shamble with feelings of sickening horror and disgust; tenderer emotions, however, ensuing as distance interposed between her and the harrowing spectacle. Without well taking note of her route, which was devious and circuitous, she at length found herself in the vicinity of the Red Cot, as if some resistless instinct had conducted the maiden unheedingly thither at that particular hour. The day had been well advanced when the young lady set out in the hopes of carrying some solace to poor Betsy Bayley; and now, in the evening,—this being inviting and friendly to thoughtful exercise,—she, with more than her usual sentimentality, prolonged her walk all alone, as was most agreeable to her at the time, in an especial degree, excepting that Cerberus, the inseparable companion of the lovely young schoolmistress, was at her heels or disporting himself around her.

———

CHAPTER XXXII.

THE CANINE GUARDIAN.

ADELAIDE'S canine companion was a very noble creature to look upon; being large, handsomely shaped, and every way just such an animal of his species as any person would like as a companion when no human associate was near. We might descant upon the sweep and luxuriance of his tail, the muscular strength of his frame, the depth of his chest, and the lion-like form of his legs and paws. But it was his majestic head, the sagacity of his expression, and the general composure of that intellectual countenance,—conscious, as he seemed fully to be, of his powers and his rights,—that the observer had most satisfaction in noting.

We have said the general composure,—for such was even his habitual state, although pestered by curs and other inferior dogs; his reproof of these mostly consisting of silent disdain or an authoritative and dignified look; or, should such admonition fail, the weight of his paw would drive the troubler from him, or drive the froward one,—belly upwards,—into the mire. Cerberus, unless provoked beyond all bounds, or in the execution of an imperative office, would not open his capacious jaws to inflict exemplary punishment by means of his formidable teeth. But to see him once aroused to wrath, and to have a work of stern duty to perform!—Oh! then he was terrible to the eye, and deadly to the object of his fierce indignation,—it might be, of his awful vengeance, or retributive mission.

"Eccentric man, yet wondrous benefactor!" muttered Adelaide to herself, as she once more stood upon the spot to which Peter Plumtree lifted the maiden when taking her from the broken-down carriage, — having rescued her from imminent danger,—as she, with her pretended mother, first neared Wartham Hall. "I can never forget the singularity of the recluse's appearance and manner that day, much less his species of surprise and the peculiar exclamations, as he gazed upon me. It seemed to me, at the time, that there was mystery in some way enveloping me,—ay, and in relation to the oddity before me, and it so appears to me still. I have a liking for this quarter; and yet, I think, I must tear myself from it and its neighbourhood. Perhaps this is the last occasion for a long time that I shall behold it; perhaps the last for ever. Well, then, let me take a fond lingering farewell of the spot."

The young lady did as she counselled herself,—experiencing the soft melancholy pleasure of which her plaintive mood at the moment was so susceptible; and as she leisurely moved towards the deserted Red Cot itself, her meditative abstraction gathered power and tension.

Twilight was upon the scene, a sweet serenity reigned, and pensively she responded to the genius of the hour and the influences all around.

"Surely," thought Adelaide, "were he who is of savage nature here he would be tamed, the cruel subdued, the profligate reproved, the wicked won to peace and virtue."

And yet it was the very same evening in which Jobson and Chesters stealthily threaded the thickets of Wartham woods,—the very same in which they lurked near to where the maiden communed with nature and herself, as unthoughtful of near and approaching peril, as she was susceptible of the serene feelings she cherished.

Adelaide was by this time so near to the Red Cot as to be within the stretch of its far drawn shadow, when the sun shot the last rays upon its roof. Nearer and nearer she glided, soon entering the grotesque enclosure which surrounded the fantastic fabric. She looked into such nondescript outbuildings as it had been the eccentric owner's taste to erect, and tarried over this inspection an unusually long time. Something like a strong presentiment of taking a last look was within her, which deepened and enchained her the more, the longer she pondered over any familiar object.

"What ecstacy would it be!" thought the maiden, "did Peter Plumptree surprise me here at this moment. To what flight would all my late despondency be put! How quickly would my pensiveness be turned into exuberant joy! The serene would have to give place to the tumultuous, I know. Ha! there are steps; it is not the sound which my canine guardian makes by his approach. What then?"

No, it was not Cerberus; for, impelled by some fancy the dog was nosing elsewhere, and not within the ordinary call of the young lady. Much less was it the owner of the Red Cot himself, whose appearance at the particular juncture would indeed have been little less than miraculous. It was the cut-throat ruffian, Jobson, who, though clad in Chester's fashionable dress, escaped not the instant recognition of the maiden; the dread and foreboding which simultaneously shot through her, taking away for a minute or two all power of lending vocal expression to her dismay and alarm. Even some seconds sped before the transfixed Adelaide could move from the spot; during which interval Jobson bolted the gate through which every one had to pass ere reaching the little court where both he and the object of his murderous intent had got enclosed.

This precautionary proceeding of his was conducted with comparative composure and deliberation, for the villain had made himself previously well acquainted with every turn, corner, and outlet connected with the place. The leisurely and regular manner in which he went to work recalled Adelaide to herself; and although she felt at the moment that it was a hopeless attempt, yet she now flew in a state of desperation farther away from the ruffian, rushing into a stone-girt and stoutly-roofed outhouse in which Plumtree was wont to keep his fuel and miscellaneous lumber, and which was lighted by means of an opening several feet high in one of the walls. It required a violent effort for the young lady to lay hold of the outer angle of the sole of the unglazed window; and even had the opening been within her reach, it was positively too small even to receive her frame, so as to allow her to pass through it.

But the cut-throat has overtaken the distracted fugitive,—his hands are upon the fair victim; and with a man's strength, he lends himself to the work of wrenching the maiden from the hold to which with a death-grip she adheres till the blood spouts from her finger-ends. Meanwhile, the monster feels sure of not only having his prey wholly within his power, but in circumstances as to hour and place he had not, even when the murderous wretch indulged the most sanguine hopes, and pictured to himself the readiest escape from accusation, calculated upon or at all anticipated.

"No;—not a drop of blood shall be shed," he muttered, as he was dragging the girl from her hold. "All will be done quietly and summarily;" the monster, although actually armed with a poniard, not now conceiving it to be possibly necessary to have the weapon unsheathed, or drawn from its keeping-place about his person. "The stupifying perfume and the poisoning acid," he added, "will do all the business quickly and without much trouble,—nay, without leaving any external traces to tell an ugly tale."

During the brief struggle which took place in the fuel-house, what could Adelaide do but cling as long as her muscular power, in her desperation, was able, to the stony angle, and to give voice by such shrieks as echoed through the neighbouring woods, to her terrors and agony? It was well that the seldom-straying Cerberus heard those screams, and fully knew whence they came. But it is dreadful to think that, though the animal bounded with unparalleled haste for him towards the gate which Jared Jobson had barred within, the framework of that barrier was not only impenetrable by the good dog and infrangible, but of a height which no reasonable being could have expected the creature to clear.

Cerberus thought and felt differently. On finding the wooden framework shut, he, like others of his species, took a run backwards; and, having with instinctive accuracy measured the proper distance for the achievement of his feat, he most gallantly sprang over the barrier, and next moment was in the fuel-house. It was the moment, too, when Adelaide's last piercing shriek was simultaneous with the exhaustion of her clinging strength and of her dropping to the ground. Nay, more,—it was the moment when she felt herself released from the arms of the ruffian cut-throat, for the execrable villain found of a sudden another kind of conflict to wage than what he had, with such assurance of success, been engaged in a few moments before.

And now, too, there was a change of voices and of appeals; for while Cerberus gave, in the much darkened place, unmistakable proofs of his worrying procedure, the prostrate villain bellowed, as long as he could command utterance and breath, calling alternately for Ches-

ters to come to his rescue, and imploring the maiden to withdraw the dog. But even the breath became wanting, for life was ebbing,—was extinct; Adelaide, while assured of this issue, which was quickly brought about, hurrying from the place, after unbarring the gate.

The lurkers in the woods of Wartham Hall had naturally, in pursuance of their design, kept mostly at a quarter whence they could have their eyes upon the Red Cot and its limited grounds. To the unmeasured delight, at least, of Jobson, when it was beginning to be dusk, they descried their intended victim sauntering about an outskirt of the tongue of land; their vision and previous acquaintance with the appearance of the young lady assuring them that it was no other than Adelaide herself. But somehow they took no note of Cerberus; the animal being generally excursive in his visitations whenever he came to his master's property, but never more vagrant than on this evening.

"Truly the girl must have grown more hardy than usual," observed Jobson, on first catching a glimpse of her, "otherwise she never would venture alone so far from her home as where she now is, and especially at an evening hour. But mark! she actually makes for the Red Cot, and what if she should take it into her head to go within its droll enclosures, fancying herself as good as mistress of the place already. It is clear that she thinks herself snugly and secretly situated in the neighbouring town, at least as regards certain of her former acquaintances. Wish yourself joy, captain! She opens a fantastic gate that leads to only one or two outhouses, in a little court from which there is no exit except by the same way that she enters. My mighty service for you is as good as done," added the execrable monster. "Hold yourself where you are; I'll be back in some five minutes or so;" and away went the cut-throat ruffian with a speed and alacrity, as if he had been on an embassy of mercy.

As for Chesters, he neither distinctly knew what had just been said to him, nor where he was; his less practised mind in the darkest atrocities, and some confused impressions that Jobson was inveigling him more deeply and wofully than ever, by each new step he took, nearly bereaving the Life-Guardsman for the time of all intellectual perception. He stood by, or rather clung to, a sturdy tree, like one who was stunned or stupified; nor did he start into anything like lucid consciousness, until, to his surprise, and his misgivings as to the issue of the murderous enterprise, he heard shriek upon shriek, that in his experience had never found a parallel, excepting on the night when Adelaide was beguiled away from the Opera House, and when the same voice gave forth the sounds of agony. But the dismay and distracting convictions of Chesters were doomed to reach a still more awakened condition, on perceiving a huge dog burst suddenly, —apparently in response to the wild cries,— from a neighbouring covert, and bound with extraordinary speed and the most manifest tokens of fierceness towards the scene of the intended tragedy.

"The murderer will be assuredly and instantly mastered!" ejaculated the tortured accessory, who, had he been armed with a loaded pistol, would probably have discharged it within the cavity of his mouth, thereby scattering his brains around the spot where he shuddered. "Our plot will be discovered as well as baulked; and the gibbet will have me, and the annals of Newgate be enriched with the story of the Life-Guardsman's end."

With what intensity of gaze did the captain follow the dog! and with what misgivings did he behold the furious creature clear the gate at a bound! And then not a minute elapsed before the guilt-stung wretch found that the bellowings of a masculine voice came instead of the piercing cries of a shriller utterance, this agonized roaring growing feebler every moment, till at length it ceased altogether. A few seconds more, and Adelaide is seen making her escape with apparently as firm a step as ever from the scene of meditated assassination, her canine guardian speedily following, in order to escort and protect her, and by his motions apprizing Chesters that the animal considered himself triumphant and worthy of the gratitude of her whom he served.

And now came the climax of the Life-Guardsman's dilemma, as well as terrors and horrors. Would it not be best to fly and leave Jobson to his fate? But then the captain was moneyless,—the other having abundance, and what was still worse, the cut-throat had exchanged clothes with him; his own being easily recognisable by many in London, while that of the impostor,—as the Rev. Jeremy Blight,—was a no less explicit tell-tale. How Chesters writhed, groaned, and cursed his infatuation whilst he contemplated his exterior, —that is, the other's attire.

"I'll have my own back again, whether the fiend be dead or alive," said the captain, grinding his teeth, and off he hurried like a madman to make his threat good; a very short time sufficing to bring him to the fuel-house, within the little court, the usual barrier of which stood wide open.

The excited and terribly perturbed man took not so much leisure as to pause for a moment, unthinking of the kind of spectacle that was to present itself to him, and only intent on having his raiment back again, and to be away from the neighbourhood with the utmost promptitude; dreading the early coming of such people as the escaped Adelaide might arouse against her foiled persecutors.

The night was rapidly throwing its mantle over all things, and within the little court of the Red Cot there was still greater dimness than without. On coming to the fuel-house, such was the obscurity of the place, that Chesters could not discover whether his late associate had maintained his conflict there or not, in so far as the eye could inform him amid the darkness. Repeatedly he called upon Jobson by his name, without obtaining the slightest response, or receiving any such sign as to tell him that the fellow was within hearing, or at all alive. To grope with his hands, and run the risk of laying hold of a corpse, were thoughts which made the Life-Guardsman quake.

"I must be a coward to hesitate now, espe-cially when every moment is so precious," at length muttered the captain. "Ha! I forgot. The ever-resourceful Jobson armed me as well as himself with the means of striking a light and igniting a taper, saying that the articles might be serviceable in the case of accidents. A cunning, contriving fellow was Jared; but somehow I have a notion that he tried his talent at trickery once too often. Ha, ha, ha!" the soliloquist, while he thus made an effort by a species of swagger to keep his courage up to a sticking-point, busying his hand in putting to trim and kindling his lighting-gear.

No sooner had he completed this operation, and turned the taper's rays towards the interior first of one roofed spot and then of another,—the second of his eager and panting inspection being the fuel-house,—than an exclamation of horror burst from his breast, and he turned him round as if he meant to quit the place for ever and as soon as possible. But other things suggested themselves, with what appeared to him an amazing rapidity and clearness, that restrained his retrograding race.

"My clothes, to be sure, are torn and gory, and cannot be used by me," thought the tortured Chesters. "But then I am moneyless, whilst there is about the other's person a sum sufficient for my present necessities; which to leave for others to appropriate would be a folly betraying greater weakness than my tremors. I'll rifle the corse—I'll plunder the cut-throat ruffian, as the scoundrel named himself."

With a desperate energy,—a reckless sort of hardihood,—the Life-Guardsman drove into the fuel-house, and stood over the dead. And a most ghastly spectacle it was,—a revolting horror, so that with a kind of devouring greediness he contemplated the sight,—he holding himself to the spot like to something rooted in it; the ordinary course of humanity being so congealed within him that he did not even sigh, while making the glare which the taper shed in the murky place traverse slowly from head to foot, and from foot to head, of the disfigured body.

As the light was made to rest by the half-stooping inspector upon the different consecutive parts of what might be regarded as a mangled carcass, the throat first arrested the captain's gaze, riveting his distended eyeballs, seeming to brutify him the more the longer he looked upon that region of the yet warm body. The agony which was depicted on the visage,—the muscles having taken a corded and rigid shape, with the mouth open, as when it essayed to make way for the last but checked cry,—was woful. The throat, which Cerberus first of all assailed,—having no doubt been in a twinkling bared,—presented the most unmistakable evidences of a vigorous worrying, being lacerated and laid open, as if with an utter disregard to the butcher's skill.

How long the strangely enchained captain might have remained in the fuel-house, lighted taper in hand, he being held as if by some mocking demon's spell,—or whether he ever could have wrenched himself from the spot but as a howling maniac, had not some potent appeal been made to him, by means of a very plain agency,—cannot be told. It so happened, however, that while his vision principally dwelt upon the last frightful proof of the canine guardian's proceedings in the conflict, there offered themselves to the sight of Chesters several gold pieces which were strewed upon the ground. In an instant the Life-Guardsman was recalled to himself, and to think of his imminent danger as well as distressing necessities. He went down upon his knees; he gathered up the coins with the certitude and celerity of a miser; and knowing that a good deal more remained unscattered by the dog, he dug into the pockets of the dead man, though they were saturated with life-blood,—rolling the body over and over, as well as searching every nook which could be conceived to form the hiding-place of purse or pocket-book.

Having reaped a not insignificant harvest in this way, and believing there was little left for gleaners who might come after him, the captain rushed from the fuel-house at as madlike a rate as had marked his race thither; not only alarmed lest he might be caught on the premises of the Red Cot or in its vicinity, by ministers of justice, but with terrors lest a supernatural pursuit should be instantly instituted against him.

"The worried and disembowelled Jobson himself is at my heels," the fugitive, as one in mortal terror, muttered with a shudder, as he sprang into open ground from the little court within which the fuel-house had its entrance. "The yells of infernal spirits are in my ears, doubtless in full chase of me."

The wretched Chesters being under these terrors, and now the subject of the most violent nervous reaction, ran he knew not whither, and at a speed such as only insanity or deadly terror reaches; the longer he held on, the madness gathering wildness and strength through the mere vehemence of his physical action in order to gain distance from his imagined pursuers.

Onwards he bounded, at times uttering sounds which, owing to his state of desperation and his exhaustion of breath, seemed of unearthly origin. It was while thus scouring along,—and it happened to be now upon the beautiful and spacious road which skirted one side of old Plumtree's tongue of land, and which also led directly to the principal gate and avenue that introduced the visitor to Wartham Hall,—he clove into a crowd of people, some of them armed, others with lanterns; the distorted vision and the demented mind for the time, having, it would seem, made the fugitive attribute to the crowd the character of angry demons. "Avaunt ye, you hell-hounds! Chesters defies you!" were his cries as he drove through the startled number.

"Jobson and Chesters,—Chesters and Jobson, are the names the persecuted young lady mentioned as those of her enemies," exclaimed several of the amazed multitude. "Murder, or its intent, has made him mad. After the runaway, some of the lightest-footed of you, and, if caught, let him be brought to the Red Cot. He cannot long hold out at the speed he is making. He already foams horribly at the mouth."

These hasty and various observations came from the lips of different individuals, just as each conjectured and felt in their singularly aroused state. And away in pursuit of the guilt-stung and infatuated Life-Guardsman sped some half-dozen of the younger ones who had seen him in his miserable plight; obeying the instructions issued by older members of the crowd.

It was now night, for Chesters remained a good while longer at the fuel-house than he had any clear conception of. The moon in her fulness was also by this time majestically rising above the horizon, and acting as if in concert with those on earth who had a mission of solemn import to perform. The queen of night favoured the purpose of the pursuers, and ere long they had the object of their ardent exertion full in view of them, as he flung forward along the spacious avenue that led to the stately Hall,—a way he had often trod with leisurely steps, and a lofty, self-possessed mien.

The wretched fugitive's race, though impelled and sustained in his demented condition by something akin to a supernatural energy, could not very long continue to outstrip every one of the number of fresh runners after him, the stimulus by which they were actuated being of no ordinary kind. Chesters, in fact, was becoming exhausted; indeed it could have been no great wonder had he fallen down dead in the course of his terrific distraction and agonizing efforts.

Still, he had some advantages over the pursuers. He had been acquainted with every corner and retreat of the ornamented grounds of Wartham Hall from his boyhood. He was familiar with every turn of the meandering paths, and could strike to the right or left as best suited him, so as to get into such thickets and groves as greatly baffled those in chase; such coverts rendering the moonlight but an uncertain conductor. On the other hand, in his frantic state, the captain more than once either nearly threw himself into the hands of the pursuing party, or came into such a predicament as all but brought him to a dead halt. Then the rustling of branches as he drove amid numberless growths was frequently a continuous tell-tale to his extreme jeopardy.

The contending conditions had lasted in the manner described for some considerable time; the feelings of the chasing party becoming gradually more and more heated as they found themselves foiled, and sometimes by the most narrow escapes of the fugitive.

"Would that we had a bloodhound with us," cried one of the pursuing number, on finding that, in consequence of some expert movement or concealed turn, Chesters eluded his grasp when almost within a hair's breadth of him.

"What say you to calling in the aid of Cerberus, the canine guardian who has already done such excellent service at the Red Cot, upon one of the intending murderers, in behalf of the young lady?" was shouted by another; the distracted captain, where he lay shrouded by a dense forest of shrubs and foliage, hearing every word which had been thus spoken, and thereupon taking greater alarm, if possible,—looking for the literal fulfilment of what was said on the instant.

"I have a last resource even of deliverance

from bloodhounds and such like!" exclaimed he, as he shot from the place of his concealment, dashing as if with a refreshed vigour straight away from the spot, and in a direction too that revealed his route to those who pressed on after him.

"He cannot escape us now for many seconds," was the observation of one runner, who had some knowledge of the locality. "He makes for a quarter where he will find himself hemmed in on all sides except the one that we shall occupy. It has long been the favourite scene of all in these beautiful grounds, as have a romantic taste. It gets the name of the Cauldron Cliff."

All this was spoken by one of the pursuing party, as breath served him, whilst he and the others held steadily on and with the utmost certitude.

"What can be the object of the Life-Guardsman's resort towards the brink of the dreadful precipice?" was the ejaculated wonder of a runner.

"He thinks of Adelaide's marvellous escape when he himself drove her over the cliff, as has been currently reported," was the remark of another.

"I rather think that the demon has a hope that some of us, in our heedless haste, and ignorance of the place at such an hour as the present, will come to an awful end, whilst he gives us the double," was said by a third.

Onwards went the fugitive, and after him pressed the pursuers, each of the latter at a loss to conceive what might be the object of the chased one,—whether an artful stratagem, such as a diabolical nature would meditate, or the infatuated proceeding of a being driven madly desperate.

"Hither with you, ye hounds, that I may grapple with the first assailant, and go headlong to perdition with the fool," were the daring and awful words which Chesters uttered as he stood at bay on the loftiest point of the cliff, and within a pace or two of the precise spot from which Adelaide had been precipitated, as told near the commencement of our story.

"There's a way to deal with the fiend, without risk to any of us," said one of the pursuing party, who was not only more courageous than his associates, but more fertile of resources. "I'll grapple with the monster, and capture him to the bargain, unless he is prepared to for a headlong fall, such as he intended the fair and innocent maiden should have experienced when he treacherously dealt with her at this place. Hands to hands, my friends, and thus stringed together, keep me to my footing while I close upon the villain."

Quick as had been the thought of the rustic tactician was there a serried row of men tied into a retreating line from the object of their pursuit; the most valiant of the party, thus supported, taking his position within a few feet of the terribly beset one, who, in spite of all his frenzy, quickly discovered how unavailing it would be to contend longer against his fate; the grinding of his teeth and the gnashing of his convulsed jaws indicating that the libertine was forced to his last resource.

"Give me line, my friends," was the word of command which the resolute rustic issued, when he found all ready to enable him to grapple with Chesters; the outstretched row instantly obeying the order, but yet not so quickly as was the measure which the wretched captain adopted.

"Follow me a fathom further, if you dare," howled he, as he turned his back upon the others. "Meet me at the bottom of the Cauldron Cliff, where I'll bid you still wilder defiance."

As the last of these words escaped his convulsed organs of speech, he made a desperate bound aloft and away, so as to clear entirely any obstacle that might have kept him within reach of his pursuers.

CHAPTER XXXIII.

THE FATED FULFILMENTS.

A CRY of horror and dismay was raised by the witnesses of the suicidal act before the wretched Chesters had well disappeared in the moonlight; a second burst of feeling following on their hearing the crashing sound of some heavy body striking the rugged floor below. The rustic number were quickly at the spot where lay the victim of his own hideous infatuation.

"He groans! he writhes!" said the men, as they bore their broken burden along towards the Red Cot, where they found the rest of the party from Wartham. Nor sooner was the captain brought to the remarkable spot, than it was ascertained he had still life within him, although evidently he had but few hours, perhaps, minutes, to live; the marvel being that he breathed at all.

The people of the town of Wartham who were now at the Red Cot had not been provided with any regular means of entering the habitable portion of the premises; so that in seeking for a place where Chesters might in a measure be screened from the keenness of the night air, they had no other resource than to plant the dying Life-Guardsman in the fuel-house, where were the torn remains of the monster Jobson.

"They were hideous associates, we have been told, during a portion of their latter lives," ejaculated some one; "and, in their deaths, they are not likely to be far separated."

But we have not yet got to the climax of the sad and solemn occurrences of that night, as witnessed at old Peter Plumtree's cot; for quickly after the arrival of a medical gentleman, and his administering of a stimulant, the dreadfully wounded one gradually recovered his senses; the more rapidly, it was supposed, in consequence of his blood beginning to flow freely in response to the application of the lancet. The eyes were opened, the ear took in the words which were gently addressed to it, and the lips came into motion. At length there were breathed utterances, which, as soon as they could with any distinctness be heard, showed that the mind had recovered its intelligence. Nay, it appeared to be with a remarkable clearness and rapidity that his recollec-tions ran over the events of the evening, from the moment that Jobson had left him at the edge of the wood, in order to assassinate Ade-laide, down to the suicidal leap which he himself took from the top of the far-famed cliff.

"Such sudden gleams of intelligence after a state of mental insensibility and also of wild delirium," whispered the doctor, "are some-times the almost immediate precursors of death. I like not the symptoms in the present case, unless as it may allow the miserable suf-ferer a short reprieve, which perhaps he may employ in order to make his peace with Heaven."

"Doctor, hold me up, and let me see where I exactly am," were at once the breathed ex-pressions of the sufferer which reached the ear of the medical gentleman.

"I dare hardly put you to that incon-venience,—to the agony which what you ask of me, Captain Chesters, must cause," said the surgeon. "I can inform you where you are, and that without putting you to more of bodily torture than what, alas! you already endure."

"What is the bodily torture to a fellow who has brought himself to my present pitch, when compared to that of the mind?" somewhat an-grily demanded the wretched Life-Guardsman, speaking feebly, but yet with volubility. "Thought I that the raising me up, so as to see clearly around, would hasten my departure hence to my proper place elsewhere, I would insist the more on your obeying me. I wish to know who is my bed-fellow, although I have a guess about the matter even as the evidence already stands. Yet I must be assured through the testimony of my own sight and touch. Lift me up, I say, until I be in a sitting posture. If you refuse to favour me by such a simple act, I'll wriggle myself to the desired point, even although fractured ribs should pierce heart and soul that instant."

There was as much of desperation in the manner of the miserable man as his weakness of frame could put on; showing that his spirit was in no genial condition. However, it was judged necessary to accede to his angrily-urged wish; nor had he been half-way raised to the posture named by him, before his gaze fastened upon the dead cut-throat with a frightful ten-sion, which seemed to indicate that the eager-ness was sustained by the dark passions of hatred, revenge, and malice.

"Hold out my broken right arm, which hap-pens to be nearest to friend Jobson," said the Life-Guardsman, a demoniac smile coming in the place of the other terrible expressions of his face. "I wish once more to touch the clothes that are upon his vile carcass, for they happen to be my own, although somewhat spoiled for use,—more misused, in fact, than his, which are on my back, even after the tear and wear the gear got in my jump."

There could be no harm in allowing the suf-ferer to have his way in the manner desired, it was thought. The powerless hand was guided to the dead ruffian, and permitted to rest upon the body for a second or two in obedience to the understood will of its owner.

"Faugh! let me have my limb back again," groaned the sufferer, the agony which the out-stretching process had occasioned extorting the sounds. "Faugh!" repeated he; "I have had Jobson's gore already upon my fingers, al-though none of you can well know when, why, and how;" referring, no doubt, to the rifling proceeding earlier in the evening.

"Ha! ha! ha!" added Chesters, after taking breath, with a mocking attempt at laughter. "It was an exploit well thought of, and cle-verly achieved; although, as matters have un-fortunately come to pass, of little avail to poor Captain Chesters now. Nay, I rather expect that the cut-throat who has so often kept me in bondage to him in times past, will hold me to an accounting throughout the future, know-ing, as I do, that we must for ever companion it together. Ha! ha! ha!"

"He cruelly exhausts himself," ejaculated the doctor. "He is growing delirious; he will rapidly sink. We must lay him down."

"I'd die as I am, in your arms, rather than give up the ghost stretched out at full length at the side of that carrion there," hastily in-terjected the wretched sufferer, who had not only taken up the import of the doctor's ob-servations, as with a dying eagerness,—which for a few seconds restored him to himself,—but who still at a moment of such extremity had some recollection of what was his condition by birth and profession. "Besides, before going, I have to look upon another sort of sight than that of a cut-throat ruffian in his gore; although that sight scathe my own, and quickly blind it for ever. Look! behold! who have you there?"

The eyes of all who had been witnesses from the first of the wretched Life-Guardsman's condition and conduct, since being brought to the fuel-house, had fixed upon him such a riveted gaze that they saw what had occurred in a very narrow line. They hardly ever looked sideways, much less behind them. Hence it was that Adelaide had got into the rear of the spectators unobserved, whence she might have departed without any of the party having the slightest idea that she had been at all present, and without their knowing that the death-scene of Chesters had not yet reached its climax.

"Look! behold! who have you there?" were his hasty words, uttered with all the force and wildness of a shriek of affright and con-sternation which the conscience-stricken and remorseful wretch could throw into his attenu-ated breathings. "The Cauldron Cliff, Ade-laide,—the Cauldron Cliff has but left it for thee to slay me outright by that blanched look of thine, which sorely upbraids me, seem-ing to be that of the accusing angel who will arraign me at the Eternal's bar, and sink me to the lowest, to consort with the spirits of such cut-throats as he whose loathsome carcass here beside me already offends the sense."

"Had I known that I was to add to the torment before the time of one of the pair who have been the most unrelenting of my foes, I should not have hurried hither this night," said Adelaide. "On the contrary, I came in the hope, should the Life-Guardsman fall into your hands, good friends, that I might be the means of delivering him; being horrified at the thought that I should have in any measure been the occasion of his associate perishing in his sins, and anxious to prevent a like catastrophe."

"It is the last thrust!" feebly shrieked the miserable man, opening his languid eyelids at the same moment; enabling him to obtain a final glimpse of the young lady, as she glided away from the place. "She has dealt me the slaying stroke, and hereafter never more is there compassion for one who made shipwreck of his own soul with the most wanton hardihood. Now lay me down to die!"—an injunction which had not been well uttered, nor fully complied with, when he breathed his last.

Instead, at this late stage of the story, of dilating upon the prostration of health and spirits which overtook Adelaide after the long series of vicissitudes she had encountered,—commencing with her flight from Wartham Hall, and finding their climax at the Red Cot on the evening that Jobson and Chesters were so hideously cut off from the land of the living,—it is far more gratifying to hasten to the period when fortune ceased to frown upon her. Accordingly, the narrative has to be wound up with these few particlars:—

Some ten days or so after the occurrence of the horrid events at the Red Cot, which have immediately above been recorded, three gentlemen, on their arrival at Dover, and almost simultaneously with their rapid glance at a file of papers, started from that port posthaste for Yorkshire,—for Wartham, in short; even the intelligence that Sir Vaux Waldgrave had breathed his last failing to detain Montague Mildmay, who was one of the impatient party. The appearance of these gentlemen in the presence of Adelaide worked a more speedy and perfect cure of all her ills than any professional doctor could have done. But we need not further particularize than to state, that while Newcomb Neville found a

daughter, and the young lady a husband, old Peter Plumtree seemed in a measure to have recovered his youth, living for years thereafter under the roof of Wartham Hall, as if with his children, and as if he had been the hereditary owner of that lordly mansion; the Red Cot having been levelled to the ground, and the tongue of land upon which the fantastic fabric stood, annexed to the splendid estate whose compactness had hitherto been somewhat marred.

As to the less prominent characters in the tale, it is satisfactory to learn that Hector Hastings became the husband of the amiable Paulina Pegsworth, to the no small disappointment of his clerical brother. Poetical justice in another way overtook Mrs. Puffendorff and her two inseparables. At the dining-table, the Dutchman's widow received the tidings of Adelaide's good fortune and restoration to her rights; the surprise and vexation thereby caused, with a surfeit of the luxurious things in which now was her chief enjoyment, inducing an apopletic fit which instantly ended her days; Ladies Lymington and Gorewell, her almost constant associates,—both of them by this time widowed,—being the witnesses of the awful visitation. It may be added, that these gossips, neither of them being well provided for after the decease of the husbands, for a while domiciled together with a view to economy, but never without bitter wranglings and disgraceful recriminations.

Even the villain Norland, and his companion, the artful and worthless Julia, met what was their due; having been, shortly after the marriage of Adelaide and Mildmay, sent to a penal colony, there to drag out their wretched lives; Wartham Hall being meanwhile the seat of happiness, and an abode celebrated for the enlightened liberality of its possessors, and the centre of intellectual enjoyment.

THE END.

www.ingramcontent.com/pod-product-compliance
Lightning Source LLC
Chambersburg PA
CBHW080830250626
47160CB00008B/2890